LA
PROTAGONISTA

Pru Jones

Copyright © 2017 Pru Jones

ISBN: 0974712566
ISBN 13: 9780974712567

"I hold it true, whate'er befall – I feel it when I sorrow most – 'tis better to have loved and lost than never to have loved at all."

– Lord Alfred Tennyson

WEDNESDAY 1 NOVEMBER 1780

S ails thumped with the shifting wind. I happened to look down at the railing. The scratch Armando made on the back of my hand at our blood ceremony had healed. How long would it take to fix the hole he cut in my heart?

A fly sitting on a lily pad was safer than being aboard our stench-filled floating prison creaking with each swell. Not that I cared. Standing over the sloshing wake against the hull below, I couldn't imagine my beloved Armando staring out at a sea desert reflecting colorless sky. Yet, I knew he had indeed made the trip.

My trust in Maximo waned with every turn of the hourglass. His misgivings, whatever they may have been, had taken charge. The man couldn't lift a three-tined fork without losing his temper.

Lost -- a word no one dared say would've been the way to describe our whereabouts. We'd been forced to rely on dead-reckoning for nearly three days, when a thimble-sized cloud-opening spattered light on a sail. Like a shot, the deck behind me pounded with barefoot seamen. That poke of sun punching a hole in the sky was all we needed to figure out where we were, provided they could find our commander, the only one on board who could navigate worth a plum pie.

Nearly three hundred years of making the crossing, Spain surely would've figured the whole thing out. But, slamming a mug of grog on the galley table, gravelling in a rasp from years of yelling commands in the salt air, the *Santa Dolorosa's* captain said, "No matter how many times you sail the Atlantic, it's always the first time."

Not caring if I lived or not would soon come to an end. Everyone on board but me was about to die.

SUNDAY, 13 AUGUST 1780

Mother sucked a lace handkerchief to her face, concealing the contagious grin from my future family.

Throwing the Limoges gilt cup at Miguel probably wasn't the best idea, but the toss felt like the soft whites pushing through the crack of an eggshell that had boiled too long. I picked up the nearest thing and flung it at him. How I managed to hold in the ensuing urge to laugh was miraculous.

The unbroken saucer, a reminder of the incident that disgraced the pristine parlor wall of Casa de la Colina, and the Lizarraga family name, was good for nothing more than a potted plant.

The over-wound-pocket-watch throw that sent my fiancé's eyebrows as high as mine the first time I jumped Artemia over the winter woodpile, sped past Miguel's brow with a miss so narrow, his forehead could've easily been bloodied with a nick worthy of bragging about to drinking buddies as a dueling mishap, had there been the remotest possibility he'd be company to either.

As the cup whistled by, my promised ducked the depth of two heads, an impressive feat most likely perfected at the university after sidestepping heckling regarding his flawless attire.

One good thing did happen by leaving the scene -- the worry I created erased punishment for my behavior.

The squabbles with Miguel over our twenty-six-month betrothal usually blew over. However, a stray ember of assertiveness sparked to flame during that particular disagreement, a display during morning tea that solidified his penchant for the unremarkable.

Our families would've been happy about the marriage, had there been one. Papa had eyes on Lizarraga's private stock for years. It wasn't already enough to be producer of the finest carriage horses in Europe with buyers coming from as far away as Moscow, Papa knew the Andalucian studs mixed with our bloodlines would've produced an even higher-quality animal. Pissing-off Miguel's father was not about to help acquire the stallions, a bargain so vital Papa sold his only daughter for them.

After the incident that nearly bloodied his son's face, Lizarraga easily could've cut off the source of Spanish stock we'd already been importing to France, broodmares that were the cornerstone of Monsieur Chevaleaux's highly prized teams. And a little payback like that may have ruined a lifetime of work that afforded us to live in near luxury even though we came from generations of peasant farmers.

My throat burned with rising fluid every time someone said, "You are such a fortunate young lady. So many girls would love to be Señora Miguel Nuñez y Lizarraga." Indeed, Miguel was very nice looking and he came from an excellent line of near-aristocrats who somehow wound up at the same table with nobility even though they had no actual title, a position not easily accomplished without being breeders of fine horseflesh, in addition to an enormous talent for bowing while smiling.

Agreed I would be marrying above my station, but I told Papa that I had no interest in entering into a union without love and passion. To be with a man otherwise would be the same as being a whore. Every time the subject came up, with the same goatee twirl he would give Mother when there was about to be a confrontation of some kind that he was trying to avoid, Papa would stare the other way and pretend he didn't hear such things from the mouth of his progeny.

The first celebratory clink to Miguel and Madeleine should've been a clue of things to come. The newly betrothed couple tipped their Burgundy-filled glasses, right after which the crystal smashed in their hands spilling purple spirits everywhere. My reaction to our stained finery appeared somewhat inconsiderate in light of the fact that as I flopped backward into a chair and laughed so hard my stays nearly ripped open, Miguel's hand was bleeding.

He had no difficulty seeing his fiancé as a woman who could put on the white wig. But he refused to accept that she was also the girl in men's pants with horses between her legs.

Even though he didn't approve, Miguel never said a word about it until we were in the company of all four parents. Standing with one hand resting on the table and the other on his hip, Miguel looked right at me and said, "If you do not obey my wishes, your parents will send you to St. Mary's Ascension Cloisters for Women." He apparently suffered a bout of stage-fright since the admonition was delivered with a momentary crescendo of falsetto when he reached the word "will." His voice went so high, he sounded like a girl pricking her finger on the needle in the middle of a stitch. Had he made it through the entire sentence I may have been more inclined to take him seriously, but as it came about I could barely keep the corners of my mouth flat.

What stung the most was not that he was behaving like a jackass, but the fact that he didn't come after me when I ran out of the house.

Around mid-morning I made the first tug of the day to pull my sweat-dampened chemise from my chest. Laundry was hanging straight on its line. Had there been a momentary breeze, it was nothing more than a taunt from the devil with a bellows in hand. Tempers rose with the heat of the sun, things went awry, and I just wanted to hide in the thick woods outside Sevilla. The forest seemed like the perfect place to disappear even though the wind from Artemia's gallop would be the only thing preventing beet cheeks and a dripping brow.

Colorful reference to peril on the roads, a topic usually included in Andalucian conversation along with Spain's reputation for risky travel, seemed to be nothing more than washerwoman talk. Nonetheless, my brother's well-worn pants that had already provided years of scatting the side-saddle also served as a suitable disguise for a single woman.

Soft patting of hoof beats in the dirt reminded me of riding with Rene. The bout of dysentery, although not the pleasantest of ailments, was not fatal. Rene's life had been cut short by someone's half-assed notion to put him in the tubercular ward, a stupid move to accommodate the last empty bed. Had the hospital been staffed by the competent, my brother would've been a few years Miguel's senior and surely would've interceded on my behalf. I stopped myself from going any further with the lingering thoughts I harped on regularly, as if revisiting the scene over and over would bring him back to life.

Tucking her haunches under like a rabbit, Artemia took off with echoing hooves banging on the stable-yard stone, loud enough to drown out a laugh. During my rapid departure from La Colina, the stable boy smirked when he saw that as she vaulted off an upside-down bucket onto her readied mare and closed her pant-legs on the grey filly's flat sides, the distressed fiancé was wearing a grin.

To take a coach ride in any direction, one would've found it difficult not to cry. Crisp butter-colored crops lay horizontal in their fields. Those who could afford to eat during the rainless summer had to pay dearly. And for the less fortunate, food was scarce. What God had planted managed to survive since most of the trees were still green. But the seeds sown by man just couldn't take it.

Following our rapid departure and a good walk to allow the mare sufficient time to regain her wind, I gave Artemia her head.

Like Flamenco on a tabletop, a syncopated heartbeat, or a ticking clock gone mad, but consistent in its insanity, the mare's hooves hammered the hardened path with a gallop, flying the long feather in my cap flat and sucking tears across my cheeks.

Ignoring the sting from the cuffs of my father's white muslin shirt snapping on my arms, I glanced down past Artemia's vibrating gray shoulder turned nearly black from sweat. The ground was a blur. I wasn't sure if someone was on the path ahead or not.

The mare's ears pointed back, questioning the tug of leather sliding through my fingers with a tiny grab on her rein. She slowed with a bounce or two and I steadied my gaze on the traveler. His hair was longer than mine. Even tied behind his head with a cloth, his brown locks were nearly to his waist. Yes, definitely a man. And he filled his clothes well. Perfect hips and thighs packed into close-fitting black pants without an inch to spare, swaying side to side with each stride of his mount. I popped a grin. A black, flat-brimmed hat that I doubt would have been appropriate anywhere besides Spain was not upon his head, but instead hung around his shoulders by a neck-cord. Why did he bother wearing it all?

A little buffoonery seemed in order. I laughed. And, in the final seconds before the event that would change my life, a tiny sting landed on my tongue as an insect blew into my open mouth. I spit it to wind and kicked the mare on. The stranger still didn't turn around. Ignoring the deafening hooves slapping the rock-like dirt behind him, he kept looking straight ahead, calmly walking on as if he owned the road. Should the man have been deaf, he might've been oblivious to the mischief, having long grown accustomed to that sort of thing, so I found it necessary to take the less-than-admirable gesture even lower. Merely charging by at a gallop wasn't enough. It would be far greater sport to lightly brush the black horse with a little bump from Artemia and then vanish into the woods.

The Limoges was still flying across the room. My heart beat faster with each stride that took me closer to the stranger. During the time a drop of water could splat-sizzle into a heated pan, I hatched the entire scheme. The speed of our gallop, however, turned out to be a hair brisker than necessary. The contact that was supposed to have been a little bump came with such force, Artemia nearly dumped me. We collided and my leg wedged between both steeds. I screamed. And instead of galloping away in glee, I struggled to find the flopping stirrups. The mare's sweat had slipped the girth and the saddle went crooked. I had to dig my knee into the horse's shoulder, and grab the seat with my heel, or I would've been riding the dust. Lord only knew what the mare thought I was doing. Luckily, she didn't slow down, even with me hanging over her side.

Pulling myself back up, bumping my crotch on a twisted seat, I took a quick turn to see my handiwork. The black had buckled to his knees and catapulted the stranger onto his horse's neck. The man pushed himself back into the saddle, pulled his mount's head up by the reins, and came after me like a bolt out of the sky. I kicked Artemia, hard. Her lungs roared. Froth oozed from the sides of her neck, making the reins slippery white. My legs flew straight out before landing repeated kicks, but the mare was no match for the black. Every time I found a moment to turn around, my pursuer was closer.

I prayed for a miracle. A blink-of-an-eye choice had to be made right then. The road ahead veered to the right over a primitive bridge. And a gallop over the flimsy wood planks might spook my horse. The only option was to leave the road and sharply turn down an embankment that led to a dry river bed. We would soon to be upon it one way or the other. The shorter, faster route required brazen-faced aplomb that would've allowed us to cross the ravine and pick up the road on the other side in much less time. Besides, no sane person would follow. I took the short cut.

The sweaty reins slipped through my fingers as I yanked on the bridle. The tired mare couldn't slow down. I yelled, "Arête." She finally locked her hocks just moments before missing the only spot on the ledge that allowed us a way to cross over.

Sliding to a stop in a tiny puff of dust on the edge of a dirt chasm that was practically ninety-degrees straight down, I finally got a good look. What probably had been under water before the drought looked all that much higher from atop a horse. My gut twisted into a knot. From a distance, it looked like the drop was nothing more than a small bank, but when I pointed Artemia's nose down the hill I saw the descent that easily equaled my mounted height.

Fire raced through my veins. With a loud splat, I slapped the end of the reins on Artemia's wet shoulder. We'd jumped that sort of thing before, but I could hardly blame the sweaty gray girl for questioning my sanity. I slammed my heels into her ribs. She danced in place on the edge of the precipice, jingling the bit in her mouth with each toss of her nose. The savvy little horse had to blindly trust me, since the angle of the drop didn't allow either of us to see where we would land.

I pushed my ass deep into the saddle. Crouching down to take the bank like a cat ready to pounce, Artemia shifted her weight onto her hind legs. The big black was almost upon us. No time to hesitate. I screamed, *"Alle!"* Artemia vaulted away, hard.

During a thin slice of a second, while she was struggling in the dirt to find her legs, I thought we would be fine. But, the wax seal broke on the envelope. The bank gave way and we slid down the incline. With each attempt at staying upright, we only sank deeper and deeper. Lowering her head to keep her balance, the mare pulled the reins through my fingers. Her dappled rump bumped the dirt behind us, buckling her legs. She went down to her shoulder. I fell with her.

Musty, brown foliage, crisp from a lengthy death filled my view. Everything was quiet. I tried to get up. Sharp pains stabbed me, while bits of blue punched random cutouts through branches swaying in a momentary breeze. Birds happily flittered from limb to limb. I hurt all over.

Feeling around for my cap as I lay there, I wound up with a fistful of clumped leaves nearly the same color as my hair. I was about to get up when rustling got louder. Thank heaven, the mare didn't run off. The gratitude was, however, short-lived. The sound of leaf movement coming closer was not from the hooves of my horse, but from human footsteps accompanied by a panting four-legged animal.

Lying perfectly still, peeking through my lashes, I hoped he couldn't hear my heart beating a hole in my chest.

My dagger along with my dress had been forgotten on the bed at La Colina. However, the oversight was not without a historic event. I actually regretted not taking Mother's advice, something that probably had never happened before. The Gospel according to Anne almost always included the concealing of a knife. Even if a girl lacked merit, she should at least keep up the appearance of virtuosity by carrying a weapon.

Mother's tiny gold earrings jiggled with the movement of her jaw when she'd say, "Always carry a dagger, Madeleine. Don't go anywhere without it."

One boot firmly planted at my hips and the other at my shoulder pointing up the hill, the victim of my prank was standing next to me.

A lustrous pair of tall black boots with huge over-the-knee flaps turned down at the top of the calf had blotted up large amounts of someone's spit. Was it his or another's that had done the polishing?

Like a bunny reflected motionless in the sparkle of a hound's eye, except for my heaving bosom, I didn't move. The charade, however, ended abruptly, when the stranger's dog wet-poked me in the face with his snout, mopping my cheeks and eyelids with an enormous tongue while I was trying to appear unconscious.

Almost as is if chasing a mouse in my clothes, the man put his hands all over me. I squealed like a schoolgirl. Being pawed like that seemed harmless, except that he targeted my privates with exuberance unbecoming of a gentleman. I didn't dare look at his face, but could feel him smiling as he palmed me all over. Darting from one place to another, he grabbed both my breasts. I swung my arms, managing to slap him several times about the shoulders. Then he put his hand directly between my legs. I screamed.

"Adelio, I think our friend is very much alive," he said, to the sizable fine-boned hunting dog that had wandered away for a sniff of the ground where Artemia went down.

Hoping he hadn't felt the little involuntary contraction of approval, I pried the stranger's probing palm from my crotch by his wrist and yelled, "Unhand me, Señor! Are you not a gentleman?"

He gave me another little squeeze between the legs, laughed, and said, "It doesn't appear as though you're a gentleman, either."

Then he made some silly reference implying that he was merely checking to see if I was hurt, but I wasn't about to let his ridiculous excuse pass. Pushing myself up off the ground, I said, "Señor, it is quite doubtful you would've checked another *man* for broken bones, in the manner in which you violated me. You took advantage of an unconscious woman just so you could steal a feel."

"I assure you that if I was going to feel a girl, I wouldn't be stealing it. And, I may not be one-hundred-percent certain, but I don't think those who've been rendered unconscious are quite that capable of kicking, clawing, cursing, and scratching."

I brushed the debris from my clothes, and he started in with me again, adding a hint of sarcasm.

"You've taken quite a spill. For a while there, it looked like you were actually going to make it. You handled that mare pretty well for a girl. Where did you learn to ride like that?"

"…On my own. And I am not a girl. I'm a woman."

Batting me around like a mouse under a cat's paw, he said, "Really?" And, with a huge pause before finishing his sentence he closed in for the kill. "What's the difference?"

"Maturity."

Looking straight up to the sky, he laughed loudly and replied, "Yes, I see that now. How could I have made the error?"

I gave my sweated collar a tug away from my neck. "Voltaire said that a witty saying proves nothing."

The stranger quipped back, "Voltaire also said that anything too stupid to be said is sung."

The additional blow of slipping on the incline of dead leaves and falling on my ass failed to subdue my waning enthusiasm. "What does that have to do with anything?"

Then, as if he had suddenly become concerned with my unsteadiness, he lost his smile, reached down to help me to my feet, and said, "That's exactly my point."

I pulled my arm away and snapped, "It amazes me how quickly you've become tiresome. Where's my mare?"

"Probably back in … where is it you're from, France?"

"Casa de la Colina."

"Casa de la Colina? Lizarraga never mentioned a daughter. However, if the clandestine child has returned, after having spent even such a brief time in her company, I completely understand why he wanted it kept quiet."

It was probably a good thing I was so dizzy, I aimed a slap at his face and promptly lost my balance.

The stranger grabbed my arm to keep me from falling and in a newfangled tone of seriousness said, "I will take you to Casa de la Colina."

"I can walk, thank you."

Letting go of me, he replied, "Well, I'll be off then. Surely you'll be fine walking for hours in this heat. Shall I ride ahead and tell Lizarraga you'll be late for supper?"

Wobbling up the hill by myself, I got to the road after slipping onto my palms only once or twice.

I had taken but a few steps and had to stop.

Keeping up his master's annoying tendencies, the dog with a wide silver collar engraved with some sort of monogram was right there beside me, panting and poking his nose wherever he pleased.

I took a few more steps and stopped to wipe my brow with my shirtsleeve, bent over and put both hands on my knees, only to endure another lick in the face.

The curve ahead that had previously gone by in a blur was leagues away.

The jingle of the steel bit, sweet scent of a sweaty horse, and gentle sound of hooves softly pressing into the sand next to me shouldn't have been a surprise. I was grateful I hadn't been abandoned, yet kept looking straight ahead as if I were alone.

The hoof-beats stopped. I expected a clever quip of some kind, but the man silently slipped his boot from the iron, placed his leg forward of the saddle, and reached down to me. I took his hand and slid my foot into the silver stirrup of a nobleman.

Pulling me up onto his horse with him, the stranger said, "It might be to your benefit to stay on top of the animal this time. Hang on to me."

Taking him around the waist was embarrassing. But the longer I held on, the more I wanted to.

In the tiny silence before the black's next hoof touched the earth, my hand was pressed into the flimsy barrier of a moist muslin shirt. Underneath, unyielding flesh made me wonder what the stranger's bare skin felt like.

The lullaby of repetitive horse steps convinced me to rest my head on his shoulder. Closing my eyes, I felt as though I were falling into a badger hole and onto the pages of a little-girl's story book. As I am running down the darkened palace steps toward a golden coach, one of my shoes slipped off. Frantically looking around, I let go a sigh of relief. There it was, sparkling in the torchlight. I picked up the glass slipper.

TUESDAY, 15 AUGUST 1780

A cool, wet, dab on my lips and a little noise similar to the squeaking of a rusty door hinge opened my eyes. The dog was sitting on the floor, and still able to put his long skinny gray snout on the linen to stick his huge black nose in my face.

I had never slept on such a soft bed, nor had such finely spun textile next to my skin, and certainly not greeted to waking by an enormous dog nozzle on a hound the size of my first pony.

The hottest summer anyone could remember seemed almost pleasant in the tiny room with a disproportionately steep roof.

Leaking through an open window covered with fine-spun lace curtains, the faint odor of lemony sour-grass perfumed the air along with the blissful aria of a songbird like the whack of a mallet on my skull.

Searching for something to throw in hopes of convincing the happy fowl to go elsewhere, I spotted two young servant girls in smocks and bonnets, peering in around the edge of the partially open door, cupping their hands over their mouths in a ridiculous attempt to conceal giggles. The splashing water from a fountain echoing off the courtyard walls behind them was loud enough to drown out any whisper.

Seeing me trying to get out of bed, the girls ran off one behind the other, yelling, "She's awake! She's awake!" their cries gradually fading in what I surmised as being an imposing house purely by the amount of time it took for the voices to disappear.

I threw back the bedcover, when a not-very-tall-wet-nurse-buxom woman carrying a tray came in.

With a yellow Asphodel yet to wilt tucked inside the comb holding her dark tightly pulled back, braided hair, neatly balled up behind her head, she would've looked clown-like had her facial expression been anything other than as kind and endearing as it was.

She smiled, sat down on the edge of the mattress, and with arms that had blossomed with ample flesh from the testing of numerous culinary endeavors, waved to the dog and said, "Go to your place, Adelio." After which the animal obediently, left the room nails tapping on the tile.

Pushing the tray in front of me, and mindfully arranging the dishes to make them more appealing, the woman took my hand, cracked the corners of her mouth into another smile, and then over-accentuating her words as if I were an infant or an idiot, said, "My name is Maria. You are here at Hacienda Sagrado del Corazon, the home of El Conde Armando de Velazquez. Your parents left about an hour ago to get your things from Casa de Colina. They will return soon. You gave us all quite a scare. Now, please you must have something. The physician said you are to eat and drink, should you" -- Then lest there was a chance I that I might not have, she pushed the tray closer and corrected herself to say, "... *when* you wake up."

Grabbing the spoon, I was about to take a gulp of soup, when I dropped the silver on the edge of the bowl with a clink and said, "Where's my mare? Where's Artemia?"

"She's fine. She's here. Your father brought her over yesterday when el conde offered the services of Carlos, our horse-master. Showing up at Casa de Colina by herself with torn reins, covered with scrapes and dirt, the little horse scared the blazes out of everyone."

Acting as if she were imparting gossip, Maria leaned closer, made superficial hand gestures, and lowered her voice. "The mare has some minor cuts and bruises, but she's in the stable and doing very well, you needn't worry."

"Papa brought her here yesterday? What day is this?"

"You were already asleep when el conde brought you home on Sunday. This is Tuesday," she replied, going to the window to pull the dark curtain closed, leaving a thin slice of sun to narrow and widen with the breeze through the lace underneath.

The woman sat down on the mattress, watched me dunk the heel of a crusty loaf into the milk and saffron sour-grass broth like a street beggar and stuff it into my mouth with no regard to what fell on the linen.

"You have quite an appetite for such a skinny girl," he said with a huge smile.

I never saw him come in.

My cheeks puffed up like a squirrel getting ready for winter, and the very man I made subject of buffoonery was standing across the room. Not only that, he was the best-looking man I'd ever seen. I couldn't take my eyes off him.

With my mouth so full, all I could do was fake a smile between swallows and eat crow along with the soup.

He was older than I first thought, very faint lines formed shallow creases on the outside corners of his eyes and unlike any nobility I'd ever been company to, his skin was sun-drenched brown.

I tried to glance away from his thighs, but his tight pants tugged at my vision like the rope that winds a bucket out of a well, and a peek at his privates happened on its own -- after which I quickly looked at his face before making diversionary aimless roaming searches as if merely surveying the room.

Praying that my wandering eye went unnoticed, I couldn't keep from admiring his body. How could God have created any man who looked that good?

On his sparsely haired, sun-darkened chest, peering through the front opening of a deeply-slit shirt, a silver cross hung around his neck.

Heel-clicks on the floor brought him closer. He stood next to my bed. His pants tightened even more as he shifted his weight to one leg. Then, resting his hand on the hilt of his sword, he parted his full lips into a half-smile, and looked right through me with sparks in sea-green deep-set eyes, the color of which belonged on a cat.

Across his chest, the slice of sun coming in reflected the crisp white linen of his shirt onto his face as if he were an actor glowing on stage in the foot-lamps, and he said, "So… it looks like you're going to live, after all."

I was searching for a witty reply when a servant girl slipped into the room, lifted her pristine white apron, curtsied, and announced, "Señor Conde, the Señorina's parents and Don Miguel Lizzaraga are here."

Pushing the door wide, billowing past Papa and the servants, Mother pressed ahead of everyone else, and shouted, "There she is! And she's fine! Just as I said she'd be! Madeleine, my beloved, have you any idea what you've put us through?"

The tiny room got even smaller.

Several young servant girls stealing wide-eyed peeks from the courtyard took turns popping white bonnets into view and disappearing again as Papa took Mother's arm and said, "Anne, let's allow Madeleine to rest, we'll have plenty of time to talk when she's feeling better."

As usual, Mama did whatever she wanted anyway. Flopping onto the edge of my bed, she leaned over, kissed my forehead, gave me a hug, and began talking so fast, no one could possibly interrupt.

"We brought all your clothes. And of course, I brought my things, too. Has anyone told you that el conde has invited us to stay here in his home until you're completely well? He has! And not only that, his personal physician has seen you several times, the monsignor has been here, and Artemia has been given the run of the stable yard. Papa will be taking care of whatever it is he has to with the La Colina horses, but I'll be here with you," she said, patting my knee through the linen, conveying the familiar loving touch she always had without realizing she possessed anything special.

Miguel's appearance went almost unnoticed. But there he was, wedged just inside the doorway of the shoulder-shrugging close quarters, squinting with his palm in front of his face to block the annoying slice of sun across the back wall.

Armando touched Maria's shoulder as if she were family, and said, "Have Madeléna's belongings taken to the Dolorosa room. Señora's things are to be taken to the guest chamber. And dinner will of course include the addition of our new guests."

Then on his way out Armando stopped to talk to Miguel in what sounded as though the continuation of a conversation that had already taken place. "We dress for supper, Don Miguel, why don't you come back around 8?"

Maria announced that I needed to rest and shooed everyone from the room.

Miguel turned to the head housekeeper and said, "I wish to speak to my fiancé, alone."

"It's all right, we'll keep it brief," I told her.

She was reluctant, but accommodated my wishes anyway.

The furrows in Miguel's brow looked more like lines of annoyance than worry. He stood at the foot of the bed, stamped his foot on the floor, slapped his sides, the jabot around his neck twitched, and he said, "I can't believe it was Velazquez who found you. Why in God's creation did it have to be *him*?!"

"He's been very kind, Miguel. Why is that wrong?"

Then as if I was supposed to know the answer, Miguel looked around the room as if searching for something, raised his voice slightly, and said, "Why is it wrong?…his reputation! El conde has a reputation, that's the problem. It's his reputation."

"You shouldn't speak of him like that in his own home, Miguel."

"My fiancée is in his house, in bed. I think I can speak any way it is I want."

"It's not like I'm in *his* bed."

"Oh, you *will* be…."

My eyes went wide with a huge grin. Biting my lower lip, I said, "I think you're jealous."

Miguel's tone was a scant more than irritated. "Madeleine, what *did* happen in the woods?"

It was the first time I really liked Miguel. "You *are* jealous," I replied, with a laugh. After which my head hurt so much, I winced and grabbed the back of my skull.

The self-petting and soft rumbling purr of a black and white cat, first rubbing one way and then quickly turning to rub the other side of its skinny body along the bottom of the wall next to the door was interrupted by Maria's closing hands around its belly as she gently placed the cat out in the courtyard and said, "Go find a mouse."

Miguel took a step toward the door as if the head-housekeeper's reappearance meant he had to leave.

"Come home with me to La Colina, Madeleine."

"I will, Miguel, when I'm better."

He was walking out when he confirmed why he was never to be my husband. Turning to me one last time, he said, "I won't fight for you, if *that's* what you want."

19

Truth was I felt well enough to have gone with him. And, by late afternoon they couldn't keep me in bed any longer.

I could've easily made it without any help, but Maria and Mother escorted me upstairs hanging on as if I were to fall at any moment.

The Dolorosa chamber at the top of the central stairway was like a bedtime storybook, were it not for the tyrannizing, weeping Virgin on the massive armoire.

Mother went right for the bed so big, six sailors could've easily slept on it with no difficulty. Shaking the white silk netting tied to the twisted posts, to see if anything would fall out, she inspected every piece of furniture, empty drawer, and crevice she could find. And with a final pat, Mother batted the velvet drapes on the balcony doors overlooking the cobblestone between the main house, the stable, and carriage house, happily wiped her palms into applause, and commended Maria on her staff, since not one bug was to be found.

The bump on my head didn't stop me from being packed into the green silk off-the-shoulder gown, an eighteenth birthday gift from parents envisioning their child being entertained by royalty.

"Madeleine, I just knew you were going to need this dress," Mother said, lacing up my stays so tight I couldn't take a full breath.

The garment had been deliberately made to make my waist appear only slightly wider than my wrist. And with the words, "Take a deep breath, my precious," I lost my grasp on the bedpost with the final yank from both Mother and Maria.

Even with the top of the corset cutting into my breasts, after slowly lowering onto the edge of the bed, all I could think about was food. And with supper still hours away, I did what any respectable houseguest would. I snooped.

Discolored walls and filled-in patches didn't quite match the two-hundred-year-old stone-work. With a mark hither and gouge there, Hacienda del Sagrado Corazon, breathing a scarred life of its own, whispered generations of Velazquez. And, at the heart, water splashed over the edges of a three-tier fountain so loud, I couldn't hear my own footsteps as I walked by.

The pale glow of the lime-washed walls surrounding each lantern replaced the final light of the day as a servant lifted a long silver rod to light the last in a row of ornate tin Moorish sconces lining the passageway. I found what was soon to become my favorite place in the house, a covered stone portico facing the carriage building, with a railing perfect for leaning against if one happened to be wearing a dress too tight to sit down.

Insects and frogs in the tall grasses beyond were getting louder with the brightening lamp-glow as workers across the cobblestone went about their nightly check of the stable horses. None of them noticed me, tugging and fidgeting with the mid-section of my gown, searching for a scrap of silk that would allow me to breathe. I smoothed the bodice over my tummy as though I had accomplished something.

"May I be of assistance?"

My heart jumped into my throat, I turned so fast. My host was standing barely half an arm's length away.

"Señor Conde, you've already given me more assistance than I could ever thank you for," I said, mustering the same tone of sarcasm I'd been subjected to more than once.

"There's no need to thank me. I did for you what I would've done for anyone," he replied, actually sounding serious.

"Really? Is that so? Would you have carried home a complete stranger, to be tended by your personal physician, have your servants satisfy his every need, and entertain his parents, too?"

A boyish grin sank the dimples in his cheeks. "Were you not a stranger two days ago?"

"Well, stranger or not, I'm going to thank you anyway," I replied, plunking my hands on my hips.

"You don't want to thank me."

"Yes, I do."

"The Moors left us with more than just stenciled walls, they ruled hospitality into law. If you thank me, you will be obligated. And, if the gracious gesture for which you would be bound were to have been for something such as…maybe saving your life, your debt would be fittingly proportionate. So, you do not want to thank me."

"I never mentioned anything about saving my life. I merely said, thank you."

Armando's green eyes punched a hole in the night. "What do you think would have happened had I left you in the woods? Perhaps you would've struck your head again, or gypsies might've found you lying on the side of the road. The forest is thick with vagabonds. Do you know how to dance and tell fortunes? Well, you're a quick study, I'm certain the learning period would've been brief. Actually, you probably wouldn't have spent a great deal of time with the itinerants. It would've been far more likely that you'd have found your way across the Strait to the slave auction. By then, I know you would've learned how to dance quite well."

"You're admonishment is most kind, Señor Conde. I already have a father, thank you."

"…And a fiancé, both of whom will be here in minutes," Armando replied, with a chink of his scabbard chain hangar as he pushed me to the stone wall.

A wisp of hair fell from the comb on top of my head and jostled over my cheek.

I was pinned to the cool, rough limestone by the weight of his body. His hands clasped my palms on either side of my face.

Armando's arousal penetrated our clothes as he slowly lowered his head to bring his mouth to mine. Beads of sweat ran down my throat, dripping between my breasts as a three-day old beard briefly scratched the corner of my upper lip. I could almost taste him. But, the kiss didn't come.

"How do you think a woman should repay a man who has just saved her life?" he said, in a low, deliberate voice.

"What would Miguel and my father think if they saw this?" I said with just enough vibrato to give away my apprehension, as if a shaking body wasn't enough.

Armando's lips touched mine for the briefest of moments, leaving me quivering like the middle of winter. He pulled away.

"What would they think? They would think you were being compromised," he whispered, looking down at me as if he still wanted to put his mouth on mine.

Wheels rattled on the stone drive in front of the house. Armando took my hand and led me to the main entry with such huge strides, I could barely keep up.

"*Bienvenidos!*" he shouted as guests arrived in clusters. The third coach was Lizzaraga's.

Naturally, Miguel and Papa stopped to greet us. With a quick shake of my head, I flipped the stray lock dangling in my face behind my shoulder. Father gave me a hug and pat. All I got from my fiancé was an icy stare. Surely, he'd seen Armando holding my hand.

"Well, it looks as though you've recovered nicely," Miguel said.

"Yes, I'm doing very well, thank you, Miguel."

"Had you listened to me none of this would've happened. But you insisted on behaving like a child."

"Yes, you're right, I behaved like a child," I replied, sucking in my lower lip.

Armando's dimples sank as he looked right at me with a smile and said, "That's the first thing Madeléna said when I found her. She told me she was behaving just like a child."

Lord knew Papa could mediate, having been married to Anne for so long. Pointing the way to supper, he said, "There'll be plenty of time in which to discuss such things. Let's enjoy the evening, shall we?"

Descending the stairs right on cue, Mother made an entrance as only she knew how. Stopping at the landing, she raised a gloved arm, and loud enough for everyone to hear, including those just stepping out of their carriages on the drive, announced, "My whole family is here, present and future!"

Ignoring everyone but her host, Mother planted her hand inside el conde's arm, giving him no choice but to escort her to dinner.

My fiancé made some feeble attempts at apologizing for letting me run off after our argument. His timing could've been better. We were following behind Mother's over-accentuated gestures walking arm-in-arm with Armando, and I couldn't take my gaze off our host's shiny silver scabbard swaying with each step he took in his tight black pants.

The austerity of a hanging tapestry or two was completely overshadowed by the dinner table that seated fourteen.

Maria wasn't still for a moment. Darting from kitchen to table, supervising staff and inspecting tray after tray, she made sure guests were treated to nothing less than perfection.

Wine and sherry from Armando's vineyard flowed freely from cistern-wielding servants, tending to every culinary desire imaginable, all presented with highly polished silver goblets, plates, fine linen, and crystal.

The only thing that wasn't perfect was Miguel's constant gibbering. Though I doubt I heard a word.

Armando and I stole glances throughout the night. And since my dress was too tight for me to eat more than a bite or two, all I did was look forward to another flicker to come my way from the opposite end of the table.

During the pretense of listening to whatever Miguel was going on about, I caught Armando looking at me during one of his transparent peeks in my direction.

Miguel took notice and said, "Did he just stare at you? I saw him look right at you."

"That's ridiculous. No such thing happened," I replied, searching Miguel's blabbering face. *This* was the man I was going to spend the rest of my life with?

I actually considered running away, a solution that would've been easier than explaining the nullification to my parents. I went so far as to imagine being in bed with Miguel, a scenario that would likely go along with being married to him. I just wanted to run upstairs, rip off my too-tight dress, throw myself on the bed, and cool off to a blissful night's sleep in Spain's August inferno.

Eternity had passed before the after-dinner decanters had been emptied for the last time. The men retired to the library for cigars, and the ladies went to a corner of the great room for gossip and idle chat.

Midnight had come and gone long before the last guest finally went home. After saying good night to Miguel and Papa, Armando, Mother, and I watched and waited outside until Lizzaraga's coach driver had taken the lively team of gray mares off into the darkness. The crunch of wheels was a distant faint grind when the three of us went inside.

The house lived a different life at night. Servants with long brass snuffers scuffed their tired feet over the tile, darkening patches of glowing flames on the limestone, extinguishing lamps one by one.

Savoring an embarrassing amount of time in which she held the back of her hand to Armando's face for a kiss, Mama was about to climb the courtyard stairs to retire for the night when she seized the chance for one more gratifying moment. Only after her host's lips had administered additional concessions did she continue up the stairs, cross the upper corridor, and disappear into her room with a click of the door-latch echoing below.

I expected Armando to say goodnight at the foot of the staircase, and then maybe return to the library for a final smoke or sherry. But Mother hadn't been gone more than a minute when the chain holding Armando's scabbard softly jingled with the motion of his hip as he put a boot on the second step.

His already close-fitting black pants tightened around his thighs as he leaned forward to rest his elbow on his raised knee.

I didn't wait for the hand-kiss. I tore my gaze away from the lower half of his body, and placed a green silk slipper on the first stair.

Armando gently grasped my wrist. A rush of blood poured through my veins as he lowered his head and whispered, "My door will not be locked. Come to me, tonight."

THURSDAY, 17 AUGUST 1780

With his invitation to bed the night before, Armando's charming manner was a sip of chocolate from a cup gone cold.

The man must've had quite the opinion of himself, to think I would just show up under his linen at the mere asking. My consolation was the hope that he had spent as least as many sleepless hours anticipating my arrival as I passed lying in bed wondering if he was awake.

The regular swordsmanship lessons that lasted anywhere from two to three hours during the hottest part of the afternoon had been rescheduled in order to accommodate a visit to the match at the bull ring in Sevilla, a little jaunt probably originally planned as an apogee to a night of mad love-making.

It would've been safe to say that Armando's confidence wasn't merely restricted to the bedroom. The fencing maestro wore a leather jacket in spite of the heat, while el conde's only protective measure was to strap on a pair of leather gauntlets merely a few shades darker than his sun-drenched skin. The highly-decorated cuffs having acquired an unsettling number of gashes, worn edges, and dark crevices, revealed their true worth, having thwarted past potential wrist-vein slashes.

Sitting in the shade of the portico, staring at the unveiling of a newly cut diamond, I watched Armando walk through waves of heat squiggling above the cobblestone.

His long shirt tails covered his ass for a moment after he pulled the garment from his pants, flung it over his head, and tossed it to the side of the courtyard. All the while his nearly waist-length long brown locks tied together by a black cloth waved back and forth, brushing his naked skin before falling around the top of his shoulders, glistening in the sun.

How would his flesh would feel under my fingers?

Waiting for his student in the center of the courtyard, the fencing maestro was making a final inspection of his sword grip as if something were wrong with the weapon when Armando, naked to the waist, lifted his blade in a mock-kiss of the hilt and sliced the air with one quick cut, making a noise similar to that of a carriage whip.

Returning the salute, the maestro yelled, *"En Garde,"* after which the echoing clangs of steel were loud enough to squelch the smith shoeing horses next to the stable.

The exchange between teacher and student looked more like a dance than a fight. Neither man's weapon was permitted to land. Instead the word touché was spoken while leaving the blade just shy of its target.

The sight of watching sweat dripping from my host's sun darkened bare torso until the waist of his pants had become blacker than black, caused me to nearly bite a hole in my lower lip.

The silver cross around Armando's neck flopped side to side. Veins on the inside of his upper sword-arm bulged. And, at times, his utterances made me think of what I might've missed in bed with him the night before.

Flashes of steel swatted the sun so blinding I had to look away before being able to see again. Yet I couldn't look at anything but Armando.

Contrary to my prior assessment, his body was not perfect. A huge gash of shiny discolored flesh spanned nearly the entire width of his upper abdomen just below his chest. And that wasn't all. He had a well-healed slice barely visible on his lower back. How did he get hurt so badly? He could fence like blazes.

A break was called, at which time Armando, far less exhausted than the maestro, clicked his boots heels in my direction.

My heart found an extra beat as he reached over the railing, picked up a blue and yellow porcelain milk pitcher from the table, and tossed his head back.

Nothing existed but Armando's throat, pulsing with each swallow as he emptied the container. A narrow white stream caressed the chin that would soon require a razor before running down the corner of his mouth and dotting itself on his sweat-soaked chest. I could've easily reached out, swiped the droplet with my little finger, and pressed it to my lips.

Armando lowered the pitcher and said, "Good morning, Madeléna."

"You're being very coy. You didn't call me Madeléna last night."

"Léna, my beloved, if I am formal, it's because I must be. Allowing my true feelings would mean that I couldn't be next to you for very long without putting my hands on you."

"I thought you were a strong man."

The milk-pitcher softly clunked to the table. Leaning his forearms on the railing, with a sigh that easily could've been mistaken for an exhale of exasperation, Armando looked away in thought for a moment. He sank his dusty-emerald eyes deep into me and said, "I am a very strong man."

Standing impatiently with his sword tip to the ground in the middle of the courtyard, the maestro cleared his throat and yelled, "It's time, Señor Conde."

Armando hurried away without another word. But, it wasn't to be long before his aloofness would come to an end.

Having never been to a bull-fighting match, I was of far greater innocence than being a virgin. So, with the sole purpose of attaining worldliness, I agreed to witness the massacre disguised as sport.

Miguel and I had been invited as a couple, along with Armando's closest friend, Maximo Zequeira and his wife, Luisa.

I intended to enjoy myself regardless of the awkward social situation. The smoldering exchanges Armando and I had already enlisted, in addition to the fact that he had chosen to be without an escort, made the afternoon sticky, to say the least.

Wearing tall black boots, close-fitting black pants, and a large white full-sleeved muslin shirt with a long slit down the front, through which his sparsely haired chest continually distracted my attention, el conde's attire was no different than that of a commoner. Were it not for the elegant transportation of the fully enclosed coach with the black and gold Velazquez family crest on the doors, no one would have a clue as to his station.

As usual, Miguel kept himself on a tight rein. The rest of us were more like a wild band of street-urchins swiping cakes from carts in the market.

"How is it that your coach is bigger than your house?" Maximo asked, handing the sherry bottle to Armando, who was standing in the center aisle with one hand on the hold-strap. The foursome was hell bent.

Leaning over to keep from bumping his head on the roof, our host replied, "This *is* my house, man. It just looks big, because the wife and kids aren't home."

In spite of the rutted road and galloping team, Armando poured without spilling a drop of spirits. Until we hit a hole. Sherry spurted from the bottle. We all got wet but the only one who cared was Miguel. He brushed the libation from his white lace jabot as if a horse had just snorted on his finery. The rest of us laughed louder than the deafening wheel-rattles and hooves.

Armando skillfully served what was left from the bottle into the tiny silver goblets we swiped from the tableware chest during a bit of pre-jaunt mischief, where I lifted my dress and stashed the vessels into my underskirt pocket.

We hit another rut and Armando seized the chance to dump sherry on his best friend as if had been a mishap.

"Watch it, man!" Max shouted.

With a tussle of her lace cuffs, pushing on her husband's arm as if the splatter had been his fault all along, Luisa squealed and wiped the spill from her eye.

Maximo wasn't laughing. He cupped his hand beside his mouth and yelled, "Tell the driver to slow down!"

Armando tried to hide his amusement as he stretched out the window and shouted to the driver to take it easy. Minutes later we were still swaying back and forth as fast as the highly-conditioned steeds could froth. El conde must've hollered out the window half a dozen times. But each attempt at communicating with the driver went unanswered.

The carriage kept rattling on at full speed and we roared with laughter.

As we passed the old Roman viaduct, the scenery was a blur. Armando grabbed the top sill and started to climb out. A universal expression of disbelief was shared. No one expected him to do it. Turning and sitting on the top sill, Armando yelled to Max, "Hang onto my leg, will you, man?"

With one boot-heel up on the edge of the open door-window, Armando's thighs came into view at eye-level, leaving his most private part directly in front of my face. I wanted to look but Miguel was sitting right next to me and Luisa was smirking. What could I do?

Armando took a fast duck back inside to escape a low-hanging tree limb. The near miss only seemed to amuse him even more as he hoisted himself up top.

The sherry bottle chinked on the edge of the goblets several times, but I just stared out the window. I was falling in love.

We got to the new bullring, and acceptable or not, finding the row of privies behind the arena was the first thing to take care of.

Mother, a woman who had smoked a cigar in public on more than one occasion, said that only a tart would relieve the need near a public forum. However, when other women saw the bold new standard venturing into socially forbidden territory, they too dared to wait in line with the men along with me.

It wasn't the sort of place to have a meaningful conversation, let alone a hand touch of my shoulder from behind.

"Have you seen the city, yet?"

I spun around. Maximo was standing closer than he should've been.

"Miguel has invited me to dinner in Sevilla several times," I replied, taking a half-step back.

"You should let someone with more experience show you around."

"Is there someone in particular you have in mind?" I said, wishing for a hand-fan to wave furiously in my face.

Maximo's grin exposed an upper missing tooth. "I know where there's a street-musician with a huge music box on wheels. We could leave now and be back before the final match is over."

"You're serious, aren't you?" I laughed.

"Very," he replied, pulling a small engraved snuff box shaped like a tiny coffin from his pocket.

Dipping his little fingernail that had been grown disproportionately long to accommodate the habit, he scooped a speck of powder and held the offering in front of my nose.

"I have an idea," I said. "Why don't you run up to our seats and tell Armando, Miguel, and your wife that we'll see them later? I'm sure all three will be fine with that, and then you and I can be off alone, together."

Max stuck the snuff up his nostril with a loud whiff and replied, "I prefer a pleasant vice over an annoying virtue, don't you?"

"Your familiarity with Moliere is commendable. But the playwright also said a learned fool is more of a fool than an ignorant fool."

The hold Maximo took on my arm bordered on frightening.

"Let go of me!" I shouted, trying to yank my arm out of his grasp.

A curl of locks fell over the furrow of his brow. He clenched his fingers tighter. Jerking me closer, he glared down his nose and said, "Heed my warning, Madeléna. Do not fall in love with Armando. If you do, you'll disappear."

Pulling out of his clutch, I made my way to a privy that had just become available. When I re-emerged, Maximo was nowhere to be seen.

After having disappeared for longer than necessary for just about any purpose other than deliberating making himself unavailable, Max made an appearance from one of the ancient Roman-theater-style tunnels under the stone benches. Squeezing past my curled knees to get to his seat next to Luisa, he dispensed a lingering stare in my direction like a howl in the night.

Armando's title allowed us to watch the match from the Royalty box over the Picador gate. But there we were, sitting pressed up against each other, elbow-to-elbow with the commoners on the no-room-to-spare benches.

With the music, fabulous costumes, and fancy riggings on the horses, my cheek welcomed the occasional scratch from a face that needed a razor. The cheering was so loud when the bull charged Armando had to practically put his lips in my ear to explain the finer points of the sport, which represented no sentimental or moral considerations, just man's bravery to cope with danger and death.

Miguel didn't say or do anything. He sat straight upright on a backless bench, gripping his knees until his fingernails had left little dents in the fabric of his pant-legs.

The advertising on the billing posts showed a drawing of the matador with his feet tied to a chair while challenging the bull. Unfortunately, I never got to see it. Right after the pica was thrust into the bull's hump, blood spewed, and I ran.

Amongst rows of carriage teams waiting outside, the occasional hoof stomp in the dirt, jingle of harnesses, and swat of a fly with a tail was like home.

Our driver was off somewhere while the four blacks had been left with the brake on.

Catching my breath, I leaned on the Velazquez coat of arms lacquered onto the coach door and looked down between my arms at the pebbles scattered in the dirt.

I didn't have to look up as someone ran toward me. It had to be Armando. He put a hand on my shoulder, and said, "What's wrong, Léna?"

Pulling my chin around with the tips of his fingers, Armando looked me in the face. I couldn't say a word.

He took my damp hand and whispered, "What's wrong?"

Tears burst. I shook my head and replied, "I ...cannot...see... bleeding, animals."

Armando smiled with a look of relief, reached out and pulled me to him. Like flashes of lightning in a distant night sky, his arms around me and his moist chest on the side of my face stirred my heart.

Under the crease of his neck, Armando pressed me closer and said, "Léna, you mustn't see the bout through the eyes of the bull, but through the eyes of the man. After being gored, few ever return to the arena."

We waited for the match to end sitting inside the coach. Armando held my cheek to his chest, stroked my hair, and kissed the top of my head as if I were a hurt child.

Cheering came from the benches and he whispered, "I should like to kiss you."

"What's stopping you?" I replied, pulling away to look into his smoky green eyes.

"I don't know whether you want me to, or not."

"What is it you think I might want?"

Armando paused. The corners of his mouth softened. His eyes sparked as he took a tiny nod, and in a deep morning voice replied, "I think you would like to taste it all."

My heart pumped my veins with a flood.

"You should learn to have greater faith in your instincts, Señor Conde."

Armando's emerging beard scratched the corner of my mouth as he put his lips over mine. Tenderly prying my mouth open with his, he slipped inside and took a gentle suck of my tongue. I'd never been kissed liked that. I had no idea where I was.

The kiss went on through the crescendo from the bullring, signaling the end of the match.

Like a sleeping person drawn to wakefulness by a silent stare, I happened to open my eyes without knowing why. Armando ended our embrace when he felt me tense.

Miguel was standing outside the coach watching us through the window.

Finding the calm usually reserved for physicians and judges my betrothed stabbed me with a stare, and said, "I thought it might've been in our best interest to come after you this time."

Calmly stepping outside, as though the incident had been an unfortunate necessity, Armando said to Miguel, "We're going to leave as soon as Max gets here."

Just as the words were spoken, from between parked carriages Maximo appeared with Luisa in tow, holding her skirt over her ankles to facilitate the hasty pace. The draw-string satchel on her wrist bounced back and forth with each hurried step as her husband pulled her toward the coach. Not quite close enough yet for normal conversation, Max shouted, "This looks like a ménage à trios! Am I too late?"

Clearly annoyed, Armando quietly said, "Get in, we're leaving."

The ride home was about as much fun as a muddy calf-birthing in a downpour. Babbling about nothing, Luisa was the only one who talked. Armando rode up top. Maximo occasionally glared in my direction. Miguel wouldn't even look at me. And all I could think about was the kiss.

Lathered in their harnesses, the foursome puffed to halt in front of the house. It was the driver who took my hand to help me out.

Waiting until I stepped to the ground, without a hint of emotion Miguel said, "I don't think we shall ever see each other again."

FRIDAY, 18 AUGUST 1780

The last dinner guest had gone for the night. Mother, Armando, and I went to the library for a few final drops of sherry, some late-night conversation regarding French cuisine, art, journalism, politics, and a cigar or two, of which Mother pretended not to want one of her own. Brazenly taking the rolled-tobacco from Armando's mouth, she sucked several puffs before gently placing the cigar back between his lips as if she were feeding a baby. I was mortified.

After saying goodnight at the top of stairs, Mother strolled off to her room, barefoot, swinging her slippers in hand as if everything was fine, obviously knowing nothing about Miguel having broken off the engagement.

Armando was about to head across the upper corridor to his chamber when he leaned over and whispered, "Meet me on the portico."

My heart nearly banged its way through my chest as I walked to my room and stood behind my closed bedroom door.

Waiting what I thought was sufficient time to make it appear as though I had gone to bed, I sneaked out.

Blossoming thorny citrus trees filled my nostrils. Insects in the grasses beyond the lawn noisily rejoiced. The blistering day finally had become tolerable.

I turned the last corner. Standing at the railing, facing the carriage house across a tarnished silver moonlit courtyard, Armando turned to greet me with a smile that lit the night.

He put his arm around me and the tiny goblet and bottle in his hand clinked behind my back, leaving a cool spot above the top of my off-the-shoulder gown.

"All of Sevilla must know by now," I said, taking hold of his arm. "My family shouldn't have to pay for their daughter's indiscretion."

"The kiss wasn't meant to hurt you, Léna. Your family will be fine."

"Lizzaraga will cut-off Papa the instant he finds out that his former-future-daughter-in-law was kissing el conde."

With one arm still around me, Armando lifted the crystal stopper from the bottle with his free hand, tucked it between his fingers like a magician, and poured liquor into the tiny silver goblet.

"Señor Lizzaraga and I had a little talk last evening. Would you care for some sherry?"

"You talked to Miguel's father? That must've been the first act of Tartuffe," I replied, laughing from nerves.

"Lizzaraga is a businessman. He saw it upon himself to make his private stock available to the Chevaleaux farm."

"You can't be serious. Those stallions have been off-limits to Papa and everyone else."

"As it so happens, I'm Lizzaraga's favorite client, and should I stop buying horses from him, others would too." Armando grinned, and I almost cried.

"You did this for my family?"

"Sherry?"

"Yes, please."

I was about to take the goblet, when instead of handing it to me, Armando took a sip and said, "Look up, Léna."

"Look up? ...in the dark?"

"The Moors left their visiting card on the ceiling. Why don't you enjoy the view?"

The low rumble of distant thunder teased with precious rain that never came. Armando held me around the waist as I leaned back to take in the sight of brightly colored Moorish tiles between the ceiling beams, merely vague shades in the dark.

"Don't move," he whispered.

The lip of the goblet cooled my throat below the chin. A trickle of sherry ran down my neck. "Mon Dieu," I whispered, grabbing Armando's forearm.

His tongue licked across my chest like a mother cat cleaning her young. The wet swipe sent a wave of bumps up my arms as though it were the middle of winter.

Armando poured again. Chasing the sherry between my breasts with his mouth, he administered a tickling slurp at the little indentation below my neck. I wanted to laugh, but was on fire.

Leaning further back to keep from falling, I grabbed the elbow rests of an ornately carved bench. Filled and emptied again, the sticky brew was licked from my flesh.

Why could I not by chance fall out of the gown, innocently freeing my nipples to the night air? Weakness raced up my spine.

He pulled away.

Placing a knee on the bench, Armando sipped sherry as though I weren't there. He knew what he was doing. How could he leave me like that?

Armando put his mouth on mine, sucking me into his world with the sweet sting of sherry. The lingering taste went on as I felt the warmth of his breath through my dress with a kiss of my breast.

The game was over. Breathing as if he couldn't get enough air, Armando pulled me to his chest.

A loud pop sent decanter splinters echoing across the cobblestone, followed by a series of hollow, high-pitched rings. The silver goblet bounced and rolled up against the bottom of the railing. The stable dogs let go a few insincere barks from across the courtyard. Quiet returned, only to be interrupted by the soft jingle of Armando's scabbard chain as he pressed his hips to mine.

Feeling his way over the stays covering my breasts, he whispered, "How can you wear this thing?"

"I have no idea," I replied with a tiny laugh that sounded like I'd been awakened in the middle of the night.

Armando's rough palm was halfway up the inside of my left thigh.

"Please don't," I said, grabbing his wrist.

I expected him to insist, but he didn't. He took his hand away. Armando's enthusiasm, however, was still very much alive.

He kissed my throat and whispered, "I want you to touch me."

I knew what he meant. I was terrified. We were fully-clothed and I still couldn't do it. He had to take my hand and put it where he wanted it to be. I'd never felt a man before. But the desire to have him eclipsed the fear. I allowed Armando to pull my hand to him and touch him through his clothes. It set him further ablaze. The buttons on his pants were about to rip themselves from their holes. He held me tighter. Moving his mouth down my shoulder, his lips left gentle puckers all the way to the crease of my arm, where he kissed the inside of my elbow and said, "I can give you pleasure like you've never known."

Telling him no would end it. I let him touch me anywhere, as long as it was through my gown.

Armando's fingers knew where to go, and exactly what to do when he got there.

The fibers of his shirt began to rip in my grasp as he moved his fingers faster.

"Say my name," he whispered.

I could not utter a thing. All I could think about were his fingers.

"I will keep you like this until you say my name."

I said it. But it came out more like a moan than his name.

"Say it again, Léna. Say, my name," he said, intensifying the little circles of his fingers.

The quakes met the final gratifying tremor that took over at the precise moment I bellowed, "Armando!"

The new day brought enough light to see the dimples in his cheeks.

"We probably shouldn't be here in each other's arms, still dressed for dinner, when the blacksmith rolls his cart in and the chambermaids come to collect bed-pots," he said with a tiny tightening of his embrace.

"Did you plan this?"

"Did I *plan* trying to get into your clothes? Is that what you mean?"

Whipping a fake slap in the air as if to actually hit him, I said, "No, silly, the sherry? Did you plan to pour sherry on me?"

Armando smiled, and replied, "I planned for us to have refreshment on the portico. Drinking from your décolletage? Well, that…was improvised."

Sweetly brushing my cheek with the lightest feather touch from the back of his hand, he looked right through me and said, "Léna, please, you need to know something. And it's very important. Nothing is going to happen unless *you* come to me. I cannot go through another night like this one, and I won't allow it to happen again. Should you decide to come to my bed, Léna, there will be no turning back. I *will* take what is mine. You must be sure that being with me is what you want."

"Armando, I've never done it before."

"I know." He nodded.

"You know! How is it possible you could know?"

"If you were not a virgin, you'd already have opened your legs for me."

I couldn't be annoyed with him despite his arrogance. Just the same, I wrinkled my nose and got up to go.

The sun was peeking over the garden wall when Armando took my wrist, gently tugged me back, and put his mouth on mine for one more kiss.

SUNDAY, 20 AUGUST 1780

It was his house. He had to come home eventually. I went mad anyway.

Lord knows I should've seen him. I stared out the balcony doors all night before finally falling asleep with my cheek pressed up against the scratchy rug.

The early evening had been magical, a quartet of strings played the entire time we dined. All through dinner I did nothing but look forward to everyone going home so I could be with Armando.

Following a very brief episode of drinks and cigars in the library with the men, he disappeared. By the time I checked the stable to find his horse wasn't there, Armando had been long gone. Every scenario I came up with to explain why he left was worse than the one I'd just imagined.

The morning sun was streaming in when I picked myself up off the floor to go to bed. I happened to take a casual glance out to the courtyard. There he was, boots confidently clicking on the cobblestone.

I tucked behind the drapes while the source of my discomfort walked from the stable to the house. The face that craved a razor never even looked my way. I was glad he was home…and fuming.

The plan was to act as though nothing had happened. I didn't even go downstairs until late afternoon. Then, we accidentally met in the cocina while Maria was preparing supper. He was talking to her about some such thing or other and didn't look at me. It was like being hit with the skinny end of a whip. I didn't say good afternoon or make pleasantries of any kind. Throwing my arms wide, I practically screamed, "Where were *you* last night!?"

Maria ran out so fast, she dropped a batter spoon on the floor and just left it there.

The servants probably were listening with ears pressed up against the door, but neither of us allowed a minor detail like that to curtail the exchange. What made it particularly tough was Armando's ability to remain completely calm. I was burning out of control, hearing things from him that included the usual, you're not my wife, this is my house, and I can come and go as I please. But what took the blade to the hilt, was when he said, "Why should I stay home at night for you to keep your clothes, on?"

That's when I picked up the bowl of batter and threw it on him.

He stood there, laughing. I wanted to get even madder, but pretty soon I was laughing so hard I had to sit down. And by the time the servants walked back in, Armando and I were smeared in dough, in each other's arms, kissing deeply.

He and I had gotten closer than I expected. All was fine until shortly after dinner.

Bottle after bottle of spirits had been brought out in hopes everyone wouldn't notice how hot it was if they were sloshed. What resulted would've been considered far less than a tipping point for a duel had we been in France. But alas it was Spain, and the balderdash fuse that was lit along with a cigar turned out to be the night's premier entertainment.

44

Instead of gossiping with the ladies, I went strolling past the library, a strictly male sanctuary after supper.

Even before the spirits began to pour at the dinner table, Maximo had shown up soused. The man could hold some liquor. He drank all night long and still wasn't fall-down staggering drunk.

As I peered through the crack of the not-quite completely closed doors, the only clue that the blacksmith was pickled was his slurred speech and a tiny stagger now and again.

"Max, would you care for one of Cuba's finest?" Armando asked, creaking open the cigar-box lid.

Swaying in his boots with brow beaded in sweat, Max accepted his host's hospitality by snapping up one of the smokes and slapping the box-lid shut.

Cutting off the end of the cigar, Maximo leaned over the desk to light the thing from a candelabra flame. Following a long suck, he raised every eyebrow in the room. "So! Armando! Have you deflowered the virgin, yet?"

My heart jumped a stone wall.

Armando's irritation was completely concealed except for the appearance of one cheek dimple from forcing a half-smile. Attempting to dismiss the uncalled-for comment in front of the quieted room of stares, he replied, "Your tongue is sharper than the swords you make."

Everyone laughed, except Maximo. Steel screeched. Whipping his blade from its scabbard, a lock of hair fell over Max's forehead as he jerked the weapon from its holder.

"...Oh, really? Would you like to find out just how sharp this one is?" he replied, exploding into a lunge at his host.

Armando would've been killed had he not instantly jumped back several paces with his full white sleeves billowing wide. He stood completely still, staring down the length of his friend's sword, the tip of which had come to rest no more than an inch from his throat.

Señor Guzman, the eldest guest who had no doubt seen a dis-agreement or two in his time, quietly picked up Maximo's lit cigar that had fallen to the rug. Gently taking the blacksmith's arm, he said, "Please don't do this, Max. Whatever happens, it cannot end well."

Maximo made a quick turn and half-shrug to remove the con-solatory gesture, looking away without a word.

Monsignor Pablo Ramirez, a clergyman who had known Armando's parents and on more than one occasion seen the fam-ily through crises, with his soft, melodic voice that priests always seem to use, put a hand on Armando's shoulder and said, "Please, Señor Conde, just apologize to him and that will be the end of it. Max is not thinking clearly."

Armando calmly replied, "I'm sorry, Father, I cannot do that, for it is he who needs to apologize."

"Everyone will know *why* you apologized, my son, just end this now."

"It is Max who needs to beg forgiveness."

"For what?" Maximo snapped.

"For the unseemly remark regarding our host's houseguest," the Monsignor answered.

Maximo indignantly blurted, "Houseguest! She's not his house-guest! She's his next tart!"

Steel ripped as Armando drew his sword from its scabbard, pointed the blade at his friend, and said, "All right, we'll have it your way. The dispute is to be settled according to the rules of duel by sword until First Blood. The bout will take place now, here in this house, in the Great Room."

Replacing his weapon into its holder, Armando went to the desk drawer, took out his protective cuffs and began to strap them on his wrists. My heart pounded.

Ramirez made a final plea in the form of a one-sided conversa-tion, spoken too quietly for anyone else to hear, except Armando, who with furrowed brow, silently stared at the desktop while lacing up his leather cuffs. "Mustn't," was the only word I could make out.

The men headed for the door. And I ran.

The women in the Great Room stopped talking the instant they saw me standing there, sucking wind.

By the way her dress rustled like dried leaves with each step in my direction, Mother knew something was up. "What's happened?" she whispered, taking hold of my arm.

The little gold-drop earrings wiggled against my lobes as I shook my head trying to find a way to say something, before the approaching voices got any closer.

Leading the all-male entourage, getting louder with each resolute step, Armando's boots pounded the stone across the courtyard.

The men came in, huddled amongst themselves, and began speaking in hushed tones.

Mother hadn't yet decided to be concerned or angry. Poised to go either way, she whispered, "What's going on, Madeleine?"

Before I could tell her anything, Maximo staggered in, attempting to appear sober. Fiddling with his scabbard chain, the drunken blacksmith stood beneath a relief of the Sagrado Corazon hanging over the entry arch like a has-been actor about to take his final soliloquy before a packed theater.

The ormolu clock on the mantle chimed 12. Guzman went to the center of the huge room and readied to disclose the terms of the disagreement. Susurrations ceased.

Regardless of the quiet, the elder guest raised his already authoritative voice to make the announcement. "There has been an exception. It has been agreed to be settled by sword until First Blood. The contest is regarding remarks exchanged between Maximo Zequiera and El Conde Armando Francisco de Velazquez. The duel is to take place here and now. It has been witnessed and authenticated. The exact words said, will or will not be revealed pending outcome of the challenge."

With his weight resting on one boot, Armando stood in the middle of the room securing the laces on his gauntlets one last time. Luisa ran up to him, fell to her knees at his feet, and pleaded, "Please don't do this, Señor Conde. Whatever it was he didn't mean it. Armando, please I beg you, he's drunk!" Sobbing, she slid to the floor. Holding onto Armando's boot with her arms around his knee, she mewled, "He can't fence you when he's sober."

Armando never looked at her. "Do not beg me, woman. Beg your husband. It is he who has forced this upon me."

Mother grabbed my elbow and whispered, "What's going on, Madeleine?"

"Maximo called me a tart."

"So they're going to kill each other?"

I nervously pulled the top of my sweaty bodice away from my chest and replied, "There could be something else, I don't know."

House servants, having learned of the duel, mixed with guests congregating along the walls. No one was about to miss the settlement.

Waving a damp nose rag as if she were summoning a coach driver, Luisa reached out to her husband. However, Maximo went without as much as a glance at his wife. Scuffing his way to the center of the room, pulling his sword from the scabbard and snapping it back into place over and over, it looked as if he had a case of the jitters. Truth was, Max was too tanked to have enough sense to be nervous.

Guzman reached into the fireplace, took out a lump of charcoal, and after stepping off the marks five paces apart, drew two lines on the floor in the center of the room.

Waiting for the drunken blacksmith to get ready, Armando asked, "What's this really about, Max?"

"You know what this is about!" the blacksmith snapped.

Armando almost broke into a tiny laugh. "No I don't. Why don't you tell me?"

Maximo responded by whipping out his sword and launching a less than graceful ballestra aimed at his host. Practically falling off his feet, Max landed his weapon tip just shy of Armando's chest and shouted, "*et la!*"

Forced to jump out of the way of Max's blade yet again, Armando, cleverly backed away as three of the men ran to restrain the less-than-arrant guest.

Guzman stepped between the two and with a hand before each man said, "We'll have none of that. This is a gentleman's settlement. Let's keep it that way."

The mantle clock ticked to Luisa's whimpering through the handkerchief in front of her face, while she watched Maximo put his sword back into its scabbard.

For a few moments, it looked as if nothing were going to happen besides an exchange of glaring stares.

"Are the swordsmen ready?" Guzman said, preparing to step aside. Both nodded. And with the same sort of gesture that one would make when removing a hat from his head, Armando raised his sword and let it fall to slice the air in the customary salute to his opponent. Maximo disrespectfully threw the tip of his blade in Armando's direction merely to get the formality over with.

Guzman held up his hand, and yelled, "*En Garde...Alle!*"

Hopefully those watching with much anticipation had not expected an enormous struggle, because had that been the case, surely they were left unsatisfied.

Word was given, and without ever raising his blade, Armando backed away from a hapless lunge that nearly brought Maximo to his knees after his weapon thrust into nothing. A clang or two of metal blade against blade echoed off the limestone walls with a variety of simple parries as Armando kept his sword out of play, a tactic that seemed to infuriate the blacksmith all the more.

Then, just as Maximo was about to initiate yet another feeble attack, the whistle of a blade moving so fast it was difficult to see exactly what was done, Armando tore his opponent's shirt on the left sleeve.

Maximo dropped his weapon and held onto the bloodied muslin where he had been skillfully sliced just sufficiently to be called First Blood. And the bout, the entirety of which took no more than thirty seconds, was over.

Holding his sword-tip to Max's throat, a tiny drop of red dripped from the point as Armando said, "I think it's time for you to go home."

Luisa stopped crying, and ran to her husband. Mopping his bloodied arm with her handkerchief as if the patting that stained her dainty linen square would be sufficient, she helped her husband to the door.

Maximo, with one hand on his wife's shoulder and the other holding onto his wound, was about to walk out, when the he turned and said to his host, "I see that you've finally bedded down the memory of Blanca."

The look in Armando's eye rivaled the edge of his blade as he replied, "I have. Apparently, it is *you* who have not."

Dinner guests slowly departed amidst a muse of self-conscious throat-clearing and shirt-tucking. Everyone would've gone home immediately had they been able to create speedier transparent excuses. And although it was no more than a quarter hour, the amount of time that elapsed before they all managed to leave seemed like days.

Mother was the only one good with it all. She covered a fake yawn, downgrading the swordfight to bore, and retired to the guest chamber where nothing less than canon-fire would rouse her from bed.

Sitting in the tub, I was staring at my wet skin sparkling in the light of the chamber-stick when the tiny clock on the mantle of the Dolorosa room dinged its dainty strike. All I could think about was Armando walking out without a word. It made me want him even more. That man could have plucked me from a tree like a ripe cherry, torn off my stem, swallowed me whole, and spit out the stone. And who in hell was Blanca?

Having washed away caveats with the bathwater, I stepped out onto the darkened upper corridor. The door on the other end was barely visible. The time it took for me to get there had to have been the longest walk I'd ever taken.

If I were going to change my mind, it had to be right then. My heart was beating its way out of my chest. But it was better to sleep with him and suffer the consequence, than not sleep with him and suffer the consequence.

I quickly pulled my hand back out of surprise. The slightest push revealed the forbidden new world though the crack in the door. The latch hadn't been clicked into place.

Facing the open balcony doors, a massive carved bed that could've belonged to a king had insect netting still in place tied to each enormous post. Beside it, on a little table, glowing in the moonlight before an abyss devoid of detail, a light-blue squiggly wisp rose from a recently snuffed candle.

Armando was an artist's painting created with such accuracy as if to appear stopped in time between breaths. Motionless as the shadow of a statue, fully clothed on top of the bed with legs crossed, he still had his boots on.

The moon straining through the lace window covering complicated the design on the wool rug under my bare feet, making it appear like a child's first drawing.

I had only been standing at the foot of the bed for a moment when Armando bolted with his hand on the hilt.

Then, like a falcon leveling off after a false dive at prey, he recognized his intruder, slowly unfastened his weapon, and tenderly placed the sheathed blade on the rug. It was the first time I'd ever seen it off his hip.

Armando looked at me in the dark for a long time without saying a word. Finally he reached for the flint-wheel. Half a dozen frantic scrapes later, the chamber-stick sparked to flame. I went to his side and slipped beneath the thin linen.

With the lightness of an artist's brush on my skin, barely touching my cheek and throat, Armando's fingertips painted their way down my nightgown, across my breast, lingering at an arm, a shoulder, a hip, and then a feather touch in the palm of my hand was replaced with a kiss.

He rose to his knees, flung his shirt over his head, and let it fall to the floor. The shiny scar below his chest reflected the candle light as he sat on his heels, searching my face with a look that was neither a smile nor a frown, but more like a new mother seeing her child for the first time.

The hand roughened by a wire-wound sharkskin sword-grip peeled away my linen shield, slipped inside the front of my gown, and softly scratched my bare breast like a dry sponge.

He ripped open the front of my chemise with the sound of tearing a new rag from an old shirt. Giving my hardened nipple a fraction of a second to rest before the next finger flicked over, Armando searched my nakedness, pulled my hair aside, rendered a kiss beneath my ear, and whispered, "My God, Léna you're so beautiful."

The weight of his sparsely haired chest pressed me to the bed. Nude in his arms, I felt a tiny splash of sweat from Armando's brow on the indentation at the base of my throat.

Sucking my nipple repeatedly, he circled his mouth on my breast like a cat searching for just the right spot in which to lie down in the hay. And the motion of his head in my hands as he did it made me think he was the one with constraint.

I was with a man, not a boy. And, I wanted him so badly I completely forgot about being terrified.

Pulling away, he furiously fussed with the buttons on his pants until we were skin to skin.

The man I thought I could only be with in a dream covered me with his flesh.

Armando found me between the legs. I was soaked, but his finger wouldn't go in.

"Léna, you've got to relax," he whispered.

How in the world was this going to happen? It didn't seem possible, I was so tight.

Armando finally wedged one solitary finger inside.

He was covered in sweat, ready to explode.

Pulling my legs around his waist, he said, "Forgive me, Léna, I cannot keep myself much longer."

But each time he tried to press himself into me, he didn't get very far.

"Armando, please, just do it!" I said, clutching his forearms.

Asking gently with one or two little pushes, he made one huge thrust. We both cried out.

The silver crucifix around his neck lay motionless against my breast. Armando pulsed deep inside me. And with a salty, sweaty kiss, I disappeared.

The candle had burned into a mound of wax on the chamberstick tray. We were still in each other's arms. A few scrapes of the flint wheel to light a new stick confirmed the wetness in bed was not just sweat.

Armando changed the bloodied linen, put me in the bath, and by the time he finished cleaning me, kneeling like a maid beside the tub, the floor had been soaked by our school-child behavior.

Dunking a silver pitcher in the tub, he emptied it over my head and announced, "I Christen the maiden voyage. No, wait. Make that, the maidenhead voyage."

I squealed and pretended to hit him, to which he replied, "You'll wake your mother."

"Don't you think you might've already done that when you came?" I laughed, swatting water in his direction.

Armando plunked himself into in the tub with me, put his mouth on mine with a calculatedly crude kiss, and reached for the cigar on the tub-side table. Lighting the thing from the candle, he said, "As punishment, I'm going to smoke."

I put out the wretched stub with one quick splash of my palm, also managing to soak his face in the process.

"What have I gotten myself into?" he said, trying to keep the dimple in his cheek at bay.

"Armando?"

"Yes, *querida*?" he whispered, throwing the soaked cigar on the floor, kissing my neck.

"Who is Blanca?"

He pulled away, leaving only one arm around me. I got scared.

Leaning back in the tub, Armando somberly replied, "She was my betrothed."

Quickly putting both arms back around me, he added, "But, Niña, that was a very long time ago. It was an arranged marriage. I was only nineteen."

"What happened?" I asked, trying not to show how disturbed I was.

"She disappeared."

"What do you mean, she disappeared? She ran away?"

"She vanished. Maximo has blamed me ever since."

Armando took a deep breath, gave me a little squeeze, and looking down at my hand clasped in his beneath the water, said, "Max never came out and said it, but he was in love with her. He chose to believe that Blanca had no interest in marrying me. After she was gone, he took it upon himself to blame me, by saying I never adequately searched for her."

"She just left?"

"It was a painful time. My father was in ill health, and in order to draw attention away from it, he decided the best way to deal with dying was to have a party. So he planned an extremely elaborate masked ball."

"You're joking?"

"You would've had to have known him to truly appreciate his unique character. Dancing in Spain is taboo, so the idea of having a ball was perfect. To hedge ridicule everyone wore a mask. We made it a very formal affair, which allowed our guests to pretty much do whatever they wanted. When one is dressed, Niña, one can get away with just about anything. There was supernumerary food, a full orchestra, no luxury was spared. Everyone knew it was to be my father's final celebration. But no one ever thought it was to be the last time Blanca was seen. It wasn't until the next day when her parents discovered their daughter had never come home that they assumed she had spent the night with me. I'll never forget her father's face when he put his hand on my shoulder and pleaded with me to tell him Blanca and I had slept together. And when I couldn't produce the lie that would alleviate his suffering, he thrashed around the room breaking things. It was a tough time. My father was dying. Blanca had vanished. And Maximo and I were at odds. We never had the same kinship for each other after that. Eventually the friendship went on for the most part, unheeded. But, I'm convinced something last night had to have caused his resentment to resurface. Niña, this is not the time. Let's not talk of such things, now"

I put my head on Armando's shoulder. He ran his hand over my slippery breasts, gave me a long, slow, open-mouth kiss, and whispered, "You were very brave to come to me."

"It wasn't courage, *querido*. I came here to die," I said, afraid to look him in the eye.

Glancing down at the two pairs of knees sticking out of the soapy water, I put my hand on his thigh and said, "Had I decided to give you my virginity, there would've been a million reasons for me not to. But, if I could give myself to you without suffering the outcome, I could find the wherefore. And the only way that was going to happen was for me to end the life I knew. So when I made the choice to get into your bed, Armando, I died for you."

Drops trickled back into the tub as he lifted his arm out of the water and pulled my chin around to face him. I was crying. Then looking as though he might be the one to cry, Armando brushed aside several stray wet locks that had stuck to my cheek. Pushing the hairs behind my ear with his fingertips, he held me and softly said, "My God, I love you so."

MONDAY, 21 AUGUST 1780

She must've come in, thinking Armando had been up for hours. The hound happily trotting alongside probably just wanted to curl up on the rug. Grabbing the dog by the collar, Maria left the room with Adelio in tow as if she merely had forgotten to fetch something from downstairs.

Her unfazed exit made me wonder if she was accustomed to seeing naked women in the master's bed.

Armando and I had fallen asleep on top of the linen just as the sky was oozing pink over the courtyard wall. We'd been in each other's arms without a stitch on all night, and by the time the head housekeeper came in, the bottoms of my toes were baking in the sun streaming through the open balcony doors.

Miguel was right about one thing -- I did wind up in el conde's bed. And the proof was asleep, pressed up against my back, his arm around me.

Naked with Armando in the daylight was like seeing him for the first time. Sun-darkened from the waist up and pale as a baby's ass below the waist, I couldn't help but grin.

I tried to get up without disturbing him, but the moment his arm gently flopped from my side, he opened his eyes, creased the corners of his mouth into a tiny smile, and invited me to slide back down next to him.

"How did you get this?" I asked, running my hand over the silky scar across his abdomen.

Armando drew tiny circles on my upper arm with the third finger of his left hand, and casually replied, "…A swordfight on the way to the Mexico colonies."

"You got cut like this?

"Regretfully, one of the risks of fencing." He grinned.

"This wasn't from sport was it?" I said, flattening my palm on the healed disfigurement.

"Hardly. The swordsman who left his card is presently in hell, which is where I sent him when I put four fingers of steel in him."

"You're serious, aren't you?'

Armando leaned back on his elbow as if it was going to be a long story, and said, "The export wine route had become available to Spanish producers. So naturally, I went to the New World to secure trade with the Colonies. Being on one of Spain's best ships has advantages, but it was also a tempting target for privateers. By the time the crew sighted them, it was too late. That pirate bunch must've had one hell of a captain because the sloop was practically on top of us before we even realized we were about to be boarded. There was a distraction. I got cut."

"I've seen you fence, Armando. The swordsman who did this to you must've been very good."

"He was horrible. He fought like swatting flies with a butter paddle. At the time, I had been forced to take the foible of another rapier-flinging scourge. And, even if they were both atrocious swordsmen, Niña, *two on one* can occasionally present somewhat of a challenge. As it turned out they were a cowardly bunch. I killed one, and the rest retreated."

The tiny creases outside the corners of Armando's eyes that always accompanied his smile vanished.

"Regardless of the fact that he was about to end my life, having killed a man, Niña, was the single most sickening thing I've ever had to live through."

"How did you get the tiny scar on your back?"

"Oh, that? It was nothing. I just got a little careless one day, that's all."

"Tell me about the New World," I said, rolling onto my stomach.

"You mean after making it there alive? Well, I did the usual things I suppose one does following a pirate attack. Lifted a mug or two with the crew and went looking for a padre. The only clergyman on board had thoughtlessly died. So, as soon as I set foot on colonial soil I sought confession before doing anything else. I found a Father Juan Bautista Velderrain at a mission named for San Xavier. The padre was standing with me outside the church in the middle of the desert, and described the surroundings as being only that which had been created by God. I thought it was a clever way to see a lack of civilization, so I left something there, a gift of appreciation. Miraculously, I was home less than two days, and found myself half-out-of-mind in love with you."

Armando jumped out of bed, trying not to laugh. The armoire latch in his hand clicked open. "Confession might be in order. I'm not sure, little girl, but I think we may have sinned."

I leaned back to take in the lovely sight of watching my lover pulling on a pair of his close-fitting black pants, so snug he had to do several deep knee bends to get into them, before finding the room to tuck in the long white shirt tails.

"Did I mention we fucked all the Aztecs?" he said, pushing his pant buttons through their holes. "Of course, we made them Catholics first." He laughed.

Seeing me naked on top of the linen, Armando pulled the shirt he had just tucked in from his pants, let the billowing white tails flow down around his hips, and came back to bed. I felt the lovely pressure of his body as he pressed his lips to mine.

Following a judicious trip to my room to get dressed, I made a brief visit downstairs. Thank God, Maria had chosen to be silent about seeing me naked in Armando's bed. Not to mention the embarrassingly transparent question in front of Mother, asking if either of them had seen him. I'm a horrible liar. It must've been painfully obvious, especially since I yawned afterward and mentioned that I would be napping all day.

Truth was I couldn't wait to get back under the linen with him. I ran upstairs to find Armando waiting for me propped up on the pillow with his hands behind his head.

He smiled the moment I came in, opened his arms wide as if we hadn't seen each other in ages, and I jumped under the cover with him as fast as I could get my clothes off.

By late afternoon we saw it upon ourselves to respite. We were starved.

Two pots of chicken and greens had been left to simmer over the cocina fire. Armando took a huge wooden scoop, and more befitting a Barbary corsair than a nobleman, dumped the stew onto a metal plate, swung a leg over the narrow bench, and slapped the pewter down on the table.

Sitting spread-legged staring at each other, I couldn't take my eyes off him. How on earth did I wind up with such a man?

From the way Armando picked up the decanter, I thought the un-corked bottle was empty. But while looking at me, he flipped it upside down, pouring dark red spirits splashing over the food. Shredded fowl, potatoes, greens, and of course the wine went everywhere, splattering the table, our clothes, and the floor. I don't think I ever laughed as hard.

"Now, it's no longer too hot to eat, is it?" Armando said with a wicked grin and a nod at the remaining cassoulet that actually stayed on the plate.

I was surprised to see my lover's behavior, the likes of which he'd never allowed me to witness before.

Armando pulled his shirt over his head and threw it on the floor. Half naked, he took a little pile of stew and pressed the morsels into my mouth with his fingers. The muscle on the top of his upper arm bulged as he tilted the wine bottle to my lips. I took a sip. He leaned over, put his hands on my thighs, and kissed me.

Spellbound by his flesh flexing over his bare chest, I watched as Armando threw his head back and filled his mouth. Seeing his dusty green eyes looking at me the whole time he chewed, I failed to notice that he hadn't swallowed. It wasn't until he kissed me again, and planted his mouthful into mine.

Armando took one more swig and put the bottle down. I felt his full lips covering mine in a kiss so deep it touched every thread of my being.

He pulled me to him. Our knees touched. Taking hold of my hips, he lifted me onto his thighs, and stood up with me in his arms. Our kiss had yet to cease.

I wrapped my legs around him as he held my bosom to his chest. The table rattled with things being swept to the floor.

Putting me down on the edge, Armando's boots scraped the stone. The scabbard on his hip banged the table. Trying to make it happen as fast as possible, he attacked the buttons on his pants. My lover was inside me. I softly called out.

The pleasure ended with similar intensity to which it began. Maximo was standing in the doorway. Lord knew how long he'd been there. Mortified, I pulled my dress down and slid off the table. Armando turned away to fasten the buttons on his pants.

But, Max was the one who behaved as though he'd been caught in the act. His head twitched back and forth and his hands were shaking. "I came to apologize for the other night. I behaved abominably, and I'm sorry."

Armando picked up his shirt from the floor, pulled it over his head, landed a hearty pat on his friend's shoulder, and replied, "No concerns, all is forgiven. Fetch Luisa and come for dinner."

Maximo hadn't been gone for more than a minute and Armando began to laugh.

"What's so funny?" I asked, apparently a bit more embarrassed than he.

"Sweet Niña, Max had to have seen what was going on."

"Yes, I'm certain. But I'm not sure why you find it so amusing."

Armando put one boot on the bench, leaned an elbow on his knee, took my hand, and said, "My precious Léna, the man walked in on the very thing for which he came to apologize for insinuating."

THURSDAY, 7 SEPTEMBER 1780

Every morning, before the cock crowed, I'd sneak back to my room, change clothes, and meet Armando on the portico for breakfast, pretending I hadn't seen him since supper. I seriously doubt we fooled anyone. At least the effort was noble.

We had spent the day in the city. I was on top of the world riding side by side with Armando down one of Sevilla's streets, when in an unconcerned manner, and without turning to look at me, he said, "You should be here for Semana Santa."

There'd never been talk of a future together. But, my God, how could I possibly live without him if I had to?

Even as wonderful as it was to be with Armando, I almost cried. And it came on the heels of being completely mesmerized by the way he moved in the saddle. The scrolled intricate silver inlay of his sword's scabbard flashing in the sun, his billowing white shirt-sleeves, tight black pants, boots and bridle-work disappearing into the stallion's shiny dark coat, and Armando's incredibly long brown hair, the perfect shade of mahogany -- he had no right to intoxicate the way he did.

Inside the church where he was baptized, *the Capilla de San Jose,* I unsuccessfully tried to imagine Armando as a helpless infant in the arms of a priest. The charming little chapel was a dramatic contrast to our next visit, the enormous Cathedral of Sevilla, and Giralda tower built by the Moors, an architectural incongruity attached at the hip.

Mischievously, insinuating that we should finish our prayer on top of the Giralda, Armando led me on horseback into the church. I thought he was crazy, but the passageway had been built with ramps wide enough for two horses to go side by side, since the fat Moorish sultan who constructed the thing had to pray up there five times a day, and couldn't have made the climb otherwise. The view was spectacular, at least it was until the bells went off and the horses went insane. Cabeza reared and backed up into a retaining wall, throwing Armando over the side. And if he hadn't grabbed one of the separating columns, the day would've had quite a different ending. Other than turning the color of the limestone, Armando had managed to climb back over the wall, and became very casual about the whole thing, joking about how his destiny was not to be thrown off the roof of a Moorish tower. Needless to say, we walked back down.

Street musicians were playing near the watering fountain. Armando tied the horses, took my hand, and danced with me.

The first thing I did when we got back home was look for Mother. Even if it meant revealing that I'd given Armando my virtue, I just had to find her. The vulnerability of being in love was troubling. And she always knew how to deal with everything.

Beyond the far edge of the lawn, tall weeds slapped a dusting of pollen on my skirt after stepping off the clipped grass. Mother was sitting on a small stool at her easel with paints neatly arranged on a blanket at her feet.

She had to have known I was standing right beside her, but kept staring at her work, brush in hand.

Finally she looked up from her canvas, peeked at the pasture, then quickly looked back down at the painting and went right for the jugular. "Madeleine, you are well. But we are still here. Your father will soon be leaving for Toulouse with his new horses and he would like his family to return home with him. What shall I tell him?"

I glanced at her likeness of the green and gold flower-filled pasture with no idea what to say.

Mother took a yellow swipe from her palette, flicked her brush on the canvas with a quick snap, and said, "Have you slept with him?"

"Yes."

Her glass prism earrings jiggled from her lobes. She jumped up from the stool, and took my cheeks into her soft palms.

No lengthy soliloquy regarding the benefits of virginity when one marries, or a lecture that would've rivaled the captain of the Spanish Armada addressing the remainder of his fleet came to pass. She pulled me to her bosom and said, "Oh my God, my child, that's wonderful. I'm so happy for you."

I couldn't believe it. Following the dramatic end of my engagement to Miguel, her reaction was the last thing I expected. Maybe she was glad I ruined myself with a count instead of a commoner. Perhaps she didn't want me to die, a virgin. Maybe she was just happy. Mother hugged me until she nearly cried.

"I'm beyond happiness, Mama. But something troubles me."

"What could possibly be wrong?"

"It's something Maximo said. He told me not to fall in love with Armando, because if I did, I would disappear. I didn't think much of the comment at the time. But, then I found out that Armando had a fiancé named Blanca, who disappeared and nobody knows what happened to her. Maybe Maximo meant something else. I don't know. I'm just worried, that's all."

Mother sat back down on her little stool, squashed the bristles of her brush into a dab of red paint on her palette, and added a flower to the canvas from imagination, for clearly there were no red flowers blooming in the pasture. Swabbing a spot of rouge, she said, "Maximo meant that to love a man like Armando, you could easily lose yourself. It's nothing more. You needn't fret about it, Madeleine."

MONDAY, 11 SEPTEMBER 1780

Having suffered ample humiliation at the nimble sword-tip of his student, wincing from sweat dripping into his eyes, the pomegranate-faced maestro pulled the soiled edge of his white shirt collar away from his neck and called an end to the session.

Reaching out for the customary handshake following the final salute, Armando's firm skin, a shade darker from the baking sun, was soaked in sweat, although he looked as if he could've easily continued.

There were scores of things to do before retiring to his private quarters to find me waiting in his bed, naked under the linen.

Waiting to hear the confident footsteps with long intervals between heel-claps on the stone, the sort of stride that would make you think he was much taller, was maddening.

Exactly when he would arrive was not to be predicted. But I knew the hunger would be over, when during the brief pause before the door opened, by mere fact that I'd witnessed it so many times, Armando performed an exercise with such regularity that I doubt he was even aware. For in the fraction of a second between his footsteps ceasing and the opening of the door, he would quickly place his fingers to his lips and then touch the Sagrado Corazon at the threshold.

My loins would attest that the tiny hesitation while the kiss was administered to the symbol before the door latch clicked out of place was an eternity.

I envied the patient shirt pulled over his head and allowed to fall to the floor.

The garment had been forced to wait in a heap on the side of the cobblestone while the sword-practice went on, only to be returned to life after being haphazardly thrown over his head. For the brief trip from the courtyard to the bedroom, the muslin, drenched in the juices of his skin, stuck to his abdomen and back as if it were a rival to my affection.

The shirt was also generous in that it allowed a sparsely haired portion of Armando's sun-darkened chest to show through the front opening. And, even though it remained un-tucked from Armando's pants, the shirt expressed its happiness to be against him, for that part of the fabric that didn't adhere to his flesh to mop up his sweat swayed with each movement of his body as though dancing around his hips to Pachelbel's Canon.

Giving me but a moment to feel the sticky moistness of his bare chest, Armando sat down on the bed, leaned over, and grazed my mouth with a probing sweat-lubricated kiss. His face hadn't seen the razor for three days, a regular habit that I was convinced was not to preserve his noble skin, but rather a tool by which to intensify my madness for him. The stinging, pumice-like scrape around the edge of my lips encompassing his soft inquisitive tongue was uncomfortable, but always left me wanting more.

"Did you save your bath water?" he asked, lifting my hand to his mouth for a kiss.

"Of course," I replied with a break in my voice from having been silent for so long.

"Very well then, if I cannot bathe with you, I shall bathe in you."

Why did he not just take me the moment he walked in?

By the time Armando finally slipped into bed next to me, I was all too ready to kiss and melt into an eruption of lovemaking. I put my arms around his neck, and drew myself to him.

"I have something to show you," he said, taking my hand.

"Can it not wait?" I replied, trying to pull his face to mine.

"I think you're going to like it. Please allow me to show it to you now."

The whole time we were snapping up clothes from around the room, I wondered what it was that he wanted me to see so badly.

After pulling me across the courtyard with two steps for every one of his, Armando dropped the chain at the entrance to the stable. Adelio trotted ahead to poke his snout at odd places, searching for a change in scenery had there been one in his absence, as dogs often do.

The center aisle, flanked by beautifully detailed stalls adorned with green and gold finials was home to some of the nicest animals I'd ever seen. Armando must've known I wasn't about to walk past the larger box stall without looking at the fine new horseflesh.

A gelding with a soft, dark, intelligent eye took note of my interest. His ears pricked and he pushed his muzzle to the bars for a sniff.

"He's gorgeous!" I said, stroking the animal's refined long white nose.

Armando reached up to rub the gelding between the ears. Pulling the forelock forward, he allowed the red strands to slide through his fingers a couple of times and said, "This horse has the biggest heart God ever put inside an animal. He's sensitive, smart, quick, and very strong. You'll have to be careful what you ask, because he's the sort that'll do whatever it is you want."

"You make it sound like he's mine." I laughed.

"He is yours," Armando replied, barely above a whisper.

I petted the animal's nose hanging over the freshly engraved stall plate with the name, Simpatico.

"This is too great a gift for you to give me," I said, shaking my head and nearly falling over my words.

Armando watched me petting the horse and casually replied, "Actually, I think he's quite an appropriate gift for La Condesa."

I turned to see Armando's dusty emerald eyes smiling, and asked, "What did you just say?"

He acted like all that happened was that I hadn't heard his comment and replied, "I just said that I thought this horse was worthy of being a suitable gift for La Condesa."

I cried and threw my arms around Armando's neck. The little I could feel of his moist chest on my cheek through the opening of his shirt was medication.

"I've spoken to Maria. Everything can be taken care of in a week's time. Our marriage is set for the eighteenth," he whispered, stroking my hair.

"Aren't you supposed to ask my father, first?"

"I already did."

"What did he say? Tell me his exact words, I want to know."

"At last, she's someone else's problem!"

"He did not!" I shouted with a tiny push on Armando's chest.

My future husband tightened his arms around me, and said, "Actually, your father never said a word. He almost lost his composure, and just threw his arms around me. That's all I needed for an answer. There'll be quite a bit to do between now and the eighteenth. And, of course we'll have to deal with the six-day separation."

"Six *days* of *separation?*"

"We're to be married by a blood ceremony, Niña. It's the only covenant sanctified by God. You and I must be separated for six full days prior to wedding each other."

"Blood ceremony? Please don't tell me. Make it a surprise."

"We can be together until tomorrow. Then, *querida*, I must leave until the marriage. I want for you to sleep in my bed while I'm gone. It'll be easier for me to do this if I know you're there."

"Where are you going?"

"You're not to worry, I'll be fine. Besides, you'll have countless things to keep you busy between now and the eighteenth."

"I don't like this, Armando. Why do we have to be apart?"

"We must cleanse our souls and be as empty as possible, so that when we marry, we'll be filled by the Lord. Fasting for the six days is in order as well. But you do not have to do this, Niña. I do not want you to completely fast for the six days. Eat fruits and drink water, have no meat or wine, and that's all you should do. I do not want you to fast for six days, do you understand?"

"You're going to be without food for six days, aren't you?"

"I want you to eat during our separation, Niña."

"You're not the only strong one."

Armando put his hands on my shoulders and said, "I know of your strength, Léna, there is no question about that. I don't think I would be so deeply in love with you if you were anything less than you are. Six days is a very long time to go without food, even for a man. That kind of risk is not what I want for you. Do not fast, Léna. This is what your future husband is asking."

Thoroughly intending to do as I pleased anyway, I agreed to his wishes. After which he went on to make light of the fact that while apart we might actually be able to *sleep*.

"Come, we must go pray," Armando said with a hug.

Taking my hand, he pulled me toward the chapel and said, "I've hired a new fencing master, who's supposed to be one of the best. You'll be able to speak French with him, Niña, he's from your homeland."

I heard Armando talking, but it was like I wasn't there. Six days apart overshadowed everything, good and bad.

Kneeling together at the altar, he prayed. I just moved my lips.

Armando hadn't even finished yet, when he turned to me, put his hands on my shoulders, and said, "Niña, I must leave now."

His face became a blur.

"Please, don't leave yet. We still have tonight."

"It would kill me to make love with you, sleep together, and then get up and leave you in the morning. I have to go now, while I have the strength."

"Armando, I cannot bear six seconds away from you, how am I going to be without you for six days?"

Pulling me to his chest, he put his mouth on mine and everything was forgotten. Armando saw my wet eyes and whispered, "The next time I kiss you...it will be here on this very spot. Only then, you will be my wife."

Like the ocean during that brief hesitation when the churning water comes to rest on the shore, sizzles for a second, and rolls back out, my heart was filled. The short-lived joyous swell ebbed during the time it took for us to get to the cocina.

The pounding of dough stopped. Standing over a huge ball on the table, Maria looked up and brushed away several strands of fine dark hair that had fallen into her eyes, leaving a dusting of flour on her brow.

Resting his hand on the cage hilt of his sword, Armando said, "I'm leaving until the ceremony. Maria, please see that Léna eats."

The head housekeeper resumed pounding the dough with the heel of her palms. She blew a breath up at the annoying loose hairs that had fallen back in her face and said, "I will do my best, Señor Conde, but you know this girl has a will of her own and it's a strong one."

Heading to the door with my hand in his, Armando laughed and said, "I am most well aware of that. Just try to see that she eats something."

Not even searching for Carlos, Armando tacked up his own horse in such a manner it appeared as though he were late for an appointment.

"Please, *querido*, I beg you, at least tell me where you're going," I asked, taking my betrothed's arm as he led the stud outside.

"I don't know where I'm going, *querida* -- I'm just going," he replied, giving me one last chance to see his cloudy-day-sea-green eyes.

"Aren't you taking anything with you?"

"I am taking your love with me."

Adelio, panting and circling on his master's heels, received a loving caress of the snout as Armando said, "You need to stay with the new Lady of the house."

Following a fast fix of the stirrup-hangar he almost never used for mounting, Armando grabbed the pommel and flung himself from the ground into the saddle.

"Do not watch me ride off, *querida*. It's a very bad omen."

Tugging the rein to prevent Cabeza from taking off with the feel of his rider's weight in the saddle, Armando leaned over, tenderly touched my chin, and said, "Léna, I am coming back to you. If this were an easy thing, it would be of little importance, would it not?"

"You don't have any provisions!"

The charms on the end of his spurs tinkled, and with a kick, Cabeza jumped into a gallop. Nearly drowned out by hooves echoing off the courtyard walls, my beloved yelled, "The Lord will provide whatever I need!"

I desperately wanted to look toward the fading hoof beats, but didn't dare.

I ran. And didn't stop or turn around until the heel of my palms stung a pound on the bedroom door.

It had been dark for some time. I finally stopped crying, sipped what was left of the sherry on the bedside table, and smudged out the light.

TUESDAY, 12 SEPTEMBER 1780

Mother would've encouraged the trespass under the guise of needing to borrow a buttonhook, but not having inherited her whippy conscience, I asked the dog sitting on the rug next to me if it was all right. The big hound agreed, administering a bit more of a canine tongue than I needed on my mouth, and I drew back the flange.

On the bottom shelf of Armando's armoire under some papers and pair of black silk slippers, inside a handkerchief-sized white cloth with a red cross in the center, I found a document awarding Armando entry into the Order of Santiago by birthright. His parents had been members of the highly revered society, and from what I grasped from reading the declaration, offspring of members were entitled, should they decide to join the secretive organization. Armando's signature was at the bottom of the page, next to a gold leaf seal.

I was afraid to touch the highly scrolled, silver inlay *Reinoso* pistol studded with silver and brass nails, so I stayed away from that, and picked up Armando's certificate acknowledging his completion of study at the University at Salamanca. He had mastered classes in Law, Philosophy, Arts, and Theology, and the French language.

Armando was apparently fluent in my native tongue, yet often allowed me to struggle with words in his. My smirk wasn't quite a laugh, but it was close, playing with the idea of innocent retaliation of some sort.

A highly detailed tarnished silver veneer box decorated with the Holy Trinity, descending dove and desert scenes depicting the Three Wise Men, and Stations of the Cross, caught my eye. A little jiggling of the hinges with the tip of my dagger and the bracket screws just happened to slip free of their holes.

Inside, I found a small journal and a tiny glass bottle with a cork stopper.

Taking the narrow red leather-bound diary back to the bed, two pats on the mattress was all that was required for the formerly flawlessly trained Adelio, who had never been permitted on the furniture, to vault beside me and curl up under my arm as though it had been his inheritance all along.

I opened the journal to the page that just happened to present itself. My hands were shaking such that I almost couldn't read what had been written. The words were unmistakably Armando's pen.

More than once I had to reach back to keep her from falling, leaving the reins dangling around Cabeza's neck. Were it not for his good nature, the girl and I both might've required rescuing. I held her arms around me for hours after she lost consciousness. I doubt I'd ever been so happy to set foot on the courtyard cobblestone. Servants came running the moment they saw us. Carlos rode for the physician. The messenger went for the monsignor, and Maria ran to prepare the bed in the casita while Arturo rode ahead to Casa de la Colina to let them know the girl was with us, and being cared for. Her horse had to have returned long before, causing great concern.

She was limp in my arms when I carried the young woman inside. Maria insisted that she take over, like the mother she knows how to be, without ever having been one. Waiting for the physician's arrival was agonizing. I had assumed the girl was a boy who deserved some sort of consequence for his ill-behavior. And it was I who encouraged a path that even an expert horseman on the finest mount would've been unlikely to cross. I was the one responsible for the girl. Of course, Maria accused me of being influenced by her beauty. And I will be the first to admit that the little wildcat looking so helpless in her deep sleep had charmed like no other in the few glib moments we spent. I sat on the bed with the little daring lioness with the fast tongue, who was really just a vulnerable child whose destiny lay at my hand. Between her fire and frailty, I couldn't take my eyes off her while she slept. It was difficult to hide my feelings when Dr. Sanchez called me aside and flatly told me that she could be fine the next day, or succumb to coma and death. All we could do was wait to see if her condition changes, and give her food and drink immediately if she wakes. Maria stayed up with the girl through the night, since that was to be the most crucial time.

Arturo brought home unexpected guests, Monsieur and Madame Chevaleaux, the girl's parents. I introduced myself to the couple patiently waiting in the library with faces gone pale, and lied to them with the truth. I said their daughter was sleeping. The physician ordered her to rest quietly. My head housekeeper was watching over her, and then, of course, asked them to stay for supper. As in a swordfight, the best defense is an attack, so I asked if they knew their daughter had been out in the woods riding alone. Monsieur Chevaleaux was clearly unsettled, explaining that he and her mother had lost control of Madeleine long before. I recall blotting everything away but her name. The girl's name was Madeleine. That's all I could ponder, and I just wanted to say it over and over again to myself.

Madeléna's father mentioned that it looked as though Lizarraga would join the fate of the others, meaning the arranged marriage probably had gone awry.

Had the girl been my daughter there would've been hell to pay for her actions, but it wasn't until dinner that I said to Chevaleaux, Señor, with due respect, the woods surrounding Sevilla is thick with vagabonds, and it's far more likely they would've been the ones to find your daughter. The man knew how to parry with the best. He was convinced it had been Divine Intervention that permitted me to be her rescuer.

The moment the front door latch clicked into place after the final goodbye, I made haste to the chapel. The plea was simple. The girl is an innocent. Spare her life. In payment, I commit my life to the Father to be used however willed. Sealed it in blood from a cut on the back of my hand with my father's dagger, I locked the covenant inside the old altar box, took the key and ran to the stable. A hot damp breeze had swept up and rustled the leaves of the huge palm next to Maximo's shop outside the locked gates. The Sereno, inside the city walls was chanting, *Media noche y serenauuua*. If I hadn't known those enormous Banyon roots that Maximo and I had tripped over on many occasions after lifting a mug at La Puerta Rojas, I probably would've been on my ass like we were one night a very long time ago, when Max couldn't make it home on his own. Sitting in the dark during the early morning hours, tangled in the Banyon roots, we laughed so loud when we fell, the cobbler next door was roused from bed. Getting on in years, the man had lost any sense of youthful exploits. Having failed to see the humor of two drunken young men who had endured far too much entertainment, the old buteo tossed boot forms at us from his bedroom window and didn't stop until we managed to make it inside.

That man was old when I was at Salamanca, but his guild sign was still swinging, proving that surely, ill mood contributes to longevity.

Maximo finally came to the window demanding to know what was so damned important for me to wake him in the middle of the night. He did his usual grumbling, came downstairs, let me in, and went back to bed, as I knew he would.

Firing up his forge, I hammered the altar box key into a cross. It finally cooled enough for me to hang around my neck with an old discarded lace I found on the floor. I've since never replaced the cord made from rubbish, nor have I taken off the neckpiece.

By the time I got home, Carlos had just finishing mucking stalls. He didn't greet me, a habit he derived as his way of letting me know my discretions were private, assuming I'd been with a woman all night. He would've been correct. It was Madeléna.

I shut the journal. I couldn't read anymore. A few papers that had been stuffed inside fell into my lap. Placing the broken halves of a faded red seal back together, they read the letter "B." Unfolding the letter, a lock of blonde-white hair tied together with a pink ribbon fell to the linen. I thought I would spew. She was real. The letter was dated 23rd April 1767.

"My dearest Armando, I am writing in haste, so please forgive my hurried penmanship. They are almost finished changing the team, and we will soon be on our way again. I will get word to you once I'm settled. I still have fear, and many times along route, I --"

Someone was coming. I quickly stashed the stuff under the bed. And it was a good thing because Mother walked right in without a knock.

Sticking a blasted tray right in front of me, she said, "I brought you a cup of chocolate. How did you sleep, my precious? Is that hunting dog supposed to be on the bed?"

I picked up the blue and white cup, took a tiny sip, and replied, "Fitfully. I slept like hell. And, no, he's not."

Waving a hand in front of her face like shooing a fly from her mouth, she ignored the hound languishing on the bedcover as if he were allowed to be there, and said, "It's only premarital nerves.

Not too worry. There would be something wrong if you weren't anxious."

"Was it like this when you were getting ready to marry Papa?"

With her natural talent for innocently locating the most vulnerable spot, she laughed and said, "Actually, I was fine. It wasn't until we had just finished our vows that I panicked, wondering what I'd just done. But of course I hadn't had sex with your father before we wed, so naturally, I was a bit apprehensive."

When she saw me push the cup of chocolate to the far end of the tray, she gave the dog a pat, kissed my forehead, and went back downstairs.

I never read the rest of Blanca's letter.

WEDNESDAY, 13 SEPTEMBER 1780

Adelio was about to trot into the cocina. I couldn't let that happen, so I grabbed his collar to hold him back. Arturo and Maria were talking like old married couples do, with no idea I was right around the corner. And it sounded like the less-than-spry servant man wasn't all that impressed with me.

"How do you know she doesn't love his money?" Arturo said to his wife.

"Armando would not be in love with Léna if she were that kind. And you know as well as I, if she were that way, she'd be looking forward to being La Condesa, shopping for dresses, and having a good time with friends. This one won't eat, sleep, or leave the house. Léna has been consumed with sadness since he left. And, he's going to marry her in just days. This is a woman in love. Have you gotten so old that you've forgotten how to tell the difference?" Maria said with a sparing hint of annoyance.

I stepped up my stride to make it look like we'd been walking rather than just standing outside the door. Armando's prized hunting hound-turned-lap-dog affectionately pressed against my leg and followed me inside.

Maria's face widened with a huge smile. "Adelio seems to love his new mistress almost as much as the master does. How are you feeling today, my dear? Perhaps you'd like something to eat. There's a helping of your favorite fish stew in a bowl waiting for you, it's the Algerian recipe you like so well."

"I'd like to help you fix supper, if that's all right with you." I grinned.

She dispensed a loving pat on her husband's shoulder, Arturo took the cue to go, Adelio curled up in the corner, and Maria and I stood side by side at the table plucking hens for the night's meal.

Ripping stray pins, one after the other, I tossed a handful of feathers into the bucket at our feet, and came out with it. "So, what really happened with Blanca?"

"You don't waste a moment, do you? It was Maximo who drove her away."

"That's not the story I heard."

Maria yanked a fistful of feathers and said, "No one knows for certain. But I do know one thing, Blanca was frail. And she couldn't take the bad blood between Armando and Max, especially since the friction began when it was announced that she was to marry Armando."

Just hearing the mention of Blanca and Armando as a pair made me nearly spew, but I didn't let it show, I wanted to hear whatever it was Maria was about to tell me.

Snapping quills from the bird, she went for a resistant pin feather with her thumb and forefinger and said in an adoring tone, "You should've seen the three of them as little ones, playing. They were always together. And, oh how Maximo adored precious Blanca. Growing up, the story was not quite as lovely. The shadow of class-difference meant Maximo had no chance of marrying her.

Then when Armando became Blanca's betrothed, Max... well... he went a little loco. I remember the frightening way he looked after the engagement was announced. And it wasn't long before Max took his frustrations out on Blanca. And that bashful child could not deal with it. So, I think Blanca found a solution. She simply, went away."

"I don't understand, Maria. If Maximo loved Blanca, why would he scare her?" I said, throwing another handful of plucked feathers into the bucket.

Maria raised a cleaver over the poulet head lying limp on the plank and let it fall with such a whack, the blade stuck inside the tabletop that had endured grooves over the years from similar chops. Wriggling the steel wedge free, the hen head falling to the floor, she said, "Max has a dark side."

"...A dark side?"

Maria took some pin-feathers between her fingers, gave them a quick yank. "You're going to find out eventually, so I may as well tell you. Armando's father was an expert swordsman, an attribute that must be hereditary. Spain's finest swordsmen were Velazquez. Alejandro, of course, had been looking for the best sword-maker in the world. And he found that craftsman in Toledo. Alejandro hired the man and brought him to Sevilla, a very smart move because it accomplished two things -- it insured that Alejandro would have the finest swords money could buy, and since the sword-maker could work only for the Velazquez family, no one else in the world was able to own such a weapon. That sword-maker was Maximo's father. So, with Velazquez money paying for the steel, Zequeira blades became famous. Everyone thought success was guaranteed for his son. Maximo's father couldn't work for anyone other than Alejandro, but Max was set for instant fame when his father died. Because Maximo could work for anyone, and he'd been privy to his father's secrets. Maximo readily took up the trade. But I think he was more in love with power and fame than forging. He used his father's name as the world's best blade maker in order to be close to aristocracy. But when Maximo's father died, the great Zequeria blades went with him. Even knowing his father's secrets, Max didn't have the gift to produce the truly fine swords that his father did, and his business slowly faltered until he was forced to make horse shoes in order to survive. He still forges a sword or two now and again, but the legendary steel seems to be in the grave with the sire. Maximo carries deep scars from his failure. Most of the time he's good-natured, but I don't trust him, especially in light of the fact that his father adored Armando. The elder Zequeira dreamt of a son who could out-fence anyone using one of his swords. That dream-boy turned out to be Armando. If you could've seen your husband-to-be when he was only four years old! From the very day Alejandro put a wooden sword in his tiny son's little hand, Armando showed signs of someday being a master. Alejandro ran into this kitchen and grabbed my arm. He pulled me all the way out behind the casita. Little Armando with his wood sword was parrying the blazes out of the fencing maestro. And the sword El Conde carries now, the one that is never further than arm's reach, is Zequeira's finest achievement. I remember when he made it as if it was just yesterday. He ran into the house to show Alejandro. The steel was still steaming in the tongs when I yelled at him for dripping on the rugs. He shouted to Armando's father about how he knew instantly after the blade came out of the water-plunge that it was the one. And he kept repeating it over and over, that sword was the finest weapon of his career. The man was in tears. He dropped down to his knees and sobbed. I'd never seen him that emotional, he was crying when he said that the steel in his hand was a-once-in-a-lifetime weapon. And my dear, that sword may have been the final nail, because that blade ultimately became a gift. Alejandro and Zequeira both decided that such a weapon needed to be in the hands of the worthiest, so they gave it to Armando on his fifteenth birthday, and it's never left his side since."

Maria took a deep breath, kicked the feather bucket out from under the table, and said, "Now you know why the duel they just had here in this house was so dramatic. Armando wound up bleeding Maximo with a sword made by Max's father."

"Oh, Mon Dieu." I gasped, covering my mouth.

Maria pulled two more partially plucked poulets from their hook, handed one to me, and said, "We just need to tidy up a pinfeather here and there."

Nit-picking the strays, I looked down at the fowl in my hands and asked, "What were Armando's parents like? He's never mentioned them."

"Alejandro was a quiet man, not very talkative or forthcoming. He was strict, kind, and loving, Armando adored him. To give you an idea of what Alejandro was like, one of his rules called for all the animals, especially the dogs, to be fed before any of us had our meal. He wouldn't allow a beast to watch you eat while it was hungry. Alejandro died when Armando was barely twenty. The senior Velazquez was in his thirties when his only son was born. Armando's mother, God rest her soul, was barely nineteen."

Maria's eyes glanced upward, she crossed herself, and said, "Armando never knew her. She died giving birth to him...in the same room in which you now sleep. She was a tiny thing, even smaller than you, too tiny to be having babies. It was a dark day in this house. Everyone was crying, servants and family alike. You couldn't walk down a corridor without hearing sobs coming from somewhere. At the time, I was barely out of childhood and found myself having to be a mother. I was the one who raised Armando. He replaced my dolls. I played with him, dressed him, bathed him, and fed him. It felt like he belonged to me."

Maria's smile vanished. She sucked in a drip from her nose with a sniff, tears ran down both cheeks, and her lip quivered. "My father kept warning me not to get too attached to the baby. He told me over and over, that little child you take care of is not a doll. He's going to be El Conde. But, Armando was my child."

Fluff feathers stuck to my fingers, but I put my arms around her anyway.

Maria's chest fluttered, and she cried, "Then one day…I wound up having to take orders from him."

THURSDAY, 14 SEPTEMBER 1780

Father Ramirez cut the air with a three-fingered cross in such haste one never would've known what the gesture was, had it not been attached to a *Dios te Bendiga*, and hurried out like he was needed elsewhere.

Why I do this from time to time I will never know, but one of those moments came to pass where I was unable to resist making a comment without considering the consequence. I replied to the monsignor's question asking if I would be willing to offer my body to Christ by telling him that I would gladly commit my body to Christ, however, I'd already given it to Armando. Right after which Ramirez made the rapid departure with his robe sash flying side to side all the way out.

The splash of the courtyard fountain through the open library doors was interrupted by a tray of rattling dishes. Maria always seemed to be cooking or carrying food. Just seeing that woman would make me hungry. But Armando was starving somewhere, and that was enough for me to stay on the fast.

"Where's the monsignor?" she asked, setting the overloaded tray on the desk in front of me.

"He had to leave for another appointment," I replied as she began arranging dishes of fruit and bread.

"Well, how did it go?"

"The usual, I guess. Do I love the Lord? Do I love Armando? Be ready to take the Marriage Communion. You know, that sort of thing."

"Why don't you go for a walk around the property? It's a lovely day," she said, probably for want of something better.

Mother had gone into the city to shop. And what began as a brief jaunt around the perimeter of the lawn to make it look as though I'd taken Maria's suggestion became the perfect excuse to wander off the hacienda.

Somewhere in the woods on the fringes of the orchards, I stopped to push up my sleeves and pull the bonnet from my head. Rustling leaves waned and I was certain -- I heard music.

Lured like a sailor to the sirens, I followed the narrow footpath winding its way from the road into the deeper woods.

In a small clearing, at odd angles from each other, four brightly painted wagons, highly detailed with scrolls and flower-like designs of red and yellow, stood around a cooking fire.

Children played chanting games, count-every-rib dogs roamed with an occasional sniff and restful flop under a wagon, while women hung laundry from a tie line.

Paying no mind to the stranger who had wandered into their camp, the vagabonds went about the daily chores of life, peacefully accompanied by quivering, sorrowful notes from the strings of a violin on the shoulder of a man who must've learned to play the instrument the way I learned to ride a horse. He would've been nice-looking were it not for the huge knife-fight and pock-mark scars on his sun-darkened clean-shaven cheeks.

Swaying his body with each stroke of the bow, he closed his eyes to savor the sadness.

The infamous, dirty, dangerous, thieving, Andalucian gypsies, refusing to conform to anyone's ways, lived in a place filled with the laughter of frolicking children, music, and a mélange of food smells coming from a huge blackened pot sitting on top of the flames instead of hanging from a hook.

The supper, no doubt intended for everyone, filled the air with a mysterious aroma, rising in a plume as it cooked, unattended.

One wagon in particular caught my attention. Someone had carefully bathed it in several fresh coats of blood-red paint, applied thicker than necessary to merely keep out the rain, and added detailed black scrolls mimicking vines on bright yellow spoke wheels.

Peering through the rear door as if casually taking a peek while walking by, I saw just about all one might require for living. Gaudy clothing and trinkets hung from ropes strung over sconces. A blue, green and gold cloth with embroidered red roses and long black fringe covered a small round table. All sorts of things were piled and packed everywhere.

"I already know your future. I can tell you what is. Or, take it to my grave."

"I'm sorry," I replied, searching the wagon's interior to see who was there.

Curled, dark hair flowing from beneath a brightly colored scarf made the rather large woman nearly invisible amongst the piles of colorful things strewn everywhere. She leaned forward from her stick chair. "Do you have a piece, my dear?"

"I don't have any coin with me."

"Well, surely you have something of value. Come in, child," she said, motioning to the empty chair opposite her, sending the bangles on her wrist crashing into each other. "What will you trade for your future?" she asked as I climbed the three large stairs, and sat down.

Pulling the small dagger Mother had given me from inside the frog on my upper leg under my skirt, I put it on the table.

She snatched it up and held it an inch from her face. Squinting as though she couldn't see very well, the gypsy woman ran her fingers over the colored stones on the handle, put the thing in her mouth and bit down. "This will do," she said, stuffing the little knife inside the rope around her waist that could've been used for anything from hanging laundry to a goat collar.

Yanking the strings tight on her black bustier, she reached over to a small trunk behind her. She pulled out a beaten and dented tin plate, put it on the table in front of me, and said, "Spit in the dish."

"Excuse me?"

Her dark eyes opened wide. Speaking very slowly as if talking to a deaf person who needed to see the words being mouthed, she took a nod at the tin, and said, "Take-the-liquid-from-your-mouth, permit-it-to-depart-your-hole by forcing-it-out-through-your-lips. Aim for this!"

Had I realized the scene was going to turn nasty, I wouldn't have had any part of the game, but she already had my dagger so I spit on the plate.

Running her fingers through my saliva, she swirled it into a pattern and stared at it while I folded my hands in my lap and surveyed the wagon.

Quickly looking up, she flatly said, "We'll do the cards."

Reaching for a deck from inside a brown velvet sack, she placed the well-used hand-sized images on the table in front of me. "Touch the top card," she said.

Fearing another mordant description as to exactly how I was supposed to accomplish the request, I merely tapped my fingers on the deck like the drum of a tabletop and hoped it would make her happy.

"Do you want to know everything, or just the good stuff?"

"Tell me everything."

One might've thought her eyes couldn't open any wider, but they did. She looked at me as if I were the only one who'd ever wanted to know everything.

The moment the third card had been turned over, she began speaking in low elongated words like an actress taking the stage for the first time. "You -- are – in – love. Very-much-in-love," she sang. Then with a grin that revealed two missing upper teeth, she added, "And, he is too."

She pulled her chair closer to the table. "There is much wealth. You have want for naught. You will marry this man."

Turning over more cards, she leaned back as if the reading had ended. She slapped the table and said, "You will take a trip, by sea…no wait…a trip by land…no, it's by sea. You will meet *another* man…"

Two more cards went face up, the gypsy raised one eyebrow, nodded, and with guile in her tone said, "…You will sleep with him."

Going on as if she never noticed I was trying not to laugh, the gypsy woman said "There are jealous women…many jealous women. The betrothed…he is attractive, is he not?"

I nodded, and couldn't help but grin.

"Many jealousies…not good…this is very bad. It can be very dangerous." She got up, went to a small box, pulled out a tiny blue glass eye, and handed it to me. "Carry this with you, all the time."

I took the amulet and put it in my pocket, just to be polite.

The fortune teller turned over two more cards, and yelled, "Beware! There will be someone at your marriage ceremony who intends to do you harm!"

Another card was placed on the table, and she seemed even more confident than she already was. "There will be more than one that means you …and your husband, harm. He, especially, will be in grave peril…take heed."

I tried not to be obvious about the struggle to make out the faded images I was forced to see, upside down.

Turning another picture, darkness befell her. She swept up all the cards into a pile, and said, "There is no more…nothing else… the reading is over!"

I strained to see the final card, but the woman waved her arm, pointed to the stairs, and shouted, "The reading is over, leave!"

I got up as slowly as I could, trying to get a better look at the final Tarot. People were falling from the windows of a tall, round, narrow structure engulfed in flames. The upside-down lettering beneath the image read: "The Tower."

MONDAY, 18 SEPTEMBER 1780

Hunters risked their lives snaring a sea tortoise and bagging an elephant, after which an artisan probably went blind carving the thing into such an intricate work, only so that I could drop the mantilla of tusk and shell, and crack it down the middle.

It was the perfect excuse for another cry, not that I needed one. Of course, Mother came to my rescue as she had done so many times, with the same comfort that had been administered for a scraped shin or cut finger or falling from my pony, and Lord only knows what else my childhood had put us though. Getting married was no different.

"Let me see what I can do with that," she said, taking the broken comb from my trembling hands. Then with the expertise that always seemed to accompany the role of motherhood, she wedged the two turtle and tusk sections back into one piece and got it to stay on my head.

"I thought you'd be happy beyond description today, my precious. Why are you in tears?" Mama said, her little pearl drop earrings jiggling as she fluffed my locks in front of my shoulders.

"Something has happened to Armando, I just know it. He's not coming home!"

"That's ridiculous. Why are you talking such nonsense?" Maria quipped.

"I just have a feeling." I sniffled, sucking in as hard as I could since there were still at least forty or more flyspeck-sized, gray-green silk bodice buttons yet to be threaded into their loops.

Maria's reflection in the mirror was busily hooking away behind me, with the little tool that had been specially made in order to accommodate the teensy fasteners. Without looking up, she said, "I'm not supposed to say anything but I'm going to tell you anyway. I cannot see you like this, especially today. And, I'm fairly sure you'd like to hear what it is."

"Well, if you think it'll make me happy, by all means, please tell me."

"I was in the cocina this morning. A beggar showed up. I just turned around and there he was. It scared the daylights out of me. An unshaven, filthy, and foul-smelling, man in the room with me, you can imagine the start I had. Of course, I got myself together, the last thing in the world you want is a derelict to see you frightened."

"Why are you telling me this, Maria?" I asked, addressing the face reflected in the mirror.

Turning over buttoning duty to Mother, the head housekeeper shooed an imaginary fly, and with far too much glee for imparting superficial details said, "I assumed he was a gypsy looking for a handout. There's been more than one vagabond who has wandered onto the property begging for something to eat, or perhaps a coin or two."

"Maria, come out with it." Why had she brought the subject up on my wedding day?

"Well, naturally I searched for a sack for some tidbits with which to send him on his way. But then the beggar called me by name.

Maria, I need your help, is what he said. That's when I really got scared. How could a mendicant know my name?"

"Maria, what is this all about?"

She took a long huff and then emphasizing her words to make the story sound even better, said, "I recognized his voice."

"Who was it, Maria?"

"It was Armando!"

I grabbed her arms and shouted, "You've seen Armando?!"

Hearing his master's name, Adelio, patiently lying in the corner, made his squeaky door-hinge noise.

The head housekeeper started talking as fast as she could, and my heart followed suit. "Señor Conde Armando, is that you? I asked him. And when he told me, Maria, I have no time for this now, that's when I knew it was him! He smelled bad and looked worse. I didn't recognize him. I begged him to tell me what had happened. But, he just put his hands on my shoulders and told me to fetch his clothes and a razor, and bring them to the casita, and that you must not see him. I agreed that it would've been a very bad idea for you to have caught sight of him, and he told me that I have a very sharp tongue for a servant. My dear, you would've reconsidered marrying him, it was that bad."

"Maria! Why didn't you tell me this right away? Where is he now? Where is Armando?"

"He's probably waiting for you at the altar," she said, looking around the room in a distracted manner.

"You see my precious, you worried for no reason. Everything is fine," Mother said, hooking the last button.

"You're dressed and we forgot the razor," Maria said, shaking her head.

"The razor?" I asked.

"You know…for the wedding bed," she added, with a face going pink.

Stepping in to claim duty's prize while trying not to laugh, Mother took my hand, and said, "I must apologize to my only daughter for not properly relaying some of the worldly rituals that would befall a new bride."

Taking a moment to clear her throat, she said, "The wife –to-be shaves herself, so that the new, inexperienced husband is not shocked when he discovers that she has hair other places besides her head."

The stays were pinching my waist from the waves of hysteria. Finally, I stopped laughing long enough to say, "And, once the husband figures out how to do it, he discovers that the act itself, over a period of weeks, caused hair to grow on his wife's --"

Rolling on the bed, my coif fell out of the comb, and four buttons on my dress needed re-fastening, but it was worth seeing the head housekeeper's pomegranate face as she attached the veil to my mantilla. The poor woman was red as a rose when I said, "I don't think we'll need that razor, Maria, I'm fairly certain Armando has already seen a naked woman."

Arranging the delicate ends of the lace over my shoulders, Mother announced, "If Armando was not already in love with you, he will be when he sees you now."

The milliners had worked night and day to complete the gown in time. A young apprentice girl with crossed eyes held the garment, carefully rolled up in muslin, on her lap all the way from Sevilla only the day before. And they were still stitching on little pearls in an attempt to cover the entire bodice when the last-minute adjustments were being made at 8 this morning, while I stood, anxiously out of my mind, on a chair in the middle of the bedroom with the head seamstress trying not to get angry with me for shaking so badly.

There was no need to count the bells on the striking mantle clock. It was 11.

Giving my black lace gauntlets a final tug, I told the wiry hound to stay, after which he curled up in the corner and put his skinny snout on his paws.

The entire way to the chapel, with Mother and Maria, trying to keep the rustling gown's endless train of silk from dragging the floor clean, we never saw a soul. If I hadn't been so nervous, I would've laughed wondering if it was the right day.

Stopping to tap a kiss to my fingers and touch the bronze flaming heart, I pushed open the door.

Inside, the benches were filled with faceless people in their best finery, candle stands burned scores of sticks, and everywhere the eye landed bunches of flowers had been tied together with ribbons of all colors, hanging from anything that provided a place for them to be attached.

Standing behind a borrowed pulpit, wearing a red and white full robe and scapular, with his hands clasped under his belly, the monsignor saw me walking toward him and smiled.

The view of butt-length hair and firm thighs packed into black embroidered breeches nearly ripped the heart out of my chest. Facing Father Ramirez, Armando stood waiting for me.

I felt like laughing and crying at the same time. Seeing my beloved, even if the view was of his ass, rushed a flood of excitement up the inside of my limbs.

Keep walking and breathe, that's what I told myself until I was right next to him. Armando turned around, the green eyes that I had longed to see so badly went right through me, a huge grin sank his cheek dimples, and he reached out, nearly taking my sweaty hand. The gesture was supposed to be forbidden until we had taken our vows, so the clasp never came. But it was impossible to see each other and not make contact. The faint graze of his fingertips swept over me like a storm, my veil shook on its mantilla, and I exploded into tears.

The protocol requiring us to stay apart until the end of the ceremony went straight to hell. Armando put his arms around me and pulled me to his chest.

Gasps, sniffles, and soft sobbing from the benches promptly died down. Armando kissed my brow, took my hands, and looked at me as if I were the only living thing in the world. We stayed that way until I found the strength to stop crying and go through with it.

Every time my beloved moved, even slightly, the polished silver-inlay scabbard that held his precious weapon flashed light from the candelabra.

It was the first time I'd seen him in full dress. Billowing white lace shirt ruffles cascading over his chest, skin-tight black breeches embroidered down the side, pristine white stockings, and the recognizable black silk slippers I found the day I invaded his armoire, confirmed I was marrying a nobleman.

What was laid out on the altar table would've made anyone not totally in love run the other way. Three huge freshly clipped red, white, and yellow unopened roses looked innocent enough on the white cloth next to a gold chalice, an earthenware cup, wooden box, and gold cord. But the tiny vile with stopper, two white linen and lace handkerchiefs, and the bone-and-brass-handled dagger that Armando usually carried in his boot spoke different words.

Taking the gold chalice, Father Ramirez began prayers. Armando and I got on our knees. My mind was in so many places, the Magna Carta could have been recited and I never would've known.

Lifting the gold cup to the Crucifix, the monsignor drank and handed it to Armando to wet his lips with a tiny sparkle.

I couldn't even begin to imagine how starved my love must've been as he took a sip of the wine.

It was my turn to drink when Armando pulled his hair forward, picked up the dagger, and rasped a bunch of strands. Slipping his fingers under my veil, he pulled a ringlet from my comb, and sliced a lock. Tying our hair together with the gold cord, Armando handed the little bundle to Father Ramirez to be blessed.

A glance at Armando's hands and there was no question -- he was Spanish aristocracy, with skin so thin, his veins looked blue. Would our children also have Blue Blood?

The monsignor placed our hair in the wedding box. Armando lifted the ruffles of his right sleeve, picked up the dagger, dipped the blade into the Holy Wine, and cut himself on the back of his hand. I watched his blood slowly dripping into the small vile and then the earthenware chalice, a mottle of red oozed through Armando's handkerchief-bandage, and the room was spinning. How I kept from passing out was a miracle. Sweat beaded my brow, and I was shaking so badly Armando had to take hold of my arm just above the wrist to keep me still for the cut. What was I doing? I must've been mad!

For an instant I thought about breaking free with a quick yank and running as fast as I could. But Armando had undressed my hand by slowly peeling back the lace gauntlet in a motion that nearly made me swoon even though I was already out of my mind in love. And if that hadn't been enough, right where he was about to cut me, Armando tenderly kissed the back of my hand. The softness of his full lips confirmed that my fate had already been decided. I turned away for the sting. It took so long for the shallow cut to let a sufficient amount of blood, I made the mistake of looking. Tiny red drops eked out of me into the vial of Armando's blood.

Sweat dripped from my brow as the bottle was sealed and placed inside the wedding box along with our hair. A little more of me leaked into the earthenware chalice for the final covenant that supposedly could never be undone. The monsignor poured Holy

Wine into the blood potion, offered it to the Christo behind the altar, and handed it to Armando.

Knotting the linen over the scratch he made on my hand, my beloved took the vessel of bloodied wine, locked his smoky green eyes on me, tilted his head back, and swallowed thrice.

Peeking into the darkness of the half-filled chalice, I took the cup from him and drank the three sips.

United in death? How could those vows have been real? Nonetheless the pleadings we made were of a sobering nature.

Ramirez pulled the white rose petals from their stem, dropped them onto the altar cloth, and said, "May you go together in truth and purity." Plucking the yellow rose, he said, "All life is eternal." Slowly pulling each red petal from its stem, the monsignor put the naked thorny stalk on top of all the petals and proclaimed, "There is always sacrifice that comes with love, and the greater the love, the greater the sacrifice."

Final blessings were delivered, Armando helped me to my feet, and the wedding box was locked with the little gold key going to Armando. Ramirez swept up the rose petals from the altar cloth, tossed them over us, and declared, "Armando Antonio Francisco Lorenzo de Grisales y Velazquez, and Madeléna Francesca Chevaleaux de Velazquez, in the eyes of the Father, the Son, and the Holy Spirit, you are husband and wife according to the Word of the Lord on earth as well as in Heaven and beyond."

Armando and I, together, held the bloodied wine and drank our final swallow. Upon which he threw the cup to the floor, smashing it to bits under the altar.

Our lips met for the first kiss of our marriage, just as he said when we parted a week before. I was his wife.

The pews emptied. Guests gathered around us. The chapel bell rang. Horns, violins, and guitars began to play outside. The doors swung open to a sea of people waving, shouting, and throwing flowers. The wedding bargain, however, was not yet complete.

Armando swept me up into his arms and whispered, "Your feet are not to touch the ground until we consummate our vows."

Holding me tight to his chest, he carried me through the ocean of faces overflowing from the courtyard, yelling, waving banners impossible to read in the flurry, and throwing trinkets of every imaginable kind. Armando laughed. "In Spain, no one misses a wedding, especially a good one!"

Peppered with a bombardment of offerings, most of which stung like hell, the trip to bed in Armando's arms was the crescendo of the world's greatest aria. And they wouldn't stop throwing things. We were pelted with flowers, beads, buttons, berries, feathers tied with ribbon, and only the Lord knows what else.

With his left arm around my back and his right arm under my knees, snug to his chest, I kept my eyes blissfully closed with my head under his chin. Like a baby rocked in a cradle, the motion of his body as he walked with me in his arms was intoxication.

Surrounded by well-wishers barraging us with little gifts and shouting blessings of good fortune and the birthing many children, we stopped on the courtyard landing for a quick little hoist before continuing to the top of the stairs. The occasional pause when Armando needed to adjust my weight in his grasp or make an evasive maneuver to get through the crowd was magic.

Those who had not been invited, thoughtfully brought their own food. Baying sheep and squawking chickens, some terrified, scattered everywhere.

After getting me all the way to the bedroom without one of my silk slippers touching ground, Armando cleverly slammed the door closed with his foot and carried me the final few feet to the bed, where the magical nimbus abruptly ended.

Lifting me over the freshly vacated spot where Adelio apparently had been lounging, evident from the hound-sized indent on the linen, my husband allowed me to fall to the mattress like the dropping of a Kamut sack.

Armando never questioned the cave in the pillows, or my big grin the instant we came in when a large gray wiry butt and tail quickly disappeared behind the bed as the door latch opened. My husband had more important things on his mind.

Taking a leap, similar to mounting his horse without aid of the stirrup, he flung himself to my side. The duration in the air as he cast himself next to me rivaled the time he was going to spend in order to solidify our vows.

Armando was adept at quickly taking off his sword with one hand, a little talent I knew nothing about until the wedding bed.

Placing the weapon on the floor as if it were alive, a move that was the last careful one I was to see for some time, he climbed on top of me. But I was laughing so hard we couldn't kiss. The mantilla, with veil still attached, finally broke in two and fell in my face.

Were it not for the smile that Armando was trying to conceal, he would've appeared seriously obsessed. With feverish breathing practically drowning out the crowd noise outside, he tugged on my dress, then pawed the buttons on his shirt, and seconds later pulled on my clothes again, all performed so haphazardly he never removed anything.

Finally, we locked together in a sucking, warm, slow, open-mouth kiss, while beads and trinkets that had become lost in our clothing tinkled to the floor.

"I'm going to fuck my wife," he whispered, with his silver crucifix tickling my breast along with a lock of his hair that had fallen out of the tie-cloth behind his head.

He lifted himself only long enough to pull the shirttails from his breeches. Pressing himself back to my bosom, the cross around his neck blazoned a cool spot on my throat.

"I am going to fuck my wife," he repeated, ripping open his shirt, pecking an off-target kiss on the corner of my mouth.

I pulled my lower lip into a pout, immediately after which he yanked off his breeches faster than I'd ever seen and threw them across the room.

The whole thing would've been over. But the tiny silk-covered buttons on my dress were not about come undone. Armando tapped a quick kiss not intended to have anything to do with romance, and whispered, "You're going to be fucked...dress or no dress."

Flinging my underskirt up over my chest, wearing nothing but his torn shirt, he climbed on top of the silk mountain and with three taps of the silver cross on my throat with each push, Armando yelled so loud, the cry sounded like he had been burned by a pot of boiling cassoulet.

The final requirement of the covenant came to be fulfilled in a symphony of what I prayed was coincidence. For the moment Armando had looked up to the ceiling beams and let go loud enough for all to know that the act that lasted maybe as long as six full seconds was over, the chapel bell clanged, the crowd roared, and musicians began to play what sounded like the commencing of a bullfight.

Incredibly long wisps of Armando's partially undone hair stuck to his sweaty face and dangled over his shoulders, several stray strands of which affixed themselves to my cheeks as he pulled me into an embrace.

Taking a handful of wedding-skirt silk, he said, "We've got to get this thing off." A task that couldn't be accomplished by any means other than slicing off the little buttons with his beloved sword while I kneeled on the mattress facing the massive headstead, looking like a victim of the Headman's Axe.

Trinkets were everywhere. And one of them, a tiny annoying silver heart, had managed to stick itself to my ass. Armando peeled it off, kissed the charm, put it on the candlestick tray, and said, "This is the one I shall keep."

He began searching the pile of clothes strewn on the floor.

"What are you doing?" I asked.

"I must go outside for a while, it's expected. But I'll be back very soon," he replied, pulling his breeches over his thighs with a deep knee bend.

Sitting down on the edge of the mattress, Armando took my hand and laughed. "It looks very bad for the husband to remain in the conjugal bed for very long. It might appear as though he ran into difficulties. I'll make a quick appearance and come right back with something to eat."

"I want to go with you."

"It would be better if you stayed here a little longer. You're supposed to be crying...or cleaning up...or something." He laughed.

The noise outside hit a crescendo and Armando walked over to the balcony doors. Peering out he said, "You're not going to believe this, *querida*."

Clutching bed linen as a robe, I scrambled to his side to see a human ocean filling the lawn and extending far beyond the main gates.

Armando turned to me and said, "Are you as hungry as I?"

"Very, but I doubt as much as you."

"The fast must be broken slowly, or we will both regret it I assure you. I'll bring back something soon," he said, kissing my palm.

From the time the latch clicked out of place until the door closed behind him, shouts and greetings roared from the boisterous assemblage in the upper corridor.

Cracking the door barely the width of two fingers, I stole a peek. Maximo was sucking on a cigar, contorting his lower jaw in a manner that made him appear ape-like before blowing his smoke upward. Then, as if there had never been any friction between them, Max threw his arms around Armando, pushed a cigar into my husband's mouth, and lit it with the thick nubby stub that he had been sucking on until both ends glowed.

"Well, this is a happy day, isn't it?" Max said.

Armando landed a hearty pat on his friend's shoulder. They leaned elbows on the balcony railing, commended the Mother country for owning Cuba, and puffed away, side by side.

The conversation turned to hunting. I clicked the door closed, swept my hand over the bed linen to sprinkle a stray trinket or two to the floor, and climbed in.

The sight of my husband's arrival was worth the wait. Holding a half-empty bottle of wine from our vineyard in one hand, and a large freshly cooled loaf from the oven in the other, Armando bolted through the door, slamming it shut with his shoulder after having cleverly escaped guests lined up to talk to him.

Lifting the wine and bread in each hand like a prize trophy, he hurried to the bed and tossed the loaf on the linen. Pulling the cork from the bottle with his teeth, he spit it out, depositing it somewhere in the room, and said, "This is all we're going to have, today."

Ripping a chunk of crust, I stuffed it in my mouth. "No goblets?"

Armando laughed. "What makes you think there's a cup anywhere to be found? I was lucky to find this," he said, throwing his head back to take a mouthful.

"Armando?" I asked shyly.

"Yes, querida," he replied, pulling a chunk of bread from the loaf.

"Where were you?"

He stopped eating, took my hand, and said, "You were worried, weren't you? The first night was the worst. I'd gotten lost, and wound up spending the dark hours lying in a ditch holding onto Cabeza's rein the whole time. When it got light I just rode. Funny thing was, I thought I knew every place within a few days ride from here, but I'd never seen this monastery. It turned out to be perfect. The monks let me stay in the garden for the six days. They took care of Cabeza and pretty much left me alone. I filled my hands under a fountain for water. And when they became concerned that I might die, the brother's brought out a few morsels. Every morning I carved a notch in a stone to keep track of time."

"You did this for *me*?"

Armando's green eyes softened. Keeping hold of its slender neck, he set the bottom of the bottle on the linen, looked right through me, and said, "Léna, I would *die* for you. If it were necessary, I would give my life for yours. I loved you the moment we met. And I made you my wife when I realized that living without you was…well…going to be difficult."

A tear seeped from the outside corner of my eye as he put the empty bottle on the floor, took me in his arms, and kissed me.

Reaching into his shirt, Armando lifted a gold chain from around his neck, pulled it over his head, and put it in my hand. It was a small pendant shaped like an arrow.

"Oh, please put it on me. I'll never take it off," I said, turning my back and pulling my hair over my head.

Armando fastened the chain. "Eros shot Apollo with a golden arrow, and the god instantly fell in love. I came home from the New World with this little trinket in my pocket and fell in love the next day. It's yours."

Rolling me onto my back Armando clasped my hands against the bed on either side of my face. The final moment before his parted lips were about to meet mine, he quickly pulled away. Then denying another kiss, he suckled my upper lip and flicked his tongue over my moistened mouth, stopping to take a gentle suck of my lower lip. Lightly, as if to make me wonder whether they were really upon me or not, his lips tickled the entire length of my throat, finding their way between my breasts. All the while, our clasped hands remained pinned to the bed. Circling his mouth around each breast he never touched either nipple. He had to have known I was going mad.

Feeling the sting of his own doing, he rubbed the inside of my upper thigh in a series of pretend penetrations, while struggling to take air into his lungs fast enough.

I tried to free my hands. "Armando, I want you. Please, I need you," I said, my voice shaking like the rest of me.

All I got were several undulating humps and trembling similar to my own. Then he just got up out of bed. He was as ready as I, yet he quit.

I sat up like a bolt. "How long do you expect me to stay like this?"

Casually picking his shirt up from the floor, he replied, "Until after we visit with our guests."

"You're seriously going to do this, aren't you?"

Pulling my legs toward the edge of the bed, he kissed the bottom of my foot, and said, "You will find the wait most gratifying, I assure you."

I didn't know if I was going to make it to the pleasurable finale, but it was probably going to be worth it, or so I told myself, as we rummaged the room searching for something to wear.

The show included my husband, hopping on one foot to keep from losing his balance while he pulled on his pants with a lit cigar in his mouth, then squatting down twice to pack his hips into the skin-tight breeches.

"You'd better not be on the bed when we get back," Armando said to his dog.

Adelio made his squeaky door-hinge sound, lowered himself into sphinx position, and rested his long gray snout on his front paws as if he understood every word.

Flocks celebrated on the lawn outside, while most of those who had actually been invited remained within the safety of the house. People were everywhere, and it didn't take long for the newly wedded couple to be lost in the crowd.

Holding trays of food above their heads, servants struggled to navigate the crowd. Age-darkened wood sherry casks being carried to the dining hall were followed by a flurry of guests attempting to open the taps before the vessels could be delivered. A gypsy woman clapped over her head, pounding huge shoes on a table that had been dragged from the house, chanting in rhythm to the banging of a guitar. Tossing her lace skirt ruffles side to side, the blood-red fabric allowed everyone to see most of her leg.

An odd goat or chicken, lucky enough to have escaped the hatchet, wandered the masses as though they'd been named on the guest list. And, everyone was numb on spirits continually carried from the Velazquez distillery.

While separated from my husband by the crowd, Maximo inserted himself next to me, put his arm around my shoulder, and said, "You look ravishingly beautiful."

"How did Armando get that little scar on his back?" I asked.

"You don't go for small talk, do you? He would have my head if he knew I told you. I was there when it happened, about six or seven years ago. We were at La Puerta Rojas lifting a glass or two with Esteban, drinking, swapping stories. A woman came in. I don't know how we neglected to pay much mind, she was a dark-haired beauty, wearing a red smock, and an even a redder frown. She never said a word. She just walked up to the bar, pulled a dagger, and stuck the thing in Armando while he was standing with his back to her. Esteban and I grabbed the girl, took the blade away, and pushed her out into the street. She was a wild one, bit me and kicked Esteban. We got back inside and Armando had slid to the floor. Sitting there under the bar, bleeding, I don't think I'll ever forget it. Leaking blood all over the place, your husband said, 'Women! ...You *don't* make love to them, they're angry. *Women!* ... You *make love* to them, and they're angry!'"

I didn't find the story nearly as amusing as Max did. Pausing for a sip of sherry, the blacksmith made me wish his libation had gone down the wrong pipe. But, instead of choking, he laughed and said, "The way Armando carried on, I figured he'd never gotten syphilis because he only made love to married women! Ha! He did manage to find one with a knife! In case you haven't noticed yet, my dear Léna, upheaval just seems to naturally follow your husband around. It's always pretty much been a runaway ride."

Armando appeared, making his way through the madness accompanied by a man who not only towered above the heads of most, but looked all the taller by the presence of a plumed hat. The offensive feather was of the most intensely pink hue one could imagine before being considered red. And as if the chapeau that eluded taste wasn't enough, his beard had been wax-pressed into a point beneath his chin.

Presenting me to the pink-plumed Coq, Armando yelled, "Léna, this is Henri La Compte, the new fencing master, with the untimely misfortune to have just arrived."

Before I could say a thing, I threw my hands up to shield flying splinters from a goblet smashing to the floor as a well-dressed man stumbled and fell right in front of us.

Resting on the hilt of his sheathed weapon, the length of which nearly touched the floor, Henri picked up my glove to render a kiss. Peering down his arm as if I were an archer's target, he noticed a few drops of red, and said, "A blood wedding? I don't know of anyone who has actually done that, and I must say you are far too beautiful a woman to be blemished in any way."

Holding up my soiled glove, I shouted above the roar, "Oh, you thought this was blood? This isn't blood... blood is red... *this* is pink."

Armando's cheek dimples went deep as he grabbed my arm, put his face to my ear, and said, "I should probably spank you right here, but I think you've gone too long without accommodation."

Making apologies to guest after guest, vying to express their respects, he repeated, "Please excuse us, my wife needs to rest in bed, forthwith." Finally, my husband swept me into his arms and headed up to the landing.

Looking over Armando's shoulder as he carried me to our room, I saw Henri standing at the base of the courtyard stairs.

Oblivious to everything going on around him, the new fencing master stared at me, wringing his long curled-end moustache between his fore-finger and thumb in a Mephistophelean twirl.

TUESDAY, 19 SEPTEMBER 1780

Watching from across the portico table, knowing full well why I had to sit down so slowly, Armando grinned as I carefully lowered myself onto the chair.

One of the kitchen maids ran by, chasing a pullet, while a stray wedding guest or two milled about in a stupor, still too drunk to find their way home. Empty bottles, tableware, clothing, stripped bones, and unidentifiable trash sprinkled the grounds.

Letting go of each other's hand only long enough to tear chunks of bread and sip chocolate, we paid no mind to any of it.

Familiar diminutive, determined footsteps drew closer. Lizarraga's coach had been standing in front of the house for better than an hour, and we never knew it until Mother, carrying a gilt box with a folded cloth resting on its lid, waltzed onto the portico, dressed as if she had been invited to dinner with Marie and Louis.

I didn't know why I thought she was never leaving, but there she was ready to go. I couldn't help but think she was trying to downplay the whole thing by lending cheeriness. I just wanted to cry.

Armando jumped to his feet and kissed the gloved hand that had been thrown into his face, as Mama said, "My darlings, I will miss you so. But, Monsieur Chevaleaux doesn't do very well without me. I promise to visit on the very next trip to the Lizarraga farm, and stay long enough for both of you to be glad when I go."

I was sure tears would spill when a tiny line cupped the corner of her mouth, as she gently touched my cheek and pressed a kiss to my forehead. She'd been there my whole life. How was I to go on without my best friend?

"My dearest daughter, I have something for you," she said, her glass and gold filigree earrings flashing bright blue in the sun as she put the gilt box in my hand.

Lifting the lid revealed the countless tiny offerings thrown at Armando and me on the trip to bed after the ceremony, all neatly gathered.

"I'm sure there were a thousand more we didn't rescue. But Maria and I couldn't possibly bend over one more time," she said, turning to go.

Stopping mid-stride as though she had forgotten something, she shoved the folded muslin into my hand, as if it were something meant to be thrown away, and said, "Oh, this is for you, too."

Inside the cloth were five pastel ribbons I'd seen many times. The cherished silk of pink, blue, yellow, white, and cream, some frayed around the edges, all tied together. Mother had kept them since she was a schoolgirl, ultimately using them as silent signals for Father, to let him know what she wanted, or what kind of mood she was in. She wore the white ribbon on top of her head when she wanted him to know she was "right" about something. She wore the yellow ribbon when she needed to be humble. Needless to say, that one looked like it had never been used. She tied the blue one around her neck when she didn't want to make love. And I can only surmise the meaning of the pink and cream-colored ones, but I knew they were all held dear.

"I can't take these from you!" I sobbed.

"Yes, you can. Do whatever you like with them. Toss them out if you wish. And, my sweet Madeleine, one final word of advice…try not to throw anything."

"…At Armando? I don't think so, Mother."

"My dearest, what I mean is that during the heat of conversation, don't throw the Limoges. It's so expensive!"

They were securing the last of Mother's trunks on top of the coach roof as the three of us walked out to the drive.

I would've preferred Mama's touch to that of her gloved hand when she smiled and said, "Senor Lizarraga has been kind enough to arrange for my transportation home. So when the coach returns to Sevilla, I'll send something along from your father."

She acted as if she were just leaving for the afternoon. Popping up the step she quickly settled in her seat and with a flat outstretched hand blew a kiss over her palm, through the window.

The driver cracked the whip in the air and the foursome rocked back onto their haunches, took a step to the side, and jogged the carriage forward with the crunch of stones fading as they got farther and farther away.

Almost out of sight, Mother couldn't see me even if she had turned around when I threw my hand up to wave goodbye one last time.

Armando put his arm around me as we looked down the empty drive. Even with him beside me, I felt alone. How could I be so happy and sad at the same time?

I reminded myself that Mother had lived for twenty years without me, before I was born, so it was likely that we could be apart and survive. Still I didn't care for it very much.

Before returning to the bedroom, Armando and I spent the middle of the day in the shade of a big old tree with his arms around me, telling stories of growing up in the house as a young boy, medication that he must've known I sorely needed.

Three chimes had come and gone, and Henri had yet to show for the first fencing session.

Armando took me by the hand to the center of the courtyard, drew his sword from its holder, and said, "It's time for your first lesson."

"You're going to teach me?"

"My only fear is that you're going to like it." He laughed.

"Here, hold it this way," he said, standing behind me with his arms over mine, supporting most of the weapon's weight, which was a good thing since I couldn't believe how heavy it was. Armando could fling it around like a twig, yet I almost dropped the precious blade, trying to hold it up.

Demonstrating a simple parry, he whispered, "You might have to take it with both hands," in such a way I wanted to go back upstairs to bed.

"The length of a man's sword is very important -- an inch can mean life or death. If the sword is too long, it will be unwieldy and slow. A sword that is too short will make it difficult to reach the opponent. And if you must fence someone above your height, timing your actions perfectly becomes even more important. Even the finest swordsman is challenged by a taller opponent. I'm very lucky to have long arms for my height. And I'm even more fortunate to be able to fence with either hand, because a left-handed opponent creates a set of interesting challenges, even for other left-handed fencers. I rarely ever let on that I'm left-handed, that is my secret weapon. The unexpected, Niña, is what makes one successful in a fencing bout. There is, however, one critical disadvantage. Favoring the left puts the heart forward in the stance. And, usually, one doesn't care for their most vital organ to be the more likely target."

The dogs bolted from the stable, barking, running across the lawn chasing imaginary prey. I snapped a tiny smile. The maestro strutted onto the courtyard like a peafowl about to unfold its plumes.

Perched several paces away, Henri took a huff as though he had been the one kept waiting.

Armando gave me a quick kiss, and I settled into my favorite chair in the shade of the portico to relish the sight of my half-naked husband in the scorching sun.

Steel clanged against steel, and at one point Armando leapt past Henri to place his sword-tip behind Henri's shoulders. The blades flashed so fast, I couldn't really tell what was going on. Not that it mattered, it was just another practice session.

I got up from my chair, thinking it was over, and heard Henri say to Armando without as much as an ounce of sincerity, "Oh I'm terribly sorry, man, please forgive my error."

It wasn't until my husband walked toward the portico holding his upper arm, that I noticed he'd been hurt. I ran to him.

Blood was oozing through a cut in the sleeve of his shirt.

"What happened?" I implored, taking hold of his forearm.

"I made a little mistake, that's all, not to worry."

I knew very well fencing exercises were supposed to leave the weapon just shy of the target. No one was supposed to bleed during practice, especially when the cut was more than just a scratch.

During the time it took for us to get to our private quarters, Armando's whole sleeve had been bloodied.

We sat down on the edge of the bed, a trickle of red spurted from the slice in my husband's soaked muslin shirt, my stomach rose to my throat and I said, "I'll fetch a dressing."

"Not yet. Give it a minute or two, the bleeding cleans the wound."

"How on earth, did this happen?" I asked, sitting back down beside him.

"Niña, the best swordfighter makes mistakes, no one is perfect. But what bothers me is that Henri cut me by miscalculating the distance, or he did it deliberately. Either way, it's not good. t's bad...very bad," he said, reaching over to the table next to the bed.

Pulling the stopper out of the bottle with his teeth, Armando spit the cork onto the linen, took a huge gulp of sherry, and poured the rest over his wound and down his arm.

Peeling off the ruined shirt, he let it fall on the floor. "You can get that dressing now."

Mustering conversation with the new fencing master at the dinner table was tedious. After every imbecilic sentence he imparted, to accentuate his idiocy, Henri waved a lace-edged nose-rag with a flap of his hand. The fellow must've had a chest full of handkerchiefs. The bulge in his satin breeches harbored a far greater purpose for the accessory than just horn-blowing and punctuation.

Food was still on our plates when Armando picked up a bottle from the table, told the fencing master to continue indulging in our hospitality, and led me upstairs by the hand, leaving Henri by himself.

Before the bedroom door latch had been clicked back into place, I was being kissed. My mouth stayed on Armando's lips until all my clothes had been taken off, one by one, falling to the floor.

Other than the shirt that barely covered his ass, my husband stood naked beside the bed moving his hands behind his head so quickly, it looked more like he was shooing flies than braiding. His waist-length hair had been knotted into one long tail.

"How you can do that so fast? But more importantly, why haven't I ever seen you do it until now?" I asked with the corners of mouth turning up.

Armando sat down next to me, caressed my leg through the linen, and replied with a smile, "Romance has given way to practicality." Reaching over to pour a glass of sherry, he opened a red leather-bound book with beautiful gold scrollwork on the edges and said, "I'm going to read to you."

Just watching his gaze shift across the page and the sound of his voice as he read would've been fascinating enough. But the literary work cleverly disguised by its elegant cover evolved into an erotic treatise recounting the details of a captured soldier describing first sight of a young maiden who brought more than just food to his prison cell.

Reciting details of the captive disrobing the girl, Armando's hand found the inside of my thigh.

The book cover softly thumped. He reached for the sherry bottle and slipped his hand under my back. Arched over the linen, I felt the cool smooth edge of the sherry decanter and a dribble trickling down my neck.

Retrieving the liquor with his tongue, Armando poured again, this time, filling the indentation at the base of my throat. He drank from my skin, licking the sherry that escaped under my arm. I tried not to laugh.

Holding my breasts to each other with one hand, he sipped the liquor from his human chalice with a series of sucking noises that seemed to amuse him endlessly.

Flicking his sherried tongue over each of my nipples, he poured spirits onto my belly, and caught the run by licking it away from the indentation inside my hipbones.

The overflow went between my legs, stinging like a salted wound. But my husband came to the rescue with his tongue.

The pleasure of his mouth between my legs was all the more powerful by fact that it had immediately followed the burning distillation.

I looked down to see him looking up in a coup d'oeil bringing me closer.

He poured between my legs again, only to wash away the pain with the delight of his mouth. My thighs shook. I clutched his forearms. He grabbed my legs. The bottle in his hand tipped over, spilling onto the linen. He sucked harder and quickened the circular flicks of his tongue. I writhed and screamed. The decanter hit the floor with a dull thud.

Armando rolled me over onto my belly, took hold of my thighs and pulled me onto him. Filled with but three or four pushes, we overflowed.

My husband leaned over for a kiss on the corner of my mouth. I tasted myself.

Thundering insects in the grasses beyond the courtyard buzzed to the harmony of gulping tree frogs and my silent tears. Armando's wet skin against mine felt cool in the steaming night. I was sure the soaked linen was my heart that had melted.

WEDNESDAY, 20 SEPTEMBER 1780

M y husband's lips on the back of my hand opened my eyes. "Why are you up so early?" I asked, noticing Armando was already dressed.

"I won't be long," he replied, heading for the door with Adelio on his heels. "The buyer for the Alazan is coming to pick up his new mount this morning. I thought it best to hop on the animal and make sure he behaves before the man arrives. It shouldn't take but a few minutes."

Before my husband walked out, he announced that he was in love with his wife. I was still smiling when the hooves of the sale horse hammered their echo from the courtyard cobblestone.

Armando's shirt from the night before was lying on the rug. Picking it up, I held it to my face for a sniff and put it on. I could feel him as I sat down at the dressing table, pushing up the huge sleeves that would not stay rolled over my elbows.

Following a lift of the lid on the box Mother had given me, and two little swings of a satin cord holding a tiny gold heart charm, overjoyed that the bedroom latch had clicked out of place so soon, I said, "You know what I'd like to do today --"

Looking up from the small pile of wedding tokens, I froze. Before me in the mirror was not my husband, but Henri, locking the door behind him.

Dropping the charm into its box, my heart made sure I knew it was beating. I quietly closed the cover and addressed the image over my shoulder in the mirror. "Monsieur, it is not proper for you to be in my bedroom. You must leave at once."

"Here with proper intentions, my dear?" the fencing master replied, slowly walking toward me like that of a stalking predator.

"Leave now, and I will not tell my husband."

Henri stood next to me with vacant eyes like dark holes fixed on my neck as he gently pulled my hair behind my shoulder and casually replied, "Oh, I don't think you're going to tell him, whether I go or not."

The guise of coolness fell away with the increasing tone and tempo of my voice. "I don't want you here. Why are you doing this?"

Henri rested a hand on his sheathed sword-grip, and said, "Because, I want to."

"Do you always just take whatever it is you want?" I snapped, wondering if the gun in the armoire was loaded.

The fencing master seized my throat and blasted, "Yes!"

Trying to break free, I screamed, stabbing my own ears with a shriek I never knew I had. I thought he was going to strangle me.

I pounded my fists as hard as I could. But Henri burned my arm in his grasp, just laughed at my struggle, took me between the legs, and forced the tip of his finger inside.

"Is everything all right, Señora Condesa? Are you all right?" voices shouted from the corridor.

"No!" I yelled, taking another wild fling at Henri's face, only to have my hand caught before striking him.

Covering my mouth, he dragged me across the room, threw me on the bed, and said, "You'd better shut up, or you and your husband will both be sorry."

The Frenchman got on top of me and began doing whatever he wanted, when I heard what must've been Adelio growling and barking in the corridor.

Sweat oozed from the creases in his brow as Henri took a swipe of me, put his hand to his nose, sniffed, and said, "You've got some spice mixed in with that fire now, don't you, my lovely?"

I fought with all my might. Nothing worked. He grabbed my hair, yanked my head to the bed, and began fumbling with the buttons on his ivory satin breeches.

Henri was about to unleash himself when he stopped dead. Boot thuds hit the floor.

Having nearly fallen over from the momentum of his arrival, Armando regained his balance inside the balcony doors, shirt-sleeves dotted in blood. Staring at the scene on his bed, my husband stood heaving for his next breath.

Henri let go. I leapt up and scrambled for my dressing gown.

Armando's brow furrowed. Perhaps the scariest of it was that he remained completely composed.

"It's not what it appears to be!" Henri blurted.

Armando's sarcastic tone began softly, slowly elevating in volume with each word. "Let's see...my wife was screaming. The door is locked from the inside. She is barely clothed. You had her trapped on the bed, holding her by the hair with one hand --" After a brief pause, his voice escalated to a yell and his face flushed, "… And with the other, you were unbuttoning your pants! W*hat exactly is not as it appears!*"

Henri was quick. "She only started screaming when we heard you coming."

Armando snapped, "If you leave now, I won't kill you."

Without waiting for a reply, my husband grabbed Henri by the shirt, pushed the Frenchman across the room, and tossed him into the corridor.

Shuffling back to avoid the booted-out houseguest, two young maids among the group of servants assembled shrieked and clutched each other as Armando flung Henri to the railing.

Adelio growled and snapped. The help pulled the barking dog away. But not before the hound had left a trace of blood on the wrist of the Frenchman who didn't budge an inch to go anywhere. Henri merely straightened himself up, gave the waist of his pants a tiny tug, and shook his ruffled shirtsleeves as if he were the one who had been maligned.

Armando gave my hand a gentle squeeze. I thought it was all over. But my husband began pacing back and forth in front of his fencing instructor.

"I might have understood you wanting my wife. I could not blame a man for that. However, when a lady says no, it *means no!*"

Henri pulled his upper lip high, looked down at me with disgust, and lifted his fingers to his nose. After inhaling an inappropriate length of time, he sneered at Armando from boots to head and said, "Your wife, Señor...she is no lady."

The Frenchman hadn't already done enough to get himself killed, so he turned his head in my direction, and spit on me, dampening the bottom of my robe.

Gasps were drowned by steel scraping out of its sheath. With sword in his left hand Armando pushed Henri to dueling distance. "En guard, Señor!"

Fear tore through my veins. The shiny cherished blade I'd only ever seen used for practice and a ridiculous duel against Maximo was pointed directly at the instructor's throat.

"Perhaps you didn't understand. Draw your weapon, Señor!"

The splash of the fountain from the courtyard below was the only thing to be heard. Henri stood motionless, as if he'd just received an unexpected guilty verdict from the Royal Court. Blanched as white as his deflated satin pants, the fencing master did nothing but stare at his student.

Armando responded by slowly inserting the tip of his sword into Henri's nose. Twisting the blade a quarter turn, he said, "Draw your weapon, monsieur, or you'll have the convenience of another breathing hole in that beak of yours."

Henri slowly pulled his sword from its holder. Armando exploded into a lunge. The fencing instructor jumped back in a split-second, avoiding death on the spot. Armando's sword-tip rested no more than two fingers width from Henri.

Armando hadn't recovered from his lunge when he was almost knocked over by Henri's clanging blow which my husband answered with a fast, high twirl that nearly slashed the Frenchman's face.

Each ring of sword strikes fouled the still morning in a duel unlike anything I'd ever seen. Ear-stabbing clangs of steel against steel, powerful enough to take a life at any moment, came and went so fast it was next to impossible to see who had struck whom's weapon.

Armando landed a barrage of attacks, backing the Frenchman down the stairs one tiny step at a time, thusly granting Henri the opportunity to fence a taller man. Soon after which the maestro lost his footing, stumbled a stair or two, and fell onto the landing.

My husband lowered his sword. Standing over the fencing master, Armando's sweat-soaked shirt revealed his sun-darkened chest, rising and falling with each heaving breath as he looked down at his opponent sitting spread-legged on his ass.

My relief, thinking it was over, didn't last long.

Pacing one way, then the other, Armando ordered Henri to pick up his weapon.

The request went unsatisfied. Henri just sat there as though nothing had been said. My husband's rebuttal was a flick of steel over the fencing instructor's left arm just below the shoulder with a precise flip of the blade as if merely opening a letter.

The Frenchman clutched the cut seeping red between his fingers.

"Are you deaf, man? Pick up your sword. Your right arm has yet to bleed!" Armando shouted.

The varmint got to his feet, groaned like an old woman picking up her bonnet, and slowly bent over to retrieve his weapon. His fingers had barely closed around the handle when he exploded into a lightning lunge thrusting steel at Armando's face.

My throat skinned itself with a scream. My husband flew back to avoid the skewering and fell onto the staircase. Keeping his sword pointed at Henri, Armando scrambled backward up the steps with one hand, while the fencing master swung his blade again and again. Armando was regaining his footing at the top of the stairs, when a wild swipe cut a split in the top of his boot.

I forgot to breathe. I thought I was going to faint. Bracing myself against the wall, I watched my husband, with torn boot-leather flapping away from his leg, bolt straight down the stairs for Henri. The fencing master casually stepped to the side, laughed, and danced all the way up the stairs.

Looking like a mockery of his former appearance, the maestro's long curled mustache had lost its stiffness. Henri distorted his voice like a bullying child, and shouted down to Armando, "Come and get me!"

Armando took the stairs three at a time, but instead of engaging steel, stopped a few steps below the maestro. With a slice as simple as the cutting of a scone, the student whisked off the tip of the instructor's slipper. The blue goatskin shoe rolled onto the second stair-step with the Frenchman's big toe still inside.

Henri screamed like a girl and headed straight for Armando. However, it was the shortened foot that had taken the first step.

Thud by thud, the maestro tumbled the length of the staircase, dotting tiny red spots in various locations.

Sitting spread-legged on the courtyard stone, Henri ripped a bandage from his shirt sleeve. His bloody foot oozed into a shapeless pool on the floor.

I almost felt sorry for him, wrapping the end of his foot while Armando stood over him, holding the sliced-off slipper tip.

"I'm no longer in need of your services, Monsieur Le Compte," Armando said as the Frenchman tried to get up.

Armando snapped his fist shut. "Aren't you forgetting something? Actually, you probably have no need for this any longer. And, I don't believe the swine have been fed yet. Rest assured it will not go to waste. It's time for you to find a new pupil, monsieur. You've been dismissed."

The fencing master of the briefest employ slowly got to his feet.

I ran to my husband and was about to put my arms around him, when Henri's blade whisked a cut in the air like a naval court marshall captain's cat 'o nine tails. Armando ripped his sword from the scabbard where it had been sheathed only seconds, pushed me out of harm's way, and executed a stunning, decisive slash that made everything he'd done before look like a mask for his real talent. Steel clanged to the tile, echoing against the lime-washed walls of the silenced house. It happened so fast, I didn't know exactly what had been done until blood began to pour from a gash just beneath the pit of Henri's arm.

The Frenchman's final attempt at proving his worth gave up the ghost as his clothes quickly drenched red, spilling onto the courtyard tile. The expert that had made his reputation known as one of the so-called best blades in Europe had been rendered incapable of lifting a sword.

"Get him out of here," Armando ordered.

One never witnessed such a scurry. Servants that had gathered to see the settlement vied to aid the departing maestro.

"Yes, Señor Conde. Yes, Señor Conde," was heard over and over as Armando's boots clicked the floor.

"Today's fencing lesson is over," Armando muttered, walking out without so much as a glance at his former sword-master, or anyone -- including me.

Holding a bloody rag to his gushing slice, Henri was lifted by each arm, and carried away.

I stood and stared at the pool of blood on the floor. It wasn't until servants began cleaning that I went looking for my husband.

The blacksmith slammed a horseshoe in front of the stable, ringing steel to anvil as though nothing unusual had taken place.

Armando was crouched down over a wooden bucket with a flask of oil. Plunging a rag into the water, he wiped the steel in his hand, then dunked the cloth and did it again, never bothering to look up.

In the heavy morning air that would be unbearable by noon, I stood beside him, silently watching the cleansing of his weapon.

Finally he said, "Do you have any idea how much I hate to wash blood from my sword?" Armando took a quick glance in my direction, saw part of my leg showing through the robe slit, and said, "Léna, go get dressed, you're going to cause a scene with the help."

Everything I'd been holding back until then crashed into a wave of tears and I ran. I was at the edge of the cobblestone when I heard, "Damn!" followed by a bucket tumble and splash. Armando's boots banged the stone behind me. I was at the stairs when he grabbed me and pulled me around to face him.

"I'm sorry, Léna. I'm so sorry. I was caught up in myself and completely forgot what you'd been through," he said with eyes filling.

"You blame *me* for this!" I blurted.

Armando pulled me to his chest. "No I don't. I do not blame you." Gently rocking me in his arms, he softly said, "I blame myself."

I wanted to say something, but all that came out was tears.

Armando picked me up and carried me to our room.

Sitting against the pillows on the bed with my head pressed to his chest, he gently stroked my hair and said, "Léna, I cut a man. And, I cut him very badly. He may not live. If he does make it, he'll most likely never be able to lift his arm. And, I cut him, knowing exactly what I was doing. I lost my temper while I had a weapon in my hand."

Pulling my head from his chest to see the green eyes I loved to gaze into, I reached up, took his face in my hands, and said, "*Querido*, you did it for honor."

"I could have let him walk out of here, but I didn't, Léna. I cut him."

"You *did* let him walk out! Perhaps, he needed a little help…"

We both tried not to laugh.

Armando tightened our embrace, kissed the hair that had fallen over my ear, and whispered, "God, I love you."

A knock came on the door. It was Maria from the corridor with trepidation in her voice. "Señor Conde, there is someone here to see you."

"The buyer for the horse, I almost forgot," Armando said, jumping out of bed. "Why don't you get dressed and join us, niña?"

During the time it took to throw on some clothes and run downstairs, maids were still sloshing soaked rags and scraping twig brushes over the stains where Henri thoughtlessly bled onto the tile.

In spite of the unusual efforts going on behind him, Armando was carrying on a normal conversation with a finely dressed man, who seemed quite distracted by the efforts of far more servants than needed to merely wash the floor.

"Ah! Here is my wife! Léna, this is Don Hernando Martinez," Armando said, putting one arm around my back and the other hand on my upper arm, presenting me as if I might've been the Mozart child after my first virtuoso performance.

"I didn't know you had a wife," Martinez replied.

"I do! And this is she! You've come to see the horse, haven't you? I'm afraid I have a bit of bad news, man. I rode him this morning and apparently, he's a much finer animal than I thought, so I've decided not to sell him. Why don't you stay for dinner? I'm sure we can find another mount in my stable that perhaps suits you better."

Stopping mid-stride before reaching the final landing, several maids descended the stairs carrying a trunk of Henri's personal effects. Dropping the end she was carrying with a clunk, one of them asked, "Señor Conde, what shall we do with this?"

"I don't care, just get rid of it. You'll have to excuse us, Don Hernando, we've had a guest leave unexpectedly," Armando said with a smile.

"Anyone I would know?" Martinez asked, nervously adjusting his jabot as a bead of sweat ran down the side of his face.

"Not unless you're familiar the Maestro Henri Le Compte," Armando replied.

"He's not that fencing master who ran into a bit of trouble some while back, is it?" Martinez said, returning to life.

"Trouble?" Armando asked, raising an eyebrow.

Don Hernando scratched his goatee and replied, "It was a year or so ago, Monsieur Henri made a rather ugly advance to someone's wife. A challenge took place. And rumor had it, Le Compte apparently hired someone to shoot his opponent in the back while they were hacking it out during a duel by sword."

After an uncomfortable moment of silence, Don Hernando's voice broke when he asked, "Was that Le Compte, who just left here? Well, I must be running. Thank you for the dinner invitation, perhaps next week, sometime. We'll look at another horse, then."

Hurrying to make an exit, Martinez nearly ran into the three-hundred-year-old suit of armor next to the door. Armando and I could barely hold our laughter.

Maria set a lye bucket on the floor next to the scrubbers. Swiping her hand across her brow and pointing to an older spot on the floor, she said, "Señor Armando, I'm afraid the floor is permanently stained. We never the other one out."

"It's all right, Maria, don't worry about it, just send for the monsignor," Armando replied, taking my hand.

"You are shortening that man's life," she replied, going to search for the messenger.

We should've been praying at the chapel altar, instead, we stared lovingly at each other. Sitting next to me on the rug, with one knee pointed toward the ceiling, Armando ran his fingers lightly up and down my arm.

"Slicing off Henri's toe was very clever," I said, touching my brow to his.

"That which does not kill you, makes you fence like shit." He laughed.

"Armando?" I said as innocently as I knew how.

"Yes, *querida.*"

"How did the floor get stained, the other time?"

He pecked a kiss and said, "The duke and I had a little disagreement a couple of years ago when he and the duchess were here for dinner one night. The seating arrangements called for the duchess to sit next to me. And, before the duck was brought out, her hand was on my knee under the table."

"You can't be serious?"

Armando's cheek dimples appeared. "I did my best to ignore it. But, by the time sherry was served, her hand had made its way up the inside of my thigh."

"No!"

"...And when the bottles were empty, she reached for...well, let's just say it became necessary for me to curtail her enthusiasm."

"Armando! ...she didn't!" I shouted, grabbing both his arms.

My husband laughed and said, "I didn't think anyone had actually seen her grab me under the table. But the duke had gotten out of his chair and walked past just as his wife had latched onto me between the legs, and it was at that exact moment that I had grabbed her wrist to push her away. I suppose it might have looked like I was the one who had put her hand where it didn't belong."

"*Mon Dieu!* I can't believe it, Armando! What happened?"

"The duke made it look like he wanted to fight. Although, I doubt he really did…at least not for the hand-under-the-table, perhaps for my political views, but surely not for supposedly flirting with his wife. Unfortunately, he had to behave like the whole thing was my fault, or the duchess would've been branded the tart that she is. So he waved his sword around, and the hardest part was trying to keep a serious face. During the so-called duel, I had to be sure to cut him where it wasn't life-threatening."

"You cut him on the ass didn't you?" I laughed.

Taking a few seconds to enjoy the memory, Armando laughed and said, "But Niña, he bled like a barrow!"

"What other things am I going to find out about my husband?"

Armando put his brow to mine, smiled, and said, "I think it's time for you to see the legacy."

WEDNESDAY, 20 SEPTEMBER 1780
LATE AFTERNOON

A rmando found me playing with the pounce pot on the library desk. I could only imagine how he had described the dismembering of Henri's toe to the monsignor.

Through the open door, Ramirez was crossing the courtyard, shaking his head as he probably had on more than one occasion after a confessional visit.

We went through metal box after metal box of papers, none of which I wanted to see. But, Armando insisted I learn the aspects of the business -- how the vineyard was operated along with the olive presses, and distillery, where all the money was kept, and the various details of our livelihood, as well as the concerns and operations of Hacienda del Sagrado Corazon. It was difficult to deal with, especially since the implication was that I would outlive him.

"I can't do any of this," I said, Armando's certificate of nobility shaking in my hand.

"Yes, you can. I wouldn't have married you, if you couldn't. It's very simple. Arturo, Maria, and Carlos handle the workers. All you have to do is oversee things once in a while. But still, you must know how everything operates without them…and without me."

"*Querido*, you handle everything, and that's the way it's always going to be."

"Niña, you are my wife, all I have is yours. You have to know how to run the business, should something happen to me."

"Happen! We are going to grow incredibly old together. You will deal with whatever needs to be dealt with. That's what's going to happen!"

"You don't want me to keep any secrets from you, do you?" He grinned.

I did what Mother would've done. I put the parchment back in the box on the desk and changed the subject. "How did you know Henri was attacking me?"

Armando laughed. "You were paid back for letting the hound on the bed. The dog! He was the one who knew. Adelio started growling. I didn't think much of it at first. I naturally assumed he caught scent of boar or something. But then he bolted for the house. I spurred that horse so hard the nag practically leapt out of the tack. We took the fence, and by the time we reached the court-yard I couldn't get him stopped down, so I leapt off, dropped the reins, and ran. By then I knew it was you screaming. Adelio must've already been barking outside the bedroom while I was taking the stairs, five, maybe six at a time. The help was standing around not having any idea what to do. The door was locked. I could hear what was going on inside, but I couldn't get in. So I jumped the railing, somehow landed on my feet, and ran back outside to climb that big citrus tree of unknown bitter genealogy, the one next to the balcony. That's how I cut my hands and tore my shirt. The blasted thing is covered with thorns."

Armando must've noticed the water welling in my lower lids, because he took me in his arms and said, "Never mind that now. Let's go see what you've inherited."

We rode for better than an hour before we got to the main wine press, grain mill, and anchor olive presses on the north perimeter of the hacienda, which was far greater than I'd ever imagined.

Crops lay dead from drought, but on our land, orchard after orchard was filled with deep-rooted older trees yielding, regardless of the rainless summer.

Workers, never having seen Armando, stood on ladders against tree-trunks tossing olives to the ground while others tugged rakes over layers of cloth under the branches, gathering the ripe and yet-to-be-ripened. None of them realizing it was the master riding by with his new wife.

The western sky had turned the color of smoke before we knew. Only a tiny slice of remaining sun perforated the charcoal horizon.

"We'd better hurry," Armando said, kicking his horse to a gallop.

The skin inside my knees rubbed raw from riding bare-legged astride when we came upon a round polished granite building in the middle of a parched pasture.

Shouting above the torrent that spilled about a minute too soon, Armando took my reins and said, "Go inside. I'll take care of the horses!"

By the time he joined me, he looked like someone had dumped a bucket over him.

Roaring rain softened for a moment, and the flapping of wings and cooing of pigeons roosting on a ledge outside softly echoed, along with the trickle of a gentle stream seeping down the wall. Rain, like tears shedding down a cheek, pooled on the floor beneath a circular stained-glass ceiling of the three Magi following the Bethlehem star.

Standing behind me, dripping onto the white and sand-colored tiles of the centuries-old Velazquez mausoleum, Armando was warm where his wet body touched mine. Clasping the back of my hands, together we walked the labyrinth inlaid into the marble floor, ending in a blossom at its center.

His new beard gently scratched my face as he planted a kiss on my ear and said, "We call this place, Dragonfly. It has four wings, just like the insect."

I could feel him through our clothes and said, "Armando, not here...not in the crypt...please."

Lifting my hair, he rendered a kiss to the back of my neck and replied, "The same blood flows though my veins as did those who rest here. They will understand. Besides, legend says that something wonderful will happen when you reach the center of the maze."

"I think the legend is referring to greater awareness." I laughed.

"Come, see how you will be enlightened," he said with his sword guard brushing my upper thigh as we slid to the marble.

Looking down at me beneath him, a droplet from his hair fell onto my face. I closed my eyes and another landed on my lid.

Armando freed himself with a quick one-handed unbuttoning of his pants, and pressed my mouth open with the grating edge of lips that would turn to silk the next time he shaved.

"Is the floor too hard?" he whispered in his love-making voice.

I nodded.

He rolled me over and pulled me on top of him.

I wanted to touch the flesh under the muslin stuck to his sun-darkened skin, but had to settle for my thighs cooling against his soaked clothes.

Armando took me by the waist, lifted me, and said, "Just relax, *querida*. I will do everything."

Holding me exactly where he wanted, Armando slowly lowered my body onto him. At first it was only a fraction, but each time he went deeper.

Even when his arms began shaking, he didn't stop. Slowly lowering me onto him, Armando was there inside me, over and over.

Finally, when we couldn't take much more, he permitted the full weight of my body to settle with all its force, pushing him so completely inside. The moment gravity took over we both called out.

The birds on the ledge outside flew into the rain as waves of medication flowed through my veins.

Armando pulled me down into a kiss. Our lips became one.

"Oh, I'm terribly sorry. I beg your forgiveness."

Maximo was standing in the doorway, a small bunch of scraggly, carelessly plucked, wildflowers shook in his hand.

Armando quickly buttoned his pants under the cover of my skirt, got to his feet, and reached down to help me up. The blacksmith just stood there in a trance-like stare. With the stems trembling in his fist, he finally said, "I've been looking for you everywhere."

"Obviously you *have*! How in the world did you find us here, man? *We* didn't even know we would be here," Armando replied.

Trying to look at anything but us, Max replied, "Well, you weren't anywhere else. So you had to be here. I just wanted to let you know there's a casual hunting group going out after breakfast, a friend of Esteban is bringing his falcon, and we'd like you to join us."

"Why don't you come by in the morning and we'll see," Armando said like admonishing a child.

"I'll be there when the chocolate pot is on," Max snapped, on his way out with the drooping flowers about to be crushed in his grasp.

As Max rode off, Armando stared out the door and said, "Sometimes, you and I get in bed at night, and I want to look around to see if he's there!"

"What in the world was Max doing all the way out here?"

"Leaving flowers, I suppose."

Down one of the narrow corridors we stopped at a plaque yet to be inscribed. Nodding at two sarcophagi, one above the other, my husband grinned." You and I will be here someday. Do you want to be on top, or the bottom? Wait, don't tell me. I already know."

"I don't think it's quite that humorous."

"Would you rather I'm melancholy? I can be, if you want me to."

I completely forgot what I was going to say. Practically in front of my face was an elaborately decorated wall next to a row of unmarked crypts, and the name Blanca de Velazquez was chiseled in one of the stones. I felt like throwing up or maybe shouting something like, what in Hades is this! But I sucked it in and calmly said, "I thought you never married her."

"I didn't."

"Then, why is her grave inscribed with the name Velazquez?"

"Her parents had the sarcophagus made after our engagement. She disappeared, and I never had it taken out. If I did, niña, it would've shadowed their hope of her ever coming back," he replied, leaning a hand against the blasted wall.

I wanted to say that we could just carve out her name when I noticed crumbled brown flowers on the floor.

Armando stared down the corridor, appearing to be deep in thought. "There is one thing that troubles me. It was pouring. But when Max supposedly walked in on us by chance, his clothes were dry."

THURSDAY, 21 SEPTEMBER 1780

Armando was unsuccessful at only one thing -- hiding his amusement. Sitting on the edge of the bed, he picked up the white gauze dress I wore when we made love in the crypt, leaned an elbow on the mattress, grinned, and said, "Here, wear this."

He'd been thoroughly entertained watching me dress, only to try something else.

"I will," I replied, taking it from him. It wasn't even completely dry, having gotten rain-soaked and left in a heap on the floor all night, because we couldn't wait to get in bed.

Looking like hell at his doing amused us both, so I put on the damp dress, blew him a kiss, and tied Mother's ivory ribbon with the secret meaning around my neck.

Droplets splashed out of the fountain with a brief hot gust. The two or three steps I took on the wet stone as we walked past felt sticky until my bare feet dried on the warm tiles. I'd never been so happy in my life.

Next to a plate of oranges, a pitcher of milk, and a bowl of butter, the chocolate-pot was waiting on the portico table along with

Moorish flatbread that Maria no doubt had just pealed from the oven wall.

Armando and I both got it in the face when I opened a fruit with my thumbs. Juice sprayed everywhere.

We finally stopped laughing, and wincing. I opened my stinging eyes. The love of my existence was sitting with the sun at his back, hair glistening like a halo.

Armando leaned across the table, put his mouth on mine for a kiss, tasted my lips, and said, "Orange."

Dipping the corner of his napkin in the water pitcher, with one finger my husband wiped my mouth, pressing the cloth slowly around the outline of my lips.

I could still feel the pressure of the touch that had circled my mouth even after he had finished.

Armando took my hand in his.

We stared at each other without saying a word.

Maria was pulling empty dishes from the table when she said, "Your guests are here, Señor Conde."

Armando got out of his chair. An uneasy feeling raced up from my toes. I grabbed his wrist and said, "Wait, I'm coming with you."

Esteban and Maximo were waiting on the drive with horses in hand. A third man, whom I didn't recognize, sat mounted. Oddly, the hooded falcon perched on his arm was looking around as though it could see, in spite of the little black bag over its head.

Armando's rough palm caressed my cheek. "I'm not going, niña. I'll tell them to hunt without me today. We'll finish breakfast."

All I had to do was say don't go. But I didn't want him to give up something he really would've enjoyed because of a wife. I faked a smile, gave his arm a loving squeeze, and said, "Don't be silly, I'll be fine. Go ahead, have a good time."

My husband put his arms around me, dispensed a quick peck on my mouth, and said, "I won't be long." I thought he was going to join the others, but he pulled me into an embrace for an embarrassing length of time.

Armando's moss eyes trenched deep as he whispered, "I'm coming back soon, even if I have to leave the others in the woods. I love you, *querida*, more than you know."

Adelio trotted up to dab his wet nose on several wrists, ahead of Carlos, who was walking across the lawn with Armando's hat hanging over his arm, and Cabeza, flapping his mane, jingling the bit in his mouth. A highly decorated rifle and powder horn had been attached to the saddle riggings.

Taking the reins, Armando pulled the hat's neck cord over his head, held onto the grip of his sword to keep from striking his horse, and vaulted into the saddle.

A crater opened in my heart.

It didn't help my dismay when Adelio snapped and growled at Maximo, something that had never happened before. Carlos took the normally congenial hound by the collar, as the four headed for the woods, hooves crunching gravel before muffling into dull thumps on the grass.

It was the first time Armando and I had been separated since we married. I felt sick. And the worst of it was the instant it was too late to say or do anything, my gut twisted. I wanted to run after Armando and beg him not to go. Why hadn't I just looked him in the eye, and said please stay? It was too late, they were out of sight.

I sat alone at the portico table, ripping the hardening flatbread into tiny pieces. Poking a dent in the crust of my chocolate, I wiped my finger on a napkin without licking it off, and told myself, Armando will be back soon, and everything will be fine. When that didn't work, I tried to visualize our children playing in the courtyard. Finally, to the imaginary applause of a faceless audience, I danced barefoot around the fountain with the skirt of my dress waving around my legs.

The peaceful day broke with a sudden gust. Wind roared, whipping the hair into my face. I ran upstairs.

Gasping for breath, I yanked open the balcony doors.

As I looked out from the narrow landing the white muslin of my skirt blew through my legs violently flapping behind me. I could hardly stay on my feet, it was blowing so hard.

Far off the outer edge of the lawn four riders were approaching Something was wrong. I ran.

Hurrying past the fountain spraying water in the wind, I cried, "Oh Lord, please let it be nothing, I beg you."

I could hardly breathe by the time I reached the courtyard between the house and stable.

Hooves landed a deafening punch on the cobblestone.

Esteban and Maximo were riding closely on either side of Cabeza, holding Armando in the saddle. My husband's white shirt was drenched red.

I let out a scream. Dogs ran around, barking like their aggression had purpose. Servants came running.

Wet palms and feet, a dry mouth, shaking hands, and legs numbed -- a cave gaped inside my chest. My vision narrowed.

"What happened! What's happened!" I shouted, clinging to Armando's thigh as they pulled him from the saddle. His leg was moist. Blood was pouring from his chest. He couldn't move, his face was gray, and he could hardly take a breath. An arrow was lodged in his left side.

Punching the air with each huge stride, Carlos ran from the stable.

Adelio, ears laid back into the grey fur on his head, bolted from the carriage house as if chasing down prey for the kill. Teeth gnashing, the hound growled and pounced onto Max, taking an arm in his mouth.

The blacksmith threw Cabeza's reins to Carlos while trying to push the dog away. "Get the physician. Ride as fast as you can, man."

Carlos vaulted onto Armando's horse, dug his heels into the animal with a pounding thud, and with hooves like canon-fire on the stone, blasted into a full gallop by the second stride.

"Somebody, get this dog out of here!" Max shouted.

Adelio wouldn't let go, shaking his head with Max's arm still in his mouth. It took two servants to pry the hound's grip open. Adelio braced his paws against the stone, barked and growled at Maximo the entire time he was dragged away.

The softest sound blared. Max must've thought he was whispering to Esteban in private, but I heard every word.

"Ride for Ramierz, and be quick about it," he said.

I scraped my knees and felt nothing as I dropped to the stone to touch my husband lying in Max's arms. With bloodied hands, I cried, "My God, what's happened!"

Armando tried to sit up, but every time he made the effort, red leaked from a crossbow arrow pointing to his heart.

"Oh my God…my beloved, please hang on, I beg you. The physician is coming."

Lifting his hand to touch my face, Armando parted his lips as if he was about to say something. He could only wince in pain.

"No, don't say anything, *querido,* it will fine, you are going to be all right. Nothing can take you away from me."

Lord knew how I held my tears back. None of it seemed as though it was really happening. I had to have been living a dream, or someone else's life.

Servants gathered. A voice asked, "What happened?"

The man with the falcon replied, in a hurried nervous manner, "A hunter's arrow must've gone astray. It was windy. I don't know… we don't know."

Sitting on my heels next to Armando, I held his hand to my cheek. His palm was getting cold. My eyes completely filled as I kissed his fingers. Everything was a blur. All I knew were indistinct legs and apron-covered skirts standing around me.

Maria choked back her wails as her tender hand touched my shoulder from behind. Pressing her apron to her mouth, she prayed out loud.

Armando tried to move, but the arrow dug into his side seeping an even greater flow of blood from between his ribs into a pool on the stone. I leaned over, put my cheek next to his ashen face. He forced a whisper in my ear. "…To live for you-- to die for you."

The noises I made upon hearing those words were not like crying, but more like the sounds I made when we were in bed together. I put my mouth on his lips for a kiss. Armando's warm breath filled my lungs. His head fell to the side. I grasped his hand. My voice rose until the words became indistinguishable sobs. *Cielo de mi vida. No puedo vivir sin ti! No puedo vivir sin ti!* Don't leave me. Don't leave me, Armando. Please, dear God, you cannot leave me! I cannot live without you!"

The dogs ran around barking in search of the unseen assailant. Armando's grasp was gone. Had I not been holding his hand, it would've fallen to the stone.

I reached into my husband's boot and ripped out his dagger. Flinging it high over my head, I pointed it toward my heart. Maria screamed. Maximo dropped Armando and tore the weapon from my hand. I collapsed on my husband's chest. The arrow-shaft in his side scratched my face as I pressed myself to him and clawed at his shirt until I was covered in blood and my throat scorched from screaming and crying so loud nothing else could be heard other than my wild sobs.

Maximo tried to pull me away but gave up far too easily. Holding onto the wound that Adelio had left him with, Max began to deal orders as though the hacienda was his.

Waving for the aid of servants who found it within themselves to comply as if their prayers had been answered for someone to tell them what to do, the blacksmith hollered, "Get the rest of these dogs out of here!"

Trying to grab a dog by the collar, the help complied with their command as Max took hold of Armando's arm and quietly said to his falcon friend, "Let's take him inside."

Armando's sword tucked inside its scabbard swung from its hangar and his spurs made soft jingling noises with each step as his lifeless body was carried to the chapel. Choking back the avalanche, I hung onto his hand the entire way.

The men gently placed him on the rug in front of the altar. Armando's spurs made their final chink, and I let out screams that rasped my throat raw.

He looked as though he were just sleeping. The agony that had been on Armando's face before our final kiss, had been replaced by a look of peace.

Workers stayed to pray and express their grief, but eventually I was alone.

Holding my husband's palm to my face, his skin was still moist and warm, but not as warm as I remembered. Armando looked alive. I gently placed his hand to his side and then back again to my face, as if the motion itself would restore life. I did it over and over and over until his flesh was cool.

Rocking on my knees singing a song Mother used to sing to me when I had hurt myself as young girl, I sat on the same rug upon which Armando kissed me right before he swept me into his arms and carried me to our bed just days before. The farther I got from sanity, the less I cried.

The candles went out, the sun set, and the cold came. My damp, bloodstained dress made it feel all the colder. Alone in nearly total darkness, I talked to the Cristo above the altar. Looking at the Lord bleeding from His Crown of Thorns, at first my words were calm.

"How could You do this? How could You take him from me? Are You jealous because I love him more than I love You?"

Shivering in the chill of my blood-soaked clothes, I dry-sobbed in the dark until my eyes had finally run out of water to spill. I cried for Armando, and for having said what I did to the Lord.

Maria came in more than once. Each time she shuffled her weary feet to my side, she desperately tried to get me to leave Armando, change clothes, rest, and eat. I couldn't even look at her let alone do what she asked. Finally, she came back and put a goblet of water on the floor next to me and covered my shoulders with a wool wrap.

Adelio had wedged his way through the open door and went straight to Armando. The dog began to lick the blood-soaked shirt and I exploded into tears.

"Please Maria, take the dog, he mustn't see his master like this."

Adelio let out a tiny whine as Maria put her hand inside his collar and pulled him along with her. Through the closed door, her sobs gradually melted into the house.

During the late hours, I was still sitting on the floor next to my husband when I looked up and squinted with the torchlight from the courtyard. The silhouette of a figure was standing in the doorway. Ramirez finally showed. Carrying a chamber-stick, he came in, put the Scapular cloth around his neck, and after setting the candle on the altar, reached down to take hold of my arms.

I pulled away, and wailed, "I'm not leaving my husband!"

"Léna, just allow me to deliver the Final Sacraments, that's all."

"You're too late, he's already gone…and without your help."

What might've been considered trivial to some would've been a nightmare for a Spaniard with less than Armando's bravery, the Sacraments had to be delivered well after Armando had no choice but to enter the vast unknown without having received the blessings of the Church beforehand.

The monsignor performed Last Rites while I sat staring at the floor. Armando's body, not his love, was cold.

Ramirez tried to get me to go to bed, or at the very least, eat something, quickly giving up once he saw his efforts were to no avail.

Making the sign of the cross at the door, the old padre muttered, "*Dios te bendiga.*"

"I want my mother. Please, I beg you, send for Anne," I cried.

He told me he'd be back in the morning, and the door softly latched into place.

I wanted the night to be over, and the pain to go away. Staring at the floor, I sat beside my husband's cold body in the light of the monsignor's solitary flame. Under the altar table, a stray shard of the earthenware chalice that Armando smashed during our wedding ceremony caught my eye just as the wick ran out.

I was alone in the dark.

FRIDAY, 22 SEPTEMBER 1780

T he ignorant sun leaked a new day's light under the door. From the other side, the sill brightened and darkened with the shadows of moving legs.

Maria pleaded in a rasp, "You mustn't tell her, not now. For God's sake, please I beg you, don't tell her."

Still in my blood-soaked dress, barefoot, freezing and exhausted, I lay beside Armando.

I had been in the dark so long, I was nearly blinded when someone came in. Through a squint, I looked up. It was Miguel.

He'd paid particular attention getting dressed that morning. Hurrying to me, he dropped down on one knee. The scabbard holding the sword he rarely touched, let alone wore, softly clunked on the rug. From the vacant surprise on his face, he never expected to find what had become of the girl he thought he knew.

Miguel put down his plumed hat, took both my arms, and said, "Léna, you've got to get hold of yourself, you cannot do this."

My head wobbled like I was drunk.

"I want you to come home with me to La Colina. My family will care for you until you can go on with your life. This is a terrible thing. I had no idea what had happened."

"Why then did you come?" I asked, my eyes half shut from the annoying light.

Miguel took a deep breath, and replied, "It's nothing you need hear about now. Léna, I had no idea Armando had been killed. Please come home with me. Any disagreements you and I may have had will be left aside, I promise you. Just come back to La Colina."

It was the first time I thought he actually cared, but Miguel's concern came far too late. I turned to Armando's lifeless body and said, "This is my home. I will not leave my husband. If you didn't come to pay respects, why did you come? It must be important, you dressed for the occasion. Tell me why you're here, otherwise Miguel, whatever it is, I will never forgive you for keeping it from me."

"Now is not the time, the news can wait," he insisted.

"Now is the time!"

As with on many occasions, Miguel's short-lived moment of standing-his-ground went away. Getting to his feet, he blurted, "Your mother has been killed."

A punch hit me in the chest. Then, I didn't feel a thing. I just stared without looking at anything.

Miguel fidgeted uncomfortably and came out with it. "The coach was held up by highwaymen. A scuffle took place -- Anne was killed. Please come home with me, Léna."

I pulled the end of the blood-stained ivory ribbon around my neck and let it fall. Miguel didn't seem to worry about getting blood on his clothes. He got down on one knee, and put his arms around me.

Maria had come in to set a plate of bread chunks on the floor.

"Where is Maximo?" Miguel asked.

"He's here somewhere. He hasn't left since --" She began to cry.

146

"Armando must be interred today, Maria. I will handle most of the preparations. We've got to get Léna upstairs. Enlist three servant girls to help. And find Maximo! I'll wait here with Madeléna."

There was a speck of comfort in the way Miguel took charge. That, and the fact that I had become so weak, by the time Max and two maids showed my former fiancé had already headed upstairs with me in his arms.

Without recollecting how I had gotten in bed, I slept for hours. When I woke, I thought I was home in Toulouse. It didn't take long to be pounded to the anvil. I quickly remembered everything.

Where that woman found the strength, Lord knew. Maria went on, even though I heard her sobbing softly to herself as she sat sewing back on the last of the buttons Armando had cut off my dress. I was to wear the wedding gown at the funeral, a Spanish custom for widowed brides.

"Why must we do this so soon?" I asked.

"It's not soon," she replied, holding back her tears.

Sitting on the edge of the bed, staring aimlessly at the floor, I offered very little help. Maria managed to get me dressed, anyway.

"Will you be my mother, now?" I asked, reaching out to her apron.

She stopped fidgeting with the mantilla, spilled tears with an enormous hug, and replied, "Of course I will."

Sweeping her cheek dry with a single finger, Maria took the black veil that had been folded over her arm, attached it to the comb, and said, "There now, no one has to see your face. You can cry all you want."

As if I'd been sucked dry from losing so many tears, my mouth clicked every time the gravel drive crunched with carriage wheels. People kept coming.

Maximo and Miguel took me on the endless walk to the chapel, the same journey I had made only days earlier, only this time the corridors were lined with unfamiliar faces.

A strange woman reached out and touched my hand. Another tried to give me a flower, and began to cry.

The chapel benches were filled. Many stood wherever they could. People were everywhere, most of whom I'd never seen before.

Inside a black and gold casket at the altar, a single lily lay across my husband's chest. He was at peace.

Grateful that his last experience of this life was our kiss, I was supposed to be crying. But I didn't.

In the middle of the service, when Father Ramirez, remembered Armando's christening as an infant in his arms, the monsignor broke down and had to stop for the longest time before being able to continue.

Women sitting somewhere in the back of the chapel softly sobbed. I wanted to laugh with the depraved thought that they might've been Armando's former lovers. Surely at least one unfamiliar woman who had come to pay respects had also known the pleasures of being with him.

Before they closed the coffin, I took Armando's dagger and rasped a handful of his hair. It was only the second time during his life it had ever been cut.

After a lift of Armando's crucifix, just to feel it one more time, I put it back where it belonged on his chest.

Ramirez administered the final blessing as the lid was lowered and secured. I still hadn't wept. It was the clunking of the poles being inserted into the casket holders for the trip to the Velazquez crypt that were the final cataclysmic bang that pushed me over the edge. Maximo had put the sword his father made in my hands. I felt the heavy, cool, steel that Armando never went anywhere without, and exploded into tears, nearly dropping the weapon that was my husband's most cherished possession.

The thought of going back to the mausoleum where Armando and I made love – was it just yesterday? I couldn't breathe, everything looked hazy.

Miguel jumped up from the bench, took hold of my arms, and asked, "Are you all right, Madeléna."

Before I could respond, a strange man pushing his way past mourners came toward us, shook his fist in my face, and yelled, "El Conde is burning in hell!"

Max grabbed the intruder just as the spinning room went black.

SATURDAY, 23 SEPTEMBER 1780

The linen was cold when I reached over to my husband's side of the bed.

I opened my eyes to see a gray needle snout attached to a rather tall, lanky, hunting dog sitting on the floor resting his face on the edge of the mattress, staring at me.

"It's all right Adelio, the master won't know," I said, patting the cover.

The dog jumped up, flopped down, and licked the tears from my cheeks.

Up against the wall in the corner of the room, the shiny steel that used to make the loveliest of dull thuds as it was placed on the rug at bedtime had become a lonely blade with no purpose other than to confirm Armando's death.

On one occasion, I made fun of the fact that he even took it with him during his private affairs, but he quickly pointed out that the privy was the number one place for assassinations. Armando had an explanation for everything. Why was there no account for this?

I'd never been alone with the sword before, and as ridiculous as it may sound, I felt unfaithful by picking it up and holding it. There was an inscription on the ricasso.

"*No Me Saques Sin Razon*" (Do not draw me without reason) "*No Me Embaines Sin Honor*" (Do not sheath me without honor).

I wanted to cry, but the tears had had enough. The cure for a dry eye was the fresh cigar next to the sherry chaser bottle that Armando drank from in order to get rid of the foul tobacco taste I hated. I could see his hair flopping over his shoulders as he'd toss his head back for the swig before kissing me.

I picked up the smoke and put the disgusting thing in my mouth. Tears rushed and I couldn't stop. I could hardly catch my breath. Grabbing the decanter, I sloshed a good one, nearly spewing the whole stinging mouthful. Nothing would stop the pain.

Maria came back upstairs to see if I'd eaten, or perhaps tried to kill myself. I think she was relieved to find that all I did was ignore the tray she'd brought up earlier.

"You must have something, Señora Condesa -- it's been days," she pleaded.

Just to make her happy I picked up a small chunk of bread and took the tiniest bite possible, after which Maria came forth with the real agenda.

"Father Ramirez is waiting for you downstairs."

"Tell him he's going to have to come up here and see me in bed," I said, putting the piece of bread back on the tray.

She went to get him. And, right before the knock came, I heard her whispering on the other side. "I think it was better when she was crying, she just stares. It frightens me."

"I will see what I can do," the monsignor replied.

Ramirez welcomed himself, and following a scouring glance at Adelio lying on the linen under my arm, the old padre sat on the edge of the bed.

I couldn't decide if his smile was real or if he was forcing the corners of his mouth up. From having spent a lifetime as a clergyman, he probably knew how to fake just about anything when he had to.

"You must let Armando go, Léna," he said, giving my hand a tiny squeeze.

I didn't respond.

The monsignor squeezed my hand again. "Lena, Armando could've had any woman in the world -- including royalty. But, he chose you."

"Armando didn't choose me he fell in love with me!" I replied, tears spilling onto my cheeks.

"It's the same thing, Léna, there's no difference. Why do you think Armando fell in love with you? You were the only one who was strong enough to be his wife. I knew him his entire life, perhaps better than anyone, including his own father. Armando was an intensely passionate man. He would have given his life for you, Léna, he loved you that much. What do you think Armando wanted for you? Not this. Not what you're going through now. You must honor him, and you must do it…by living."

I'm far from strong," I sobbed

Ramirez got up and walked around the room, glancing at things as if strolling through a museum. Looking back at me sitting on the bed with my face in my hands, he said, "Madeléna, only a very strong person can love as you do, for love is the greatest vulnerability there is. If you are capable of loving so powerfully, you have the strength. Armando arrived home from the New World and came to see me. We talked of many things, but I clearly remember him laughing about some treasure he left in New Spain, for the love of his life to find. I didn't think much about it at the time, and I don't remember his exact words. Only that he said something about this prize and I thought it odd that he fell in love the following day."

"Where did he leave the treasure?" I asked, sweeping a tear from my cheek.

Ramirez gave his goatee a tug. "It was somewhere on the Northern Frontier of New Spain. Armando spoke of a Basque padre at a mission called...what was it?"

The monsignor crossed his arms in front of his chest. Giving his gray goatee another squeeze between his fingers, he finally pointed up into the air and said, "Oh yes, I remember now. It was a mission named for San Xavier.

SUNDAY, 24 SEPTEMBER 1780

Camp was being torn down, horses hitched, and fires doused. The vagabonds were packing to go. What if I couldn't find the fortune teller? But, there the wagon was, still parked right where it had been.

The gypsy woman was stuffing clothes, tins, pans for cooking, food, knives, and whatever she happened to pick up all into the same trunk, her bracelets crashing into each other, jingling with each spastic move.

The way she looked up and waved her hand at me, as if I were a fly on a plate of cask, made me think she was about to lose her temper.

"We're leaving. What do you want?" she snapped.

"I brought coin."

Pointing to the chair at the little round table, she said, "We can leave a little later. Tie your horse, sit down."

Eyeing the lonely coin I put on the on the table, she made a face and turned away. I quickly put two more pieces in front of her.

Bangles collided as the fortune teller swept up the money, stuffed it in a small pouch, and said, "It's too late. Isn't it? You didn't listen to me, did you? I knew you wouldn't."

Waving her hands over the glass ball in the middle of the table, she began to speak in song. "Your pain is deep. You don't want to live. He's given you the greatest pleasure you've ever known. And, he's also given you the greatest agony."

Leaning on the table cloth that smelled of suppers past, I pressed my forehead to my folded arms, and cried. There was no one else to turn to. I didn't know what to do.

She stared at the crystal globe and said, "There are rewards to be found. But first you must go through an initiation. Conquer that trial and you will find treasure."

I popped my head up. Both the monsignor and now the gypsy came out with the word "treasure." It had to have been some sort of message. That was all I needed.

A moment of bravery surfaced as I was about to step out of the wagon. I turned and said, "I was wondering if…if I could have my dagger back. I'll buy it from you."

"I don't have it anymore. I traded it for something," she snapped.

It was like losing Mother all over again. The tears returned.

"You shouldn't have given it away if it was so important," she said in a slightly less harsh tone.

My foot was on the first step, and the gypsy spit out, "You don't have to look for it. New love will find *you*. But watch out. I foresee betrayal that comes with a kiss."

By that time I had little interest in anything she had to say.

"You don't understand. My husband was killed. He's never coming back. I don't know what to do without him. I have no idea how I'm going to make it through another minute, let alone another hour or another day."

"You mustn't do anything now. Do nothing," she insisted.

"I rode all this way, paid you good coin, and you tell me to do nothing?"

"Love is from the universe. It is yours whether you are with someone or not. Just be happy there's money. You already have *everything*, yet you insist on *misery*. Go away. Go home and stay there. Your god has forsaken you."

I had taken all from that woman, I cared to. I stepped to the ground and she shouted, "You want answers! Leave your horse tied right where he is now -- to the back of this wagon. Leave everything and come with us." Slowing her words, she nodded, and concluded, "You will find your answers."

I turned my back on her, untied Artemia, and put my boot in the stirrup to mount up.

The gypsy didn't quit. "Ah! I see that you're not willing to give it all up, are you? Go home! Come back when you're serious!"

I had picked up the reins to ride off when I heard bracelets crashing into each other. The fortune-teller lifted her skirt and pulled the dagger Mother had given me from the frog on her thigh. Waddling over to the back of the wagon, she handed it to me. I pulled open the strings of my pouch to give her something, but the woman shooed her palm at me, yanked her fingers away like she'd been stung by a hornet, and said, "Keep your money. Just take your precious dagger and go."

The gypsy went back to her trunk and began stuffing things inside. I pulled Artemia's head around to leave. The woman looked up. Sounding sincere, she softly said, "In the end…torment will have unlocked all doors."

MONDAY, 25 SEPTEMBER 1780

"That's very troubling, Léna, please stop."

I glanced across the portico table. Miguel had folded his arms like an annoyed schoolmaster. I let go of the arrow pendant I'd been pulling back and forth over the chain around my neck. The grating-of-nutmeg rasp stopped and I said, "I'm going to San Xavier."

Yet again, insisting that I leave Hacienda del Sagrado Corazon, and return home with him, the crease on my former fiancé's brow deepened with the widening of his eyes as he put his chocolate cup back on its saucer and finally asked, "Where in creation is this San Xavier place, anyway?"

"…On the Northern Frontier."

"…In the New World!" he almost shouted, turning away to look out across the courtyard. Miguel was silent. His eyes met mine and he replied, "You've gone mad."

"That may very well be. But I'm going, anyway. I don't want to become an old woman and never know what I might've found there."

"Well, if you *do* go, you never *will* become an old woman! Léna, this is insanity, the Northern Frontier is the single most dangerous place in the world. Do you have any idea what you'd be getting yourself into?"

Maximo and Luisa's timing couldn't have been better. They waltzed onto the portico.

Miguel turned to the blacksmith and said, "Lena wants to go to the Northern Frontier. Tell her she's out of her mind."

"Armando left something at San Xavier del Bac, I must find it, whatever it was," I said, looking straight at Miguel.

"Isn't that the mission in the colonies where Armando was confessed?" Max beamed, overzealously flipping a chair around to sit astride as if he had just placed a bet on a cockfight. "You cannot make this trip alone, Léna."

"Carlos or Arturo can come with me."

"*I* will go with you," Max insisted.

Miguel flattened the corners of his mouth, looked out across the courtyard, and retorted, "You've both gone mad!"

Luisa whined, "Maximo! No!"

The blacksmith got out of his chair and took hold of his wife by the shoulders as if he was actually being sincere. "Armando was my closest friend, my lifelong friend. He would've been the one to do this for you, if need be. I must be the one to take Léna to the New World."

Luisa ran, wailing, into the house. Max, not only didn't go after her. He didn't wait for me to say yes. He began spouting plans for the pilgrimage as if the whole thing was his idea, and he was the one in charge.

"You don't have to do this, someone else can take me," I replied, glancing toward the servant quarters over the carriage house.

Miguel interrupted. "Well, it's not going to be me," after which he got up from the table and walked out mumbling, "I cannot toy with suicidal behavior."

"I'm leaving at first light, Max. I doubt you'll have time to make arrangements for your family," I said, attempting to discourage him.

Despite Luisa's sobbing leaking from inside the house Maximo carried on as though the trip was only thing in the world.

"You're not going alone. I'll be back at sunrise," he said, getting out of his chair, heading for the corridor.

Hugging the chocolate pot, Maria took a quick step sideways to avoid the blacksmith. "Where is he going in such a hurry?" she asked about to pour.

"To go pack, I suppose. He's taking me to the New World."

She bent over, picked up the yellow flower that had fallen from behind her ear, and said, "You're going to the New World with Maximo?"

"Maria, I admit the idea is mildly unsavory, but I must keep the orchards and presses running while I'm away. Arturo and Carlos need to be here."

The head housekeeper plopped into a chair as if her day was over, slapped the table top with a tiny whack, and said, "This is not the way to deal with your pain!"

"It's exactly the way to deal with it. That's why I'm going."

"And you're taking *Maximo!*?"

"I can assure you, Max is not my first choice."

"If your mother were alive, God rest her soul, she would tell you the same thing. Listen to me, Léna -- Señora Condesa, your first mistake is running away, your second mistake, which is even bigger than the first, is taking Maximo with you!"

"I went to see the gypsy woman."

"A beggar told you to go to the New World – those people are liars and thieves!"

"Maria, I did not listen to the gypsy woman, blindly. And I am not running away. She said something that made sense. She told me I would find answers by leaving everything. Besides, the monsignor mentioned that Armando left some sort of treasure at San Xavier. My sweet surrogate mother, I'm not going to stay there. I'm coming back home."

"This is loco. The monsignor is an old man who doesn't even remember the names of his own relatives, let alone something Armando may have told him months ago. And Maximo is not the good friend you think he is. Not to mention how dangerous a trip like that is for a man, let alone a young woman who happens to be beautiful ….and wealthy."

"What do you know about Max?"

Maria sighed as if there were new promise for me not going and said, "There isn't any one thing I can put my finger on, but I can tell you this for certain, that blacksmith would have little difficulty assuming Armando's fortune. And even less difficulty assuming Armando's wife."

THURSDAY, 2 NOVEMBER 1780

B arefoot seamen climbed the damp riggings like monkeys --
you'd never know the decks were slick as slime. Overnight,
it had gotten warm enough for sleeves to be rolled. We'd finally
made it to the cerulean waters of the Caribbean.

After weeks at sea, the stink wasn't so bad. Except when the
wind was directly in your face, the stench of the confined, vermin-
infested, *Santa Dolorosa de Hispania*, rivaled the smell of the back
streets of Cadiz, a lovely reminder of the city from which we set sail.

Floating home to criminals, scholars, refugees, the adventur-
ous, those seeking anonymity, and everything else in between,
along with the confluence of smells, sweet and foul, hugged by
marred and gouged darkened timbers, the *Santa Dolorosa de
Hispania*, had been on the waters for quite some time.

The odors that one had no choice but to accept -- shit, piss,
puke, rotting food, chicken and pig pen remains -- rose from the
glistening green bilges on the lowest part of the hull below the
waterline, together with the body odor of un-bathed crew and passengers, the sweet smells of freshly cooked peas and onions, salt

air and damp pine, were a mélange for the senses. And everyone had nits.

There had been some sort of problem with one of the sail riggings, a complication that made us late in getting off at Cadiz. The captain vowed to close the distance separating us from the other four vessels in the caravan, a promise that was unfortunately never satisfied. There we were, on the doorstep to the New World, and we still hadn't caught up.

It was considered far less dangerous to travel to New Spain than sailing back on a ship laden with treasure. Lagging behind shouldn't have been much of a concern, having sight of the ship ahead. Even if only a dot on the horizon, they would've turned around if we'd have disappeared from the spyglass. Or at least that was the story we heard.

Everything had gone smoothly. The Spanish made a big deal about it too, pennants were flown, a band of musicians played, and the local clergymen performed a brief ceremony in which the ship, its crew, and passengers were blessed and absolved, all coming about without a hitch.

There was, however, one brief moment that, in spite of my overwhelming desire to make the journey to San Xavier, I got cold feet. It came on the heels of the prayers that were my final plea to the Lord for a sign that I shouldn't go. Just prior to the plunk of the heavy boarding rope being thrown from deck, down to the floor of the longboat that had taken us out to ship, stomach fluid rose to my throat. The feeling only lasted a second, but at that particular moment of realizing there was no turning back, I nearly threw up.

Grief, boredom, and sea-sickness were second only to Maximo's constant doting. But, as nauseating as the month at sea was, it could've been worse. Max and I were the only ones besides the captain to have a private cabin. The rest of the ship's passengers and crew were forced to sleep wherever a place to lie down could be found.

Our tiny accommodations weren't much bigger than a double privy, with barely enough room in which to stow a bag or two. The few stolen moments of cradle rocking and creaking of the Dolorosa flexing on the rolling waters when I could be alone on top of that itchy gray wool blanket were a God-send.

I heard Max come in so many times, sparing myself the dark comedy of his endless fumbling. I stayed facing the wall, scrunched up with my arms to my chest.

Wood rammed against wood, pounding another notch in the wall behind the door, batted open with far more force than necessary. Immediately after which Maximo twisted sideways to give himself enough room to slip inside, and finally, the shutting of the door, bending over to pull off his boots, and bumping of his ass on the wall. I didn't need to look, I knew exactly how it went.

Max climbed onto the bunk. Embracing me from behind, he dried his sweaty palms on my arms and said, "Léna, Armando and I were very close. I can hardly recall a time he wasn't there for me."

"You don't have to tell me any of this, Maximo. I know."

"Armando had everything, Léna. I had very little. But I never envied him."

The long pause that screamed of a confession coming made me feel like it was a good time to be stricken with sea-sickness.

Maximo gave me a damp squeeze and said, "When you came into my life, Léna, I completely forgot about Blanca. And the night I got drunk and behaved like a fool, and challenged Armando to a duel, I went mad because I knew he'd already had you, or was about to. And I couldn't stand it, Léna. I've been in love with you since we met that day at the bullfight. I was probably in love with you before he was."

Maximo pulled me around to face him and planted his mouth on mine. I clenched my lips shut. Luckily, it didn't last long. He pulled away and yanked the shirt over his shoulder, showing me the scar Armando had given him during their duel.

"This is you. The fight was over you, Léna. I wanted him to kill me. I didn't want to live without you."

"Maximo, you're scaring me. Stop, please."

"There's something else, Léna, something I must tell you."

"Please, Max, you don't have to do this. It's over."

Almost crying, he said, "Léna, my soul is contaminated. I'm going straight to hell, I know it. But I would do it all over again for you."

"Max, I don't know what you're talking about, and I don't want to. Please don't tell me any more of this."

Clearing the lump in his throat, Max hugged me tighter and said, "Do you know why I'm going to go to hell? Because I'm glad Armando's gone."

Max broke down and cried out loud. My mouth had begun to water in anticipation of a vomit when he got himself partially together.

"Léna, we don't have to go back to Spain."

"Max, I can never be with another man, there was only Armando. There is only Armando," I said, my eyes pooling.

"I'm happy just to have you in my arms," he replied, giving me another nauseating squeeze.

My God! Would Max just take his sweaty hands away!

The deck timbers above pounded. Shouts cried, "Repel boarders! Repel boarders!"

Max must've punched the wall with his elbows a hundred times, hurrying to put on his boots. Grabbing his sword, and scabbard, he jammed a pistol into his belt and said, "Stay here, Léna! Do not leave. Do you hear me? Don't go anywhere until I get back!"

Passengers and seamen, anyone who could wield a sword, rushed up the tiny stairs to the deck. Maximo shut the door and yelled from the other side, "Stay there, Léna!"

Pistols fired, metal against metal clashed, and very soon after the timbers resonated with bodies hitting the deck.

Castilian shouts became fewer and fewer. English, of which I understood very little, was taking over.

I had to do something. I couldn't just stay curled up on the bunk hugging my knees. Slipping out the cabin door, I hid under the stairs. Through the open hatch, filthy tarred-hair thieves armed with grappling hooks, pistols, cutlasses, and whatever they could find hoisted themselves over the sides to join their buddies already battling the remainder of our crew.

The setting sun washed the deck dampened by Spanish blood in pink, orange, and purple as the *Dolorosa's* captain pulled grenados from a box.

Handing the gunpowder-filled metal balls to his first mate, he yelled, "Why were the anti-boarding nets not in place? Why didn't you fire the canons or deploy the yardarm barrels?"

The ghostly faced first seaman took a grenade and shouted, "We didn't have time! They came up the stern! Their vessel is below this one. If we'd fired, we would've blown a hole in the Dolorosa!"

A pirate ran up behind them with an axe in one hand and a huge double-edged knife in the other, put his filthy anchor-tattooed arm around the first mate's upper chest, and slit the Spaniard's throat with a single swipe of his blade, like the cutting of salami against one's thumb.

Two pirates grabbed each of the captain's arms, stuck a blade in his belly, and yanked off his jacket. Ripping away his sword, dagger, and pistol, they took the captain by the ankles, his head struck the deck with a whack, and they dragged him to the edge of the ship. After his pants were pulled off they lifted the commander onto the railing and tossed him overboard with a splash that sounded like the anchor. One pirate snagged the captain's hat from the deck, waved it in the air, and ran off yelling.

English were all over the place, carrying clothing they'd taken from Spanish bodies along with whatever they could steal. The ship's wheel had a ragged tar-head behind it. Privateers were everywhere, yelling, climbing riggings, and furling sails. The *Santa Dolorosa* had been taken.

But a few Spaniards stood their ground fighting on deck. Max among them, swinging his weapon as though he anticipated surviving. His shirt, spotted with blood and dirt was torn at the sleeves. Holding a cutlass-waving pirate at blade's length, Maximo's hair flew into his face with each thrust of his sword.

The blacksmith slashed an English to the deck with no more than a half second to get his wits about him before the next pirate started in. And then more came.

Max's stand was reduced to cutting the air with wild flails of his sword, spinning in a circle with sword-arm outstretched while the privateers laughed with weapons lowered.

Foot thumps pounded the steps. Boarders descended the creaking ladder. One of them spotted me under the stairway. Grabbed by foul hands, I was carried topside. But it wasn't without a fight. I screamed and punched with everything I had. Little good it did. They shoved me around like a child's toy. A tar head grabbed the top of my chemise. I screamed and flung my fists.

Maximo's hair flopped over the side of his face as he snapped his head around. It was in that split of a single heartbeat that his eyes met mine, and an Englishman thrust a cutlass into him.

Blood seeped down his shirt, over his stomach, and onto his pants. Clutching the blade stuck in the middle of his chest, Max slid to the deck.

Lying there, bleeding, helplessly watching the pirates carrying me below, he could do nothing but die.

Shouts of victory to the tune of random splashes of Spanish bodies thrown overboard poisoned the still evening. The deck banged with English, yelling, hugging each other, and running off with whatever they pleased.

The only survivor of the *Santa Dolorosa de Hispania* was dragged along the corridor to the ship's galley. And the darker it got, so went my hope.

The largest of the lot, stinking from tar, tied my wrists, pushed me onto the table, and tossed the lashes over a beam. All I could do was stand there, helpless, while the apes took turns jumping up to squeeze my breasts.

The fat one deliberately tore my chemise, and stank so badly, I couldn't help puking. My unwitting aim couldn't have been better. I got him right in the face.

In terms of entertainment, the vomit superseded a nearly bare breast. The English went wild, yelling, stamping their feet, swatting their hands on the table.

The pissed privateer swiped his sleeve over his brow and raised his arm. I turned away for the strike that never came.

Except for the occasional creak of the Dolorosa, it was dead quiet. The privateer first mate had walked in on the game. Pulling his knife, he cut the strap that held my hands to the rafter.

The fleeting thought of having been saved as he lifted me off the table was further abbreviated, when burning my wrists under the lashes, I was dragged to the captain's quarters.

Falling to my knees on the timbers was a hell of a way to see the inside of the commander's cabin, a sight I'd been curious about until then. There wasn't much -- a slanted row of windows on the stern viewing endless sea, a small desk with plume, hourglass, charts, spyglass, a few books, and an astrolade.

I climbed onto the bunk, tucked my knees to my chest, and heard boots pounding the corridor timbers outside. The footsteps stopped. The cabin door creaked open. Too scared to look, I turned away, feeling his stare.

Grabbing the ties that bound me he shouted, "I do not wish to speak Castilian. Do you understand anything else? Somali would be good. French, Russian, Latin...anything but the language of those Spanish bastards!"

Shoving me back onto the mattress, he went over and glanced out the windows, giving me the chance to steal a peek. From the frilly jabot hanging around his neck to the hilt of the Toledo weapon on his hip, the man had to have had breeding of some kind. Other than a rather awkward-looking hat with the largest brim I'd ever seen, there was no hiding the fact that he was an officer, not a scoundrel.

The assuming leather head covering, far wider than necessary, had shabby edges, frayed as if having been chewed by a small puppy, and was disproportionately curled up on one end, a deformity that most-likely occurred from having been set down against something for a long period of time.

He turned abruptly and said, "Actually, now that I think about it. Things would be better if you didn't talk at all. I don't think you'll find it difficult to understand what I want."

I found it within me to look him in the eye.

Lost in the overgrowth that had missed a razor for weeks, what was visible of his face was striking to say the least, a Persian-looking goatee, so dark in color it appeared black next to fair skin that could've been on a Scandinavian.

I nearly laughed, imagining the fierce pirate plaiting his hair in the mirror every morning. Tied in back with a cloth in the usual style, two long thin braids dangled on either side of his face, providing a more piquant solution for a windy deck, than tarring.

With his lips inches from mine and his braids tickling my cheeks, he pressed me back onto the bunk and climbed on top of me.

His not-blue-nor-quite gray eyes sparked. "I am going to take you. You have no choice about that. There are two options -- you may relax and enjoy every moment of it, as I will, or you may kick, scream, and bite, in which case I will enjoy it even more."

I got in a good swat before he caught my hand.

"My precious little shrew, keep in mind that if you are placing a wager on the eventuality, you will lose unless you bet in favor of me having you any way I want. I am taking you. You belong to me, to do with as I wish."

He was too close to land a decent blow, but I swung my fists, regardless. Following a few more unimpressive slaps to his face, he acted as if he liked me hitting him and just laughed without even trying to stop me.

Holding my wrists over my head, he put his lips below my throat. My nipples, having found their way over the torn bodice on their own, itched like mad against the knotted buttons and loops on his wool frock coat. I screamed. I didn't know what I expected. But it certainly wasn't what I got. The wetness of his kiss dampened a spot on my neck as if he was tenderly making love.

"You're not a virgin, are you?" he whispered, sounding as if not being one was virtuous.

His face turned to benignity. He pulled the hat from his head and let it fall to the floor. Sliding down next to me, the privateer navigated my body with his eyes before putting his scratchy beard between my breasts and his hand up my skirt.

"God, help me, please," I muttered.

"He's not going to help you," the pirate whispered, sucking a nipple upright and pulling away to admire his handiwork.

The cabin door banged open with a short series of thumps on the wall behind. A seaman was standing at the threshold with sword drawn.

Exerting himself no more than to lift his face from my bosom, the pirate said to the intruder, "It's generally considered a gesture of civility and a congenial custom to knock before you enter. It's also a good idea *not* to piss off one's commanding officer. What in hell do you want, Armitage!"

The seaman made a threatening poke in the air with his sword, gave a nod in my direction, and shouted, "De la Cruz! You said we would get more money for a virgin. You took the woman! And now, it would appear you are about to damage the goods!"

The captain leapt from the bunk, ripped his blade from its holder, and engaged steel in the tiny space too confined for such an attempt.

The bout would've looked real were it not for the fact that the captain talked the entire time weapons clanged.

Without taking his eyes off his adversary, de la Cruz, parried the mutineer and calmly said to me, "As long as you're asking the Lord for help, as you did a moment ago, you might also ask Him for assistance in winning this challenge. Because should an outré turn of events take place and I do not succeed, the entire filthy English crew of this ship will do with you as they wish. And I think it's a well-known fact that the English have not bathed in, what is it? …two? No, I'm pretty sure it's been three centuries since the English last bathed, even then it was only one Englishman who'd forgotten tradition after being struck in the head during a pub brawl. Speaking thereof, I try to avoid having sex with English women without at the very least dumping grog on them first."

Looking as though he were in his natural state of being, de la Cruz, forced the first mate to back away and said, "Armitage, you fence like shit. And I won't ask when you bathed last …or if ever. More importantly, and completely irrespective of the woman being a finer example of the female half of the species, the real agenda here is the fact that I haven't laid a woman down in more months than I can count, so it will be no surprise that I am taking this one, simply because I want to, and I can. I am captain of this ship and I will do whatever I please. She is mine!"

With a final reposte landing his sword tip a paper-thickness away from Armitage's throat, de la Cruz pushed the subservient seaman into the corridor outside, and said, "Now get out of here, Minoan whore's bastard!"

Slamming the door shut with his boot, the pirate captain slid his sword back into his scabbard and bolted back to me as though nothing had interrupted him.

"I know of one decent Cretan whore, but we won't go into that," he added with a grin, pushing me onto my back.

Untying his jabot, he threw it to the floor along with his coat and climbed on top of me. The swordfight had been nothing more than foreplay.

I had just about given up hope when a small gold crucifix next to a higa on a chain around his neck fell out of his shirt.

The cross was dangling in my face along with his braids as I flipped my head to avoid a kiss.

"What kind of man wears a crucifix and does this to a woman?" I blurted.

He kept trying to kiss me as though I hadn't said a word, so I asked again, louder, "What kind of man wears the Cross of the Lord, and violates another human being as you are doing now?"

He stopped. Completely serious, he looked me in the eye and said in a quiet, controlled tone reserved for tea gatherings, "What kind of man, you ask? What sort of man wears a crucifix and violates another at the same time? A priest. I see by the look on your face, in your frozen state, that you find what I've just said unbelievable. Well, perhaps that's because you're not Spanish. Yes, I'm afraid it's obvious. Your Castilian is horrible, you don't look Spanish..." Swiping me with his tongue in a lick that went from under my chin, over my throat, and down my neck, he looked up and said, "You don't taste Spanish."

The chance to blaspheme the Mother country apparently was of greater relish than having sex. He got up from the bunk to pace. Regardless of sentences crashing into each other from enthusiasm, like a racehorse given his head, de la Cruz's mouth ran with astounding elegance.

"Yes…*a priest*. How could that be? You must be asking yourself how a priest wearing the sign of the Lord could possibly violate another human being. Why don't you ask Spain about that! They wrote the book. You are luckier than you know, little girl," he said, walking back and forth in an agitated manner.

"I hate Spain. Had you been Spanish, I would've given you to the crew. Spain has, dare I say, gained a fly-dot of knowledge about the violation of human beings. Unless you consider forcing men to choose between God, their country, and their lives, a minor inconvenience of pledging allegiance. Contrary to what the public has been led to believe, it's not about gold nor power, it's not even about politics, or conquering the enemy, it's about man's right as a human being to make the most significant choice he can make… all stripped away. The killing…? Well, that was supposedly done in the name of the Lord, which makes it completely acceptable, even righteous. Spain has murdered in the name of God, explained away by being the part of a larger plan, a plan that somehow includes burning human flesh at the stake. I humble myself before the King. Yes, please forgive me for being so blind as not to see the 'Greater Plan.' The inability to visualize the more perfect state of existence was definitely a weakness. My lack of insight needed to be shown the door of excommunication and exile, while bowing humbly in gratitude for the sparing of my life, a greathearted gesture from Spain by request of the Clergy based on my years of faithful service. Yes, I am indeed blessed. So to answer your question, what kind of man violates another? In Spain, it is a man of God."

"You're a priest?" I asked like an idiot.

"Not anymore!" He laughed, looking up to the rafters, showing a row of nearly perfect teeth. "I like your mind. You thought I was an ordained priest about to rape you after just having pirated the Santa Dolorosa. You catch on fast, little girl. The Santa Dolorosa and everything on it now belongs to England. Except for you, I've officially taken you from England -- you are mine."

"Nobody owns me. And what does England have to do with it?"

"You still don't get it. I work for England, and your luscious little ass is my personal property. You are the possession of a privateer, legally employed in writing by orders from King George III himself, and my new mother country, England. I was hired to loot, steal, and harass Spanish ships. And take an occasional prisoner for a slave if I want. I'm permitted by law to pretty much do it any way I like as long as it's on the high seas. It's all legal. I love my job. England gets the money. I get a cut along with the satisfying opportunity of expressing my humble ex-communicated opinion about Spain. The marriage works very well. And the joy is solely in making Spain suffer, screw the money."

Assuming a humble tone, he added, "Besides, they should've known better than to fuck with a Basque anyway."

De la Cruz dropped to one knee next to the bunk, put his face in my hair, allowing several strands of locks to sift through his fingers, and whispered, "What's your name, little girl?"

"Madeléna de Velazquez – almost everyone calls me, Léna."

"…de Velazquez? How did you get this name? Never mind, I do not wish to hear of this now."

De la Cruz climbed back on top of me, nuzzled his face to mine like a purring cat, and said, "I don't want to talk anymore -- I want to fuck you."

"What about your vow of celibacy?"

He laughed so hard, he nearly fell off the bunk. "Celibacy? My dear Léna, when one gives up the priesthood, which do you think is the first vow to be discarded?"

Captain de la Cruz was about to embrace me again when we heard things being tossed about and broken, along with heated voices, heckling, and cheering coming from the galley.

Shouting, "Mother whore," he got up, pushed the top pants button that he had just finished unfastening back through its hole, and quickly tested the ease of drawing his blade by sliding it half-way in and out of the scabbard on his hip with a tug, push, and clack. Tossing a blanket over me he walked out, and slammed the door.

I hugged the itchy cover on the bunk. It was dark. A few ridiculous thoughts of hiding or trying to escape disappeared. Facing the wall, I cried.

SATURDAY, 4 NOVEMBER 1780

If there were a benefit to being prisoner of Captain de la Cruz, it was his mandated, subservient call to personally see to my needs, a must in order to keep me away from the others. And after going on about how I was going to have to wait to get the fuck of my life, and aside from the fact that he had to navigate the dense fog we'd gotten ourselves into, he brought food, water, and the trunk with all my belongings, at which time he also smartly instructed me not to get the three wooden buckets -- chamber pot, drinking water, and bathing water -- mixed up.

I had been left alone the entire time my captor navigated the soup. The sun finally showed itself and only one thing entered my mind. Holy Jesus, I'm still alive.

De la Cruz walked in swatting the dark braid that would not stay out of his face and said, "We're going to do it in a real bed. Grab what you will, we're going ashore."

"We're near land?"

"It's on the other side of the ship, little girl." He laughed, scouring the cabin for a bag. "If this lot doesn't lay down some women soon," he said, picking up an old sack from under the bunk. "I feel sorry for the bitches whoever they may be. But as luck would have it, Nassau has one or two willing to lower their already scurvy esteems. I'm not captain of a ship. I'm mother to a flock of sons-of-whores that always need something!"

Leading me to the window, he allowed me to press my forehead to the glass and looked all the way to the right to barely see the edge the island.

Sinking his face into my hair, de la Cruz took a deep, long breath, let several strands of locks slide through his fingers, and said, "You washed, didn't you? Personally, I would've preferred you un-bathed. But, I'm one lucky salt of a dog. You're in Nassau, little girl. You'll be dirty in no time."

He pulled me to his chest and said, "I should just take you right now. As a matter of fact, you're probably wondering why I don't just fuck you witless where you stand. To satisfy your wonder, the only reason you can still sit is because I wish to be in a real bed when I do it until I can no longer entertain the notion. How many fucks in a row do I have in me? I'm not certain, but I assure you the number will be great. Take what you will, we're leaving!"

De la Cruz was ready to walk out when he turned to a tall seaman on his way in, and with a quick nod in my direction said, "Hang onto her, Rodrigo, we're going ashore. Oh, by the way, I'm making you first mate. Armitage doesn't know it yet, but we're leaving that mongrel of unknown heritage here in Nassau. Let him bum a ride home."

Sails were loosened and furled while de la Cruz, stood on deck beneath his enormous shabby-brimmed hat keeping a watchful eye on his empire.

I had ripped my dress at the shoulder seam, climbing down to the longboat with Rodrigo and our captain. But the sun on my skin through the torn fabric felt warm as the handful of seamen with us swished the oars toward the dock on the north end of Nassau Island.

For the moment I'd forgotten about making a break for it. I just gazed at the sparkling ripples on the sandy ocean floor, happy to be alive.

De la Cruz lifted me out of the boat onto the flimsy landing, and if one hadn't seen my tied hands, surely they would've thought I was a bride. Not that Nassau would anywhere a newlywed couple would want to be.

The main thoroughfare was no more than white sand flattened from use, and so bright in the sun I could hardly keep my eyes open. Decaying water life, refuse, and the unrecognizable remains of storms past littered the shoreline smelled vile, and then went with the sweet shifting breeze only to return again a moment later.

Roaming street dogs came up for a sniff, ignoring the flies likening their scrawny flesh. Black children in tattered clothing smashed fallen fruits in the shade of a palm. A coal-skinned, shoe-less woman wearing a worn skirt pulled forward through her legs and tucked into itself at the waist, briskly passed by holding a huge basket on her head that stayed perfectly balanced with each step. No one so much as gave us a glance.

The sailors who came ashore with us as reward for being the least unruly of the lot, shuffled close to the dock like scolded school-children. They had been ordered to wait for our return while de la Cruz, and the first mate with me in tow, headed for what there was of a town -- a row of decrepit buildings. The houses must've been pleasing to the eye at one time. Some of the paint still remained -- white, pale pink, blue, and light green -- patched in numerous places from storms, brawls, or both. One house with closed window shutters bore a crudely drawn sign that read: "The Tankard."

With a creak of wood, de la Cruz shifted his weight on the walkway and looked into the dark nothingness past the threshold. Not one thing inside could be seen beyond the narrow pair of open doors.

"I'm going to arrange for a bed. Take care of Señora de Velazquez for me if you will, Rodrigo."

Like an idiot I blurted, "*Señora Condesa* de Velazquez!"

I could have slapped myself. De la Cruz dispensed a lengthy raised-eyebrow stare and said, "I believe my personal worth has just increased from only a moment ago. Hang onto *La Condesa* if you would be so kind, Rodrigo."

The ex-priest, having learned a tawdry thing or two since leaving the Catholic Church, took a dagger from his boot, clasped the handle in his palm, and with the blade stuffed up his sleeve disappeared inside.

When he re-emerged with sparks flashing in his eyes, he held up a large key and snapped, "I have us a bed."

The Tankard was where I intended to find someone to help me get away, but once my eyes adjusted to the dark, clientele far seedier that my captors constellated the makeshift tavern.

Staring our way, a black keeper with a shaved head and swabbing-rag over his arm stood motionless behind the gouged bar. Maybe he just liked the feel of a straight edge scraped over his scalp, but more likely it was because he didn't want anyone to grab him by the hair. Sleeves torn off at the shoulder revealed muscles that had no doubt ousted a few in their time.

An old ship's rail on the floor allowed patrons to put a foot up while sloshing back grog, everything else in the place was junk. Spirits were sipped from an assortment of broken mugs and glasses, tin, pewter, and various earthenware containers, some missing a chard, anything that didn't have a hole in the bottom, and some that did. A few sticks of what had been real chairs scattered the cave-like room with the only illumination coming from the open door, a lit stick or two, and the thin lines of light leaking through several seams where the wooden wall boards met.

Not one of the few squinting souls sitting on broken crates at rum-barrel tables seemed to find a woman being tugged along with hands tied in front of her unusual.

I was ready to order a drink when de la Cruz pulled me straight for the tiny crooked staircase on the far wall of the tavern's only room. He had but one thing on his mind besides drowning the nits in a bath.

Following a few rattling twists of the key in the lock, the door at the top of the wobbly stairs creaked wide. Stepping aside as if pointing the way to the nobility theater seating, my capturer joined me in the moldy room not much larger than the captain's quarters on the Dolorosa.

Dirty, torn, muslin curtains hanging from a rope nailed to the wall waved back and forth in front of an open window. The so-called real bed was no more than ropes strung from primitive timbers silvered from age and salt air.

Taking me in his arms, de la Cruz put me on the bed and climbed on.

Pulling the folding knife from his belt, he cut the lashes from my wrists and dispensed a barrage of meaningless kisses.

"We can get this over with very quickly. I assure you it won't last very long, at least not the first time."

"There will never be another for me," I said, turning my head away to cry.

De la Cruz rolled off. Sitting on the bed with his knees tucked inside his clasped hands, he took hold of my wrists, pulled me to his chest, and put my hands around his waist. I cried even harder. Sweetness was the last thing I expected.

Stroking my hair, he softly said, "You don't have to love me. I just want to… you know… do the old in and out. All you have to is lie there."

Something about the way he said it started me laughing.

"So that's how it's going to be, is it?" he said, putting his hands on his hips. "I'm going to the bar."

"I'm coming with you," I replied, clearing a sniffle.

"That is definitely *not* going to happen," he said, rummaging through his bag.

"Why can't I go with you?"

Pulling a rope from his sack, he looked up and said, "Aren't you in enough trouble already? Now you want to accompany me to a room filled with ex-patriots, thieves, murderers, and plunderers, half of whom are frothing at the mouth for a woman and sucking down enough grog to render a legion unconscious. You haven't got an ounce of sense inside that beautiful little head, do you?"

"Please don't leave me here. I'm scared to be in this room alone, tied up. What if somebody finds me? I promise to be good. Just take me with you. I'll behave. I swear."

De la Cruz hesitated. "You are not to say a word unless I talk to you, do you understand?" he said, pretending to be disgusted.

Pressing my lips together to keep from smiling, I nodded several times in quick succession.

"And the very last thing you are to ever say is, Señora Condesa, because I can assure you that those very words would probably be your last. If the supposed nobility thing came out, the situation might outweigh my capability to protect you, my dear Léna. You are in the kidnapping-for-ransom cooking-pot of the world. For all we know the Tankard is where meals begin."

"If I'm going to make love with you, shouldn't I at least know your first name?"

"So now, we're going to make love? Allow me to go over the details of your obligation. We are not going to make love, we're going to fuck. And we're going to do it as soon as we get finished with our drinks. I don't care if you do cry. And you don't have to know my name."

"It would just be nicer if I had something to call you in the heat of passion, besides de la Cruz, don't you agree?" I smirked.

"I'm going to regret this," he muttered, stuffing the rope back in his bag.

"When you were a priest, did everyone just call you Father de la Cruz?"

"I'm already regretting this, you're going to be a problem," he said, throwing the bag on the bed.

"No, I'm going to be good, I promise," I replied, quickly changing my tone.

De la Cruz dumped the bag on the bed and began to sift through parts. Putting new flints in two pistols, he stuffed them into his pants. Then, pulling a huge doubled-edged knife from the holder on his belt, he slowly ran his thumb over the edges and tucked the blade back into its sheath.

He was checking the small dagger in his boot when I asked, "Aren't we just going downstairs to have some drinks?"

"That's why I'm only arming myself lightly."

Had it not been for the dim light of a crudely cut tin reflector on the wall, we would've had to carry flame. The place was pitch, except for a spot of sun on the dirty wood floor in front of the doorway to the street.

"Just tell me your name, for my journal," I said, stepping onto the landing.

The first stair creaked, and he quietly, replied, "Salvador."

"Salvador? Your name is Salvador?"

He turned around and glared. "What did I just finish telling you?"

"I'm sorry, I'll keep quiet, I promise."

"And don't do anything fast. Even the slightest unintended gesture could be misinterpreted as a threat and spark violence on a whim. Don't look at any one. Even a harmless glance could set off these drunks. I must be mad taking you down there."

Surprised to see us so soon, the privateer first mate jumped up from his rum barrel in the corner.

"What would you like to drink, Señor Capitan?" Rodrigo asked.

Loosening his pouch strings just about the time onlooker interest had returned to their mugs in hand, de la Cruz pulled out coin, handed over the money, and said, "Rum for me, whatever it is you'd like, and Esperanza will have wine."

"I want rum, too!"

"We haven't been down here two minutes and already you're making noise. She's drinking wine, Rodrigo."

"I'm sorry, Salvador. I just wanted what you were having."

Rodrigo grinned and said, "Salvador?"

"Just take the coin and get the drinks, man."

From the looks of things, Nassau wasn't the perfect place in which to make a run for it. I was safer with de la Cruz than without him.

Feeling the fine hairs exposed by his sleeves having been rolled to the elbow, I tenderly took my captor's arms and said, "I have a proposal."

"I knew letting you come down here was a bad idea. What is it, woman?"

"Take me to San Xavier and I will fuck you like you've never been fucked before."

"Done! Shall we draw up a contract? Or simply honor the agreement by word?"

"You gave in rather easily. Especially since you already planned to have sex with me anyway," I replied, trying to hide my astonishment.

He leaned closer, gently took my face by the chin with one hand, and said, "I've found that sometimes, my dear Esperanza, it's best to fuck it all and take the very next thing that comes along no matter what it is. And, now is exactly such a time. Besides, in order for you to fuck me like I've never been fucked before, you're going to have to find out all the ways I've already been laid down, and that may take a rather lengthy time."

"How long can it take? You were a priest for… how many years was it?"

He didn't answer right away, so I added, "You're thirty, aren't you? You're over thirty!"

De la Cruz sat there playing with my hair. Allowing a few strands to slip through his fingers, he said, "I'm wondering exactly how you planned to get to this San Xavier without me. More precisely, how did you think you were going to go anywhere by yourself, and with no coin I might add? We might just as well go back upstairs right now. I doubt you know very many ways to fuck anyway. But that's not a problem. One way over and over will do just fine."

"You *are* over thirty!"

"If you're trying to see how tolerant I can be, I will advise you that my sense of humor extends just so far."

Rodrigo slapped two mugs down on the barrel top, nodded in the direction of the bar, and said, "I'll be over there."

"Where is this San Xavier that you must get to?" de la Cruz asked.

"You agreed to take me and you don't know where it is?"

"Well you were going there, weren't you? How tough can it be?" He laughed.

"I think it's not too far from Mexico City."

"What did you do, get on the first ship sailing to anywhere and hope to find it?"

"It's here in the New World," I replied, experiencing a twinge of distress.

De la Cruz lifted his broken mug, threw his head back, and after the bump on his throat rose and sank several times, he wiped his face with his sleeve, and yelled in a baritone becoming a best opera star, "*Viva España!*"

Rodrigo slumped forward over the bar like he'd been punched in the gut, banged his glass down, and sprayed a mouthful.

De la Cruz shouted again, "*Viva España!*"

Everyone able to lift his head was looking. The whole place quieted. Then from the darkest corner of the room, indistinguishable murmurs, much slower than one would normally talk, were spoken in such a manner that almost made the patriotic phrase sound maligning. *"Vi–va Es–pañ–ia."*

"Your angel awaits," de la Cruz said, taking me across the room by the elbow.

The shadow in the opposite corner turned out to be just another drunk.

Spitting out another *Viva Es…pañ…ia,* the pickled patron plunked his face to the barrel, the mug still in his hand tipped on its side, and dripped whatever it was he'd been drinking onto the floor.

De la Cruz reached over, pulled a lit stick from the end of the bar, and held the light over the wassailed shirtless man wearing what looked like the remains of a military uniform. His jacket with the distinguishable red Spanish collar was missing the sleeves, probably torn away to accommodate the warmer temperatures of the Caribbean, along with tattered blue woolen breeches ripped off at the knees.

The fellow's face, distorted from being pressed to the barrelhead, could've been the Prince-Bishop of Würzburg for all we knew.

De la Cruz leaned over and shouted in the drunk's ear, *"Por Favor, mi amigo,* we are compatriots in need of some assistance. Can you tell us how to get to San Xavier?"

Squinting in the light, the drunk not only couldn't hold his head still, the *Santa Rosa* embossed on the leather bandoleer across his chest swayed side to side as he tried to bring forth conversation. His jaw poked the air and he catted over the barrel top.

De la Cruz jumped back to avoid the barf ambush sprinkling the tip of his boots.

The soldier wiped his mouth on his arm as if he still had a sleeve, and slurred in Frontier slang, "Well, how'd ya git har?"

"Never mind how we got here. We need to find San Xavier. Can you tell us where in New Spain it might be?" de la Cruz, replied.

The drunk flopped back against the rickety slats of his chair and said, "It's on the Northern Frontier, man…in Bac. Just go north as far as you can. Then go west as far as you can. You'll run right into it."

I turned to de la Cruz and said, "That can't be right. Armando went there on his way to Mexico City, I'm sure."

Two smirking drinkers at the next barrel overheard the whole thing. The scenario was just too good for them to stay silent. One elbowed his buddy, pointed at us, and said in barely understandable Castillian that lapsed into English and back again, "There'll be jus' a little more to worry 'bout than jus gettin' thar."

"Yeah, if the smallpox and Injuns don't git ya, Sugar Jack will!" the other said. They both laughed.

"Who is this Sugar Jack, may I ask?" de la Cruz inquired.

"William Neal! Yup, that be his real name. Dey call him Dos Dedos on the Front, 'cause his flintlock exploded while he fired at a kid."

Nodding like he was remembering the occurrence firsthand, the first man said, "Sugar Jack likes killing the little ones. Powder done took his right eye, his thumb, and da first two fingers of his hand. He done got da name Jack, you know, like da cards, one-eye Jack. It's kinda easy ta spot 'im." He snickered. "The French call him Sucre Jacques…lures babies with candy. Hung 'round Mobile Bay playin' da French and British agin each other, selling guns to da Injuns, an' making money off da Rev'lution. Been all over the Frontier, mostly sellin' pox-fested blankets to the savages. Gits 'em for nothing, since no one wants a blanket from a dead person done died 'o disease. Then he sells 'em to the Injuns, and from what I understand, Sugar Jack's blankets are da only wee anyone can git those savages! Word has it, da Brits used the pox to git the Col'nists. And dey paid Neal ta spread it. Yup, gettin' all da way 'cross the Frontier should be the easy part, if ya don't git lost, da savages don't kill ya…or the pox. Or, Dos Dedos!"

De la Cruz turned to the drunken ex-pat and said, "How do we get there, man? Can you take us?"

"I left my tour of duty somewhat un-dismissed. I don't think I'm going anywhere near New Spain. Just git youself to *La Bahia*. If you can pay, someone will to take you to Bac."

The soldier's lids drooped half shut and his head was about to sink to the barrel again, when de la Cruz grabbed him by the hair and shouted, "*La Bahia?* Where is *La Bahia?*"

The drunk muttered, "*La Bahia Espiritu Santo,*" and passed out with, his head hitting the wood with a thud.

"There's a map on board. We'll find it," de la Cruz said.

I felt something behind me between the butt cheeks. I screamed and bolted around. A bearded man in a ragged, dusty uniform of some kind had taken it upon himself to feel me by tucking his first finger lengthwise between my buttocks, pressing the muslin of my skirt into the crack of my ass.

The trembling began with my hands and quickly spread to the rest of body. But, de la Cruz was cool. He acted like it wasn't a big deal. As if only slightly annoyed, he turned to the molester, and said in a very casual tone, "Go away, man, this is my wife."

The stranger kept touching me.

De la Cruz added a note of displeasure in a few more languages. And without understanding a word I could tell the exchange was escalating.

Two other filthy English walked over to join their buddy. De la Cruz didn't take his gaze off them for a moment. And it didn't help me any to see the cool captain beginning to get jumpy.

De la Cruz's head twitched a couple of notches and his fingers splayed, waiting for the right moment. It was going to be one against three. Scanning the trio, the priest-turned-pirate watched their hands and yelled, "Rodrigo!"

No reply came. De la Cruz yelled louder, "Rodrigo!"

Our assistant had chosen the worst time in which to go leak somewhere.

De la Cruz had to do something, and do it soon. With his hands down and his arms quiet at his side, his fingers began to move like tapping on a table top in rapid succession.

"Rodrigo!" he shouted, as loud as he could.

The brazen English began to play with my hair. De la Cruz shoved him away. But, just as the molester's shoulder had been flung back, it was defiantly pulled forward and the scoundrel picked up my hair, again.

It went so quickly, it was impossible to tell exactly what had happened. The English drew a blade. And just as rapidly the favor was returned. I never saw him go for it, but somehow de la Cruz already had a knife in hand, whipped his arm, and slashed the dagger so fast it whistled before ripping the molester's mid-section open. Letting go of the blade stuck in the English's abdomen, de la Cruz pulled both pistols from his pants and fired into the belly of the second English with one shot and with the other, fired into the chest of third English, who had just drawn a short-sword.

During the time it would've taken to inhale and exhale a normal breath, three men lay dying at our feet.

Not one of the Tankard's drinkers had paid any mind. Those still conscious slowly lifted mugs to their lips as though nothing out of the ordinary had happened. But, in the blink of an eye, my captor had killed three men.

De la Cruz made the sign of the cross drawn in the air so fast, if one hadn't been totally focused on it, she'd have missed the gesture altogether.

The scoundrels were leaking the last of their lives onto the floor when the privateer took several coins from his pouch and put them on the bar.

Picking up the silver as if it was payment for a mug of rum, the keeper tucked the coin into the purse on his waist and swabbed a rag over the bar as if there was no other mess to clean up.

De la Cruz complacently turned to me and said, "One of the niceties of the region is the considerate custom of leaving money when one leaves bodies."

SUNDAY, 12 NOVEMBER 1780

I t was a miracle we made it anywhere. The celebrating had gone on night and day since hightailing Nassau, a little gratuity to the crew for having missed shore leave. And since most of the seamen were carrying on with less-than-normal brain function, de la Cruz who had brazenly kept the sails set for a week, decided to drop an early anchor for fear of running aground.

Nassau had no authorities, a bonus that lured all sorts. And even though there was no one to formally kick us off the island, de la Cruz cut the stay short.

He enjoyed making it sound like anyone but him was to blame for leaving in such a hurry, the story varied depending upon who did the telling, however, the decision to leave forthwith had been solely his. Who was going to argue with him?

Anchored in the silted waters far off the edge of Corpus Christi Bay, standing at the same spot on deck we'd watched the Nassau harbor get tiny on the horizon a week earlier, de la Cruz leaned his elbows on the railing, looked out across the bay, and went on about the incident that had forced us back out to sea.

189

Threatening a smile, the pirate said, "It was the first real bed I'd seen in months. I'd already paid for it! And we wind up getting into trouble, the worst of which...besides having to say, *Viva España*...was leaving that shitty mug of rum on the barrel."

I reminded him that we had plenty of rum on board, but he just liked complaining about the one he paid for and didn't get to finish.

One thing he particularly loved about our swift departure was leaving Armitage behind. Not only did the former first mate have no idea it was going to happen, the scene as we were leaving was especially memorable. Right after de la Cruz told his former first mate that he had been relieved of his duties, the oar-men began rowing like mad to get out to ship while Armitage, with his street-dog under-bite flapping away, was left standing on the edge of the dock, shaking his fist, yelling and snapping comments about his former captain's heritage, while two black women with their heads wrapped in white bandages were screaming. One of them had sliced the head from a pullet and was waving chicken blood all over the pissed-off seaman, a scene de la Cruz relished re-living more than once.

Other than the unforgettable exit and the three dead men in the bar, not much else happened. There had been, however, some signs of possible ill-will. The local religion made its presence known by leaving a small crudely carved statue of a deity or demon of some kind inside a ring of lit candles in the middle of the street, not far from the dock.

We walked past the Despacho, a black woman ran up to us yelling and waving her hands, and de la Cruz figured that one pissed native with a pagan offering was enough. So with the flames licking our asses, we got out of the devil's bed, but not before acquiring a few necessities. Besides fresh fruit and pullets, we secured a few items we dare not return to ship without. Especially since the announcement of cancelled leave ashore meant that the crew was going to have to find carnal bliss at sea. Luckily, they didn't seem to mind where they debauched. Several barrels of rum and two native women were brought on board, a diversion that left no one sober.

The funny thing was, Rodrigo had no difficulty buying women, but acquiring horses was another story. He tried to get three and when that proved to be impossible, he settled for the two weedy animals that would've left Papa in tears had he seen them. The skin-stretched-over bone creatures didn't look like they could carry a thing.

It would've been tough for healthy horses to manage balancing themselves at sea for a week, let alone wobbling flimsy legs weakened even more from the trip. But the animals were still alive and that was all that really mattered.

Rodrigo banged a fist on the door of the captain's quarters and said, "We're ready to hoist the beasts over the side."

I couldn't believe it! De la Cruz was really going through with it.

Seamen, selected for their ability to appear somewhat sober, led the skinny pair to the deck and harnessed the rope riggings.

The first horse was lowered into the longboat without a snag. Unfortunately, that was anything but the case with the other little gelding.

Four of the less-drunken groaned with each tug on the yard-arm ropes that held the horse with head, neck and legs dangling. All had gone well until just as the beast was being lowered over the side, the longboat began to drift out of position.

The crew, shouting to the seamen below, attempted to steady the suspended animal while the longboat was maneuvered back into place. The hollering and sudden change of motion panicked the little horse. Writhing to get free, the pony flayed his legs and twisted his head until the men couldn't hold the lines, the rigging gave way and our second mount dumped into the sea with a loud splat and splash, after which the beast went under.

De la Cruz grabbed a rope hold, leaned out over the side, and shouted, "Hail Jesus, Mary, and Joseph, that son-of-a-bitch didn't catch a leg."

Following an unnerving amount of time below the water's surface, the froth cleared and a long slender nose with eyes glaring their whites poked through the briny. The little guy's nostrils were flaring and snorting seawater like dragon-breath, and he began swimming toward shore.

"And he can swim!" de la Cruz, shouted.

But just as he mentioned how fortunate we were, for some reason that animal flipped around and headed out to sea.

"Mother whore!" de la Cruz yelled, bending over to pull off his boots. "That nag's headed back to Nassau!"

Flinging a leg up onto the railing, he vaulted off the *Dolorosa* and dove straight into the sea, disappearing for nearly as long as the little horse. I just about swallowed my heart. Finally, de la Cruz surfaced, shook the water from his hair, and swam like hell, as only one who grew up near the sea could have.

The little gelding was about to have his mane grabbed, when suddenly the pony flipped his head around and turned toward shore. De la Cruz yelled and went under. I screamed.

Rodrigo was already at speed from across the deck, yanking off his boots on the way. He leapt over the side, hit the water, and made a bunch of dives before getting the white-faced captain above.

Having caught a stray kick in the gut, de la Cruz could barely take a breath when they pulled him into the longboat.

His recovery was brief. The pirate, apparently, was more enthusiastic about going to San Xavier than I, and he didn't even try to hide it. De la Cruz got some color back in his face and without bothering to change clothes, started going over maps.

Leaning over the captain's desk, he ran his finger along what looked like mountains on beautifully drawn parchments with curled edges. By the way he touched the paper it was obvious he loved to handle the charts.

De la Cruz was one hell of a seaman, that's for sure. He'd gotten us to Corpus Christi from Nassau in record time, having ordered the sails to remain unfurled at night, a tactic considered dangerous by just about every sailor in the world, except him.

The ex-priest never mentioned what the big hurry was. So, he probably just did it because he could.

When I brazenly queried him about how he became such an expert, I discovered that de la Cruz and I had something in common. We both had fathers who used their God-given talents to lift themselves up to become extraordinary.

"How is it that a priest can know how to master a ship as well as you?" I asked, not thinking the question was a big deal.

He laid the brass divider that he had been measuring distance with down on the map, looked at me, and said, "Caviar."

After allowing me to stand there with question marks in my eyes, a droplet from his wet sleeve fell to the floor and he said, "Being a clergyman isn't hereditary. Being a natural born seaman is, especially the only son of a royal fisher."

"There's such a thing as a royal fisher?" I asked.

"Well, there is when he continually brings home nets filled with sturgeon, even if he is a Basque." De la Cruz laughed.

Looking down at the charts, as if he were shy about speaking of his upbringing, he scanned the maps and said, "I grew up tossing about on a little pond called the North Sea, waters that make sailing the rest of creation like navigating a bathtub. My father was the single-most-successful fisher of sturgeon the world has ever known, an achievement that made him rich enough to send his son on to an education with Jesuit warriors of Christ and sword, the likes of which few have realized. Others baited sturgeon and pulled up empty net after empty net, scouring the ocean until their sails were in shreds. My father, being cursed with the same daring streak he passed on to his progeny, knew all the tricks. He used mutton for bait, a little tidbit sturgeon find as much a delicacy as their eggs are to us. My father's real talent, however, was in knowing *where* to look for the prized female *fishies* -- a secret he never shared with anyone but me. I have no notion as to how he figured it out. I always explained it away as some sort of Divine gift."

"So, you're not pirating ships for the money, are you?" I said with a smile.

Unfolding the knife he kept tucked in his belt, de la Cruz reached over to the wood bowl on the desk, grabbed one of the apples we took off the island, flipped the fruit up in the air like a juggler, and the instant it fell back into his palm, rasped a slice.

Holding the blade's edge to his mouth, he pushed the sliver in with his thumb and said with a crunch, "There's more to life than wealth, my dear Léna."

He stopped eating. Putting the seedy core on the desk, he looked closely at the map of the Northern Frontier.

"What is it?" I asked.

He didn't say a word.

On the other side of the cabin door, drunken seamen were laughing and singing some off-key tune referring to wine, women, and the god Neptune. I didn't understand all the words, but it sounded like every other barroom drinking song no matter what language it was poorly sung in.

De la Cruz kept looking at that map, maybe hoping for the picture to change. But no matter how the parchment was viewed, Bac was on the other side of the world, with no roads leading there.

"I don't see how San Xavier can be so far, Armando never said he had trouble getting there," I cried.

Having already heard far too much about my brief marriage, the pirate acted like he knew what he was talking about, first-hand. With his fingers on the map, he looked up with eyes that rivaled the color of the sky on top of the water and said, "You were married to him, yet I know Armando better than you. Stop me if I'm wrong. Your husband was deeply religious. He had killed a man. Never mind that it had been in self-defense, it was still a killing. Confession wouldn't have been enough for a man such as him, so Armando picked San Xavier Mission *because* of the difficulty in getting there. The *journey* was his penitence, Léna."

Jolly voices wailing the pitch-less tune of drunken bliss echoed in the corridor.

My stomach panged and I spilled tears. "Armando never said how he got there. He never mentioned an ordeal, or danger, or anything like that. Why didn't he tell me?"

Laughter and slurred words accompanied a thump that sounded like someone outside the cabin fell against the door.

"Go away!" de la Cruz shouted.

Wetting my breast with the sea-dampened muslin of his shirt, the priest-turned-pirate put his arms around me and said, "Armando *never* would have told anyone about his penitence...not even you."

MONDAY, 13 NOVEMBER 1780

The eeriness of rummaging dead people's trunks lessened after scavenging the first few bags. But worst of it was most of what we found on the *Dolorosa* was meant for anything but the outlands.

De la Cruz snagged a pair of buckskin breeches with black embroidery and silver conchos down the side of the legs, perfect for keeping the stinging thorns from scratching, even if he did look as if he were going to a wedding.

The pirate pulled the blanket from the bunk, cut a slit in the middle with his folding knife, held it in front of me, and said, "Here, put your head through here. You'll appreciate it when the wind blows, and probably a bunch of other things we haven't figured out yet. If it has more than one use, we're taking it."

Without a third horse, there wasn't much to pack. But we were not for want of weapons. In addition to an escopeta, pistols, extra flints, a sword, daggers, and the like, de la Cruz brought along an Espada Ancha, shorter than a regular sword, but wieldy as hell and prized as the preferred weapon in New Spain.

One thing could be said in his favor -- the man was creative. Not to mention how skilled he was with a needle. De la Cruz cleverly stitched doubloons into both saddle blankets, a little trick that expertly concealed more than enough gold to pay for everything we could possibly require, and more. We probably could've bought the entire Frontier with the coin he was taking.

Unfortunately, no amount of money in Nassau granted better mounts. The two weedy horses we acquired would've needed weeks to fully recover from having been at sea, but spouting concern about the weather turning, de la Cruz wanted to ride right away. At least that was the story. He probably just couldn't wait to start another adventure.

The first step out of the longboat sank my boot into stinking silt. Corpus Christi turned out to be nothing more than a foul-smelling name on a map that made the confining stench of the *Dolorosa* seem like Versailles.

The swamp, which had a particularly bad odor wasn't squat more than dark sandy marsh, twisted trees, and prickly scrub -- the sort Papa would've ripped up had it grown anywhere close to the house.

Crewmen, who had spent the night on shore looking after the horses, aimlessly wandered the beach with backs dusted in sand, while de la Cruz gave a few last-minute orders to Rodrigo.

The ex-priest secured the Espada Ancha to his saddle, picked up something in the sand, and vaulted into the saddle.

I pulled the neck cord of Armando's hat tight under my chin and took a final peek at the ship out across the bay. I have no notion as to why I felt sad, but I did.

We rode north with nothing but the sound of hooves pressing into the dirt, light wind whistling in the grasses and the squeak of leather. The pirate pulled out his map, let his reins dangle over the horse's wither, and while looking over his chart began to thread the shell he found when we first set out.

"What's that for?" I asked.

"So, we can find our way."

"Not the map … the shell!"

"It's for your pilgrimage to Compostela."

"…In northern Spain?"

"That's the place, little girl. May you live long enough to get there."

I couldn't believe he was talking to me like that. I started to cry.

He muttered, "This is going to be a long trip."

"You think we're going to die, don't you?"

"Everyone dies."

"I mean now! I need support and all I'm getting is a crack that isn't even clever."

De la Cruz kept looking at his pathetic map and said, "If by some miracle we survive this hell hole, we're likely to be together for at *least* the next two and a half months. God be generous. So, should you be inclined to share, at least attempt to make it of some value."

"This *is* going to be a long trip," I mumbled.

His grin needed to go away so I said, "Maybe you could help me out. I'm having a bit of difficulty. Perhaps it's my creative short-comings, but I just can't quite visualize you hearing confessions."

"What exactly do you find so baffling?" he replied, taking the bait.

"I can't see anyone calling you Father!" I blurted, laughing so hard my horse broke into a trot.

I should have let it go at that. But instead, I tugged my horse back to a walk, and said, "As a matter of fact, you're so adept at using the word fuck, I was wondering just how you discovered it. Did you hear it during someone's confession? The larger question being, how did you learn to do it?" After which I had such a good laugh it almost felt as though I'd had sex.

Not nearly as amused, de la Cruz, still looking down at his map, said, "You're typically French, aren't you?"

"Armando, never once called me *French.*"

"Oh, this is just perfect! You're going to compare me to your dead husband all the way to Bac, aren't you?"

"There's no way you could ever compare to him."

"I can jump off this fungus-infested cur, pull you off your horse right here, and all your questions will be answered very quickly."

"So, did you hear confessions?"

"Of course I did."

"Did you give absolution?"

"Léna, I was a priest."

"What was it like the first time you made love to a woman? I mean after you gave up the priesthood. That was the first time, wasn't it? Or was there an indiscretion before you took your vows? And the woman -- was she deeply attracted to you, or just being charitable?

"You seem to be most interested in the very thing you deny me."

"I don't want to do it with you. I'm merely curious about the challenges of ending celibacy."

De la Cruz threw a leg over his horse's neck, jumped off, grabbed my leg, and pulled me out of the saddle. Holding my elbows, he pierced me with a stare and said, "Léna, I am going to fuck you. Then you will have a real comparison to your dead husband. Only I am going to take you solely for my own pleasure. Though I doubt it will be sufficient pay-back for having to endure the torture of being forced to traverse this stinking nothingness with you as company. Occasionally I am a man of my word, so I will keep my part of the bargain. But at some point, my dear woman, you will know what it's like to end a long duration of abstinence, since it will be quite some time before we reach Bac, wherever the fuck it is -- unless you provoke me to take a departure from the original agreement."

"Similar to the way you ended your obligation to the Cloth?"

The raw scrape of his beard outlined his stabbing tongue as he pressed his lips wide over mine, reached under my blanket, yanked my shirt from my pants and went for my tit.

"Please don't tear my clothes. I haven't got anything else."

During his little misplay, the horses had trotted off, which is probably what made him stop. Certainly it wasn't my plea. He took a couple of fast steps before moving very slowly in the direction of our mounts busily dining a few paces away on tall blades with far more interest in foraging than running off.

De la Cruz quietly picked up the reins lying in the dust and said, "Well, the map is gone. And it's your fault."

"My fault? You were the one holding it!"

"We'll camp here."

"We've only been riding for half a day and we're going to stop?"

He turned me around by the shoulders and said, "Look!"

"What am I supposed to see?" I said, standing there with my hands on my hips. Slapping my arms to my sides, I whined, "Oh, water? Is that it? Well, too bad it smells horrible."

"Had I known lamp oil was going to be all over the place, I would've brought one," de la Cruz replied, pulling the escopeta from the saddle.

"How do you know that stink is lamp oil?"

"I've smelled it before."

"Where may I ask?"

"…the Holy Land."

"You've been to the Holy Land?"

"And, I can curse in seven languages." He laughed.

"So what do we do now, Señor know-it-all?"

"You must be a single child. That's why I'm trying to find greater forgiveness for your behavior."

I wasn't about to bring up my brother, Rene, just to prove how wrong he was, so I let him have the last word, especially since he was about to walk off. And even as obnoxious as he was the thought of being left alone was worse.

The pirate headed into the brush and said, "The horses need to be un-tacked, hobbled, tethered to a line, and fed, a fire needs to be made, a few things unpacked, I'm sure you'll figure it out. I'm going to go kill something. I can say shit in Basque, of course. And in Castilian, those bastards, Portuguese, French, English, Somali…Latin…well, maybe not so well in Latin…"

"You speak Somali? I yelled loud enough so the ex-priest who was partially disappearing behind a bush could hear.

He shouted back, "Bernal Diaz set foot on this desolate continent with Cortez, and stated that they were here for the Glory of God…and to get rich. Well, I'm already rich! And we know what happened with my efforts to support God's Glory, so what in hell am I doing here?"

The last thing I heard as he slipped out of sight was something about palm-fronds bearing Nubians serving champagne.

After unpacking the little we had, I found sticks for a fire, hung a tie line, and plucked grass for the beasts. The sun was almost gone, and I was on the verge of getting scared when the shot I hoped was supper rang out.

De la Cruz appeared with his gun in one hand and a huge rabbit in the other, four or five times the size I was used to seeing back home.

"I killed this thing hours ago, I walked around until now so I wouldn't have to put up with you," he said, putting the bloody thing down next to the fire.

I didn't care if he called me a cow's wet-nurse, I just wanted to eat. I knew how to pluck a pullet, but I'd never done a rabbit before. He apologized for not being able to find a hen in the brush, and it was unfortunate that he hadn't, because, as it turned out, the ex-priest-terror-of-the-high-seas possessed a vaporous talent reservoir for survival outside civilization. He reluctantly came forth with the fact that not only did he lack knowledge of rabbit preparation, he also had the luck to be stranded in the wild with the only other person in the world unable to de-hair a hare.

After a valiant effort at fixing the kill, very little remained. What we didn't manage to cut away with the fur fell into the fire and caught aflame.

The one good thing that did happen was the mess stopped the friction. We laughed every time a slice slipped from the knife and fell on the ground. At one point de la Cruz even hugged me, dabbed a kiss on my cheek, and spouted, "Why is it that the women who cannot cook always seem to be the ones you want to be with?"

Darkness fell bringing an uncomfortable chill. The flames died, and the shivers got worse.

"Look at the bright side," de la Cruz said. "Snakes don't care much for less-than-tepid weather."

"At least we would've had something to eat if one showed up."

"How much do you suppose would've been left after we skinned it?" He laughed.

A pop and spark from the nearly dead fire reflected a brief light on his face as he lifted his blanket and gently ripped the head-hole a little larger. Opening his arms, he softly said, "Come here."

Pulling the wool over us, he pressed his cheek to mine. I slid into his embrace like I belonged there, and whispered, "How is it you've never had feelings for a woman."

"I never said that."

De la Cruz was leagues away. The first few words faltered as he said, "She was hardly a woman. And she was even less mine. Some might've called her a woman. But she was only a girl."

The ex-priest failed miserably at hiding his lingering sentiments. I envied the woman loved so much to never be forgotten.

"How old were you?" I asked.

"Seventeen," he said, giving me a tiny tug to hold me closer. "My cousin and I went across the strait to Morocco looking for trouble. We lost sight of each other in a large market. I wound up wandering through the holding cages of a slave auction along with buyers examining the stock. People were being sold like animals. And from the looks of things, the only difference I could see between a buyer and a slave was the luck to be on the outside of the cage."

De la Cruz kissed the side of my forehead and said, "I'd seen enough. I was about to go when a little milk-white hand covered in dirt reached through the slats of her pen and latched onto my sleeve. She didn't say a word. I'll never forget the way she looked at me. I can still feel her frail grasp. Chalk-white dirt-smudged cheeks, hair the color of last year's hay, eyes bluer than a cloudless day, and there she was in a pen, about to be sold into slavery. No amount of filth could hide her beauty. She looked like a porcelain doll accidentally painted with too sad a face. And she was the most beautiful thing I'd ever seen. The palest of skin stood in rags behind bars with two huge, black, muscled-up Moors caged on either side. *Au secours,* was the first thing she said. I almost fell apart right then. What could I do? I had to be the one to wash the dirt from the cheeks of the little blonde slave girl whose family couldn't provide for. Her name was Spring. Even to this day, I have a tough time getting past the first blossoms of the year without thinking of her. The parents needed money, so they sold their daughter to a well-to-do family they believed would take care of her. The new far-from-poor guardians smelled coin. They took an enormous sum for the little girl they had agreed to raise themselves. Spring was sold again for even more money, ultimately winding up in that Moroccan slave holding pen, about to be sold yet again. She was beautiful and she was a virgin. Someone with bags of money would pay.

In my naïveté, I told her that I would be the one to buy her, and take her home with me to San Sebastián. I'll never forget what it felt like when she reached through the slats and stroked the side of my face with those tiny, gentle hands. She smiled and I wanted to

203

rip that cage apart and take her away right then. I promised that little girl I'd be back. I kissed her hand and ran to find my cousin to figure out how much money we had. Of course, he thought I was mad. We put all our coin together, asked around to see how much a young slave girl might sell for, and begged in the streets pretending to be blind, a little part I wasn't proud of but we had to do something to be sure we had enough. Sleeping on the ground, holding her hand though the slats, I spent three days outside her cage, never leaving for more than a moment. We talked about going home together, and laughed about how my family would react. I was happy. My life was meant to be with Spring. The night before the auction, I told her that I was falling in love with her.

Spring said that she didn't know why she picked me out of the crowd, but the moment she touched my arm, she knew she loved me. That night lying beside her, holding hands through the cage, she whispered my name and put her finger over her lips for me to be quiet. I'd never seen a woman. She untied her robe and let me feel her unbelievably beautiful, bare flesh though the bars of her cage. I felt her throat to her new breasts, down her belly, and lightly brushed the soft fine hair between her legs with my fingertips. I almost cried. From inside her prison, she gave me the only thing she had. I needed every ounce of strength I had to keep from ripping the slats apart to get her out of there right then. But I kept my head and swore that once I freed her, legally, I'd take care of Spring for the rest of her life.

Two men carrying flame showed and she quickly covered herself. Don't get too attached to this one, she's going to bring a tidy sum, one of them said to me. He squeezed her breast, laughed, and carried her off. I wanted to kill him. But I was going to put an end to her nightmare in the morning and my anger went away. The sun came up, my cousin and I counted our money. We tallied those coins what must've been a hundred times, waiting for the sale to begin. After sitting through nearly the entire thing without seeing her, I was covered in sweat, afraid she was gone. All sorts of things ran through my head. I was about to lose my mind.

Finally, they brought her out. She was the last slave offered. I couldn't believe it. The filth-smeared girl I had fallen in love with was dressed in the finest silk, laden with jewels, and not only that, she didn't look like a child anymore, she looked like a woman. The ringlets of her hot-iron-curled flaxen tresses bounced with every move. I almost didn't recognize her. Spring was the most beautiful thing in the world. Buyers showed up from out of nowhere. She was introduced as a virgin. And whispers came out of every mouth in the crowd. The bids got higher and higher. Each time I raised my hand I was squelched by a larger purse. I'd even bid the money we saved for the trip home. I was desperate. My cousin and I begged strangers in the street. Maybe we got a coin or two, but it wasn't nearly enough and it came much too late.

I got back to the sale just in time to see a fat, bearded, over-dressed man in a turban being awarded her possession. He waved his hand in the air for two of his servants to carry her off. All I caught was a glimpse of her screaming my name from over some ape's shoulder, right before she disappeared into the street crowd. I threw my arms up and shouted. But she had vanished.

Sometimes, I still hear her crying my name. What's even worse than not having been able to save her is living with the fact that she must've thought I abandoned her. I've never been able to deal with that. I got home and had no trouble making the decision to become a priest -- and even less difficulty eventually breaking those vows."

The pirate's forehead pressing against mine felt too soft to belong to the son of a fisherman.

One faint orange ember from the remains of the fire glowed brightly, popped, and left us in the dark.

TUESDAY 14 NOVEMBER 1780 AND WEDNESDAY 15 NOVEMBER 1780

I could've eaten my saddle. When I heard a cow, de la Cruz made a smartass quip about me being so starved I was hearing food. But just as it was getting dark, baying cattle were everywhere. And right in front of us, perhaps only half a league away, the dim glow of torches at the front of the fort at La Bahia Espiritu Santo softly spread to the other end as more lights came aflame.

The Basque somehow got us there, without the Grace of God, or a map. The first presidio and mission on the Northern Frontier was gleaming in the distance, with as many as a thousand head and maybe fifty families living in stone houses sprouting beyond the stockades.

Two days in the saddle, sore, tired, and hungry, the place looked great. Any place would have. And all we had to do to get a meal and a bed was tell the guard that we were seeking sanctuary within Spain.

Our nearly lame horses practically pulled the reins from our fists to get through the stabling gate. Open covered stalls with straw bedding looked as good to them as the good sniff of beef steeping in a broth pot from a summer kitchen nearby that made my mouth water.

We were pulling off saddles and sorting bags when Lieutenant Eugenio Fernandez came to greet us. He wasn't even wearing a shirt, let alone a full uniform. And, the man had non-human primate chest hair. Surely, he could've at the very least buttoned his jacket for heaven's sake.

Wiggling his thick untrimmed moustache, the soldier said, "El Capitan would like to see you."

"Of course," de la Cruz replied, taking me by the hand.

Walking toward the captain's quarters, we saw dirt everywhere, the presidio was covered -- livestock in their pens were coated with dust, and those we passed by, kind-hearted souls who welcomed us with a pat on the shoulder or handshake, had most-likely stopped bothering to brush the sand from their clothes long ago.

Dust puffed around his fist as de la Cruz pounded a knock on the slatted wood door with light leaking through the seams.

"Come!" a robust voice shouted from inside.

The door wouldn't open. The pirate put a shoulder to it, and after a loud scrape on the walkway, he about fell over as it suddenly swung wide.

We stood there for a ridiculous length of time, while el capitan, seated behind a carved Spanish writing desk with a few parchments scattered on top, along with a tri-corner plumed hat next to an ink bottle, stared down at his paperwork without making any effort to see who had walked in. The commander finally looked up. His gaze immediately found me.

The man might have seen as many as forty years, but it was most likely the toll of the Frontier that made el capitan look older than he was. Somehow he was attractive though, in spite of the circular scar on his left cheek, later described by de la Cruz as the sort of disfigurement one might acquire from being on the losing side of a bottle fight.

Nearly shouting, el capitan said, "So! What brings you to La Bahia?"

With a look in my direction, similar to the one he dispensed in Nassau when I vowed to be good, de la Cruz turned to the officer and replied, "We need fresh horses, provisions, and someone to lead the way to Bac."

El capitan's stare widened. Stealing another glance at me, he asked the pirate, "Do either of you have any notion as to exactly where Bac is?"

"We've seen it on a map," I replied, tired of hearing how far and dangerous it was.

"*Both* of you are going to Bac?"

"Yes, both of us," I said.

"Why, may I ask?" he replied more like a command, than a question.

"It's a pilgrimage."

He got up from his chair, walked around to the front of his desk, and the rich voice sounded as though it were coming out of the wrong person. The rather short-in-stature commander elongated his reply as if employing a slow torture. "I see."

El capitan lifted his chest, hiked his pants, and pounded the floor with heel claps, pacing back and forth. Stopping abruptly, he turned to look at us and said, "The smallpox outbreak is supposedly the Brits secret weapon in America. Whether it is or not, it's all over the frontier. So be advised. I'm telling you this because I don't want you griping out on the trail somewhere, saying I never explained what it was going to be like. Getting to the other side of the outlands is likely going to be the single-most difficult thing you've ever done. You have, however, accomplished the first task -- you found someone who can get you there. But it's not going to be a picnic."

"So you're taking us?" I asked, afraid to smile too soon.

"Your arrival is timely. I'm leaving in the morning to return home to my rancho in Tubac to begin my political career. As luck would have it, Tubac is on San Xavier's doorstep. You are both welcome to accompany me. But, it'll cost you."

Clasping palms with de la Cruz, the commander said, "Don Juan Diego de Anza, everyone calls me Anza. You and your wife must have supper with me this evening. It might be our last chance to sit at a table for a while."

Accepting the invitation, the pirate didn't rebut the inference about husband and wife.

Anza sat back down at his desk and said in a tone that whittled my elation, "There's something else you should be aware of... the savages."

"...The Indians?" I asked, giving de la Cruz an appropriate look for the occasion.

El capitan took a huff and said, "Comanche can be a problem. Apache *will* be a problem. All right then! Now you know! Let's have supper."

The dining hall, like every room in the fort, shared a wall with the stockade. Also like every room at La Bahia, not much was in it.

Pewter tines that looked as though they'd been used to battle Indians along with dented tin plates were set out on the long table where we sat with a few upper-ranking officers, while soldier's wives and a native woman served the one-pot beef supper.

Several minutes of focusing on nothing but my food elapsed before I caught Anza staring at me from across the table. The dark eyes that sank deep into his skull came my way more than once.

How much of a problem are Apache?" de la Cruz finally, asked.

Anza clacked his tine to the plate of half-eaten stew in front of him and said, "How formidable is a charging heard of buffalo? Those relentless bastards hate us so much, it's lasted two hundred years. I may as well tell you, since it's far from secret anymore, Spain has finally had enough. Military support is no longer being dispatched. Some presidios only have fifteen maybe twenty soldiers, where there were once hundreds. And with the soldiers, so go the people. Not many are crazy enough to stay. The last residents here are those who refuse to leave their homes, or they're just plain insane. The worst of it is Apache need no reason to kill, but they do. They thieve our livestock along with whatever else they can help themselves to and murder in return. Twenty of them won't hesitate to attack a cavalry of sixty, if we still have that many men in one place at the same time. I've studied Apache my entire life. There is no way to conquer them. They're godless people. They've refused everything we've tried to teach them at the cost of thousands of Spanish lives. And as long as there's one of them left alive, they'll keep their ways.

"What has Spain done about it?" de la Cruz asked.

"We've given them guns."

"You've given Indians *guns?*" I spouted.

"Yes, guns. You may find that foolhardy, but it's quite the opposite. Apache can ride a horse at a full gallop and deploy arrow after arrow, while a Spanish soldier is still aiming an escopeta. So, to even our chances, we've given the savages guns, hoping they'll use them. I didn't say we gave them *good* guns." He grinned.

"Has it worked?" de la Cruz asked with an ounce of sarcasm.

El capitan laughed and said, "Hell, no! But one thing has... *liquor.* Whiskey and smallpox have been the only successful weapons against Apache. They can't handle either."

"If this was their land when Spain laid claim, maybe they just want it back," I said.

"My dear woman, Apache have no permanent structures, they're nomads. They came down from the north about the same time Spain set foot here, the land was never theirs, nor do they believe *any* man has a right to it. And, I think they hate us simply because...we build houses."

Three little vertical lines appeared over de la Cruz's nose as he said, "What are our chances of running into Apache before we reach Bac?"

Anza shook his head and replied, "Chances, you ask? We *will* cross paths with Apache. You can put money on it. And it'll happen before we reach Fronteras, I promise you that."

Everyone was already talking about it, so what the hell, I got right to the point. "What kind of meet up will it be?"

The candelabra flame on the tin sconce in the center of the table sparked in el capitan's eye. "It'll be a confrontation of some sort. How we cope with it will depend on my ability, luck, and the Grace of God. One thing you have in your favor, woman, is that I lay claim to being the single-most-successful Apache-fighter alive."

De la Cruz and I looked at each other in disbelief as Anza rested his elbows on the table and added, "If we were to be travelling with a cavalry, even with the dust cloud from so many horses, there would be an excellent chance of victory pitted against Apache. We'll only have five horses, giving us a greater chance to remain concealed. However, should we be attacked? Well, that's another scenario."

Turning to de la Cruz, as if there were no more to his story, Anza asked, "So, what is your profession, Señor?"

The privateer leaned back in his chair and without so much as a flinch replied, "I'm a political emissary between England and Spain."

I practically lost a mouthful of the dreadful wine.

But Anza played along and said, "Other than Spain hating England enough to lend a hand in the revolt, I didn't know there was any interest in maintaining relations."

The ex-priest broke a shallow grin and said, "There isn't."

"You must've made a stop in France," Anza replied, looking my way.

"Madeléna and I met aboard a Spanish ship," de la Cruz replied, as if he were serious.

"Have you been married, long?" Anza asked.

I kicked the privateer under the table as he lifted his glass for a toast. Lovingly staring into my eyes, he said, "We've only been hitched to the cart for a short while, even though it feels like a lifetime. I'm sure that's because how much in love we are."

It was hard to say which was worse, the pirate's off-center humor or the vile wine, a distillation so horrible any true Frenchman would've spit it across the table after one sip.

Anza took his cup, saluted us, and said, "To the newly wedded couple, then!"

Stinging like the tart swill on our lips, de la Cruz kept his gray eyes on me and wouldn't shut up. "It was a beautiful ceremony, wasn't it, Madeléna, my love?"

The bottom of my glass went high. I daintily patted the corners of my mouth with a napkin and following a mock pucker as if I were about to kiss him, replied, "As lovely as a freshly opened bottle of spirits."

Trade beads made noises like a child's wooden game pieces. Dressed in a blue and red presidio solder's jacket, a tri-corner hat, fringed buckskin breeches, and deerskin slippers, strands of native trinkets dangled around the Redman's neck along with an ornate Spanish crucifix on a leather cord. A single waist-length braid fell over his shoulder as the dark-skinned native leaned over and whispered something to Anza, who stopped the private conference and announced, "Escucha is the savviest scout on the frontier... perhaps, the world. S'cucha, I'd like you to meet our companions to Fronteras, Señor and Señora de la Cruz. They'll be making the journey with us."

Pulling the tri-corner from his head, Escucha looked at me and said with surprising command of the language, "It will be an honor to accompany you. I will do my best to make the trip as comfortable as possible for a woman with child."

Taken aback, since I was the only one who could've possibly known I hadn't gotten my monthly since Spain, and I certainly wasn't fat, yet, if... My God, could Armando be alive in me?

"By what magic have you asserted that I am with child?" I replied.

Escucha smiled. "It's in your eyes, Señora."

"Pick out two mounts for our guests," Anza said, taking the scout's arm.

The Indian announced that he would select a suitable horse for a woman, to which I replied, "No, just select a *suitable horse.*"

I could tell by the way he poked his hat-brim with his finger and grinned as he headed for the stable that I'd won his approval.

Anza tipped his chair back onto its rear legs, put his hands behind his head, and said, "Besides being my scout for a good many years, Escucha, is a friend. He's a Renegado. Even after all this time we've been together, I have no idea why he was ousted from the tribe. Scucha's been baptized. He claims to see it from the white man's perspective these days. Though I suspect he's not completely relinquished his Apache ways."

"He's *Apache?*" de la Cruz asked.

"...One hundred percent."

"So, they're all not bad, are they?" I said, looking right at Anza, who nearly lost his balance on the two rear legs of his chair.

Talk turned to how late it was getting and we promptly retired to our luxurious accommodations for the night, which by some miracle we didn't have to share with anyone.

In a row of small rooms on the outside wall of the fort, the bantam quarters had been graciously vacated on our behalf. The mattress, too narrow to fill its own frame, was somewhat better than sleeping in the dirt. And the pirate, who usually slept in fits of conscience, had fallen asleep like the cover shutting on a book.

Still awake, I had one arm on the bare ropes and my butt up against de la Cruz when lowered voices leaked from the next room.

I got up and pressed my face to the planks of the separating door. Peering through one of the cracks, I saw Anza and the scout looking at a map. Escucha ran his finger over the parchment, turned to Anza, and whispered, "You're taken with the girl, aren't you? That's the reason they're coming along. You're not doing it for the money."

Anza kept looking down at the drawing. "You're wrong, Escucha, it's the money."

"Señor Capitan, I know you very well. You have little interest in the money anymore. You want what men cannot have. No such women like her exist here on the Frontier...young, beautiful... spirited."

"Escucha, even if there were truth in what you say, she's married to de la Cruz, a union with her would be highly unlikely."

"She is not married to him."

Anza rested his palm on the map, stared at the Indian, and snapped with intense interest, "How do you know that?"

"Even you should be able to see that easily, Capitan. If the señora was your new young wife, how would you behave? Wouldn't it be different than the way he acts?"

"Escucha, not all men conduct themselves the way you think."

"Yes, they do." The Indian smiled.

The sun came through the tiny window. I felt as though I had only been asleep for a few minutes. The ropes poking creases in the thin mattress under me had greater appeal than getting up.

De la Cruz tossed back the moth-eaten cover, threw his feet over the side of the bed as if he were actually rested, wiped the floor-dust from the bottom of his stockings with a brush of his hand, and leaned over to pull on his boots.

He stopped tugging, turned around, smiled, gave my knee a gentle touch through the blanket, and said, "The love-making was particularly good last night, don't you think?"

"Very special," I replied, thwarting a grin.

Stretching out to enjoy the view, I watched the muscle on top of the pirate's upper arms tighten and soften as he searched for the sleeve of the shirt he had left tucked inside his jacket the night before.

"Don't you ever take off your clothes one piece at a time, like normal people?"

"I'm wearing the same thing I did yesterday. And probably will be wearing again tomorrow, and most likely the day after that. I wouldn't be surprised if I don't take my clothes off at all between now and the next time I'm lucky enough to see a bed. So why should I separate my shirt from my jacket?"

"I just wanted to see what you were going to say." I laughed.

De la Cruz leapt back onto the bed, reached under the vermin-eaten cover, and pinched me until I laughed so hard my stomach hurt.

"Stop! Everyone will hear!"

"We're newly married, remember?"

"Oh yes, how could I forget? The happy couple's bridal tour was spent traversing the disease-and-savage-infested, Northern Frontier of the New World."

De la Cruz picked up his saddle bag, threw it over his shoulder, and gave a huge tug on the door wedged against the dirt floor. "If you don't get going soon, I'll take the faster of the swamp-stomping nags."

I threw the pillow at him just as the door scraped shut.

By the time I made it out there, they were all ready to ride.

Anza and de la Cruz were standing side by side in the middle of the presidio in some sort of deep discussion. From the casual head nodding and fingers pressed up against a chin now and again, they behaved as if they'd known each other a lifetime. The padre from the mission was flinging dots of Holy Water on everything, granting absolution, and the Indian, with all our horses in hand, stood flipping the ends of the reins around like a toy. Four of the five animals were saddled, and the fifth was fully packed with provisions tied to a carrier-harness.

The Renegado saw me, tipped his hat, and along with my horse, handed me a tortilla for breakfast in the saddle and a narrow, braided cord that he said was an amulet for the journey. Made especially for me just that morning, he'd gotten the hair from some prized war-pony horse tail.

"Señora, the wearer of this neckpiece will have the power and swiftness of the animal from which it came. My former people believe that a woman who knows how to ride a horse goes where she wishes to go."

"It's lovely, Escucha, you are very kind," I replied, tying the gift around my neck.

I was just about to slip my foot in the stirrup, when de la Cruz spit into his palm and swirled his fingers over the seat of my saddle until the spatter disappeared with a squeak.

"What are you doing? I asked.

The pirate leaned an elbow on the gelding's rump, looked down at me with those gray eyes sparking under his huge, tatty, wide-brimmed hat, and savoring every word, slowly replied, "Making the leather less slippery."

THURSDAY, 16 NOVEMBER 1780

We spent two days of hard riding, a night sleeping on the ground, and not one Indian or bad-man showed. We didn't see a soul for that matter.

I hoped Josefa's rancho was going to live up to the kinship Anza and Scucha had, since all they did on the trail was talk about the place.

By the time we pulled up the sun had dipped below the trees and the chill of dusk was getting colder by the minute. I was ready to be out of the saddle.

Most homes on the frontier were small structures made of rough stone held together with cactus-juice mortar. This one had an upstairs and freshly axed bark-less supports holding up an extended roof that covered the entire front portico.

Two barns, corrals, and several tiny rock casitas radiated around a stone-topped well in back. The snag was prickly paddles and bare-branched thorny gnarled scrub trees popping up everywhere, just waiting to catch our clothes.

Escucha collected the reins and led the horses to the stable, leaving us to be cold-nosed on the back of our wrists and the toes of our dusty boots drooled on by two panting dogs.

Having regained some of his vigor, Anza hopped up the three stairs, just as the door creaked open. Fresh-baked dough smelled good enough to make me cry.

At the threshold, the silhouette of a sturdy woman with a crooked knotty cane stood in the shadow of hearth light.

Anza outstretched his arms, and said, "Josefa Sancha, you are filling your clothes well these days!"

The old woman didn't lend many clues as to her age, other than it had been years since she was young. She did possess a pair of sparkling dark eyes that had no notion of time.

Stepping aside, she gave el capitan a tiny affectionate slap on the shoulder and pointed inside with the darkened walking stick, smoothed by the rasp where branches once sprouted.

Waving the end of her cane to discourage the curs from trying to get into the house, Josefa took another loving swat at Anza and sounding as if she smoked several cigars a day, jovially said, "Somehow you always manage to make it here when the tortillas are ready to be lifted out of the pan. Come in! Introduce your companions! Sit for supper. Antonio Federico is home!"

"Is he now? So, the Prodigal Son has returned," Anza replied, giving her a pat on the shoulder as if she were a man. A moment later, the Apache-fighter pulled off his hat and squeezed the old woman like a long-lost love.

"I bet there's a story that came home with Antonio, too, isn't there?" Anza said with a speck of sarcasm, as she cut off the embrace.

Josefa Sancha de Ontiveros was a Puebladora. The title sounded far more impressive than it was, since Spain had difficulty finding anyone willing to inhabit the outlands. Her family had status high enough to be granted land as a gift from the king, plus the fact that women were scarce on the Northern Frontier made Josefa such a rarity, she easily won her territory. And the land she got for nothing was about equivalent to the size of some small countries in the Old World.

Following Anza's announcement that de la Cruz and I had recently married, he went to help Escucha with the horses, a story that was most likely an excuse to go have a quick swig with the vaqueros.

The creases of the old woman's smile cracked wide, beaming with the chance to give us a gift. She insisted we sleep in her private quarters. I tried to make excuses, but Josefa Sancha wouldn't have it any other way. No doubt, the priceless joy of knowing the newly wedded couple would make mad love on her linen had a reward all its own, because she insisted we have the best bed in the house.

"You'd love a bath, wouldn't you?" the old lady said with a smile.

"That would be wonderful, Doña Josefa."

"You're in the New World, my dear, formalities are long gone," she said with a pinch of her gray, yellow, and red striped wool skirt, which must've been a blanket before it was cleverly crafted into clothing and worn along with a pair of soldier's boots. She waved her cane to beckon help from the kitchen and added, "It truly is a new world. I'm going to have one of the girls put a bucket on the fire for that bath of yours."

De la Cruz took me by the hand, grabbed my saddle bag, flung it over his shoulder, and we started up the stairs that had been built without a railing. We were on our way up when an exceptionally nice-looking man with complete disregard for the intimidating drop to the hearth-room floor below shuffled by, practically knocking us over.

With a fast-half-hearted bow, he said, "Sorry, I didn't realize you were coming up."

He jumped the last few steps down and darted across the room.

The mother's favorite boy whose name we'd already heard a dozen times had made it to his mid-twenties, but acted more like an energetic child trapped inside an adult body.

Josefa lifted her cane and said, "Anza is here! Where are you going?"

Antonio cut his bolt for the door short and spouted, "I know, Mother, I saw them from the window!"

Quickly taking off again, he was just about to run out when he turned and said, "There's not much more satisfying than scaring an Indian and the self-proclaimed greatest Apache-fighter, both at the same time. I'm going to sneak up behind them..."

"Come greet our guests. I recall bringing you up with some manners," Josefa said, exuding adoration for her son with every word.

Antonio ran back, took half the steps in a single bound, reached up the rest of the way, and stuck his arm out for a handshake with the ex-priest. "Pleased to meet you," he said, clasping palms.

"De la Cruz."

"Sounds like a man of the Cloth!"

"I did take some religious instruction." The pirate grinned.

"Well, I've been to confession," Antonio said.

"I have too," de la Cruz replied, with a smirk.

Josefa waved her stick. "Let's allow our guests wash off the trail dust."

I doubt I'd ever been so happy when I saw that bed. Albeit a smudge guilty for acquiring the outrageously extravagant-for-the-outlands accommodations by means of a lie, but I intended to thoroughly enjoy it, regardless.

Wormwood wine, ready to be poured, sat on a little table next to a large bed with lovely old turned posts, a huge stuffed mattress covered with lots of pillows, and linen with lace edges that reminded me of the sort we had back home in Toulouse. A fresh night gown had been laid across the bedcover by one of the adopted girls, busily going about filling the tub. It was perfect.

That is, until de la Cruz let our bags thud to the rug. Taking me in his arms as if we were lovers, he inched his hands down over my ass and pressed his lips to mine, probably knowing full well I had to oblige in order to keep up appearances. The girl who had come to prepare the room turned as red as a cherry. Having witnessed the kiss, she ran out shielding her face with the brim of her bonnet.

I pushed de la Cruz away and said, "You scared that poor girl."

"She has to learn sometime." Heading for the door, he announced, "You and I deserve a quarter hour away from each other, don't you agree?"

"Where are you going?"

Walking out, he laughed and said, "Baby girl -- wearing these old boots, how far could I possibly go?"

I had completely forgotten about escaping.

Claiming it was cheap labor and a guarantee of life without loneliness, Ontiveros took in orphans. Youngsters of mixed sizes and features showed up at the supper table. Whatever she said was the reason for adopting them, by the way she looked at the little ones, speaking sweetly to them while administering gentle caresses whenever possible, it was plain to see Josefa Sancha loved children.

The smell was incredible. Corn powder, sprinkled with water and flattened in a hot pan. The frontier lived on tortillas. Soldiers at La Bahia squatted around a fire, cooking the flaps on the inside of their shields. There was no guess as to what was going to be served.

Oddly, the grain only fed to swine back in the Old World was beginning to take on appeal. I thought about telling Mother, and nearly laughed, because she would've feigned horror. How could I have forgotten she was gone? Just the same, I wanted to write her a letter. Then I began to worry about Papa.

Had I managed to explain my state of affairs, Mother's little pearl earrings would've jiggled with a grin, along with some clever epigram she always managed to muster even in the dreariest of times. Who was it tougher to live without, Armando or Mama? I swiped a tear and stole a dab from the mound of butter that had been set out for supper, sucking it off my finger when no one was looking.

Ornately carved chairs, accompanied by a piece or two of fine old furnishings from Spain that hadn't become warmth for winter, looked ridiculously out of place amidst unsophisticated furniture made from scrap. Somehow it all worked.

Escucha took his supper to the barn, for a pass of the jug with the Vaqueros and a little knife tossing into the straw. The rest of us grabbed a chair while the two older girls pulled apart slabs of well-cooked beef and piled the shreds on top of a huge tin plate.

The former priest was getting ready to take a seat at the table. He would've benefitted from a shave. Shabby as he looked, I was happy to see the scoundrel.

Fortunately, manners were casual. Reaching across the table to twirl our three-tines into the meat and fold forkfuls in tortillas, de la Cruz and I must've looked like prisoners set free.

Wearing a rolled white cloth around his forehead to keep the pale, curly locks out of his face, had it not been for the gray hair or two over his ears, the dearest of Josef's own flesh would've looked too young to have grown the sparse beard on his face trimmed in all the wrong places. Antonio Federico was the old woman's last-born son, and despite the affection she bestowed upon him, he acted as though his mother's loving concern was just the way it was supposed to be.

Antonio's father, an aspect to one's heritage of the highest significance in the Old World, apparently was of little importance on the frontier. No one said a thing about the man, whoever he was.

Josefa tipped the spout of an old silver-inlaid glass decanter from the Old World over my glass and said, "It's still not broken. And, neither am I. Would you care for libation with your supper?"

"You have wine?"

"I'm fortunate to have several bottles."

The first swallow immediately brought comforting warmth. "This is excellent. I don't think I've tasted anything like it since Spain."

"Perhaps that's because it is from Spain. We've finally begun to import decent spirits here."

"This is Spanish wine?"

Josefa leaned on her cane to lift herself out of her chair at the head of the table. Tapping with each step, the extra leg helped her to the hearthside where she searched a shelf of crocks and came back with the original bottle. Lowering herself into the chair, she handed it to me and watched my face shadow as I read the label.

It was as if someone had punched me in the gut. I covered my mouth. Sucking air, I couldn't say a word.

"What's wrong, my dear?" Josefa asked as de la Cruz moved his chair back from the table, and put his arm around my shoulder.

Having swallowed proof that Armando had indeed secured the trade agreement, I cried, "I'm drinking my own wine!"

Josefa raised her glass. "Well then, you being here is providence!"

Anza walked in, pulled a chair from the table, sat down, and stuck his hat on his knee. He didn't look happy. "One of the horses has a stone bruise. He's probably not going to be able to go on for days, maybe weeks. So we'll be short one mount. Unless Josefa Sancha allows us to borrow a fresh animal," he added with a grin, looking at the old lady.

"I've already loaned you far too many horses. And you've managed to kill most of them!"

"Nonsense, I did no such thing. I never killed any of your horses. They merely decided to die while they were in my possession."

Josefa cracked a few more smile lines. "I'm *not* giving you any more horses. But you are welcome to stay as long as you like."

De la Cruz put his wine-goblet down on the table and said, "We can pay for fresh horses, it's no problem."

"Keep your coin. I have no need for your money, but I do need my horses. Just make yourself at home. Surely, your journey can wait a little longer."

"Well, it looks like it's going to have to, doesn't it?" Antonio said, with an ounce of what sounded like revenge.

Anza leaned way back into his chair and casually said, "So what brings you home from London's Circus? Did they kick you out when you opened your mouth with that accent?"

"There are two kinds of people in the world -- circus people, and everybody else. There's no discrimination among a breed unto its own," Antonio replied, sounding serious for the first time.

De la Cruz couldn't hide the fact that he loved a good pissing-contest. He picked up the wine bottle, tipped it over Antonio's glass, and said, "What *are* the old Red Coats up to these days?"

Antonio flung his hand over the mouth of the goblet. "None for me thanks."

Anza's eyes got wide. "You've stopped drinking, Antonio? Now *that* sounds serious. What gives?"

Antonio's claw-foot chair screeched against the floor as he stood up. Pausing only to flip a dark stare in Anza's direction, he left the table and pounded the stairs.

FRIDAY, 17 NOVEMBER 1780

The renegado was supposed to be keeping an eye on me. Crouched down several paces away, aiming and tossing a small knife into the sand over and over, the world's greatest scout looked like he wasn't concerned at all.

I thought about telling him the tip of his long braid was brushing the dirt. But I didn't.

He wasn't even interested in why I was laughing. It just so happened I was amused by the possibility of a sudden gust of wind blowing the patches and powder horn that I'd placed on the well ledge down the hole.

If the Indian was to be questioned as to why there was no danger of the implements falling into the water, he'd have said something like, I knew it wasn't going to happen, so why worry? Escucha always had some weird sort of native reasoning for everything, and apparently he was right about so many things, after the fact I might add, that he had everyone hoodwinked into believing he was harboring some divine gift.

Josefa yanked me out of bed at dawn after banging on the door with her cane. She even went so far as to come in and pull the covers off us. Half-asleep, de la Cruz went for the big old double-edged knife he always kept under his pillow, but the feisty old witch whacked him a good one with her stick, told him to go back to sleep, grabbed me by the ear, and said, "This one's coming with me."

The woman didn't even let me get dressed. I had to tuck my night shirt into a pair of pants and go out back with a case of re-load cartridges and a dusty muzzleloader.

The renegade, enlisted to watch over me to make sure I didn't shoot myself or anyone else, stayed too far away to do any good, if you asked me. But since nothing blew up in my face, he'd have insisted he wasn't neglecting his duty. Even though all he did was delight in watching the tin white woman run after the firing ball rolling around in the sand so many times, dirt couldn't pack another grain under my fingernails. The whole time, the Indian was hiding a smirk. Perhaps it's an old native means by which to laugh at someone without getting killed. Escucha could ensconce a grin in such an unperceivable way, his talent surely must've been hereditary, no white man could do it the way he did.

The day had its rewards, the priceless honor of hammering the ball in with the ramrod while staring back at the Indian.

Wrapping that blasted ball for the millionth time, I ripped a long narrow rag strip and put the swatch in my mouth.

The wise ex-Apache brave said, "If you're loading to keep from getting killed, pray you'll be near a stream. Your mouth will be too dry to get the patch wet."

"Don't your knees hurt?" I asked.

"My knees?'

"Squatting down like that, doesn't it hurt your knees?"

"Only white men's knees hurt from squatting. White men cursed by centuries of chairs. Now they cannot squat."

It was a good thing Josefa came down from the house when she did, because the redskin had pushed me too far.

The old lady lifted her cane, pointed to an old broken bucket full of holes sitting on a corral post that looked like it must've been used to teach all her children how to shoot, threw the muzzle-loader back to me, and said, "Load as fast as you can, and hit that as quick as you can."

I fired until the infernal gun was too hot to hold. By the time the sun was low in the sky, Josefa went so far as to say that she thought I showed some natural talent.

Wiping the sweat from my brow, I was silently thanking God I was finally finished when the woman came back out there with a horse. She put the reins in my hand, and said, "Okay – now do it from a gallop."

She didn't let me stop till that horse was frothing between the butt-cakes. My arms hurt so badly I couldn't hold the gun up or take a swing at the Indian who certainly deserved it after watching me struggle all day long. I easily could've smacked the smile right off his face when Escucha so graciously took the reins from me and said, "Allow me to help you, Señora."

He only turned around once on his way to the barn to see if I was pissed. Lord knew I had it in me to show him. But, I didn't say a word to the ex-Apache brave walking off with the lathered nag.

Back home in Toulouse, other than the horses, some hens, a milk cow, and a small garden, we didn't have much in the way of a farm. We did have an endless supply of grazing. How Josefa's rancho survived on sand, cactus, and weeds was miraculous.

It was my job to cut a few thorny paddles for supper. Cooking the prickly plant was another story, but I agreed to gather a stack for the girls to make.

Behind the barn, next to the last pen of flat-nosed hogs peering through the slats in hopes of a handout, a rather large cactus was sticking out of the sand next to a huge old gouged door.

I was wondering how to cut off a paddle without getting stuck when someone behind me said, "Forty-two feet."

I turned to see, Antonio, wearing a fancy hat.

"Forty-two feet?" I asked.

"That's how wide it is," he replied with a tiny stagger.

"I don't think it's quite that wide." I grinned.

The long white theatrical plume went high as he pulled the hat off, raised his arm, took a deep bow, and nearly lost his balance. Bent over, swaying in his boots, he snapped his head up, looking into the crowd waiting for applause. He'd been drinking.

"Alastaro the Great, needs quiet from the audience! Alastaro must concentrate," he announced, falling on his ass, barely missing a thorny paddle.

Sitting spread-legged in the dirt, looking around in a series of pullet-searching-for-scratch, jerky head motions, Antonio patted the ground and said, "Nope… no scorpions, come sit."

I put the seat of my pants down next to him. His breath about knocked me over.

Reaching for an old thumb-handled crock, he took a gulp, wiped his mouth on his sleeve, dangled the jug in front of me, and said, "Be my guest."

"What is it?"

"I don't know what it is. Makes you feel really, really good, though. Tastes like shit. But, who cares?"

"I don't think so, Antonio."

"Go on, try it! Spit it out if you don't like it," he replied with a crooked smile, tipping the spout to my lips.

I took a swill, winced, and sprayed. "You drank that?"

"It's all right, you don't have to. My sweet Phoebe never drank, either."

"Who's Phoebe?"

"The ring is forty-two feet wide."

"What ring are you talking about, Antonio?"

"The circus ring…what other ring would I be talking about?"

"Yes, tell me about the circus. I hear they're going to have one in Paris, soon."

"My boss…or I should say my former boss, Astley, was a trick-rider. He made this big discovery. Run a horse around in a circle forty-two feet wide, and you can do all sorts of things, like stand on its back, hang off the side, whatever you want, and it's easy. Of course, he must've figured all this out by riding horses in circles." Antonio laughed, waving the jug.

"Astley told everyone the forty-two-foot circle was his invention. There's something about forty-two feet that keeps you balanced. I don't know why anyone would want to do anything but sit on a horse, instead of hanging upside down, unless they needed to pick up something and didn't want to get off. Try it sometime. I have. Hey, you wanna get a horse and do it now?"

"Who is Phoebe?" I asked, again.

Antonio took a huge gulp from the jug and said, "Who *was* Phoebe, not who *is* Phoebe? She's dead. Phoebe's dead."

"I'm so sorry, Antonio. I had no idea. What happened? How did she die?"

"I killed her."

I didn't know if he was joking, but my heart pumped anyway in case he really was a murderer.

"What happened, Antonio?"

"I can tell you. Everybody knows. It's no big secret. I mean, everybody in London knows."

He just sat there staring at the ground. Suddenly, he looked up and began to ramble, "The sawdust smelled as good as a swig. Messing with knives was the first thing I remember. I started playing with them when I was just a kid. I could hit anything straight on with the tip of a blade. When we got lucky enough to get cobbler shavings, Astley had the roustabouts mix it with the sand in the ring. The theater smelled nice and the horses had better footing.

That freshly ground pine hit my nostrils, the torches blazed, and I was the only man in the world -- like Jesus on the mound. All eyes were on me. I melted into somebody else...something else. The ringmaster bellowed as loud as his lungs could yell...And now, all the way from across the world -- from the untamed savage wilds of New Spain -- Alastaro the Great!

"I never looked at the faces in the crowd. That scared me. I didn't want to see them. I didn't want to know what they really thought. My sweet Phoebe had skin white as cream. Except for her cheeks, she pinched them pink before every show. And she always looked right at me when she smiled. I could tell she forced it sometimes, but she did it anyway. I didn't like her showing her legs. But, Astley wanted to give the audience their money's worth. Phoebe had to be bare-legged for me to throw a knife around her when the wheel was spinning.

"Astley had been looking all over creation for acts that didn't have anything to do with horses -- he wanted stuff that people would pay to see, acts that would make women in the audience swoon. I was full of it when I packed my blades and set out for Westminster Bridge. I knew they were going to love me. The first thing Astley asked was if I could throw a knife and cut the tip off a cigar. I said, sure no problem. Then he looked me right in the eye and said, can you do it while the cigar is in someone's mouth? I looked right back at him square in the eye, and told him I could do it, blindfolded. I was only joking, but Astley loved it. I really did it. There were drawings of me in a black blindfold, throwing flaming blades at a half-naked girl, and they were stuck on lampposts all over London. Alastaro the Great and Phoebe was the final act in Astley's Circus and everyone paid good coin to see us.

"My precious Phoebe... she was only sixteen. Her family didn't have a thing, except a beautiful daughter. They came from Catherine's Palace in Russia, ballet people turned acrobats. All they knew how to do was perform, and drink vodka. Neither

Phoebe nor I could speak much English, but we managed. To the audience, it looked like we hardly knew each other.

"Alastaro the Great would make his entrance. Then the innocent target, Phoebe came out wearing a mask. But, we'd gotten ready for the act in the same little room. I would step out into the ring and taste her in my mouth from making love to her that afternoon."

Antonio closed his eyes, looked down to the ground and pressed the tears away with his thumb and forefinger. A drip ran down from his nose. He lifted his chin and said, "The ringmaster would raise his horn, and say, Phoebe is not her real name. She asks that you forgive her disguise. But because of what you are about to see, she requests that her identity be kept secret! Every single time she flung off that red-satin lined cape and everyone saw her velvet short pants and naked legs, the crowd hummed like a bees nest. They bought the whole thing and she loved it, performing was in her blood, she couldn't help it. But Astley had to keep making it harder. It wasn't long before throwing blindfolded wasn't enough. The target needed to be moving. They built a wheel. Astley kept changing the game. The crowd always demanded more, or they wouldn't come."

The fondness in Antonio's voice was turning to pain along with the salty tide filling his eyes. "Timing was vital -- I had to hear the clicks of the moving wheel so that I would know when to throw. And if there was a noise from the crowd at the wrong moment..."

Antonio brushed away the lock that had fallen in his face and said, "One day, Astley came to my room next to the theater in a little place I rented from the baker downstairs. I was shaving. I knew it was Sunday because there were long periods of silence between clopping hooves on the cobblestone in the street below. He'd never visited me there, before. I think he was afraid of finding me with Phoebe, so he came when he knew she would be at mass. I still had the razor in my hand when I wiped a towel across my cheek to get the soap off my face. I let him in and he didn't even say hello. He just said, 'As soon as you and Phoebe are done, Peter is going to jump his horse through a burning hoop.' Then he apologized for having to take money off the top of my wages because he needed to give more to Peter, and told me that I must have a lot saved up by then anyway. And he walked out."

Several gulps dripped the foul brew down the front of his shirt with each swell of his throat. Taking one last swallow, Antonio said, "I picked up the bottle. It wasn't a problem. I could throw the knives in my sleep. April wasn't supposed to be hot in London. But it was that night. Right before we did the spinning wheel throw, Phoebe turned sideways. It was part of the act. One of the roustabouts put a lit cigar in her mouth. I turned to the crowd holding four knives in each hand and waved the blades high. The drummer tapped a long roll. The cloth was tightened around my eyes and knotted behind my head. I turned to Phoebe and let the first blade go. I lost those knives. They must've been trampled into the dirt, scooped up with the dung, I don't know. Maybe someone in the crowd ran off with them. The second blade stuck right where it was supposed to, next to Phoebe's thigh. I let the third knife go. Just as it was out of my hand, someone screamed. At first I didn't think much about it, women in the audience screamed during every show. Another woman screamed. Then, everyone was yelling."

Antonio's face distorted, and he bawled. "I ripped off the blindfold. I had no idea what was going on. People were running around the theater. A man in the crowd was yelling he hit her. He stabbed her. Pheobe had slipped to the sawdust, holding onto the blade stuck in her belly. I kept saying over and over, this can't be, it's not possible. This is not happening! They had to pull me away from her."

Antonio stopped crying and began talking as if the story was a fable. "Three days later, Phoebe was still lying in my bed. She was in so much pain, she couldn't eat. She could barely drink a sip of water. All she asked for was the opium bottle. I wanted to kill myself. Seeing her suffer was more than anyone could bear. Sister Mary Rose stayed with her the entire time. That woman's ice-cold hands were the only thing that kept me from taking my life. I can still feel her cool touch on my arm and hear her thick Irish accent, saying, Phoebe needs you alive now -- don't you let her see you like this. Every time we changed the bandages, the bed linen turned red. Three days had gone by and blood was still leaking between her legs. Phoebe's little hand was limp in mine and her cracked lips oozed white in the corners. She could hardly talk. I was sitting on the edge of the bed, she'd broken out with sweats in the middle of the night. Leaning over, I put my face next to hers. I could hardly hear her whisper to me, Antonio, it was not your fault. You are Alastaro the Great. My precious girl was trying to smile. But Phoebe was in so much pain and her gray face was perspiring so badly, I caught a sweat-bead with my finger as it dripped from her brow. The opium was wearing off. She was trembling when she told me that she had gained two inches, and changed her costume so no one would see. It took the last ounce of strength I had to ask her why she never told me. She gave my hand the tiniest squeeze. The cracked corners of her little mouth turned up just enough to force the beginning of what would have been the smile I loved more than anything in the world. Phoebe whispered with her last breath, I want to be your wife, because you love me, not because you have to marry me."

The burning brew from the toppled jug spilled into the sand with a series of glugs, each less intense than the one before. Antonio flopped backward onto the dirt covering his eyes to hide the sobs he could hold back no longer.

I threw myself to his side. Lying together in the dirt, we cried in each other's arms.

SATURDAY 18 NOVEMBER 1780

"Your countryman, L'Abbat, swore that courage and skill is of little use without a good weapon," Antonio said, putting the tip of the blade upside-down between the first three fingers of my right hand. The knife was large enough to carve a bear. Pointing it straight toward the old door leaning against the back of the barn, he lifted my arm and said, "You can hold it by the handle, but this is the way I like to do it. The release is the easy part, getting the timing right for the distance and putting the spin on it... that takes a little practice."

Josefa's son could pick a spot on the target and throw knives in a perfect tiny circle around a pinpoint. I tossed blades everywhere. Finally, one stuck the way it was supposed to.

Antonio applauded, marched over to the panel, and with a tiny squeak pulled the blade out, handed it to me, and said, "Here's your first throwing knife. I promise it'll bring you luck. You have to practice every day. A knife isn't like a gun, sword, or bow, you have to get it right the first time, because if you don't hit the target, you've thrown your weapon away."

The old lady was coming in our direction with a flintlock in hand, leading a big red white-faced horse, sweetly allowing the old lady to move at a crawling pace without walking away with her.

That woman's going to make me fire the gun bareback, crossed my mind.

Instead, the old lady squinted with the dust cloud that had just blown up from a sudden breeze and said, "I think your husband has heard every Anza Apache story he cares to. Escucha is itchy to get going. And your horse is still lame. It occurred to me that I have the power to fix all the problems. So, I've decided to do just that. Here's what makes you equal to any man."

I just about cried as I took the weapon and lead rope from her outstretched hand. "I thought you weren't parting with any horses," I replied, stroking the nose of the gorgeous creature I was hanging onto, with my eyes ready to spill. The animal was the nicest I'd seen anywhere on the frontier.

"I said I wasn't giving Anza any more horses! I'm a woman of my word. He'll be pissed. But I don't have a problem with that. This horse is for you." She chuckled, contorting her weathered face in the blinding sun that had freed itself from behind a cloud.

On the way back to the house, I told her there was no way I could ever repay her for all she'd given me. Josefa leaned her cane on the edge of the table, picked up an old gun-worm screwing device that had seen many years of extracting unspent charges from musket barrels, and began to un-cork a bottle that was waiting along with two pewter goblets.

"You have champagne!" I nearly shouted.

"I do! We're going to share it."

"Right now, in the middle of the day, for no special reason?"

"You and I are here. That's plenty special enough."

A quick loud pop and the bubbling spirits let loose, spilling froth down the side of the bottle.

"Is Anza really the greatest Apache-fighter?" I asked as the old lady carefully poured our prize into each goblet.

She laughed and said, "He has a great deal of experience. He's still alive. So, maybe he is. One way or the other, you were lucky to have met up with him. What brings you to this part of the world, anyway?"

I could feel my face turning to sadness.

"It's a man, isn't it?" she said.

"How did you know?"

"The only souls in these parts were born here, expatriates, roamers, crooks, madmen, or those running away from something. The pain is in your eyes, my dear. What else could it be but a man?"

Placing herself in position over her chair, Josefa hesitated for a moment. Then with cane still in hand, she plopped down the rest of the way, took a long sip of Champagne, and said, "Hurt often comes from something that used to be a pleasure."

She leaned back to relax with her elbow on the arm of the chair and said, "I've been upon this earth longer than four of my five children. I've been scorned, ridiculed, abandoned, sullied, lied to, stolen from, and nearly killed I don't know how many times. But I'm still here. And those who tried to hurt me are not. When I was a girl, it might've been said that I was adorable or cute, but I would've never been considered, beautiful. I was nearly thirteen when I met the father of my first born. We were among several families up from Mexico City who settled this area. José de Valdes was only four years old. I had no idea he was to ever become my lover. He was just a child. I played with him, pretending he was mine. Years went by, there was no one I was interested in, who was also interested in me. I had reached my mid-twenties, well past marriage age. I accepted the fact that I might never marry. José came of age...well, almost of age. His boyish ways were charming. I loved him, hoping that maybe he loved me. I gave into him and bore his child. He shamed his family, and me. Later he moved to El Paso and married someone else.

"I went on to have four more children -- four different men. I've never married. I'm a landowner, rancher, and businesswoman. I'm in good standing with the church. Clergy on the frontier can be extremely understanding in light of being faced with mortality at every turn. My children married into families with social ranking. What did I need a husband for? I may have lived this long simply because I never had one! I did whatever I pleased, and I still do. I didn't need a husband to have children and I didn't need a husband to have land. Men come and go throughout your life, my dear, but who is with you from the day you were born? And will be with you till the day you die? Who is it that has always been there for you? And is here right at this moment? Rely on yourself, Woman! You will never suffer betrayal."

The door flung open. Escucha walked in backward, carrying one end of a long branch to which a bloody kill had been tied. With its legs lashed to the limb and its eyes glazed over, a huge wild boar dangled upside-down. On the opposite end of the stick, Anza labored under the weight of the hog, swaying side to side with each step, dripping blood on the floor.

De la Cruz danced in behind them with musket in hand, grinning like the slave master he pretended to be, and announced, "The losing hunters had to carry dinner home. That was the deal."

Josefa shouted, "It took three days for the three of you to kill something, and now you're bloodying my floor! Get that thing out of my house! Take it to the cool-room. Bring me the ribs -- we'll have them for supper,"

The old lady turned to me and said with a change in tune, "Why don't you go get acquainted with your new horse."

"What's his name?"

"We called him Rojo. You can call him whatever you like. He belongs to you now."

237

"Then, that's what I'll call him, Rojo," I said.

Anza flattened the corners of his mouth, gave the old woman a raised eyebrow stare, and said, "Lena has a new horse?"

Mother used to say anyone could make an entrance, the real talent was in knowing when to make an exit. I picked up my hat and ran out the door.

Antonio was still behind the barn with his elbows on the top rail of the corral fence, watching Rojo twisting his body and kicking up his heels like a foal discovering his new legs for the first time.

"My mother must've taken a liking to you. This is the best horse we've got on the place," he said without turning around.

"I don't know what it is that I did."

"I think you remind her of her."

What will you do now?" I asked.

"I guess I'll become a farmer."

"There's that circus starting up in Paris." I smiled.

"I would like to go back over there. Maybe you and I will meet one day."

"Perhaps we will," I replied.

"Now that you have a ride, I imagine you'll be leaving soon."

"Anza will probably make us head out before the sun comes up. What is it with you and him anyway?"

Antonio took a quick visual survey of our surroundings and replied, "One day I was out here rewinding a handle on one of my knives. I overheard Mother and Anza talking in the barn. She asked Anza pretty much the same question you just asked me. Of course he denied having any differences with me. Then she told him she thought he and I were always at odds because I was his son."

"You're joking! Anza is your father?"

"I wish it was a joke. Anza made excuses saying that he was only fifteen that one time in the hay barn. Mother said to him, that's all it takes, once. Funny thing is I know my mother wouldn't have said anything unless she was sure. I've always given doubt the up-per hand, but if Anza really is my father, it would explain why I've fucked up my life so badly. Never mind all that. I have something for you."

Antonio reached into his shirt and pulled a crucifix on a cord over his head. "Look," he said, holding it up so I could see how it worked. "You can lift it off the strap in a second, and push the little button on top…"

With a click, a blade popped out, instantly turning the cross into a knife.

"The Corpus on both sides makes it perfectly balanced if you have to throw it. So, if it looks like turning the other cheek isn't going to work…" He laughed.

I was ready to cry. "Antonio, I don't know what to say."

"How 'bout just saying thank you?" he said, with a grin.

I threw my arms around his neck and gave him a kiss that was more than I would've given to my brother but a little less than I would've given a lover.

Lying in bed, flicking the button on the crucifix knife, pushing the blade back inside the cross, I amused myself until de la Cruz rolled over and in a muffled voice from his face being in the pil-low said, "We have to ride for eleven years in the morning. Will you stop that and douse the light?"

Snuffing the candle, I thought, what if one April day I got up, threw on some clothes, and went out back, swinging a bucket. The sun would be warming my shoulders while the girls wet down torti-lla flour and stoke the fire under a hanging tin of coffee grounds. Each pulley-squeaking tug of the rope over the well would send blackbirds flitting from tree to tree, squawking and spotting the sand with their droppings. Looking up, I couldn't help but smile. Shielding my eyes from the bright light, I'd catch a glimpse of Antonio, laughing from the upstairs window, shouting, "I can't wash this soap off my face without that water!"

SUNDAY, 19 NOVEMBER 1780

I had to look to see if I was still holding the reins. I couldn't feel the leather in my hands. Rain was coming down so hard, the brim of my hat flopped waves around my face, the red gelding under me had turned umber, and the fiery sting of cold just about knocked me out of the saddle.

Shaking like I had the fits, I managed to keep my eyes open. The horses ahead were barely visible. It wasn't until Anza was right beside me that I realized who had turned around and ridden back.

Giving his reins a sharp tug to keep his horse from bolting off with the chill, he hung onto his hat, yelling above the deluge, "I'm sure we can make it to Candelaria before nightfall."

Splashing muddy holes that filled instantly, he galloped back to the lead with Escucha.

How we found the place was a miracle. Getting dark, with rain still coming down, we couldn't even see the abandoned settlement until we were practically on top of it.

The shell of what was once a flourishing mission had been empty for nearly a decade. Without support from the Spanish government, the people left. From the remains, it looked like they took off in a hurry.

All three men had to get on their knees in the mud and dig with their hands to dislodge the silt around the old doors. Several times they stopped to put shoulders to it, only to get back down on their knees and paddle the soggy earth again. Finally, the gates gave way with a crack loud enough to be heard over the torrent.

I didn't get off my horse until I rode into the church, after which I promptly fell on my ass. My feet had gotten so numb, I couldn't feel the floor when I landed.

Adding to the enchant, de la Cruz leaned over to help me up, water rolled off his hat and dripped all over me.

"Thank you very much." I laughed.

"Oh, I'm terribly sorry, did I make you wet?" he replied with an insidious grin.

Escucha was stringing a tie-line in a corner of the chapel for the horses, while Anza and de la Cruz, smashing old brittle pews for firewood, carried on about the lack of available slave labor.

The padre's quarters where we planned to sleep was smaller and had suffered less erosion, so it was bound to be warmer.

Laying my soaked clothes in front of the fire, I wrapped myself in the driest saddle blanket we had, and got as close to the flames as possible without setting myself on fire.

I finally stopped shivering, lit an old nub, and explored the adjoining chapel.

A few sticks of furnishings not worth taking along were all that remained. The roof was leaking in a bunch of places, and the clay floor had hardened in various locations from the continual stream every time the skies opened up.

Brightly painted walls faded to nearly colorless, revealing various icons outlined in primitive floral patterns almost beyond recognition. A canvas of the dagger-hearted Dolorosa had been left leaning to one side, defiled with bird droppings and feather fluff.

A hand grabbed my breast from behind. I almost got a scream out, but he covered my mouth, and whispered in a graveled voice, "Don't turn around. Don't make a sound. Just do as I say. I only want to touch you."

I didn't dare make a sound when he let go and began feeling his way over my serape, coaxing my nipples with a squeeze through the wool. He drew little circles on my throat with his fingertips, banging extra beats from my heart for fear he might strangle me.

Sliding his hands underneath my blanket, he whispered, "Ever done it with a stranger?"

"No, I haven't," I replied, trembling.

"Would you like to have the excitement of not knowing my name or seeing my face? Just feel me inside you. What if I fuck you right now?"

He was hard in the crease of my ass when he found the exact place that felt so good I couldn't do much of anything else except allow him to violate me with his fingers.

"Someone might see us," I said.

"If they do, they will quickly leave," he whispered, lifting my leg.

Placing himself where he wanted to be, with just a little push, he'd be inside. I thought he was going to do it. He let go and pulled away.

I turned to see the man buttoning his pants in the shadow of the firelight coming from the Padre's quarters.

Splashes were falling around us from the leaking roof. Two drops landed on my face. I almost didn't recognize him. I was angry, but kissed de la Cruz anyway, and reached up for a feel of his soft bare cheek.

"I didn't know you ever shaved it all off," I said.

"I religiously shave my whole face, every three, four, maybe five months," he replied.

Anza appeared in the doorway, leaning against the beam support. "I need to see you in here right away, de la Cruz."

I opened my blanket in front of the hearth to steal another dose of heat while they stood with lowered heads over a busted table in the center of the room.

El capitan pointed a finger somewhere on the parchment, the crease in his brow deepened, and he said, "Late tomorrow, we'll be on the leading edge of the most dangerous Apache territory on the entire frontier."

TUESDAY, 21 NOVEMBER 1780
SAN SABA

The sliver of a moon had clouded over and we couldn't see a thing. Stumbling around in the pitch, tripping over rocks and juts with horses in hand was crazy. The truly insane part, was according to Anza, the lack of sight protected us, since Apache supposedly never attack after sunset. So we wound up wandering around like a bunch of idiots in the dark. Too bad I never felt as safe as he said we were. De la Cruz, of course had his own take on the situation, saying we'd probably be the first white men lucky enough to be sniped by savages at night.

We couldn't light a torch, to which the pirate pointed out the absurdity of worrying about being sighted if Apache weren't going to attack anyway.

What made it especially harebrained was we were risking our asses purely because 'Scucha sensed an uprising. There was no real evidence, at least that was what he told us. The forecast was based entirely on just a feeling he had.

The renegado must've seen something, some sign or mark. As ridiculous as it may have sounded to de la Cruz and me, Anza had come to trust the Indian's offhand predictions. So we pressed on to make it to San Saba before sunrise.

The sky turned a hair-shade lighter. There it was, like a tiny ember in a dying hearth, the watch tower torch of the San Saba Presidio.

Exhausted as we were, the horses still came first. My saddle thudded to the ground.

"I think I'm going to skip a bath and go straight to bed," I said to the pirate un-tacking his mount next to me.

"I've never known anyone who washes as often as you. We're in the outlands, and you can't wait to find the nearest sliver of soap." He laughed.

"Don't Basques have bath tubs?"

"Actually, not. We tossed them all across the border into France."

Anza came into the corral. The sun was getting ready to show. Leaning an elbow on Rojo's rump, he said, "I'm going to service at the mission, the two of you should come along. It's half a league up the river. Gonzo's going to give us a ride. We'll sleep later."

I had no desire to tell El Capitan I wasn't going to church with him, and although de la Cruz hasn't got much of a problem saying anything to anyone, he elected to go. The bath, food, and bed were going to have to wait. I wasn't about to be left behind.

Gonzalez, the mule driver, greeted us with a huge smile consisting of the few tobacco-stained teeth he had. The man was too scrawny to be loading or unloading anything, but the little wiry old guy with a nose that belonged on a much larger face could lift his own weight. Gonzo was pulling the last barrel of provisions from his wagon when the four of us climbed into the back.

The mule driver took his seat and announced, "These here is my maiden jennies, Ruth 'n Ester," to which the long-eared girls, hearing their names, bayed on cue.

"They do the walkin' and I do the talkin'," Gonzo said chewing on the leaf in his mouth.

He slapped the ladies on the behinds with the long reins and headed down the rutted road beside the river.

Unable to hear much else than the noise, we banged our asses on the bare floor of that old rattling cart.

With another flap of leather on the jennie's rumps Gonzo laughed and said, "Tobaccy is the only reason I got any teeth left at all."

One of the donkeys bayed with her head high in the air, to which the mule driver took a break from being amused by his own wit. "Now you stop complainin', Ester. This cart for sure ain't near as heavy as it was b'fore. You git goin,' girl."

We hadn't been on our way more than two minutes when de la Cruz stood up, and said, "Pull over here man, I have to leak."

Gonzo tugged leather up along the tall river reeds, and with a sing in his voice said, "The girls won't be squawkin' bout a chance to rest. For that, ey'll be on their best behavior."

De la Cruz was somewhere in the swamp a long time. I didn't know if I should come up with a clever quip or start worrying.

I was ready to say something when the tops of the reeds moved violently against each other. A moment later, stumbling his way back to the wagon, de la Cruz came into sight. He didn't look happy. The tall brush behind him stopped moving and three Indians emerged right on his heels, toting long guns and spears, making aggressive gestures in our direction with their weapons, arguing amongst themselves.

One of them shoved the pirate along, in a manner much like a master's discontent with a tardy schoolboy. From the expressions on their war-painted faces, they were more annoyed than de la Cruz.

Having the good sense to keep his mouth from flapping while Anza and Escucha stood up to get a better view, Gonzo sat quietly holding onto his long reins, taking a brief head-turn a couple of times to see what the Indians were doing before looking away again as if none of it were his business.

Scucha talked to them in his own language. It seemed the conversation was friendly. De la Cruz had mostly likely done something harmless to piss off the savages, and nothing more. But whatever it was the renegado said, the braves weren't in the mood, and their intentions were becoming clearer by the moment.

I suppose I felt mild terror -- truth of the matter was that riddled with fatigue, I was just plain too tired for any of it to be happening.

The illusion of being able to roll off on our way with just a slap on the jennies' behinds with the reins quickly died. One of the Indians threw his spear into the ground. With his bone necklace rattling against his bare chest, he climbed up onto the wagon, grabbed the collar of my chemise, and ripped it to my waist with a welting sting to the back of my neck.

I screamed and threw my arms around myself. De la Cruz flung off his jacket and covered me while the Indians stood there, laughing.

Hopping down from the wagon, the renegado pointed his finger at the Apache, and said something in their native language. They backed away. Why in hell didn't he say whatever he did the first time?

Anza put a hand on the old man's shoulder and calmly said, "Drive to the mission."

"Get on now, girls!" Gonzo yelled.

The mules tightened their harnesses and tugged us forward with a squeak and rattle.

The three Indians stood on the edge of the bed like we were their prize.

Leaning to the center of our huddle, Anza whispered, "Two of those dogs were set on killing de la Cruz, the third said no. It wasn't because he was being noble -- the killing would've ruined their surprise."

De la Cruz muttered, "You know what the worst of it is? I never got to leak."

"Don't worry, you'll be pissing in your pants along with everyone else very soon," Anza replied, sounding serious.

Escucha pushed the front point of his hat high. "Did you notice anything unusual about these Apache, Capitan?"

"You mean the Comanche war paint?" Anza replied.

Escucha lifted his head just enough to place the brim of his hat in position to protect his eyes from the rising sun and simply said, "Yup."

"Don't you think we're just a bit too far west for Comanche to be carrying French guns," Anza added with a nod in the direction of the Indians.

"At least there are only three of them and five of us," de la Cruz said.

"For every savage you see, there's a bunch more you can't," Anza said, pulling his hat off, dragging his sleeve over his perspiring brow.

More Indians appeared. Up ahead on the left side of the road, four barelegged Apache dangling their limbs over tack-less slab-sided war ponies, stood looking at us. The horses had their flanks, shoulders, and faces painted with strange symbols in bright colors, and ropes tied around their lower jaws for reins.

Those Indians didn't move. They just kept watching with their heads following the wagon as we went by.

More Apache appeared. Angry painted faces came through the tall grasses by the river. Savages were everywhere.

Wiping my sweaty palms on my pant leg, I tied the torn ends of the chemise around my neck. My mouth was dry as cotton. Dozens more were standing along the short road to the mission.

"What's going on?" I gasped, twisting around hard, having forgotten how tired I was.

Where there had been no one behind us, warriors appeared. Apache hung from tree branches along the water. Indians were everywhere. My heart was about to beat its way out of my chest.

The mission walls came into view on the bluff. For a second there was a moment of relief. It didn't last long. The security we'd hoped for within the stockades turned out to be a bit shortsighted -- hundreds of mounted Apache were already inside. Behind us, scores of Indians had cut off the road back to the presidio.

More and more of them appeared, tens became dozens, dozens turned into hundreds, until in every direction all that could be seen was Indians.

Worry trenched Anza's face as he put the hat back on his head, turned to Scucha, and said, "How many, do you think?"

The unruffled renegade matter-of-factly answered, "How many do I see? Or, how many do I think there are?"

"How many *are* there, 'Scucha?" Anza asked.

Holding up this hand to cover his eyes where the hat-brim failed to shield the sun, Escucha took a long squint, surveying the landscape. "Fifteen hundred, maybe two thousand, it's not only Apache, Capitan. Other tribes are here, too."

Anza took a slow turn of his head to look at each of us squatting low in the wagon bed and quietly said, "How many Spanish soldiers did we leave just now at the presidio, thirty maybe?"

The jennies turned through the huge open gates. Indians were all over the place. The mission property was filled with them. Not only were warriors inside, the stockade was surrounded by painted faces, all carrying bows and arrows, spears, guns, or hatchets.

Father Miguel Herrera and Ignacio, the mission's Apache interpreter, were standing in the center of the courtyard surrounded by savages, negotiating with the Indian chief when our cart rattled in.

Obviously, Herrera had no notion the entire rescue entourage was before him -- he came to greet us, robe sash flying side to side, outstretched arms, and a huge smile. Embracing Anza, Father Miguel said, "They come in peace."

"They're covered with war paint, and you just let them in?" El Capitan replied, with canon-fire in his eyes.

The natives who supposedly meant no harm were masked as animals, or had faces covered in black and red. All of them had weapons.

Anza leaned toward Scucha and whispered, "Are you buying any of this shit about coming in peace?"

The renegado looked down to hide a smirk and said, "I can see how one might think that scores with painted faces and guns came to pass the calumet."

Two young Spanish boys dragged supplies from the storage house as part of Father Miguel's attempt to divert an incident by adding more gifts to the dusty pile of tobacco boxes already at the chief's feet.

Four savages absconded with the containers, hollering as they ran off. The chief let go a vicious outburst of laughter.

The sea of Indians, rapidly losing patience with white man banter, crowed around us like flies on a three-day old rump hanging in the sun. Apache thrust weapons in the air, and all the while the supposed negotiations were taking place, horses were being stolen from the mission corral.

A scuffle in the gathering came closer. It was a Spanish soldier squeezing his way through the herd of angered warriors. Clutching his bloodied shoulder, he leaned over and whispered to Anza, "They're not here in peace, they lanced me at my canon station for no reason."

"Go to the church and instruct the padre to dismiss mass and prepare for attack. This bunch will not to be placated much longer."

Settlers from the pueblo outside the mission stockades were trying to get through. A few villagers managed to make it inside. The less fortunate screamed as they were slashed to pieces by Apache.

Anza turned to me and said, "Go to the church with Herrera and the sentry, now!"

"If I am going to die, I'm not going to die with strangers!"

Ignacio relayed Anza's message to the chief, asking, "What is it you want?"

"More horses," the chief grumbled.

"You've already taken all the horses. We cannot give you what we don't have," Anza replied.

The moment Ignacio had finished passing along Anza's response, Indians took off in every direction, waving weapons, screaming, and making away with whatever they could grab.

De la Cruz turned to Anza and said, "Wrong answer."

Gonzo ran up to one of the braves struggling with the wagon rigging trying to steal the mules. The jennies bayed with their heads in the air and wouldn't move.

Anza grabbed the old man's arm and shouted, "Leave the animals, save yourself, man!"

Apache placed their guns to the heads of the docile, faithful mules refusing to budge for anyone but their master, and shot them right in front of us. Gonzo dropped to his knees, hanging onto to one of his beloved beasts that went down in her tack.

There was no waiting around to see what was going to happen next. Scucha grabbed the wailing mule driver hugging the jennie who had fallen to the dirt in her harness, and dragged the old man away.

There would've been no way for me to keep up if de la Cruz hadn't been pulling me faster.

Gunfire pops and Apache ranting drowned out the sound of our own feet pounding the ground.

"Do you still have to leak?" Anza shouted.

"Do you?" de la Cruz yelled back.

I thought my lungs would explode. Wisp, splat, an arrow struck the arch over our heads. Anza shoved the chapel door open with his arm out in front of him like a battering ram.

"In back...the president's quarters...*vámonos!*" he shouted.

Lowering the barricade bar, we ran down the aisle. Padre Santiesteban was kneeling in prayer at the altar.

"Father, come with us!" Anza cried out.

The stubborn old man of the Cloth kept his head bowed over his clasped hands. Without looking up, he said, "The meek shall inherit the earth."

"Someone has to stay alive to tell them what to do with it!" Anza yelled, bolting through the doorway behind the altar.

We were all inside when one last time Anza shouted, "Please, Father, I beg you, bring yourself to safety!"

Santiesteban continued to pray before the Christo. He looked up for an instant, and our eyes met. The expression on the padre's face was the sort that haunts a man long after seeing it. Bowing his head down again, I heard him say, "...I relinquish myself into your hands."

Slamming the door shut, the men began barricading the place with trunks, furniture, whatever they could move. Chairs and boxes were dragged to each window to support what weapons we had. All I could do was stand there like an idiot.

De la Cruz stopped pushing things around, put his hands on my shoulders, and with his eyes smoldering into mine said, "Lena, we're never going to be apart. Do you hear me?"

Gunfire popped outside.

"We're always going to be together. I promise you that," he repeated, squeezing my arms.

Savages were flinging torches to the base of the fort wall, setting fire to the stockades. Scucha was closing off the final window. A bang came on the blockaded door. No one moved or said a word. I thought I was going to faint.

A shout came from the other side, "It's Steward Juan Antonio Gutierrez!"

"Thank God! Let's get him in here now!" Anza shouted.

The men frantically moved everything that had just been put in place.

The door stayed open only long enough for the soldier with a bloodied leg to slip inside.

Anza came alive. If I hadn't known better, El Capitan seemed to be enjoying the scourge. Skillfully deciding on a whim which weapon to deal each of us, he handed out firearms from an armoire on the back wall.

"We're not going to use the slow-loading rifles unless we absolutely have to have the accuracy. Fire muskets until I say otherwise. We will not play their child's games. Do not fire unless our safety is about to be compromised."

My job was to reload. I was given an embroidered velvet sack bearing the Bourbon Spanish Coat of Arms, looking more like a fine purse worthy of the best milliner in Paris than an ammunition holder. The *Caja de Cartuchos* that appeared to be a lady's accessory was filled with lead and gunpowder casings.

I felt like I'd forgotten the first thing about it. I talked myself through -- shake a round from the small wooden cylinder, tear off the end of the lead's paper with my teeth, pour gunpowder into the half-cocked lock pan, the rest goes down the barrel. Slide the lead ball in, stuff the paper down with the rod, and hand the weapon to the next man reaching for a gun.

My hands were shaking so, I spilled more gunpowder on the floor than into a weapon.

Anza, de la Cruz, Escucha, Gonzo, Gutierrez, Ignacio, guards Reyes, Valdes, the wounded sentry, Villareal, even Father Herrera fired at Apache. It went on for hours, palms sweating, and thirst that never ended.

The sun slipped low. Shots were still exchanged.

From the charge of a small canon on the top of a chest at the window, almost single handedly Gutierrez penetrated Apache attackers as if it were a child's game. If the soldier fired, an Indian fell. And he did it with his right thigh oozing blood from gunshot.

The silence was eerier than the noise that preceded it. For but a few stray pops of gunfire, it was quiet.

The room glowed orange. Reed fires were burning along the river. Our water was gone. Sliding to the pounded earth floor with the empty pitcher in my hand, I cried, shaking like the coldest day of the year.

De la Cruz set down his gun, took me in his arms, and pulled my head to his shoulder. Stroking my tangled hair, he kissed my cheek.

"What have I gotten us into? I'm terrified, Salvador." I sobbed.

Contently gazing back at me as if relishing a newborn, he pressed me to his chest and whispered, "Even if we were to die now, I'd have no regrets being here with you, Léna. It's going to be all right. I know it. I can feel it. I don't know how. But it will be."

The air was thick with the smell of gunpowder. Indians outside congregated around the smoldering ashes, dancing, singing, and chanting shouts celebrating their victory as the last inch of setting sun streaked through our broken window coverings, shadowing fine gold slivers on the back wall.

The few of us lucky enough to have gone without a wound were spotted with the splatter of another's blood.

A single shot fired somewhere, immediately followed by the splintering window shutter, sent wood slivers flying through the room. Father Miguel cried out. Wood chips had pierced his arm. He'd taken lead in the chest.

I flattened myself on the floor with the others. Anza shouted across the room for Scucha, who was about to fire a musket through a crack in the shutters. The renegado dropped to the floor, and like a lizard frightened by a cat, crawled over to our huddle faster than I ever thought a person could move on his belly.

The dried reed fires burning along the river bed lit the side of Anza's face as he sat with raised knee in a corner of the room. Looking directly at the Indian, he said, "Someone has to reach the presidio and let Colonel de la Barilla know we're still alive."

Scucha shook his head and said, "Capitan, there are less than thirty soldiers, they will not leave their posts."

Anza pulled his hat tight with a tug, stared at his scout, and said, "There are probably thirty or more soldiers out guarding the pastured horses, and another thirty or so with the supply train due anytime. Barilla will know how to handle this, but we have to get word to him. We need someone fast and nimble to scale what's left of the stockade and run like hell about half a league."

Flat-mouthed, the former Apache stared at his commander. Grabbing an escopeta as if it were a buzzing fly to be swooped up into his fist, Scucha slipped out the window. Making his way toward what was left of the stockade wall, like a shadow, the renegado was about to vault over when a brave sitting on the limb of a nearby tree caught sight and leveled his weapon. A shot was fired, the barrel of Scucha's gun sparked, the weapon fell to the ground, and our only hope disappeared into the dark.

Other than popping up to peer through the slats of the broken shutters now and again, for the most part we stayed huddled on the floor. All we could do was to wait.

Hours passed. The mission grounds smoldered. Still no sign of help.

Anza was about to say something when the faint jingle of tack got louder. Four mounted Spanish soldiers were approaching on the road from the presidio.

With the sort of excitement in his voice as if he had planned the whole thing, El Capitan said, "The savages are going to be busy with those poor devils. We can't waste a moment, we must go now!"

No way was Gutierrez going to make it, blood spewed from the wound in his thigh with the slightest move. Leaning on his side, stationed at his cannon, he looked the other way and said, "Go on, get out of here."

One by one, with Anza putting a hand on each shoulder to make sure no one messed it up, we slipped out the window before he followed us through.

Crouched down, sneaking across the crinkling splinters of the smoldering stockade wall, trying our damnedest not to step on anything that would make noise, we crept up to the edge of the swamp dotted by tall grass alongside the river. My heart was in my throat.

A few scraggly trees were all that separated us from Apache hiding in wait for those four mounted soldiers. The brush was filled with Indians. I couldn't even swallow hard, they were so close.

Gonzo, the wounded Father Miguel, Igancio, the sentrys, Anza, de la Cruz, and I slowly lowered ourselves into the freezing water. The blasted silt on the bottom was slipperier than a frozen lake. Had de la Cruz not been hanging onto me to keep me from falling, and worst of all, making noise, we might've never made it. Those braves would've heard us for sure when the mud gave way and I chilled waist-deep.

Waiting for just the right moment, Anza peered through the shallow wall of reeds.

The savages on the other side of our thin covering leapt out to the road, pulled the soldiers from their saddles, and slashed those poor men to death.

El capitan knew the diversion wouldn't last long. Waving us on, our leader got us out of there for no other reason than those four soldiers being killed.

Climbing out of the water at the presidio, wet, cold, and shaking, we were greeted by the fort's wood barricades glowing in the Apache fires along the river, like a yet-to-rise theater curtain in the footlights, and the beautiful stink of livestock pens.

Anza caught the attention of a guard atop the watchtower. The gates were inconspicuously cracked and we slipped inside.

People and animals were everywhere. Anyone who could make it to the darkened presidio with the few beasts they were able to grab packed the fort.

Anza led the way to the colonel's quarters walking as though he had a tall man's legs. Scucha was leaning over Barilla's desk. I ran up to the Indian and threw my wet arms around his neck.

The renegado flung off his jacket, wrapped it around me, and said, "I was just telling the colonel, there's no need to send soldiers, they'll be fine."

It was a good thing we waltzed in when we did because Scucha was getting ready to go back for us alone, against the colonel's orders. Barilla had refused to send anyone to the mission.

Thank God for a blanket, a stale chunk of bread, and a tin cup of drinkable water. Sitting at the colonel's desk, hugging moth-food around my shoulders, I was about to dunk the crust when a ruckus sounded outside.

A soldier was lying on the ground without a stitch of clothes on. Having made it back to the presidio, single-handedly fighting his way through Apache, he'd been lanced, shot, and burned.

Someone ran off to get water, and a woman standing next to me whispered, "He didn't ask for anything but the padre."

Father Miguel administered Last Rites with blood oozing though his robe from his own wound, while the soldier gave a hurried confession, probably for fear he would die before he finished.

That was it. I had had enough. I ran up to de la Cruz, grabbed his arm, and said, "I want to go home, Salvador."

"All right, as soon as the last of these Indians clear out, we'll turn around. We can probably catch a ride back with the supply train."

"So it's that simple? We're just going to leave?"

"That's what you said you wanted to do, isn't it?"

Anyone would've expected a lengthy, ear-rattling soliloquy beginning with something like, you dragged me all the way out here, and for what? But he was so blasé that I demanded to know why he came in the first place.

He took me in his arms and said, "I thought that was pretty plain. I'm here because I want to be with you."

It was next to impossible in the dark to tell if he was being sincere or not, de la Cruz was so damned good at faking both earnest and delusory statements.

He pulled away and spouted, "Why do I always become *Salvador* when you're panic-stricken?"

"I'm not panic-stricken. I'm completely in control. Panic-stricken was a little while ago. I'm fine, now!" I yelled, attempting to ignore the corners of his mouth beginning to rise. "You want to be with me, is your answer? How can you possibly say that? I was your captive -- afraid for my life, I might add. You scared the shit out of me and now you have the audacity to tell me, you want to be with me!"

"Were you more frightened than you are now?" he said, trying not to laugh.

A flute, probably carved from one of the large river reeds, softly echoed in the dark from across the courtyard, blowing music to the moans of the injured soldier being carried off.

De la Cruz casually checked to see if his blade was still tucked in his boot. Sliding the knife back down into the rolled knee flap, he said, "So, shall I tell Anza the deal is off?"

WEDNESDAY, 22 NOVEMBER 1780

De la Cruz reached over and pulled my hair back. He knew it was coming -- the series of bilious spews, so fast I almost didn't hit the pan. Barfing over the side of the bed every morning quashed any doubt about it. I was pregnant. A combination of joy and inconvenience. Mostly, just another cause for worry -- a baby I wanted more than anything.

The night before, we stayed awake long enough to take off our blood-spattered clothes and line up weapons in case of another attack. Nothing happened.

The scout from the supply train made it through a passage unguarded by Apache, and soon after everyone was safely inside.

Small disorganized groups of Indians beyond the stockades, behaving more like school children than adversaries, randomly taunted soldiers in hopes of luring them out—and that was all.

I punched the few filthy things I had, one by one, into my sack, while de la Cruz pulled our tack from under the bed.

Throwing his saddle over his shoulder by the horn, he headed for the door and said, "West with Anza, or south with the supply train?"

My bag flopped onto the tattered blanket. Staring at the sagging horsehair mashed to the ropes, I thought about going home. Lord knew I wanted to. Turning back now would mean I could make it to Sevilla in time for Armando's baby to be born.

My heart collapsed when I tried to visualize the house I loved so well. The hacienda was fuzzy. If only the pain of losing Armando was. I didn't know what the hell to do.

I picked up my bag. Repacking the clothes I had only a moment ago stuffed in like rags, in a voice not much louder than a whisper, I said, "West…we're going west."

De la Cruz let the saddle thud to the floor. He took me in his arms, my favorite place to cry, and kissed my brow. The pirate's comforting touch had become as significant as sleep or food.

He lifted my chin and said with a spark in his eye, "If you were to leave now, you'd never have the chance to try my sheep-brain cassoulet."

"How can you be so detached from danger?"

"Do you mean the Northern Frontier or my cuisine?" he replied, ruining my cry.

"Aren't you afraid to die, like normal people are?"

"You are no more at risk than when you were in swaddling cloth in your mama's arms. Everything that has happened to you during your life has led you to this place, to be with me. You got here, did you not? Therefore you've never really been a risk, have you? Aren't you here, now, very much alive?"

"I didn't know you made sheep-brain cassoulet."

His moist lips seductively pressed into the palm of my hand. I reached for his face.

Pulling away, I said, "What do you mean if I were to leave now? If I was going, wouldn't you be coming with me?"

"I'm beginning to get attached to this place. The frontier has so many opportunities. And I believe a position has just come available for a new padre at the mission."

The scoundrel managed to make me laugh and I replied, "I suppose you'd be fine as long as they don't ask for references. You're insane…and shameless!"

"Come now, my dear Madeléna, why are you surprised? I'm a commoner with the education of a nobleman. I have the wherefore without the bounds of hereditary self-preservation. And, I'm a Basque Jesuit. *Basque* alone should've been questionable enough."

"I must be the one who is insane," I said, picking up my saddlebag only to let it fall again.

De la Cruz drew me to him. The kiss was long and slow, the kind that made me feel like a paper boat in a child's bath slowly sinking as it soaked through.

Scucha popped his head around the cracked door and said, "We're ready to ride."

"We'll be right there," de la Cruz replied without taking his gaze off me.

The renegado tenuously added, "El capitan has agreed to go with Barilla to inspect the remains of the mission before we head out for San Buenaventura. The señora can wait here."

"That's nonsense. The mission grounds are on our way. I'm going with you," I said.

"Léna, no, wait for us here, please," de la Cruz said, taking my hand.

"I lived through the attack. Surely, I can make it through what I've already survived."

My gut told me otherwise once we started on our way. Clinking tack and singing birds made it seem like we were out for a pleasure ride. But the closer we got to the mission remains, the deeper my doubts about having come along.

Our boots crunched the char of the scorched earth. There wasn't much left but a few wisps rising from the blackened rubble. Three or four stray goats that had been stolen found their way home, only to have the pads of their cloven feet burned in the crinkling embers.

Ransacking the storage facility and all the houses wasn't enough. What the Indians couldn't steal, they destroyed.

Everywhere I looked my gut wrenched with the sight of a fragment of something, a devotional painting, icon, or ornament peeking through the ashes of the church, partial boxes and bales of flour, soap, chocolate, and tobacco, blackened bodies, parts of bodies, a leg, a hand, or unidentifiable portion of a person.

The blackened body of Father Santiesteban, where I last saw him at the church's altar, had been scalped. His eyes were gone from their sockets. Sticking out of his chest, a lance with its decorative feather silently moved back and forth in the breeze.

The capilla quarters where we had barricaded ourselves during the attack was unrecognizable. Juan Antonio Gutierrez, still clutching his small canon, was burned black. They even killed the mission cats.

Barilla's men were carefully lifting a partially burned, beheaded Santo from the rubble, when a small gold charm on the ground flashed a wink in the sun. Brushing the ash away, I picked up the familiar symbol that probably had been an offering pinned to a vestment. It was exactly like the flaming heart medallion on the entrance gate at Hacienda del Sagrado Corazon.

Tears didn't have a chance to flow. Rattling wheels from the supply-train wagons heading south were interrupted by thuds and hollers. A girl had jumped or fallen to the ground. Picking herself up, she wiped a hand across her face, stared at the man driving the wagon rolling off with the others, turned around, and came our way. What a sight she was -- barely into her teens, sunbaked fair skin reddened almost to the color of her hair.

"Are you all right?" I asked.

"Can I go with you?" she said, tripping over a blackened piece of something. She had a welt on her cheek that took up the whole side of her face.

"My family was killed during the attack. Dat's my husband driving away right now," she cried, pointing to the supply train disappearing around the bend. "Please take me with you. I don't care where you're going. I can't stay here a 'nother minute."

Anza was trying to keep the corners of his mouth flat, but his disapproval was beaconing. The bottle scar on his cheek distorted and he said, "You'll have to have a horse if you're going to come with us."

The girl started crying. De la Cruz pulled coin from his pouch, turned to one of Barilla's men, put the gold piece in the soldier's hand, and said, "How much for this horse? Will this do?"

The military man lit like a fire spark. Handing the reins to the pirate, he ran off before the deal could be rescinded.

Handing the horse to the girl, de la Cruz said, "You can come with us."

"Thank you, God Bless you," she wept with a smile, reaching out to touch his arm.

"I'm afraid it's a bit late for that." He laughed.

"What's your name?" I asked.

Sniffing back the last of her tears, she pulled her smudged sleeve over her brow to dry her huge blue eyes and said, "My name is Avril, but 'dey call me Spring."

A cloud swept the pirate's face.

MONDAY, 11 DECEMBER 1780

Long, low, puffy white clouds dotted the horizon like the froth of a heated beverage around the edges of a cup. The sun warmed our shoulders. We weren't getting our shoes sucked off by mud, nor were the thorns ripping us to shreds. Flies weren't stinging either. It was downright pleasant.

Pointing out the absence of speared bodies lying around, de la Cruz described the Guzman valley as the vacation spot of the Americas.

No matter how tranquil it seemed to be, the lowlands could've easily been a sanctuary or a deathtrap. There was only one way in.

Spring made the most of her time on the trail. I caught her gazing longingly into Anza's eyes more than once. And when that went nowhere, she turned her attention to de la Cruz, offering him a worthy return on his investment by claiming to be indebted to him for the horse. She never let me see that little gratitude. The only reason I knew about the less-than-subtle overtures that had apparently taken place was because de la Cruz told me. When I asked him why he didn't accept the invitation from a beautiful young flaming-haired woman, he simply replied, "Be second to Anza's disfigured face? You cannot be serious."

The privateer was, however, more forgiving than I. He dismissed it all by saying that she was just trying to survive by doing the only thing she could.

Riding side by side behind the men, happily yakking to each other to the creak of leather, Spring's wisdoms came forth in spite of the fact that she had no education.

"You was probly wunderin' why I'm here, weren't ya?" she said for no apparent reason other than the sight the pueblo coming into view.

"You don't have to tell me if you don't want to," I replied.

"My husbin' caught me with 'nother man. Or I should say, boy. An he, my husbin' never let on he done found out. 'Cause I think my husbin' was 'fraid that if he hurt me, my brother would whip his ass. So he jus' kept all that resentment and anger inside, eatin' hisself up for months waitin' to strike when I wus helpless. All my kin got killed by Apache, an' if I didn't know better, I'd say he planned that Indiun attack jus' so he could pretend for us to pack up and start a new life down in Mexico City. 'Cause he waited 'til we were headed south with that supply train before he beat me and done throw'd me out of the wagon, citing that infidelity, that I didn't even knowed he knew. But ya know, all da times I did it. I never got with child. I guess I never done it with the right one, 'cause my momma used to say, the Lord don't make mistakes wit babies."

"The timing could've been a little better with mine," I replied.

"You got a baby in you?"

"I barf every morning with the cock's crow, and haven't had my monthly since before...since being in Spain. I probably should've turned back and headed south with the supply wagons."

"You coulda gone wit my husbin' to wherever it was he was goin.'" She laughed.

"If I knew about the baby, I never would've dreamt of going anywhere, let alone a hell-hole like this."

A vulture squawked, flapped his chewed-up looking wings from behind a scrub bush, and Spring said, "Dose buzzards so lazy they won't even fly unless dere's a breeze to carry 'em 'cause they don't wanna work."

Sitting straight up in the saddle that was too big for her small ass, she opened her arm wide to display the sight, moved her hand across the sky, presenting the view as if it were her own creation, and said, "'Cept for that scraggly bird, dis here ain't no hell-hole. Look at dat!"

Mountains peeked their tops behind a distant bluff almost as blue as the sky, spring-fed pools and reed-like grasses poked through the desert flanking our sides, and up ahead the San Buenaventura Presidio and Mission burgeoned forth like a solitary jewel in the middle of untouched waste.

Wherever the mule refused to move, was where the house was built. At least, that was what it looked like. Homes sprouted up from the lifeless desert at unexplained locations.

The settlement's limestone buildings, far more refined than any of us had seen for a good long while, were so bright in the mid-day sun, it hurt your eyes to look at them.

Spring leaned back against the saddle cantle and spouted, "Oo Woman, dere's a party happenin' here tonight. And we be just in time!"

Candles wedged into the sand along the main street waited to be lit at dusk, paper flowers hung from hitching posts, decorations were everywhere.

My horse took a shy with the spark and pop of black powder set off by three young boys in front of the mission church. The celebrating had already begun on the eve of the two hundred forty-ninth anniversary feast day of Nuestra Sénora de Guadalupe, as significant to Mexico as Santiago was to Spain. And it didn't look like anything had been spared.

For a piece or two, a family of baptized Indians welcomed us to stay as long as we liked. The new husband, wife, and baby recently took up residence with the wife's sister. The extra coin was worth far more to them than the lack of room guests would create in the tiny casita.

Carrying on conversation with our hosts involved a great deal of head nodding and smiling orchestrated to make it look like we knew what they were saying, but we could barely understand a word of their Byzantine form of Castilian mixed with Indian and Aztec tongues. The deeper we got in the frontier, the tougher it was to communicate. And from the looks on their faces during the limited talk we exchanged, they probably didn't get much of what we were saying either.

Ready to go track down prey with Scucha and our host, Anza and de la Cruz acted like bringing back a contribution to the fiesta table was going to be a chore, but they couldn't wait to get to the bluff and start shooting things.

De la Cruz was about to pick up his gun when he lifted the screaming baby I had tried to quiet for nearly an hour and kissed the child on the forehead. The baby stopped wailing, smiled, and cooed with delight.

It wasn't the wink and a smirk I got that landed a punch. The instant de la Cruz handed the baby back to his mother the infant began crying.

Mumbling something about puppies liking him too, the pirate segued into a lengthy gripe about how much he was looking forward to getting back on a horse. But the spark in his eye as he tightened the saddle girth and slid his gun into its holder told otherwise.

Scucha was about to hop up onto his piebald when Spring put her arm around the Indian and gave him a kiss on the mouth right in front of everyone. The only thing that kept the red man from turning the color of his new woman's hair was the darkness of his skin.

De la Cruz and Anza subtly inferred that something must've happened behind the barn, and although they managed not to laugh, equivocal remarks followed about how the renagado had finally adapted to white man ways.

The four rode off toward the bluff looking for turkey or boar if we were lucky.

The men were still in sight when parading toward the house, a group of children from the mission singing songs and banging sticks on skins stretched over wooden buckets followed a *cortège* that had huffed all the way from the church.

Winded individuals, heaving from their labor, carried a barge holding a Santo of the Virgen de Guadalupe, while the padre waved a Holy Vessel on a chain spreading the sweet smoky smell that had become all too familiar. There was no incense, so black powder was used instead.

The padre blessed the house with a sprinkling of holy water, drew a candle-soot cross on the beam over the door, we put paper flowers from a dye bath tin the girls had on the fire next to the offerings that had already been left, and that was it. The procession departed, huffing toward the next home quite a hearty walk away. The whole thing, prayers and all, lasted but a few minutes.

Truth was I could fight Apache better than stitch. The clothes I had didn't fit very well. So, I took a stab at sewing. Several stabs as it turned out.

Getting the needle threaded while I was wobbling around on a chair missing one leg didn't help either.

Spring sat on a little milking stool next to me, watching so intently she even said "Ouch," when I dropped a spot of blood from my thimble-less finger.

The young mother and two sisters, girls who had merely ex-changed their rag dolls for a real baby, were stirring the tripe pot hanging from an iron hook over the fire. The infant was crying. I was trying to stitch. We were a family.

Pushing her wild tangled fiery tresses away from her eyes, my friend looked up from her seat beside me and asked, "You done it wit more than one guy?"

"Only one," I said.

She gave me a little pat on the arm. "What I mean is… did you have to do it a lot to get with a baby?"

"No, I suppose not," I replied, pulling a crudely made stitch through its loop.

"I done it wit so many -- it's not my fault dey like me."

"You could say no."

She widened her huge blue eyes, laughed, and said, "How ya do that?"

I picked up a lock of her tangled red hair. "I could try to get some of these knots out, if you like."

Pounding hooves out front slowed. Horses snorted to a halt.

I didn't wait to see if it was friends coming to call, I knew the men wouldn't have returned so soon. I scrambled for the Trabuco. The three-legged chair hit the floor. A huge bang swung the door wide. Filling the house with the stench of tobacco and excrement-soaked animal-skins, a mountain of a man with a patch over his right eye shouldered his way ahead of his two companions, as if he were shrugging off varmints.

Jumping to her feet, Spring's wild flaming locks distracted him long enough for me to yank my hand away as fast as I could, leaving the gun upright in its corner.

The young mother grabbed her wailing son from his cradle and hugged him to her chest. Clutching each other, the sisters screamed.

Reeking worse than a three-year-old privy, the huge man with a ratted beard melting into his buffalo cloak took up half the house. It was only when he moved you could tell where his hair ended and the animal fur began.

Walking around the room, surveying everything like he'd just taken ownership, the big one ducked for each supporting beam to keep from bumping his head, something he most likely learned to do after cracking open his brow a few times.

Who the hell was this? The monster took up the whole house clunking into furniture or bumping the wall, not only with his size but with all the junk hanging around his waist and over his shoulder.

Rattling with every step, his powder horn, trabuco, espada an-cha, knives, and pistols were in front of me more than once. So close, I could've just reached over and swiped a gun or knife as he walked by. All I had to do was yank the weapon from its hanger when he was looking the other way. But I didn't.

The stinking man leaned over for a feel of Spring's nearly or-ange hair. His clumped locks fell away to reveal a huge scar, part of which was covered by an eye patch. The disfiguration looked like a portion of his flesh was gone, and it was so big, it spanned the whole right side of his face.

"Will you look at this one," he said, taking hold of my friend's arm with a hand that only had two fingers.

One of the women screamed, *"Dos Dedos!"* And they all began rambling unintelligible appeals in each other's arms.

None of it meant anything to the outlaw who must've been the Frontier's infamous Sugar Jack. He walked over to the panic-strick-en girls, raised his arm, and pounded one of them so hard, the bones of her jaw cracked as she fell to the floor wailing.

Dos Dedos stood over his prey, looked down at her whimpering at his feet, and shouted, "Shut up!"

He lumbered back to our side of the one room house, each step swabbing the pounded dirt with his animal skin boots. My stomach bumped into my heart.

Like a half-wit, I took a fast blink at the trabuco leaning up against the wall in the corner behind the door.

The monster sloshed a splat onto the freshly whisked floor, pinched my upper arm with his claw, and showing tobacco-stained lips through his matted beard spit out, "Goin' someplace, little girl?"

The devil went over and picked up the gun. Tossing the weapon right into my hands, the badman threw his head high and roared so loud it hurt my ears. "Is this what you lookin' for? What were you spectin' ta do – shoot me?" He laughed.

Level the gun and fire right into his chest. That was what I should've done. But, what if it misfired? What if he grabbed it from me and pulled the trigger? What about the other two men? I stopped dead.

Dos Dedos ripped the trabuco from my hands, threw it to one of his compadres, and went over to the iron tripe pot that had been sitting over the fire all day. Either he couldn't feel the heat or was too stupid to realize the simmering stew was scalding, there was no telling. He picked up the handle with the bare fingers of his claw hand and tossed the cauldron onto the table with a splash.

"What's for supper?" he yelled, glaring at me and Spring.

The donkey's ass plunged the dipper into the pot and scooped a steaming ladle into his mouth.

The boiling stew had been on his tongue for two or three ticks of the clock before he screamed and spit it on the floor.

His men let loose with laughter as if seeing their boss get hurt was the funniest thing they'd ever witnessed.

The outlaw got more pissed than he already was. With a huge sweep of his arm, the two-fingered criminal growled and elbowed the pot to the floor, spraying the night's dinner everywhere.

The baby screamed. All three women cried.

Spring's rainy palm took my hand. Shaking like the middle of winter, we exchanged looks.

Our lack of reaction wasn't exactly what Dos Dedos had in mind.

"How come you're not crying?" he snapped, grabbing my arm in his scorpion-like claw. Then he took hold of Spring, shook her with a bunch of wags, and shouted an inch from her nose, "Why aren't you crying like the others?"

Fear had to be ripping through that girl but she didn't make a peep.

Dos Dedos went back to the mother clutching the wailing infant in her arms. He plucked the child from her chest. She screamed. He raised his arm threatening a strike across her face, but instead just calmly sat down at the table with the baby on his knee.

Dropping every jaw in the room, the outlaw sat there making made soft cooing sounds, bouncing the infant up and down on his lap, as if it were his own. The little one was all smiles.

We could do nothing but watch while his men ransacked what little there was, tossing pottery onto the floor, scattering chards everywhere, turning the family's meager belongings to trash.

Dos Dedos began losing interest in the game and along with his waning amusement, the roughness of play increased. The bouncing had reached a point where the fun became uncomfortable for the child. Smiles turned to tears and soft utterances became wails. The baby screamed from being jolted around. Sugar Jack did it anyway.

An empty gaze fell over the badman's face. Emotionless, he pulled a pistol from his belt and said to the child, "You don't like that? All right, we'll put an end to it."

Sugar Jack put the barrel of the gun to the baby's head and pulled the trigger. The walls echoed with shrieks. Click, snap, the weapon misfired.

The mother took leave of her wits and lunged at the outlaw.

Pushing the woman to the floor with the point of his pistol, the bad man threw the weapon down with a thud, ripped a second firearm from his belt, held the gun to the crying child's head and fired.

A stray drop of soup finding its way to the earthen floor was the only sound.

From the looks on their faces, I doubt either of his men thought their boss was going to do it. They froze and stared in disbelief like the rest of us.

Specks of blood and flesh dotted our faces, clothes, the floor... everywhere.

Empty arms dangling at her sides, the mother stood and stared. She began to laugh. The sisters, like mourners sent to accompany the sentenced up the guillotine steps, took the woman by the elbows as she collapsed, screaming and crying in their arms.

Sugar Jack's appetite had not been satiated. He pressed on Spring's shoulder until she was forced to sit down on the milking stool next to me.

Bile crept into my throat as he picked up my three-legged chair and pushed me onto the wobbly seat.

Towering over me, his stink was almost more than I could take. Spattered with baby blood, his face was right in mine, glowering like I was something to be squashed.

He reached into the pocket on his belt. Piss ran down my leg. I wouldn't even know I'd done it, had I not felt the wet. I wanted to get the hell away from him so badly, I almost went over backward, grabbing the wall behind.

Pulling out a small tobacco pouch, Dos Dedos swung the thing in my face. Then he dangled it back and forth by its tightening strings in front of Spring. He was so close to her, the scratchy edges of his beard must've tickled her chin. She didn't even flinch.

Back and forth he went with a vicious grin, taunting me, then Spring. Rubbing the pouch with his two claw fingers as if it were a magic lamp, he popped it against my nose and said, "Do you know what this is?"

Loosening the draw strings, the freak took out a wad, stuffed the tobacco in his cheek, turned the pouch on its side and shoved it under Spring's nose.

Her eyes got huge when she realized what it was. At least she was smart enough to hold her tongue, which is what I should've done.

He drew the strings closed with his teeth and swung the bag made from a human female breast, laughed, and rattled, "See, I have purpose for women. This used to be on an Injun."

I looked Dos Dedos straight in the eye and said, "Well, I suppose there is one way then that a woman would let you touch her tit."

Sugar Jack's men laughed so hard one of them fell on the floor holding his belly. I wished they hadn't taken quite such an intense liking to the remark, because the frontier's infamous ogre wasn't about to have his reputation sullied by an unarmed girl.

Growling like a mad dog, he grabbed the collar of my shirt and with a rip that stung the back of my neck, tore it half way off me with his pinching claw.

My heart beat so fast I couldn't catch my breath. I braced for the strike. But Sugar Jack never got the chance. At first I didn't know what stopped him. Then I heard the distant galloping hooves steadily beating louder. Those horses were going like blazes, too.

"See who that is!" the big man yelled.

Peering out the window, any loyalty the compadres may have had went that way. They took off wide-eyed and without a word.

Jack snapped the trabuco up from the table, grabbed Spring around the waist, and hanging onto her like a bundle of cornstalks, headed for the door.

"Put me down! I ain't goin' nowhere wit you!" she screamed, waving her fists at him.

Dos Dedos turned to me and shouted, "I'll git you -- you just wait!"

Spring was flinging punches at the badman's belly, but little good it did. He hurried out with her packed under his arm.

I ran after them, screaming, "Run, Spring...run! Run!"

The demon had her slung over the horse's neck in front of him, whipping his mount on the shoulder and under the belly as hard as he could with the whack and slap of his reins.

"He's got Spring! Dos Dedos has Spring!" I screamed, pointing to the horse headed out of the valley.

Still at a gallop, de la Cruz had his boot pulled from the stirrup and one leg over the saddle with gun in hand.

Sugar Jack and one of his men were already in a dust cloud. The third tried to make off with Rojo and spent far too long lagging behind. The Big Red wasn't having any of it. My horse had planted himself like a statue outside the corral, nostrils flaring and his head-harness dangling over one ear while the third outlaw finally galloped off on his own horse.

They were getting away by the time Anza and Escucha slid their frothed mounts with clinking bits to a stop in front of the house. Those animals were lathered and roaring wind so hard, the men were being pushed up and down in the saddle.

The first outlaw was just as good as gone but Escucha fired anyway.

Anza pulled a rifle from the scabbard on his saddle, leveled the gun, and took aim. With the click and snap of the flintlock, the hombre who had tried to steal Rojo fell from his horse, hitting the ground in a puff of dust, arms flopping like a cloth doll before rolling into a motionless pile.

The moment de la Cruz dropped the reins, his horse went to the ground with his tack on, collapsing in exhaustion.

Sweat dripped from the pirate's brow as he leveled the only loaded weapon they had, and put the sight to his eye.

Dos Dedos was getting farther and farther away. But, we could still hear that flaming-haired girl screaming.

Escucha shouted, "Our horses will never be able to go after them, take the shot!"

The outlaw and Spring were getting smaller. Still there was no fire.

Taking his finger off the trigger, agony creased the former-priest's face as he lowered the Trabuco and said, "I can't make the shot without hitting the girl."

"She's dead anyway, you know that, don't you?" Anza shouted, ripping the gun from de la Cruz's hand and firing.

We just stood there watching as the badman's horse disappeared from sight with Spring's screams fading along with the hoof-beats that left smaller and smaller puffs of dust.

De la Cruz threw his arms around me. It looked as if he were going to cry. "Thank God you're all right," he said, holding on tight.

The embrace lasted only a moment or two before he pulled away, searched my face, and squeezed me into another hug.

Anza and Scucha went out on foot to see if the downed outlaw was dead, while de la Cruz and I led the Big Red back to the corral.

The infant's father had taken his only shot at turkey on the bluff. Neither the young mother nor her sobbing sisters were able to tell him the baby was dead.

"How did you know?" I asked, pulling Rojo's head collar off, latching the corral gate.

De la Cruz put his arms back around me and said, "Thank Escucha. He was squatting down on top of the bluff, staring at the same piece of dirt for a long time. Anza made some crack about the Indian having been with white men so long he couldn't track a rabbit anymore. We thought he was looking at game trail, but it was fresh hoof-prints headed this way. Escucha knew by the way the horses had left their tracks in the sand, one of them was being ridden by a big man. That Indian had a very bad feeling about it. Anza didn't like it much either, especially with the recent talk of Dos Dedos. He couldn't ever recall Scucha having had a sense that didn't turn out to be right, so we got back here as fast as those nags could run. When we were close enough to see three horses tied up in front of the house, we rode hard."

"He said he was going to get me!" I cried.

"Not as long as I'm around."

By the time sundown came, it was as though nothing bad had happened. The celebration everyone had been preparing for went on regardless. Escucha and Anza went to the presidio to drink with soldiers they hadn't seen awhile. Our hosts spent the night with neighbors. And de la Cruz and I stayed behind to return the home's interior to as close to normal as possible.

The generous offer that no doubt surfaced during a moment of weakness in which the pirate hoped to repent for a general lack of conscience required us to collect the baby's remains for an infant-sized coffin that one of the villagers had left outside the door.

What I could not bring myself to do, I left for de la Cruz, since he was the one who volunteered for the luxury.

We prayed that Spring might have gotten away, somehow. For the most part, the pirate managed to hide his remorse, except for one time when he spilled his heart after reliving the sight of a second Spring being carried off while he couldn't do anything about it.

I was beginning to feel sorry for him when he quickly returned to his usual blasé behavior.

Surprisingly, not only did de la Cruz refrain from dispensing a barrage of opinions, he also put up with my bombardment of complaints about the distasteful nature of the task he signed us up for.

With help from a pitiful bottle of spirits, we tossed worthless shards into the privy hole, mopped down the table and chairs and finally dunked ourselves, one after the other, in a large tub normally used for laundry.

I was so repulsed, I stood shin-deep in the water and scrubbed myself fully clothed, before disrobing.

"Here, you need another swig of this," de la Cruz said, handing me the bottle as we stood in front of the fire wearing nothing but a pair of scratchy wool blankets.

"Do you itch as badly as I do?" I asked.

"We can fix that," he replied, taking my wrap, tossing it away, and pulling me under his cover. "This one's not so bad," he whispered.

Green torchlight filtered through the tattered muslin window covering giving the inside of the house an unusual appearance. Music was coming from inside the city walls.

"How do the flames burn green?" I asked.

"Boric Acid," he replied, liked he'd been anticipating the question.

The emerald glow reflected in his eyes as he took my hands. Our blanket fell to the floor.

"Dance with me," he said, bare-fleshed in the dim green light of the darkened casita.

Slowly moving together, I felt his naked body against mine and said, "This isn't dancing."

"We're taking steps with our feet. I'm holding your hands. What more needs to be done?

"How is it you know how to dance?" I asked, trying to ignore his readiness and the bare chest warming my breast.

"I used to be very civilized," he said, moving his mouth closer for a kiss.

"We can't do it now, not like this. How can we even think about it?"

"Terror is an aphrodisiac," he whispered.

"Are you mad?"

"I might be. But when one is threatened, they may react with increased desire. Were you not excited when you didn't know who came up behind you at Candelaria? Were you not excited tied up on board the *Dolorosa?*"

"You're scaring me."

"Are you not excited now?"

"Is there anything you don't know?"

"Caviar buys one hell of an education."

"Salvador, you could've done anything. Why in God's name did you choose privateering?"

As if reciting a love sonnet, he continued our skin-to-skin dance and replied, "My sweetest baby girl, I may have mentioned this before, but allow me to embellish. You can have one idea about what you think your life should hold, when in fact, God has another. So when notions turn to dust, which they always do, I say fuck it and take the next thing that comes along, no matter what it is."

THURSDAY, 14 DECEMBER 1780

Janos had a bar. Not much else mattered.

Anza had begun talking about the drinking establishment ever since we left San Buenaventura. By the time we were only a few hours out, everyone was itchy.

The blossom was off the stem. Like an old couple married too long, Anza and de le Cruz were fraying around the edges. At least I got a laugh out of riding behind the pair.

Without turning to look at de la Cruz, Anza said, "Don't you ever stop talking?"

"What makes you think I was talking to you?" de la Cruz replied.

"I dunno, maybe 'cause you're riding next to me and your mouth is flapping."

"You're not listening to a word I've said anyway, why should you be concerned if I'm talking to you or not."

"'Cause you're making noise."

"I'm making noise? What about you yelling 'Scucha at the top of your lungs every thirty seconds? I'm surprised that Indian hasn't taken a hatchet to your wig more than once."

"What's your point?" Anza asked, finally turning to look at his riding companion.

"The point is... you're pretty shitty company."

"As I recall, you didn't hire me for my talents as an entertainer."

"Oh yes, that's right, how could I have forgotten, I hired the world's greatest Apache fighter."

"You're alive, aren't you?" Anza quipped.

"Am I? You call this living! You probably got us all killed back in San Saba and what I think I'm experiencing right now isn't life at all -- it's actually hell. And my eternal punishment is to be riding next to you listening to your Indian fucking fighting crap, drinking your wretched coffee grounds, which you cannot keep out of the cup to save your life, or ours -- and to look at that bottle scar stretch out of shape every time you think you know what you're doing, which you don't. How *did* you get that cut on your face? Don't tell me, it was a bar fight where you kicked six hombres at once."

"Seven. There were seven of them. I kicked seven asses, by myself."

"Wait, don't tell me...you're the only one left alive to tell the story."

"That's exactly right."

"I can't wait to hear this."

"You're about to go to the bar where it happened."

"Well, perhaps this time you might try drinking out of the unbroken end of the bottle."

Before Anza had a chance to retaliate, Utopia appeared.

The *Real Presidio de San Felipe y Santiago de Janos* wasn't a flimsy fort like the rest. The pueblo with a reputation for having been subjected to not only the greatest number of Apache attacks, but also the worst of all Indian sieges along the entire Northern Frontier, had a bar. They needed one.

About a league south of the Casa Grandes River, Janos had been there for nearly a century. Scattered homes, each with its own garden, sprouted beyond the protective walls of the fort. Inside, was a church, a coach house, a tavern, and a general store that had but a few things on its shelves.

We were dying to have a meal, find a bed, and see what we looked like without several layers of dust. But the first order of business after taking care of the horses was drinking. The men headed straight to the bar and I took a peek around the store.

Finding a pristine chemise, felt like Cortez discovering Eldorado. Neatly folded garments, one on top of the other, were sitting in a pile on a small table just inside the door. I went running to find de la Cruz for some coin.

He probably would've just handed me the money. But I knew the pirate would be far more likely to be generous after having downed a drink, so I waited until a mug or two had been lifted before asking.

The broken-down establishment that had for days been extrapolated as the peak of our journey was a hole in the wall with a cantina sign.

Anza's boot spurs clinked on the floor as he led the way inside. He was getting good at ignoring the pirate.

But de la Cruz was ready. He put out a hand blocking the doorway and said, "Your name is probably carved on the wall beneath a little shrine. Maybe I should go first. Someone is bound to recognize the world's greatest bottle-fighter...Apache fighter, that's what I meant to say."

Playing along, Anza stopped and opened his arm, allowing his mocker to walk in first.

We stood there sizing up the place while everyone inside did the same with us.

Following the dead silence that, no doubt, was on my behalf, commemorating the scarcity of women on the frontier, we sat in the last empty corner, avoiding the middle of the room, the most dangerous place in any bar.

Anza put his hat down on the corner of the odd carved table that must've been left behind by a prominent Spanish family, turned to de la Cruz, and said, "I would be very surprised if there isn't at least one place on the globe that you're not wanted for high treason for a tidy bounty."

De la Cruz categorically replied, "The only reward would be the short-lived satisfaction of knowing you killed me, after you'd gotten the living shit kicked out of you. Handing over a dead criminal has no monetary value, whatsoever. And that's the only way you could take me anywhere. In addition, you might wish to assess whether it's worth the risk of possibly waking up one morning to find yourself looking at several feet of dirt. So! Who's buying?"

A small furry brownish-gray rodent darted between decanters and disappeared down the neck of one of the bottles of rum or whiskey sitting on a shelf hanging from the rafters behind the bar. Whether Anza saw the varmint or not, he jumped to his feet and said, "What'll it be, *amigos*? Save your thoughts, I'm sure there's only one choice."

El capitan slapped his palm down on the worm-eaten knotty bar and said to the proprietor, "Four drinks, Señor."

Knott-hard forearms that had lifted a few heavy boxes in their time bulged out of the rolled-up sleeves of the stout ruddy-faced tender leaning across the bar, plainly running afoul of Anza's space. Cocking his head to the side for a clear view of our table, the barman pointed right at the Indian scout and said, "Not him."

One of the two men seated on the other side of the room pushed his chair back and crossed his arms, readying for the entertainment.

Anza put his face inches from the proprietor's nose, took the barman's shirt in his fists, and said, "The man you just pointed to is a Spanish soldier. Four drinks, *por favor.*"

Unlike most in his trade, this drinking-establishment proprietor lacked talent for sizing up clientele. The man reached over, took hold of Anza's shirt, and growled, "Maybe you didn't hear me. I don't serve anyone who doesn't speak Spanish. Get him out of here."

Knowing firsthand how de la Cruz dealt with drinking-establishment affrays, I glanced at the pirate just in time to see him inconspicuously reach into his sleeve and check his blade before slowly walking over to Anza's side at the bar.

Scucha's chair slid back. His deerskin slippers didn't make a sound as he crossed the floor, leaned over the bar, and said to the proprietor, "Would you be so kind as to provide me with a beer, whiskey, rum, or whatever brewed beverage you might have on hand? I would be much obliged."

De la Cruz slapped his fist down with a whack on the bar and said, "He speaks better than you do, moron."

Anza yanked the ruddy man's head forward, plunking his brow to the bar with a thud, and said, "Now, serve him a beer."

De la Cruz spun around, leveled his Trabuco in the direction of one of the locals with his hand on a pistol in his belt, and said, "You don't want to do that."

Lifting his fingers from the gun, the drinker put both hands in the air, wriggled his empty fingers, and grinned.

The barman's face was still pressed to the worm-eaten wood when Anza grabbed both the fellow's ears and lifted him off the plank just high enough so that de la Cruz could get in a good shove.

Shouting to the face oozing nostril blood, deformed from the pressure, Anza yelled to the barman as if he were across the room rather than inches away, "Can you say 'stop' in French?"

The tender screamed, *"Ya vasta, ya vasta!"* as a drip of blood seeped from his temple.

"What does ya vasta mean?" de la Cruz asked.

"Its frontier talk," Anza replied, as he and de la Cruz took turns smashing the keeper's head to the bar top, blood splashing after each whack.

"So am I correct in mentioning that this gentleman definitely has not said stop in French yet, has he?" de la Cruz asked.

Leaning over the bloody face on the bar, the pirate yelled, "Ya vasta?" isn't correctly spoken, you idiot, so I guess we won't be able to stop smashing your head into this bar until we hear whatever it is you were saying in… well, we know you can't speak French, so I'm going to give you a break and accept English. Just say stop in English and we'll allow your ugly kisser to come off this splintered piece of wood."

Anza whipped the barman's skull to the wormy plank again and said, "I thought you needed to hear it in Swedish?"

De la Cruz replied, "Yes, you're right, I must've forgotten. I need to hear *stop* in Swedish."

The keeper was spitting blood through reddened teeth when he finally gave in. "I'll serve him…I'll serve him! Truth is…I'm really low on drinks right now. I won't have enough to make it through this week, let alone this month. They get hostile here when there's no drinks, but I'll serve him, I'll serve him."

Anza and de la Cruz let go.

The bar tender moaned as he lifted himself up.

"Escucha drinks for free, got that. You've insulted him. So the Indian gets grog on the house. We'll buy three drinks. My friend pays nothing. Got it?" Anza quipped, rattling coins in front of the bloody barman.

The newly cooperative proprietor spewed, "Yes, señor. Yes, señor, I understand."

De la Cruz took a tilt of the mug and said, "I like this place. It offers just the sort of thing I enjoy after a long journey."

"You make friends easily don't you?" Anza laughed.

"As a matter of fact, I do," de la Cruz replied.

"Me too," Anza said, lifting his glass with a smirk.

We didn't enjoy a lengthy sit after sloshing back drinks. We were just about to walk through the door when someone said, "If they're headed to Fronteras, they'll git what's comin'."

The man who said it was looking right at me and added, "Yeah, some girl welted Dos Dedos real bad, and the big man ain't too happy, I hear. Matter of fact, he's promising to do somethin' 'bout it and says he ain't gonna quit till he gits her."

De la Cruz ignored the secondhand threats. He had the ability to shrug off just about anything. For me, it was a different story. The innocent didn't live long in the company of Dos Dedos, let alone someone who had made a fool of him in front of an audience. Regardless, de la Cruz acted as he usually did, as if nothing were wrong.

Our boots sank into the dirt outside. The pirate turned to Anza and said, "Has there ever been a time you didn't manage to get into a fight in this place?"

SATURDAY, 16 DECEMBER 1780

The Piebald's head went high as Escucha pulled to a halt at the edge of the bluff. Fixing his gaze out across the plain, the Indian waited for the rest of us to catch up.

The presidio at Fronteras looked close, but could've been as far off as half a league, or more. It should've been an easy ride. But smoke was puffing dots into the air. And underneath the smudges on the horizon a line of twelve or so mounted Apache stood on the crest of the far ridge.

Anza dismounted. Reaching into his saddle pack, he retrieved a small brass spyglass and took cover behind a scrub tree. Peering at the enemy, he said, "Yeah, they see the white men. And they're wearing war paint."

The glass wasn't back in its bag for more than few seconds when we heard hooves thundering. Battering the sand, Apache shouting war-cries descended the bluff heading right for us.

You would've thought those Indians were already in firing range by the way Anza grabbed the packhorse's headstall and started yanking bags from her rigging. "Get this thing off her now!"

De la Cruz leapt to the ground, pulled out his dagger, and began cutting away harness straps.

"What's going on?" I shouted as our supplies thudded to the ground.

"This mare can't run worth a shit even when she's not carrying a load. With this all this stuff she'll slow the others!" Anza hollered.

Escucha and de la Cruz tucked guns into their pants and tightened their saddle girths.

Every second, Apache grew closer.

Clenching an escopeta, Anza, shouted, "We can fire two, maybe three decent shots." He grabbed my leg and tried to pull me out of the saddle.

"What are you doing?" I screamed, pulling my boot back.

"Rojo is the fastest of this lot! It's too dangerous for you to be out front. Take Scucha's horse!"

"No! I'm riding Rojo!"

"Change horses now!" Anza ordered.

"I'm staying on *my* horse!" I screamed, digging my spurs into the Big Red with one swift kick. The gelding lifted his forelegs, tucked his butt under, and ran like a rabbit that'd just seen the dogs.

"That pain-in-the-ass-girl's making dust! *Vamenos!*"

Rojo didn't even think about going around scrub. Heading straight down into the canyon, we jumped cactus bushes and everything else that got in the way.

The others were right behind us in a whirling dirt-cloud as our horse's hooves dug into the bluff's embankment. None of the others was a match for Rojo, especially the struggling little pack mare that couldn't keep up.

Winding my fingers into the red stringy hairs high on the big gelding's mane, I kept low. My life depended on staying on top of the horse. And a banging heart made me very well aware.

We got onto the flat. I gave Rojo his head. The Big Red stretched out with strides so huge, the other horses had to take nearly twice as many paces just to stay close.

With the wind whipping mane-hairs, stinging my cheeks, I couldn't keep my eyes open for more than a second or two. The ground was going by so fast down past Rojo's throbbing shoulder, everything was a blur. When I did manage to peek up for a moment to make sure we were headed toward the presidio, my hat buffeted so violently behind my head the neck cord just about strangled me.

Apache cries grew louder. Their fresh horses gained on us.

With the wind and thunder of hooves, I barely heard de la Cruz yell, "How will they know to open the gates?"

Trying to keep my eyes open for at least a second, I looked up. The presidio doors were closed! We were galloping as fast as we could toward a wall.

"They'll see us. Just *yell*...yell in Spanish! They'll open the gates!" Anza hollered.

Red was the sort that would push on with all he had until it killed him. The big horse was nearing exhaustion and if I didn't stop kicking, he might not make it. I backed off.

What in hell possessed me to look? I nearly swallowed my heart. Those Indians were so close, the paint smeared on their war cry shouting faces was plain as day.

An arrow wisped the air, barely missing Rojo's head. I screamed.

Anza caught up and put himself between Rojo and rushing Apache. Bunching his reins in one hand, he hung his heel over the horse's back and slung over the side.

Galloping on as fast as that nag could go, Anza leveled his escopeta under the horse's neck, took Apache into sight, and fired.

The Indian nearly upon us fell from his pony, hit the ground in a puff of dust, and instantly disappeared as we bolted on.

We were close enough to the fort to make out a soldier on the tower with gun in hand. But the presidio gates were still closed. And the savages kept charging.

Anza completely out of the saddle, dangled next to his horse's legs, hanging on by clenching the horn.

Escucha and de la Cruz shouted, "Open the gates! Open the gates!"

Click-pop, soldier flintlocks fired at Apache. I yanked leather with all my might. Rojo was too tired to sit on his hocks. I couldn't get him stopped down even though I was pulling as hard as I could.

We were about to hit the gate and die. The doors parted.

The seconds of relief after galloping inside vanished when I dismounted. An Apache arrow was stuck in my saddle cantle. I could hardly breathe.

De la Cruz came up beside me, horse in hand, and whispered, "That arrow was closer to your ass than I'm probably ever going to be."

"I was almost killed!"

"But you weren't," de la Cruz replied.

"No, I wasn't, but --"

"There aren't any *buts*, except yours. Close doesn't count. Nothing matters as long as you're all right. If you're unharmed, it's the same as whatever it was that threatened you never having happened, so let it go. I can't even begin to tell you how many times I've nearly been killed. See how fine everything is with me." He laughed.

The lathered, sweat-darkened horse that de la Cruz had ridden to safety moaned like a child with a belly ache, and stood heaving with legs splayed.

Pushing me wide to get me out of the way, de la Cruz hurried to loosen the saddle riggings. "Watch it, he's going to go down."

The animal buckled at the knees, fell over, and made a few disoriented kicks in the air.

"He's going to be make it, isn't he?" I asked, scooping the bridle over the horse's ear.

It took all three of us, Escucha, de la Cruz, and me, to get the tack off. A lifetime around horses and I'd never seen one tie up like that.

Setting a bucket down, the renegado got on his knees. Dipping his hands in the water, he softly chanted in his native tongue, the long braid in back of his head gently swaying side to side. He wetted the gelding's head, neck, and thighs with gentle strokes. The horse's breathing slowed and its eyes showed more brown than glaring white.

The Indian looked up and said, "He's going to be fine, just leave him right where he is."

De la Cruz took my hand and said, "Walking to Bac is rather unappealing, so I'm going help Escucha nurse my ride, why don't you go to the chapel and I'll meet you there when we're finished."

There wasn't a lack for a prayer or two -- the sight of that arrow stuck in my saddle was a little much to forget so I obliged.

A big balled-up weed blew across my path on the way to the church just about the time a tear had washed a dustless line straight down my cheek.

Over the previous days, random attempts to steal cattle and sporadic Apache attacks threatened the area in a series of events that were referred to as a minor uprising. Several had been hurt and everyone was on high alert.

I wished I hadn't looked in the font just inside the chapel door. Right after I dipped my fingers, I noticed the Holy Water was red from the wounded readying to cross themselves.

Far more people packed that tiny outland chapel than any big city church in the Old World.

On his knees at the altar, the Apache fighter didn't look when I knelt beside him. Anza was pissed. He had to have known I was right there, but he went on with his plea just the same. "... Santiago, obtain for us strength in the unending struggles of this life. Help us to follow Christ constantly and generously, to be victors over all our difficulties, and to receive the Crown of Glory in Heaven. Amen. You could've gotten us all killed. Where do you come off not obeying orders? I could take you right now and thrash you over my knee. I knew there would be trouble when Ontiveros gave you that horse. Where is your husband?"

"My husband is dead."

There was no need to peek, I knew he was staring.

Anza grabbed my wrist with a bit too much enthusiasm. Keeping me in his grasp as I knelt beside him, he looked up to the altar as if pretending to still be in prayer, and calmly asked, "Who is the man you are with?"

"He's the privateer who took me from my ship," I whispered, keeping my head bowed and hands clasped.

Striking with similar confidence to that during a surprise Apache attack, Anza said, "Señora, I offer you sanctuary."

"De la Cruz is risking his life to take me to San Xavier, and will risk his life to take me home."

"Señora, I will take you around the globe, if that is what you wish. And, should you choose to become my companion, you may discover that you do not want to be anywhere other than with me."

I didn't give Anza the immediate response he was looking for. Crossing himself, he got to his feet and walked out.

I didn't even know de la Cruz was there until I felt his arm against mine. The pirate was kneeling beside me. My stomach went sideways praying to God he hadn't heard any part of what was just said. He crossed himself, and whispered, "Anza's pissed. El capitan-the-great practically pushed me out of the way to get through the door. I don't give a bat's ass if he is in a bad mood -- I'm not looking forward to putting up with whatever happens to be yanking his tail at the moment."

"Why in heaven's name did I come here? I should've just stayed home?" I cried.

The kind eye of the Santo bloodied by a Crown of Thorns on the altar wall watched as de la Cruz took me in his arms, and with the same tone he probably used through the little confessional window at the height of his former career, said, "Léna, there is no what would've been. There is only what is. Difficult times are a test to see if you believe you're being taken care of. It's God's way of finding out if you think He's really with you."

"Salvador, I'm with Armando's child. If something happens to his baby, it'll be like losing my husband all over again."

I started crying and couldn't stop.

The pirate took me in his arms. The altar candles glimmered in his eye and he said, "Had you not come here, you'd have missed the opportunity to enjoy the pleasures of this lush, serene paradise. Maybe you should've just married that other guy; what was his name? You know the one your parents wanted you to take on as a husband. The fellow with a dozen pairs of satin pants and matching frocks. Your life would've been perfect."

"How did you know about the pants?" I replied with drying eyes.

De la Cruz put his arm around my shoulder as if he were making a business deal and said, "Let's see if I can talk someone out of a half-filled bottle of spirits and some food. We'll dine under the stars high atop the stockades, enjoying the view of the livestock pens, and the arrant epicurean cow-fart aperitif."

The priest-turned-pirate once again had me laughing through my tears.

Lord knew where he came up with that bottle.

Sitting together on the floor boards of the empty guard station lookout bridge, de la Cruz took off his huge-brimmed leather hat and poured the wine he conjured from somewhere into an earthen mug. It immediately began to leak out the bottom. Quickly lifting the spoils, the pirate allowed the scarce beverage to run into his mouth and said, "Not a drop of this distillery can be wasted. I had to pay extra for this prized local label aged inside a helmet once worn by Hernan Cortez."

He leaned over and kissed me. A cow farted in the pen below. The pirate pulled away and announced, "Dinner is served."

I laughed harder than I did in the front row at Moliere's *L'Ecole des Maris.*

"Be careful. You fall in love with the one who makes you laugh," he said, flipping his head back to slosh down the sting before handing me the bottle.

"Do I make you laugh?" I asked, taking a sip.

"Among other things," de la Cruz replied in a newly found tone of seriousness. His eyes flashed and he said, "I have us a bed. Not only did I secure the use of a mattress, it happens to be in a room with *only* eight or nine soldiers."

"Why do I feel so lucky?" I replied.

He leaned closer. Pushing his gray-not-quite-blue-eyed gaze deeper into me, he whispered, "Because you are."

We sat up there with the food he'd mustered in a bucket, and folded charqui into stale tortillas followed by the burn of the bottle until the sun was about to fall away.

De la Cruz pointed to the fading pink and orange sky hanging over the purple sand and with his scratchy cheek on the side of my face, said, "Never mind which way you're facing. Pretend this is a painting. See the tiny sliver of sun showing where the sky meets the earth? If you have no idea what time of day it is, how would you know if the sun is rising or setting? It could be moving up or down, sunrise or sunset. Am I not right?"

"I guess so, what's your point?"

"Ah, clever girl knows there's a point -- the beginning and the end are the same. You're looking at the answer to the question that has been asked since time began. It's right in front of you. Birth and death are alike. God painted the proof right there."

"Is this your serious side?" I asked, relaxing my squint as the sun dropped below the horizon.

"Occasionally I fall out of character."

"I think you might be falling into character."

"I have something I've been meaning to give you."

"Besides a hard time?"

"Léna, how can you be so unkind, I've been easy since the outset."

"Like when you tied me up and tore my clothes off?"

"You could've had my body from the moment we met. I'd say that labels me easy, does it not?"

"So, besides your body, what do you want to give me?"

"I'm only going to let you have it if you promise not to use it on me."

"Will you stop with the *Taming of the Shrew*! What is it?"

De la Cruz slid his fingers into the flap of his boot and pulled out the familiar little dagger with colored stones n the handle.

"Where did you find it? This belonged to my mother. Oh my God, Salvador, thank you all the way to the ends of the earth!"

I threw my arms around him and kissed the pirate until the desert turned blue.

De la Cruz finally pulled away and said, "Salvador?"

"I got excited. It slipped out, I'm sorry. How did you get it? How did you know it was mine?"

"I took it off one of the seamen, probably the slime that swiped it from you. Look at this thing, it obviously belongs to a girl. What kind of a man would carry such a bauble?" he said, nodding at the knife in my hand.

"I thought it was gone forever! You had it the whole time. Why are you just giving me the blade, now?" I asked, retracting a portion of enthusiasm.

"A blade? It's not a weapon. It's a trinket! The thing was designed for the pretend defending of a woman's virtue. What better place to keep up that masquerade than here?" He laughed, stretching out his arms in a mock embrace of the desert.

"I'll have you know I actually hurt someone pretty badly with that little dagger."

"I'm sure that you've hurt a good many without it!"

"I was actually thinking about doing it with you tonight. But you've ruined it."

De la Cruz leaned an elbow on the floor planks. Pulling me to him, he put his mouth on mine and felt my breasts through my chemise as if it were a necessary deed in order to kiss properly.

The power of his fingers on my belly just beneath the top of my pants gave me a twinge of zeal as he searched my eyes and solemnly said, "This should be my child."

An old man lighting sconces along the inside walls lifted his torch before inching his way to the next lamp. Branches of a scrub bush outside the stockades rustled. Perhaps it was the stir of a small animal escaping its hiding place. A dog barked. De la Cruz still had me in his arms.

We had emptied the last of the bottle when a soldier's flat-brimmed hat popped into view through the ladder opening in the floor.

The sentry placed his musket on the boards, came up from below, picked up his weapon, and said, "I'm on watch here for the night."

"I thought Apache don't attack in the dark," de la Cruz pointed out, helping me to my feet.

The sentry rested his gun on the stockade, peeked over the wall, and said, "There's more than just a savage or two out there."

"Well, it's a good thing, or you'd probably be wasting your time sleeping right now," de la Cruz replied.

The guard went on about how it was only a job and de la Cruz made several more uncalled-for comments including a quip about how all the safe careers must've already been taken.

We retired to our quarters. The pirate braided my hair and we briefly talked about riding out in the morning.

Packed together on the narrow rope-tied bunk, last in a line of at least a half-dozen or more, beneath a thin slice of wool sufficient for July, it felt wonderful to be close to him.

I always knew when de la Cruz had fallen asleep because he wouldn't be hard anymore. But for some reason he stayed awake.

The quiet was broken by singing insects beyond the stockades that refused to die with the onset of winter, an odd cough, sniff, or snore. The pirate must've thought I was sleeping because he whispered, "I love you, baby girl."

MONDAY, 18 DECEMBER 1780

Anza was jumpy. The Indians were in war-mode, and all he wanted to do was push on.

De la Cruz was of the mind that it wasn't because *el capitan* feared for our lives, but more likely because he needed to keep up his reputation. Getting scalped wouldn't have looked good on his Apache-fighter curriculum vitae.

Sieges usually came in waves. Apache would be quiet for weeks, even months at a time, then go crazy and attack over and over.

It was our luck to be in the middle of the frontier during the crazy period.

The only time Anza would relax was at night when the savages couldn't see either.

No one admitted it, but we were lost in the dark, somewhere on the edge of Apache territory between Janos and Tubac.

I'd bet anything, we walked across the same patch of soil more than once, but the renegado insisted we hadn't. One way or the other, it was starting to get light by the time we got our bearings.

Cold, tired, and hungry, the only thing worse was the sight of *char-qui* and *pinole*.

It must've been around mid-day since the shadows were short -- the renegado pulled up that pony of his that could stop and turn on a cat's whisker. Twisting around in the saddle, the fringe on his deer-skin pants flapped as he cupped his dark hand around his mouth and shouted back to us, "Take off your hats!"

Scucha told us to do something, and we did it without question. Besides it was futile to disagree with him. If the slightest doubt arose about the accuracy of one of his assessments, the Indian would somehow manipulate the facts to make it appear as though he had been right all along, a talent that won him respect from just about everyone.

As odd as it seemed, I took off my hat and stuffed it under my ass. A squashed head-covering was better than one that blew away.

Wearing a grin like he'd just won the three cups and balls trick, de la Cruz leaned back in the saddle, crossed his arms, and let the reins dangle around his pony's neck. The biggest hat known to mankind was nowhere in sight.

It was one of the few times Anza was without the tri-corner that made him look taller, so whatever was up ahead had to be serious.

El capitan turned all the way around in the saddle, put a palm on his horse's rump, looked right at me following him, leaned over, and said, "Unless you want to get us all killed, you might obey my command this time. Do not say anything. Do not look at them. Look straight ahead and keep your mouth shut."

Anza's tone got particularly scary when he inched closer by reaching even farther back on his horse's butt and said, "If you would like to keep all that pretty hair from bouncing around on the end of a hatchet, you'll do exactly as I say! You are not to look at them or say anything. *Comprende?*"

"You made your point, Señor Capitan," I replied as calmly as I could.

I suppose it shouldn't have been that much of a surprise when a group of Indians came into view. I thought I would swallow my heart at first. But the closer we got, it looked like they were more scared than we. There couldn't have been more than fifteen of them, mostly women, small children, and a few boys, maybe thirteen or fourteen years of age at best. Two of the women were mounted. The rest walked on foot with pack horses and sacks in hand.

The path was so narrow, the tapping of beaded fringe on a girl's dress as we passed by was plain as day. There was no need to look direct at them. The worried expressions on their faces, clearly visible out of the corner of my eye, made me think we probably surprised them more than they did us.

They disappeared down the trail without a peep. I punched a place to put my head back in my flattened hat, and trotted Red up alongside Escucha.

"Why did we have to take off our hats?" I asked.

Swaying his ass in the saddle with each step as if he and the horse were one, the renegado's fingertips were barely touching the reins. He looked straight ahead and replied, "Some tribes attack anyone wearing a hat. Only white men wear hats."

"You wear a hat."

Escucha took the long weed he'd been chewing on, flicked it into the brush, and gave me a quick smile. The squeak of leather with each hoof that quietly pressed into the sand was the only reply I got.

So, what the hell, I came out with the real question. "Scucha, how is it you came to leave the tribe?"

Several more squeaks of the leather went by before he softly said, "I did not leave Apache."

"But you're no longer part of the tribe, right?"

"If you are born Apache, you always will be Apache. I have taken white man ways, but I am still Apache."

"I don't think many would believe you can be Apache and be a Spaniard."

The renagado pulled the front tip of his hat down to cover the native beads strung around his forehead on a strip of leather. Flattening his mouth to hide the beginning of a smile, he replied, "You talk a lot for a small white woman."

"You're not the first to point that out. So do you still have Apache family somewhere?"

The piebald took a swish of his tail. Scucha's expression clouded, making me think I'd struck an out-of-tune chord.

"You want to know about Apache and Spanish? Both believe in evil spirits. Apache believe those spirits are to be appeased. The white man believes they are to be destroyed."

"Apache steal horses and cattle, is that not wrong?" I asked.

"You cannot own a living thing. Do you own the air you breathe? Apache believe horses and cattle cannot be owned, they are for everyone, just like the land, the air, the sky, the sun. Apache own no land. They occupy it, use it, and move on. It's the same with horses. Apache believe no one has the right to keep it from others, so they just take it."

"Well, what about the killing and torture?"

With a squeak of his buckskin pants on the leather of his saddle, Escucha turned to face me and said, "I worship your God now. And, I am not the only one. Many Apache have been baptized and taken Spanish ways. I feel about killing as you do. But you must understand that Apache believe enduring torture is bravery and courage. And death is an honor."

"What about the vengeance and killing for spite. At San Saba, they killed and mutilated without reason."

Escucha didn't come up with an answer quite so quickly. And had I not known him so well, I might not have noticed the smile he was trying to hide when he said, "No one is perfect."

Something grabbed the renegado's attention. Kicking the pie-bald into a gallop, Scucha said, "Wait here."

The Indian was still in sight when he halted in a puff of dust.

Anza and de la Cruz went to see what was going on just about the time the Indian shouted back, "Tell señora to stay there."

I wasn't about to be the one left behind. The three of them were looking at whatever it was and they were still alive, so I kicked the Big Red and hoofed sand.

The four of us sat on our horses and stared. Flies buzzed around five tall poles well over the height of a man.

It wasn't the sticks planted in the rocks that hollowed my chest, it was what was on top of them. Partially decayed, disembodied heads, covered with insects, cast small round shadows on the ground -- and Lord help us all, they had hats on. No bodies, just hats, on heads, on poles.

I could've handled the decapitated remains. I'd already seen that kind of thing at San Saba. It was those hats. There was something about seeing hats purposely put back on heads without bodies that made me sick.

Shadows faded with a passing cloud. Sweat beaded on my brow and everything went fuzzy just about the time de la Cruz leapt from his horse to grab me.

Next thing I knew, I was being pulled to my feet by the pirate and Anza tugging on each arm.

De la Cruz was brushing the dust from my jacket when we saw dark smoke rising in puffs on the distant bluff. When the wind blew just right, the faint rhythmic pounding of drums packed my heart into my stomach like the wrinkled clothes crammed in my saddle bag.

I didn't recognize Salvador. He looked worried.

Anza had seen all he needed to. Staring down at the sand, flipping the reins between his fingers, he gave a nod in the direction of the smoke signs and said, "One of two things has happened. Apache has spotted a group of Spanish cavalry...or they've seen us.

We could live with the cavalry in the neighborhood. The second scenario might not be as golden."

Following a brief private discussion with the renegado several paces away, Anza walked back to us and said, "Escucha is going to ride ahead for an hour or two. We'll break until he gets back. I don't think any of us wants to sleep tonight anyway."

The Indian flung his leg over his horse and sank into the saddle the way most would slip into a favorite chair.

It was my turn to say, *vaya con Dios*. Scucha was about to ride off, those words passed my lips, and I felt as though he wanted to reach out and touch me, maybe the squeeze of a hand or perhaps a casual embrace. But, of course he didn't.

Glancing down from the saddle, the scout tipped his hat, smiled, and said, "Have no fear, señora, all will be well."

The piebald's hooves echoed in the shallow canyon until they could no longer be heard. Scucha melted into the desert. I believed him when he said everything was going to be fine. The Indian was always right.

His hat vanished from view, and I recalled Armando before he rode off on our six-day separation, telling me it was a bad omen to watch someone you care for leave until they were out of sight. I wanted to look away, but I'd already seen Scucha disappear. All I could do was pray the scene had been the exception.

"Let's do something civilized," Anza said, rummaging the supplies on the packhorse.

Pulling out a small sack of coffee beans and a tiny grinding box, we put a few sticks together for a small fire.

The three of us drank the whole pot, and then another, and another. The sun had fallen below the sand -- Scucha hadn't returned.

I squatted down next to de la Cruz, who was tossing dry twigs on the fire to make more coffee.

Desert night life echoed when we passed the cup for the last time.

The renegado would've been back by dark. It was the first time I saw concern crease el capitan's face.

Shoveling sand with his boot, Anza covered the ashes of our tiny fire. With a final kick in the dirt he said, "*Vamenos.*"

TUESDAY, 19 DECEMBER 1780

I t looked like campfire ash. We got closer, and it was another
story. The char turned out to be the blackened corpse of someone who'd been set on fire.

Sifting the remains with his toe, Anza picked up a stick, squatted on the edge of the burned ground and poked around.

"Who did this...Apache?" de la Cruz, asked.

Anza pulled a piece of blackened metal from the ashes and
said, "I don't think so. Apache have purpose for everything. They
would've used a broken flintlock to grind corn, or Lord knows what.
It's not likely Indians would've left something like this behind."

An animal tooth on a tarnished silver band in the ash caught
my eye. I lifted the bone charm from the char and recognized the
thing right away. It was still warm.

I'd seen the amulet around Escucha's neck every day that I'd
known him. He never took it off.

I dropped to my knees and started crying.

Anza got down on one knee, put his arm around my shoulder,
and said, "Many men wear such trinkets."

"Where is he, then? Where is Scucha?" I wailed.

Anza tightened his grip around my upper arm. I knew he meant to comfort me, but his voice broke more than once.

"Escucha was a fierce survivor. It would have been nearly impossible for any man, red or white to have done him in. I cannot tell you how many times that Indian pulled us both out of a spot that would've killed anyone else."

Anza put his glove over his eyes and broke down to tears.

De la Cruz silently mouthed something that must've been last rites.

Quickly pulling in the rein on his emotions, Anza began sifting the ashes with his fingers, searching for something, anything that would've proved us wrong.

Plucking a few leaves of tobacco from the sand, he rolled the unburned flakes around on the tips of his fingers and said, "The killer enjoyed the pleasure of a smoke, while sitting here watching his victim tortured to death."

Anza's knees cracked as he got to his feet, stared out into the desert, took a huff, and said with finality, "*Dos Dedos.*"

FRIDAY, 22 DECEMBER 1780
TUBAC

A lone tree never fell from the whack of a hatchet. Maybe it was infested. Perhaps they just wanted to keep an example of what a tree looked like for future generations, since there were no others for as far as the eye could wander.

Four not-so-lucky trunks holding up the covered walkway spanning the front of Anza's enormous house had been axed into posts.

El capitan apparently had bags of money. The earthen-walled home looked like someone had dropped a ransom in the middle of the desolate plain and the home sprouted up from the coin.

We were practically on the doorstep. Nothing had been said about the woman. But there she was, waving from the front door, flapping a pale-yellow handkerchief over her head.

It was tough, but de la Cruz and I somehow managed to keep from laughing. At first sight of her, she was no bigger than a button. How in the world that woman recognized her husband from such a distance was amazing. She was yelling, "Juan Diego," right up until we pulled up at the house and even then, Anza didn't let on he had a wife.

I stood there with dried silt caked on my boots, with Señora Apache-fighter dressed for the opera. She ignored me and the pirate, gushed sonnet-like love phrases that would've turned a cobbler's face red, let alone the famous military-adversary-Indian-battle hero, and threw herself into her man's embrace.

By the way she was dressed, the doña had planned to welcome guests, but apparently the woman always looked as if going to tea.

Anza's rancho was the largest on the entire frontier. Maybe it was her money, but, wherever it came from there was a lot of it. At a time when almost everyone was in want for food, the Anzas had plenty.

Besides the usual char-qui, chile, corn, and nameless beans, they had garbanzos, garlic, onions, chocolate, sugar, honey, wine, and azafran. There was a stable, grain and hay buildings, corrals, pens, a huge herd of cattle, sheep, chickens, goats, fine horses, and at least half a dozen vaqueros tending it all. The earthen-oven spit out crisp-crusted wheat breads. Where silt was a luxury, spring water slowly dripped through a round porous filtering tub of lava stone, providing clear drinking water.

There was a house-keeper, most likely the wife or girlfriend of one of the vaqueros, but more-importantly, the doña didn't do a thing but needlepoint and get pregnant every once in a while.

We weren't yet accustomed to the idea of a Señora de Anza when we found out the frontiersman also had three children. The three sons were extremely shy, a characteristic they must've inherited from their maternal family, or perhaps another father. Anza hadn't seen his two-year-old boy since the child was in swaddling. The four-year-old didn't even recognize his father and hid behind his mother's apron every time Anza tried to hug him. The oldest was thirteen or fourteen and unlike most his age, barely spoke a word the entire time we were there. The span between the oldest son and the middle son represented Anza's longest separation from his wife, when he was solely engaged by Spain as presidio captain Apache-fighter, a stint that kept him away from home for almost a decade.

After we were introduced as Señor and Señora de la Cruz, naturally, Doña Teresa asked about the renegado. She obviously didn't know her husband very well, or knew better than to ask why, because even I could tell how painful it was for Anza when he replied, "Escucha didn't make it this time."

The house-girl was the one who led the way to our accommodations at the end of the corridor. Through a round-topped door with iron hinges, the room, exclusively reserved for guests, waited ready.

Standing inside the threshold, holding my dusty saddle bag for fear of getting dirt on the rug, I didn't do anything but look at the loveliness of it all. How wonderful it would've been to fling myself onto the bed, the likes of which I'd not seen since Spain.

Decorated with carvings of flowers and birds and an iron cross that hung behind insect netting draped over clean crisp linen, I just wanted to enjoy the mattress.

Hanging from the earthen wall above a dresser, the Dolorosa holding dried flowers was flanked by two glass-enclosed standing tin sconces with little doors that had to be unlatched before lighting the candles inside.

Anza's wife Terésa was holed up in her bedroom finishing Christmas embroidery that she'd begun in July. My bathwater was on the fire and de la Cruz had gone off with el capitan and his sons to see how the livestock had grown, when the servant girl poked her nose around the partially open door and peeked inside.

She put the garment that had been over her arm down on the bed and said, "The Doña thought you might like to borrow a dress."

"I think I remember how to put one on." I laughed.

The girl admired the cross around my neck, the one Antonio gave me with the hidden blade. I had almost forgotten it was there and replied, "I never take it off."

The tub water was cool when I finally got out and put on the freshly laundered dress. The reflection in the mirror was one I hadn't seen for a while.

Warm dark chocolate was waiting for me at the huge table in the main room of the house. Sipping the sweet, I sat there admiring the lovely furnishings.

The ticking of a clock's brass pendulum swinging back and forth on the far wall, happy voices of children playing games outside through an open window, I felt safe.

Anza appeared in the doorway. Motionless, he stood watching me lick the chocolate from my upper lip after taking a swallow. The inside of his pants down to his boots had been powdered with dust and pale gray hairs from sitting bareback on a horse.

He crossed the room, put one boot on the seat of the chair opposite me, and leaned an elbow on his raised knee. Pulling the three-pointed-hat from his head, Anza deliberately let it fall to the floor.

Watching me the whole time I sipped chocolate, he slowly sat down, never taking his gaze from my lips.

Two or three gray curly hairs amongst the dark were sticking out of the slit in the front of his shirt. I tried to imagine how they might feel in my hands. It would've been so easy to find out if they were soft or wiry. All I had to do was reach over and gently tuck them into the opening from which they'd strayed.

Anza's snug-to-the-thigh pants squeaked against the tightly stretched leather seat as he leaned back and shifted his weight in the chair. The bottle-scar on his cheek, which occasionally grew obtuse by a brief smile or frown, never changed its shape. His gaze remained fixed on me.

I popped a glance into the chocolate for one last swallow, a lame attempt at diverting my attention failed to succeed. Every time I peered elsewhere, Anza pulled my vision back by some mysterious force.

Clock ticks and el capitan's fingertips gently tapping in succession on the finely rubbed shiny dark tabletop was all to be heard.

The taps ceased. A breath-sucking start kicked my heart to a gallop as Anza's chair tipped over backward and rattled to the floor. Like escaping the pounce of a mountain lion, he flung onto the table, pawing wildly in a crawl to escape the animal's stalk. With a wild kick that thudded the candelabra to the floor, along with a blue, yellow, and white pitcher of milk splashing its drink everywhere, he came straight for me.

I jumped up and backed away, but little good it did. After almost losing his balance with one foot hung up on top of the table, he found the rug next to me, grabbed the back of my head, and pressed his lips to mine.

With one arm around my waist and his other hand feeling its way over my ass, his tongue pushed its way inside my mouth.

Laughter and light conversation was getting closer. Anza had to have heard it, but he didn't stop kissing me.

Straining to see over el capitan's shoulder while his lips were locked to mine; there they were -- de la Cruz and Terésa standing in the doorway. Nothing curbed the runaway kiss, not even my wide eyes. Then, as if merely cleaning up after one of the children, the doña stooped down and began to pick up what was left of the broken cup, dropping the tiny chards into the largest broken piece, one by one.

"Excuse us," the pirate said, grabbing my arm.

Dragging me all the way to our room, he slammed the door. "What was that all about?" he demanded, shoving me toward the bed.

"You're acting like you own me," I said, pushing the hair that had fallen into my face out of my eyes.

"I *do* own you. How soon we've forgotten, haven't we? I'm going to fuck you in Tubac, what do you think about that?" he replied, yanking his shirt over his head, pushing me back onto the bed as I was trying to get up.

"That wasn't part of the deal!"

"I believe we've passed the point at which I usually call an end to being taken advantage of."

"You're not exactly in a position to be reminding *me* about breaking *my* promise!" I shouted.

"What about that little kiss, Léna my love? Where was that going to lead? You, Anza, and the doña could live here as one big family, leaving me to be the stable boy? He had to know you're not my wife, because if you were, he'd be dead, now. How long has he been privy to that little tidbit?"

De la Cruz put one knee on the bed and began tearing at my clothes.

"You're ruining Terésa's dress."

"I don't think she cares to wear it anymore, do you?"

"All you were interested in was having sex with me. So what if I kiss someone else. Didn't the whores you were with kiss others besides you?"

He froze and then said, "You know, you're right. What could've I been thinking? Why would you be any different than just another whore?"

De la Cruz began stuffing things into his bag.

"What are you doing?" I asked, feeling as if I'd taken an unexpected poke in the stomach.

"I'm going home... wherever that is."

"What about taking me to San Xavier?"

"You're practically there, little girl. I bet you could find your way by yourself. Besides, I'm sure Anza will take you. And probably take you wherever you want to go after that."

Taking a last look around the room for a stray belonging, he headed toward the door.

Desperate times, called for desperate measures.

"Salvador, I need you. I might even love you. Please don't go. Kissing Anza didn't mean a thing."

"You can kiss -- whomever you wish."

I'd lost the pirate.

Then he turned and said, "What exactly did you think was going to happen?"

My biggest problem was trying to keep a straight face when I immediately replied, "Haven't you done anything without knowing why, totally oblivious to consequence?"

We looked at each other for about two seconds and burst into laughter.

Yanking off his boots, he sent each of them cracking into the far wall. After which he turned around, checked the latch on the door, flipped open his pant buttons, and pulled off his breeches.

Somehow, until then, I had never noticed the two sacral indentions just below his waist, like punctuation marks over his buttocks. Had they not been so masculine, they would've looked good on a girl.

"You've got dimples over your ass!" I laughed, leaning back on the bed to enjoy the view.

Putting on the face he must've worn at baby baptisms, de la Cruz slipped into the bed, pulled the cover over us, and said, "How can it be such a small girl is such a little lynx?"

"How can a caring, loving man, be such an irreverent scoundrel?"

"*Te amo*, Lilliputian lynx."

Je vous aime aussi," I whispered in his ear as he gently placed my bare thigh over his sacral dimple and covered my mouth with a probing kiss.

"Oh God, Madeleine, I had no idea it would be like this. You feel so good."

Breathing like someone who couldn't get enough air, Salvador pulled the chemise up around my shoulders, slipped his hand under my back, and put himself where he needed to be. I expected my body to resist. But it was as easy as slipping a key into a door lock. Unfortunately, the apology came sooner than anticipated.

"Lena, my beloved, I'm so sorry. No, I'm not…but I am, you just feel much too good. Oh God, I'm coming, *now*!" he yelled, sweating and shaking with the word. Everyone in the house must've heard.

"I can't believe you did that!"

"I mentioned God, they'll think I was praying," he said, collapsing on top of me with the full weight of his body.

"I can't breathe!"

Lifting himself onto to his elbows, he looked down at me, grinned, and said, "I paid for that."

"Oh, *you* paid, did you? You think you're the center of the world. You make everyone you come in contact with, pay. You're the only one who ever had anything shitty happen, and you take it out on everybody by making them responsible for your wrongdoing. You do whatever you like, and it's all right. Well, it's not! I can assure you of that!" I shouted, and he fell out.

I tried not to laugh as we spilled onto the linen.

De la Cruz confidently leaned back on one elbow, picked up my hand, and slowly opened my fist by gently moving his mouth side to side with his tongue to render a kiss to my palm.

A knock came on the door. It was the servant girl pleading from the corridor, "Señora de la Cruz, the doña would like to have her dress back, please."

SUNDAY, 24 DECEMBER 1780

A native woman with a striped serape covering her head reached into the basket over her arm, pulled out a candle, and stuck it into one of the iron holders along the base of the foothill on the eastern edge of the settlement. She was about to light flame when she looked up, saw us at the hitching posts in front of the church, and ran.

"Well, I feel welcome, don't you?" de la Cruz said, swinging his leg over his horse's neck, jumping to the ground.

Slowly, turning in a circle, to take in the sight of the deserted pueblo, he put his hands on his hips and looked up at me, sitting on Rojo.

Keeping my grin under cover, I knew it was coming. He threw his arms wide and in the usual sarcastic demeanor, which he loved to do as a sort of post-excommunicative soliloquy, said, "I can't understand why you haven't gotten off your horse. This magical paradise you risked your life, and mine, to get to is the one thing in my life that was a certainty! Because here we are – the supposed Zion of the New World, San Xavier del Bac! And, it's Christmas --how special!"

My boots hit the same dirt where Armando had been. Holding back the tears was a miracle.

It took a few minutes for my eyes to adjust to the darkened interior, but once they did, the sight after weeks of bleakness ripped a seam in my soul. Brightly painted walls in red and blue, gilt carvings and exquisite santos in keeping with any of the Mother Country's devotions came to life, San Xavier could have been the Capilla de San Jose in Sevilla or any church in the Old World.

The structure wasn't even finished yet. Shavings from the workman's bench littered the floor, triangular stencils halfway up the walls had been drawn by pencil, yet to be filled-in with color from the artist's brush and scaffolds almost blocked the view of the altar. Many carvings were bare. Nonetheless, the climax of the journey was not the disappointment it was before we went inside.

Kneeling at the font, I could see Armando dipping his fingers into the Holy Water on that very spot after dropping to one knee. The tip of his scabbard tapped the floor as he crossed himself and walked up to the altar with confident strides like those of a taller man. As though it had just happened, it shot through my chest like a stab. I couldn't breathe. How in God's universe was I to go on another second without him? I thought I was going to be sick. The pain of losing Armando ripped through my whole being. But I took my next breath and patted a drop of Holy Water onto the hidden blade crucifix around my neck before lifting it to my lips for a kiss.

Once, I told my husband I needed him as badly as I needed to take in air. He kissed me, and replied, "Yes, we require air more than any other thing in order to live, but even air we only need half the time. The other half of our lives, we exhale."

A gray-robed Franciscan padre emerged from the pulpit with arms outstretched and said, "I am Padre Ramon de Meléndez – welcome to San Xavier!"

De la Cruz got a few words in, but Meléndez talked and talked. He went on about the shifting flow of the spring that brought water to the newly relocated pueblo and a bunch of other things I missed because I was thinking of Armando.

I didn't know whether to laugh or cry when de la Cruz burst out with, "Father, I would like to be confessed."

The padre, naturally said, "Of course, my son," and led the pirate out to a small garden.

On my knees, pretending to pray at the sleeping velvet-robed saint next to the door, I heard everything.

"Father, forgive me, I have committed crimes against men, against a nation openly dedicated to God – they were not ordinary crimes, Father. The offenses were just about every wrongdoing you can think of. Disguised by the declaration of liberating men's souls, and to honor God, I've committed the worst crime of all, sacrilege. I sought revenge as a flimsy veil to cover my own misguided soul. My former life to protect and spread the Word of God was really the setting of the stage for a living death of killing, pillaging, and worse. I once was a man of God, as you are," de la Cruz said, barely getting the words out.

"Can you go on, my son?" the padre asked.

"I don't deserve to live. Suffering is my only prize. The greater my agony, the greater the justice. No amount of pain could be sufficient payback for the things I've done. There is no prayer, no Grace of God, no Absolution, no penitence. I cannot wait to see what's being cooked up for me in the next life!"

Sounding as though he'd said it a time or two, the padre replied, "You may choose God, or you may choose evil. You know what is right, and what is not. The Lord gave Himself over to evil, in order to conquer it. Perhaps it is your destiny to know both sides.

Paying for sins with pain is a sign of being worthy of redemption. The only thing that concerns God, my son, is what you do now."

"Your generosity is a scant too great, Father."

"San Xavier Mission is the source of many miracles, my son. Anything is possible here. Perhaps God favors this place because of the collective faith of those who seek out this wilderness. Whatever reason it might be, I assure you, God's force is at work here. I'm giving you absolution. Go continue your work for Him."

One offering of the many that had been pinned to the saint's red velvet vestment grabbed my attention. It was penned in Armando's unmistakable handwriting.

I plucked the paper from the robe. A small corazon that had been wrapped inside fell to the floor. Bending over to pick it up, my hands began to tremble as I unfolded the crinkling parchment.

My husband's writing filled the page around mysterious markings 彷徨人 drawn in by brush rather than quill.

"The Wanderer could be a name for Him. Was He not in a strange land? I, too, am on foreign soil, a place with peril at every turn. And it is here that --"

A two-fingered hand tightened around me, squeezing the breath from my lungs and filling my nostrils with the stench impossible to forget.

"Scream and I'll cut you right now," the voice coarsened by hatred whispered, blowing stink in my ear.

I couldn't have called out anyway, a crease was pressing into my throat, from the cold edge of a sharp knife.

With the huge blade to my neck, Dos Dedos dragged me down the aisle and out the door.

A solitary star was hanging above daylight's last slender golden strip over the hills. It was the sort of evening that would've made one feel good to be alive had she not been in the arms of a murderer.

All I could do was try to stay with the bad man's huge strides yanking me to the hitching rails, or that knife would tear the flesh at my throat.

A red and white piebald stood tied next to Rojo. Scucha's horse. There was no mistake.

Sticking the knife in his mouth, the outlaw tied my hands in front of me with some flimsy leather lash he pulled from his belt.

I looked down to see the warm trickle of blood that had begun oozing along the inside of my pant leg, darkening the top of my leather boot-leggings.

I was six or seven when my brother would gallop alongside, reach over, and pull my pony's bridle over his ears. Rene would laugh and I got mad every time he did it. One day he pulled that little trick and I showed him a few things about galloping off with no bridle.

As luck had it, the outlaw had pushed me up onto the worthiest animal for such a deed. I was sitting on the Big Red.

Dos Dedos fumbled with his reins and Rojo's tie rope long enough for me to lean over and flip the Red's head collar over his ears. The leather fell to the ground with the sweetest little thud I ever heard.

Grabbing a handful of mane, I dug my heels into that horse. Being as smart as he was, the savvy animal took off as fast as he could.

Too bad I didn't have time to see the look on Sugar Jack's face. I heard him cursing as we galloped off at racing speed, headed for the cover of the foothills.

I twisted around to see the outlaw lumbering his big ass onto the piebald.

Rojo took the first corner of the winding narrow path up into the foothills and slipped on the loose sand. Like a cat, he kept his legs under him.

Galloping like hell up the hill, we had just disappeared from the outlaw's sight when I heard a shot. I kicked Rojo harder than ever before.

The trail was getting tighter and narrower with each turn. Dos Dedos was on my tail with a belt full of weapons rattling into each other.

Our path became one continuous circle. It occurred to me that road probably wasn't going anywhere. I tried not to panic. I sure as hell wasn't turning back.

Gasping for my next breath, I prayed the piebald wasn't going to be able to make it up the hill carrying the plumped out old Sugar Jack.

Rojo slid to halt in a small clearing where someone had left offerings around an iron cross stuck in the dirt -- the road had flattened, and come to an end.

The horse under me was sucking wind, dancing on the edge of the crest like stamping on an ant hill. We were practically on top of a mountain. What the hell could I do?

Go straight down the side!

Sugar Jack was so close, I could hear him and the piebald grunting with each stride.

Stabbing Rojo with my heels high up on his flank, I yelled, "*Allez-y!*"

The horse hopped around trying to figure it out, but kept jigging in place. *Vamos!* I screamed.

I felt the top of Rojo's rump against my shoulder, as we took the drop so steep, I had to push the stirrups all the way forward and lean as far back as I could.

Every few strides down, we sank into the dirt. Thank God, the clever Red tucked his hind end under and kept us from falling.

I prayed Dos Dedos would turn around when he saw that hill. It slowed him down, but the varmint didn't turn back.

Musket-fire exploded. Pink froth spewed from Rojo's nostril. The wet splashed my arm. He'd taken the shot in his lung. Blood mixed with breath poured out of him, yet the Big Red didn't miss a stride – that animal from God kept on going.

Getting to the bottom wasn't going to be a Sunday ride in the park. The iron crosses that had been lit for High Mass were lined up aflame on the edge. There was no way to get onto the flat without going over them.

I grabbed Red's mane with both hands, and gave him a huge kick. With a herculean thrust, the gift-beast brushed his hooves on the flames as he jumped the barricade, found his feet on the other side, and galloped on.

Musket-fire exploded. Its echo rang against the lime-washed walls of the mission. What felt like the full-force strike of a club stung like blazes. Piercing lead claimed a chunk of flesh from the outside of my arm above the elbow.

Rojo threw his head to the stars and lengthened his strides. Tears flew across my cheeks. The horse's white face was pink. He had to have been in unbelievable pain, but found the wherewithal to launch us into a full gallop on the flat.

The Red took two huge full strides. His legs gave way. Down we went, hurled into the dirt so fast and with such force it was as if we'd run into a wall.

My mount and I lay together in a heap. Rojo was still alive, but couldn't move. His breathing was short and shallow. His kind dark eye glaring white as blood flowed from his nostril. He moaned and put his head down in the dirt.

I frantically pushed and pulled trying to free my leg pinned under him. I couldn't budge. All I could do was watch as Sugar Jack slowly got off Escucha's horse. The animal just about fell off his feet from the uneven weight in the stirrup as the huge man dismounted on the far side of the row of torches, with the gun powder horn bumping his ass.

Watching me squirming and pushing to get out from under Red, the outlaw laughed and went for another gun. Slowly pulling a weapon from his saddle scabbard, Dos Dedos had all the time in the world.

"God, please, if only somebody would just show up."

It was no use. I was pinned under my horse and Sugar Jack had a trabuco in hand.

He put the gun to his good eye. I could see the black hole of the barrel. The bad man adjusted his feet on the incline to keep his fat ass from falling and the powder horn that had been hanging too low on his hip accidentally brushed one of the torch flames.

A pop puffed a little black smoke cloud. At first it didn't look like much happened, other than a tiny explosion. Finally, the over-due scream that sounded like it belonged to a girl bounced off the church wall behind me.

The giant looked down at the bloody blackened flesh hanging over his pants where a portion of his ribcage was hanging loose and grumbled.

Covered with blood and soot, Dos Dedos kicked over two of the cross-torches, and lifted the short musket to his face.

My life had come to an end. But the huge man didn't fire. He lowered his gun.

The frontier's most-feared criminal couldn't resist one final taunt.

"Thought you were smart, didn't you?" He laughed, taking aim again. "I got you now!"

Sweat ran into my eyes as Dos Dedos wrapped one of his claw fingers around the trigger.

Wiping my face with a bloody torn sleeve, I un-hooked the cross from the cord around my neck and tucked it in my palm.

Blood was oozing over his deerskin pants, but the intoxication of watching me suffer kept Sugar Jack from ending the game too soon.

"I'm not going to kill ya right off. I'm gonna incapacitate ya and then mess with ya a little bit before I end it, just like I did with your friend. She was a hot one, weren't she? I wonder if ya gonna put up half da fight she did?"

Just a little more time. Faking a struggle to get out from under my horse worked.

The outlaw lowered the gun and laughed. "What are you going to do now, little girl?"

I clicked the hidden button on the cross in my hand. The blade snapped out. A tiny twist of the knife sliced the lash around my wrists.

The two-fingered bastard never noticed. He raised the trabuco, only to stop halfway and take another poke at me. "Maybe I'll just come over there and git me a souvenir before I shoot ya."

I lifted my shoulder off the ground and said, "Yeah, why don't you do that? Why don't you come over here and get a piece of me, first."

The ass growled and came right for me. The moment he was close enough, I raised the blade and let it go.

Wisp, thud, howl – his shot fired into the air. The huge man fell to the ground with the handle of the Crucifix blade sticking out of his one good eye.

Motionless in the dirt, Sugar Jack had the blood licked from his face by three scurvy dogs, sniffing for tidbits.

Still pinned under Red, I lay my head on the ground, too exhausted to look and see who it was running toward me. Then I recognized the cries getting louder. De la Cruz.

MONDAY 25 DECEMBER 1780

The native woman who helped me through the ordeal forced de la Cruz to leave, not because it was forbidden for him to be in the room, she thought he was the father, and according to custom, the father cannot be near the birth.

The exhaustion that followed my miscarriage was accompanied by sadness and torpidity so deep, I didn't care if I lived or died. Part of me was already dead, anyway. Losing Armando's baby was almost worse than losing him. And the physical pain was a little bonus that went along with the emotional agony. I barely felt the gunshot wound in my arm spurting blood with each birthing spasm that sent a rush of blood from between my legs.

The baptized Indians explained my emotional distress as a physical retention of the infant's life force still being with me. And that it was necessary to bury the placenta and anything else that had come out for the baby's soul to be reunited with its energy.

I was given a bitter herb to rid my body of all that remained inside. Oddly, following the native ceremony that I could not bring myself to witness, a hole in the ground became a little sacred grave, and the melancholia eased. The child I was never to know was with his real father.

I woke up too weak to throw the covers back.

De la Cruz sat down next to me. The mattress popped up on its ropes, and he pulled back the bloody bandage covering my gun-shot wound. "We've got to change this," he said.

With the little strength I had, gut-wrenching tears poured. Wailing, I pounded my fists on de la Cruz. "It's your fault! If I hadn't slept with you, I wouldn't have lost the baby!"

"You know that's not true, Léna. But if you want to blame me it's all right," he said, taking me into his arms.

I struggled to sit up.

He said, "You're not going anywhere today. You've lost an ocean of blood."

"I have to find the paper," I said, remembering what I had come to San Xavier for in the first place.

"The paper?"

"A parchment in Armando's hand was pinned to the saint's robe. Dos Dedos grabbed me before I could finish reading. I must've dropped it."

"You removed a prayer from an icon?" he said, shaking his head. De la Cruz burst out laughing. "You thought I was serious, didn't you?"

"I'd slap you if I could."

"I can't wait until you can."

"Rojo! Rojo is gone! That horse saved my life!" I cried.

"I'm certain that white-faced red guy knew exactly what he was doing, too. You were very lucky to have had that animal, and to have met the old lady who gave him to you."

De la Cruz gave my thigh a squeeze through the thin wool blanket and said, "Let me bring you something to eat."

"Please Salvador, look for the parchment."

He took a deep breath and said, "I always seem to be in trouble when you call me Salvador. I'll be back with food. And your paper, if I can find it."

I was feeling around under the bed searching for the chamber pot, when de la Cruz came back with a tray of little cakes on a tin plate along with a wooden bowl of soup.

"Did you get it?" I asked, already knowing the answer from the drab look on his face.

"Do you remember anything about it, other than the writing?"

"A symbol of some kind had been drawn with a brush instead of quill, possibly Japanese or Chinese, a complicated squiggle, like lettering from the Orient. Armando had written something about the Wanderer?"

"Yes, the Wanderer," de la Cruz replied as if it were common knowledge.

"You know what it means?"

"In the early days of Christianity, it was dangerous to worship the Cross, so some used the old Japanese character symbolizing the vagabond. By very imaginative terms, The Heavenly Lord was a stranger roaming the earth."

"How do you know this? Never mind, don't tell me…caviar buys one hell of an education. I'm never going to know what was on that note, Salvador. It had to have been very important. Armando never would've bothered with anything less."

"I did find something while I was on my hands and knees, "he said, sliding the plate on the tray aside to reveal a little gold heart underneath. He picked it up and turned it over. A long thin channel had been gouged on the back.

I pulled the pendant that Armando had given to me as wedding gift from around my neck. The gold arrow fit right inside the hole in the heart, clicking into the groove with only the slightest pressure. The two charms were one.

De la Cruz put his arms around me. I cried uncontrollably until he pulled my head under his chin and whispered, "He left his heart for you to find." Stroking my hair, he said, "The supply train is getting ready to head back south. We're going with them."

"I had a bad dream."

"I'm hardly surprised."

"All I can say is thank the Lord that Sugar Jack is dead, because I plainly heard that two-fingered monster say I would never be safe as long as he's alive."

"Léna, Dos Dedos may not be dead."

"That's not even remotely, humorous," I replied.

"I'm very serious. His body is missing."

"What do you mean, *missing*?"

"After we got you inside, I went back out to get the little knife you brilliantly stuck him in the eye with, and he was gone. The padre talked to the Papago, and either they didn't see him or they were afraid to say they did. Whoever Dos Dedos recruited as his new sidekick must've somehow gotten him out of here. The killer has to be blind or dead and you're probably worrying for nothing."

The freshly laundered shirt de la Cruz was wearing made me jealous with the thought that it might have been a pretty young native girl that had delivered the crisp muslin in the middle of the night. The garment was pristine, except for the collar around his neck, which was damp, as if it had been a hot day. A bead of sweat dripped from the pirate's brow.

"Are you all right?" I asked.

"Of course," de la Cruz muttered, swaying an inch or two.

Slipping from the edge of the bed, the pirate collapsed into a heap on the floor.

TOWARD SAN MIGUEL AND CIUDAD DE MEXICO BY WAY OF THE ANTIGUO CAMINO REAL (OLD ROYAL ROAD)

We found out a tad late, venturing along the Northern Frontier was a path for soldiers, Indians, criminals, and madmen. The southern route with a military escort accompanying a large group of merchants returning to Mexico City was a hell of a lot safer.

I got better, and it seemed as though all would be well. But then de la Cruz got sick. After the fever and vomiting, pustules formed on his face, neck, and arms with unmistakable lesions. The pox.

I'd broken out with small sores after having had the inoculation back in Toulouse, but it was nothing compared to what he had.

Mother was obsessed about the disease and insisted we take the repulsive treatment. Apparently, it worked, because de la Cruz was ill and I wasn't.

We were allowed to follow along at a reasonable distance and take food. The fact that I hadn't been stricken alleviated the concerns of many, but nonetheless I was the only one to care for the pirate.

My upbringing gave me the ability to hitch a wagon and drive, but the work was hard and filthy, especially in addition to everything else I was forced to do, the most difficult of which was pretending to ignore any concerns about the disease. That, and the fact that de la Cruz's needs were so unsavory, I think I would've given anything to have been anywhere else, doing just about anything other than being delegated to nurse, a task even more chilling than the Northern Frontier.

I woke up in the middle night, crying. Why the hell was it all up to me? I didn't want to be the one responsible.

Salvador took a turn for the worse. A few of the pustules had dried up, but the high fever came back. I was sure he was done for. Seeing him completely docile was frightening. But the scariest of it was having no vision of the future.

De la Cruz was burning up. I had to do something, so I laid several blankets outside the wagon, hoping the cooler evening air might lessen his fever.

Even with his arm around my neck, he needed all his strength just to stand up and when he finally did, I couldn't hold him. We took one step onto the box I laid out so he could step down, and he fell to his knee, nearly pulling me to the ground with him.

After mopping his brow with the cleanest cloth I could find, I tugged a comb through the knots that had managed to tangle themselves in spite of my daily efforts.

"We're going to have to cut these off," I said, trying to pull the tortoiseshell through the ends of his shoulder-length hair without hurting him.

The pirate reached for my arm and said, "Your presence is humbling, La Condesa."

"Go to sleep."

"La Condesea must be experiencing infinite happiness with her current duties."

"You're not making any sense. You need to rest -- now shut up."

"I'm completely yours, you know that, don't you?"

"Painfully aware."

"I know how much my good looks mean to you. So I must regretfully inform you that these lovely oozing sores may leave a blemish or two."

He began to bleed through the vertical creases of his dry cracked lips. What the hell was I going to do? I had no ointments of any kind.

A run up the path brought me to the source of the smell of cooking pullet drifting from the next wagon. Stopping far enough away for the group sitting around the fire to feel safe, I shouted, "Can you spare a wing?"

One of the men stood, smiled through lips so shiny I could see their sparkle, tossed a piece of bird, and said, "Sure, here ya go."

Catching the greasy leg, I ran back to our camp behind the rest of the train as fast as I could.

De la Cruz was lying on the ground completely still, facing the other way as if his neck were broken. My God, he's dead!

I dropped to my knees in the dirt next to him. "Salvador!"

The pirate slowly turned around. Taking my arm, he managed to lift his head off the blanket and with eyes only half open said, "Léna, my beloved, I'm not leaving. I promise you that. But why must you call me, Salvador?"

"Shut up. Just shut up."

Swiping grease from under the charred pullet skin, I gently smoothed his cracked lips and said, "My life has been nothing but shit since I met you."

"If it wasn't for all the shit, we wouldn't have lives," he replied, closing his eyes and putting his head back down on the blanket.

"Don't you die on me, Salvador de la Cruz. Do not die. Did you hear me? Don't you dare die. I forbid you!"

Barely loud enough to be heard he mumbled, "I assure you I am doing my best to accommodate your wishes."

Sweat from the pirate's soaked shirt wetted my cheek along with the tears. And with my head on his chest I cried, "No more pain. Please, God, make it stop!"

Even though she was gone, and I was sobbing in the middle of some place I never knew even existed, I could see Mama's smile. Her little earrings jiggled as she said, "Madeleine, there's your time for making things happen, and then there's God's time."

SAN MIGUEL

A well-dressed woman, having taken pity upon the couple in tattered clothing, tossed a piece through the window of her coach as it went by. Following the ring of the coin landing on the cobblestone at our feet, de la Cruz and I, not expecting a monetary kindness in regard to our appearance, laughed so hard the release was preceded by a snorting sound similar to drinking a glass of milk that accidentally went through the nose.

"Do we look that bad?" I said, managing to talk in between waves of hysteria.

"We might benefit from some new clothes...and horses. I'm voting against walking to Vera Cruz," the pirate replied, tugging the brim of his hat to the side, shielding his eyes from the sun.

"The pox scab, it's gone! The one that was on your brow, wasn't that the last one?"

"It was." He grinned, bending over to pick up the piece lying on the stone. Pulling me into a kiss, he put the coin in my hand, pointed across the street, and said, "Why don't you sit outside at that Taberna. I'll make a few inquiries about horses. We'll have something to eat, maybe a libation or two, and then shop for clothes. You'll hate it, I'm sure. Order whatever it is you want. I'll join you shortly."

San Miguel had it all. Hints of the flourishing silver and gold trade sprouted everywhere. Pink flowering vines hung over balconies and walls. Women wearing jewels around their necks in the middle of the day filled baskets in lush open markets, riding off in fancy coaches to wherever it was they were going. Shops, taverns, monuments, and government buildings. It was the first real city, since Cadiz.

Finding a seat that wouldn't wobble was becoming a task, when a bosomy bronze-skinned, reddish-gold haired woman sitting at one of the three street tables nodded at the empty chair next to her. The arm-waving Mulatto infant on her lap grasped her bosom and she said, "Jus' put youself right down b'side me, girl! You jus got here dint yous?"

A chicken foot strung from a cord around her neck flopped between her enormous breasts as she softly cooed at the baby with a little squeeze of his toes. "My name Isbelle Lambert. I'm from Novelle Orleans. I'm lookin' for Dumaine, my precious love. Dumaine come down ta San Miguel searchin' for da money. You jus' look 'round and every one doin' dat."

Three or four buzzing flies took turns lighting on a tiny dark sticky patch where something had spilled on the table barely big enough for one.

With a casual swat at the pests as if she didn't care if she got one or not, she said, "Dumaine come down here lookin' for financin' for hid boat. He's gonna set up his gamin' on da big river in Nouvelle Orleans. You know, the *Fleuve St. Louis.* It be jus' an idea right now, it be his dream. But, Dumaine says he's gonna make it happen. He wus gone so long, I come lookin' for him.

"Kin you understan' me? I knew it! You speak French, don't'cha, girl? Well, I kint help it. I go from French to Spanish to native, cept they ain't natives down here. And back to French agin and no won I run inta lately can keep up. Duamaine said he gonna call dat boat da *River Belle*, after me. My name Isbelle. He was in a hurry 'cause he said if he doddn't git it done, build dat boat I mean, someone else was gonna. Gamblas always gittin' inta truble, so Dumaine say if you got a boat, I mean ship, he gets agg-tated you keep callin' ita boat, you cun take dat ship and head outta town. Dis new steam power can drive a boat, ratha ship. He has da plans for it. Says we're gonna be real rich. But he's gotta find da money ta build it. So he come down here where's dere's plenty o money. Ma daddy was a refugee, kicked outta some country. Theys said he could live in Novelle Orleans if he be a Christian. So he said yea, and here I am! My momma was a free woman. She done tricked somebody, good, and won her freedom. She brought me up right. I had a few bad ones, but then I gots lucky with Dumaine. And I know he love me back. I been sick wit out him. But I knowed he had to come down here for da money for hid dream. And dere's plenty o dat in Zacatecas 'cause of dat silver mine.

"I know you's wonderin' cause I could tell by da way you's lookin', so I'm jus gonna tell yous. Dis is not Dumaine's baby. But he don't knowed dat."

She grinned, grabbed her baby's toes, gave them another squeeze, the infant guggled, and she said, "I love both of dem like they wus father and son. Love dis little one. He give me one heck of a time. Had hid little ass on da way down here. Dis storm rolled in and da pains begun, real bad. But I squeezed this little guy out, and he the spittin' likeness of hid daddy. Uh, I mean Dumaine. Someone in Zacatecas said they seen Dumaine down here in San Miguel, so I's figure I come all dis way, I might jus as well come here before I go home. Are you goin' to your home, too?"

She pulled a shiny pendant from under the top of her chemise, twirled the little vessel between her fingers, looked down at the little silver vial on a chain, and said, "I jus got dis, I think yous supposed to keeps poison in it. Maybe it come in handy some day!"

Her huge breasts fluttered like bathtub swells as she laughed with the baby gleefully bouncing in her arms. "I'll fill it wit chicken blood, or my own from my monthly, if I ever get it agin! My momma used to tell me, if you want a man to never forgit you, take some of your menstrual blood and put it in his coffee. But you's got ta be careful not to put too much in, or he could never leave ya lone. So I never did dat, althos I thoughts about it a coupla times. No matta how good it is, it never lasts. 'Cept for Dumaine, dat is gonna last. If I's ever find dat boy agin. You come to Orleans, girl, and you gonna see me and little Dumaine here, ridin' on dat *River Belle*. We'll be wavin' at ya from da railin'. I'll be wearing a frilly white dress with a big white hat, yous won't miss us! Yous got a husband?"

"I did have."

"He's dead, I knows it. 'Cus no man in his right mind would leaves a woman like yous! Was he un older man?"

"He wasn't old. There was an accident. He was hunting and took a stray arrow in the wind."

"Well, if ya don't mind me sayin', do you think dat sounds likely? I mean, did he have an enemy?"

"I'm afraid he may have."

The smell of oiled fishes in the pan leaked into the street as the barmaid came through the taberna door. Placing an earthen cup in front of Isbelle, the server wiped her hand on the smock around her neck and waddled back inside without saying a word.

Isbelle took the lemony leaf from the edge of the cup filled with coffee so thick it looked like chocolate, tossed the herb on the table, sipped, smacked her lips, and said, "Oo, dat good. Almost as good as back in Orleans."

Thwacking the cup on the table, she said, "Well, don't'cha think dat maybe someone done killed yous man? Dat a more likely thing than a wild arrow in da wind? And you knows what dey say, yous take on yous spouse's enemies when yous marry. Maybes yous shouldn't go backs dere. You can come to Novelle Orleans! Yous speak French so yous be welcome like family. And yous won't hav'ta hide yous religion either. Yous can stay wit me and Dumaine. And when he gets dat ship built yous can have da whole house to youself. In Orleans, a pretty woman like yous won't be lone long, if yous don't alridy got a man."

The baby made happy noises bouncing around on breasts jigging with laughter as she took another swallow of muddy coffee. "Oh, yous got one. Yous already got a man, I can tell."

Headed in our direction from the next street on the other side of the square, de la Cruz came into sight with two horses in hand, both calmly walking with heads low, snorting, clopping shod hooves with each step.

The pirate's hat that fell to the stone more than once was on top of one of the mount's heads. After stopping to pick it up for the third or fourth time, de la Cruz placed it back on the sweet animal's head, saw me staring at him, and launched a huge grin.

VERA CRUZ, SATURDAY, 3 MARCH 1781

Without taking his gaze from the tavern's sign, the pirate shifted his weight from one foot to the other, folded his arms, and said, "People usually meet in a social setting. Perhaps they're physically attracted to each other or have something in common, a love of music, literature, philosophy, something of that sort. Conversation might include such things as personal values, ideas, interests, and passions. The connection might bring the attraction past physical to an intellectual and emotional level. Outings together would allow the couple to get to know each other and see the way the other reacts in certain situations. If they get past the awkwardness and the magic is still there, physically, mentally, and spiritually, it would be a safe assumption that romance will take place. However in our case, my precious vixen, I abducted you during a coup on the high seas, after which you cleverly bargained for safe passage across a savage-infested wilderness by promise of a loosely defined sexual agreement. So where does that leave us, my dear Léna?"

Looking at the same sign he was staring at, I smiled and replied, "Even in the best relationships, it's quite common for things not to go well at first."

De la Cruz pulled me to his chest. "Madeléna de Velazquez, what is it about you? What magic do you possess that will not let me go?"

His lips pressed to mine. The inn's door creaked open. Standing behind the threshold with wet-nurse-sized breasts, threatening to rip the seams of her bodice with each breath, the doña smiled and said, "If you need a room, I have a lovely bed upstairs."

De la Cruz still had his arms around my waist and his gaze upon me when he replied, "We'll take it."

The innkeeper's three ill-behaved children ran around the room yelling and screaming, stealing a greasy wing or fistful of greens from the center of the table in spite of random scolding that seemed to be more for the sake of appearance than disciplinary measure.

Nonetheless, de la Cruz behaved as if I were the only one in the room. Staring at the collar of my chemise, he toyed with fabric as if to admire the stitching, before gently pulling back my hair and depositing a kiss on my shoulder at the base of my neck.

Beneath the guise of road-weariness, we retired early.

Belly down, lying on top of the linen with my chin resting on my hands, I watched the pirate's reflection in the mirror while he shaved.

His shirt was off, leaving a perfect view of his chest in the glass, bare back, and every other inch of him filling his tight black pants.

I observed every nuance of the scraping of his face to the silkiness of a wedding dress without touching a hair of his goatee, a feat that must've been perfected from years of being forced by fashion to skillfully keep one's upper lip and chin from knowing the blade. The rasp of the razor ceased only to be replaced by the swish of water in the bowl for a rinse of little dark hairs from the thin steel edge.

Every so often he would glance in the mirror to see me on the bed watching him, and the moment our eyes found each other, it was if he'd said, "*Je t'aime,*" before looking back into the glass for another rasp of the blade.

"Have you ever made love until the sun comes up?" I asked the reflection wiping his face dry with a cloth.

Following a moment of silence, he cleared his throat, swished the razor, looked up, and replied, "I have."

"Who was it with?" I asked, without having successfully concealed the irritation in my voice from more than just a twinge of envy in the pit of my stomach.

"Mercy," he replied, putting the razor back in the box.

I laughed with the sort of embarrassment that accompanies the fear of being perceived as ignorant. Abashed, I asked, "Are you requesting compassion?"

"Her *name* was Mercy…Mercy Knudsen."

"You made love with a woman named Mercy? You cannot be serious. Knudsen? Her name was Mercy Knudsen? No one's called Mercy Knudsen!" I replied, rolling onto my back.

He was grinning, and I all I wanted was to slap it right off his face. I threw my arms wide and repeated, "You did it all night with a woman named Mercy Knudsen? So was this before or after the priesthood?"

"You're asking a lot of questions, why does it matter?'

Flopping back onto my belly, I said, "I was just wondering, that's all. Where did you meet this woman? Was she actually Scandinavian or an English tart with a flair for the theatrical?"

"You're jealous," he said, coming over to the bed.

"No, I'm *not*. I was just wondering where you met her and how you came to share an all-night tryst."

He sat down next to me, picked up my hand for a kiss, and said, "You're jealous because the only time you and I made love, it was abbreviated."

"You're not going to tell me, are you?"

"I know you won't stop until I do. She was an actress. I sent flowers backstage. And one night after her performance neither of us went to sleep."

"I knew it! She was a tart. What play was it?"

De la Cruz grabbed my wrists, rolled me onto my back, put his soft face between my breasts, and said, *"The Taming of the Shrew."*

"You're lying! No Shakespearean actress is named Mercy Knudsen? What kind of flowers were they?"

He stopped kissing my breasts and said, "I don't remember, Léna. It was a long time ago. I had my mind on other things."

"Was it really good? Or were you just trying to impress her?"

"You become completely unraveled when you're emotional."

"I'm not being emotional! Just tell me, were you able to do it all night or was it necessary to resort to other tactics?"

De la Cruz put his lips close to mine. Taking his soft, just shaven cheeks in my hands, I pulled his face into a kiss and instantly forgot there was any other part of my body other than my mouth.

Water threatened to break loose from my eyes when I whispered, "I want you to love me like that."

"I've never loved anyone *but* you, Léna," he said, lifting the chemise over my head, brushing the outline of my jaw with his fingertips. His feather touch enticed the side of my neck, shoulder, and then down my arm where he stopped at the crease inside my elbow. Making a tiny circle with his tongue, he repeated the caresses, replacing his touch with a kiss on my ribs, hips, the outside of my thigh, and down my leg.

Barely pushing back on my hands, I captured each nuance of motion under the soft tiny hairs on his stomach, tempting my palms as he unbuttoned his pants.

A kiss was deposited inside my knee before his lips travelled down my thigh to linger at the crease inside the top of my leg.

Putting one hand under my back, de la Cruz lifted me off the mattress, rolled me onto my stomach, and whispered, "I'm going to kiss you, everywhere."

Pulling my hair aside so he could whisper in my ear, he leaned over and softly said, "We'll start here."

Drawing tiny circles on my neck with his artist's brush tongue, the pirate stroked color onto his flesh canvas.

Stretching my arms wide, de la Cruz clasped my hands and kissed my shoulder. I felt his mouth every inch the length of my arms to the tip of my fingers, licking and sucking the thin web of skin between them.

By the time he got to the bottom of my spine, I was gushing onto the linen.

Pulling open my knee to press my thighs wide, he tucked his face between my legs with a probing kiss.

He slid inside and whispered, "Just be still."

"I cannot."

"Try," he said, caressing my insides like the needle of a compass searching for north. The more I tried to comply, the harder it was.

De la Cruz hadn't quite come full circle when convulsive waves took over, and torment turned to bliss.

He leaned an elbow on the bed and began pulling aside the sweaty strands stuck to my cheek.

"How can a priest make love to a woman they way you just did?" I asked.

"I was a priest, but I am also a man."

His eyes went right through me when he said it, and I wanted him all over again. His look of adoration faded. He got out of bed and began going through his bag on the floor in the corner, as if the lovemaking had never happened.

Taking out several gold pieces, he placed them on top of the dresser, and I jokingly said, "Thank you, kind sir. Be sure to come see me next time you're in Vera Cruz."

Two more coins were laid on the dresser lace before he finally said, "That should be sufficient tender to get you home."

"Get *me* home?" I asked with a bit more vehemence than I should've imposed.

The wait for his reply was brief, but agonizing.

"I'm not going with you," he replied without a hint of emotion.

"What do you mean, you're not going with me? We've been all over God's creation, why in the world would you not be coming home with me? The Inquisition? Is that what this is about? You can't be serious. I assure you, there's no way anyone is still looking for Salvador de la Cruz, except maybe Mercy Knudsen. Spain has an entirely new stance on things. Change your name, if it makes you feel better. Just stop being silly, I'm not getting on that ship without you."

De la Cruz took my hands and with an unyielding expression that let me know how serious he was, said, "Perhaps I *can* go back. Let me put it another way. I *will* not go back to Spain."

"Are you able to stop being stubborn just once?"

Maybe he was trying to convince himself, but whatever the reason, he began speaking faster than he needed to.

"Léna, stay with me -- we can be anywhere -- we can go back to France if you like. I'm in very high standing in England -- we would have a prosperous, comfortable life together to say the least -- I will go anywhere with you -- I'll even stay here. But I'm not going back to Spain."

De la Cruz sat on the edge of the bed, looking around the room. Opening his arm, he said, "Do you realize being here in this inn is the closest we've ever come to having a normal life? I'm almost afraid to ask exactly what your vision of us together would be – the devoted husband after returning home from a hard day of looting on the high seas is greeted at the door by his loving countess?"

"Don't you already have plenty, Salvador? You could write books."

"Why didn't I think of that? Of course, I could pen a treatise. Or better yet, I might scribe instructional manuals on how to piss off clergy and statesmen alike."

"I cannot believe you're just going to let me sail out of your life."

"I saved you from a shipload of horny pirates, got you to San Xavier, and I won't mention how many times I nearly got killed carrying out your whim! Isn't that enough?"

"You broke the agreement! Remember Tubac? You talk about saving me. I was the one who saved *your* life! Who took care of you when you had the pox, half out of your mind with fever? You don't remember that part, do you?"

"Well, the part about being half out of my mind was almost correct. I must've been completely out of my mind. Truth is, little girl, I didn't take you anywhere. You took me half way around the world! As it turns out, for nothing more than the pleasure of your company – if you can call being in your company, pleasurable!

"Oh, really? Is that what you think? I could have run off with Anza at any time --but I chose you! Obviously, a decision made while I was out of *my* mind!"

De la Cruz pulled me to his chest and said, "You want me. You've wanted me right from the beginning, back on the *Dolorosa*. My dear woman, do not delude yourself, I only wanted to fuck you. And I did! The only reason why we're still together is so you can see me tortured right up to the very end, that and the fact that you were scared to be alone."

"Being without you would've been bliss! There was no danger in my life until *you* showed up. And as for being frightened, so what! Virgil said confidence cannot find a place wherein to rest in safety."

Closing his eyes for the kiss, the pirate put his lips wide over mine. A tiny tear seeped through his lashes from the outside corner.

Touching his fingers to his mouth, he reached over to the candle at bedside. With a quick sear from his thumb and forefinger, the flame extinguished, filling the darkened little room with the smell of smoldering wax. De la Cruz tightened his arms around me and whispered, "You'll never be safer than you are right now.

MONDAY, 5 MARCH 1781

The bag was too small for what little I had, not that I would've packed properly to begin with. Dropping the sack on the bed after each ram of clothing like the hammering of a firing ball into a gun-barrel, I knew something was destined to happen. De la Cruz and I were not going to be separated.

All he had to do was take me in his arms and pull me aside. Or perhaps, at the final moment when the longboat dock ropes were to be untied, the pirate would hand his horse to a lucky passer-by, casually hop on board with me, put his arms around my waist, and tell me he couldn't live without me. It was just the sort of thing he would've done, and I expected it, or at the very least something similar.

Flinging the straps of my sack over his saddle horn, he acted like I wasn't even there. The whole time we meandered toward ship, walking with the horse in hand, I looked everywhere but at his face. He must've been doing the same, because neither of us said a word.

Vera Cruz looked like Sevilla. Palm trees filtered the sun, casting feather-like shadows on yellow limestone houses with pediments over the windows. Proprietors swept the street in front of their shops at the start of another business day. Names of Saints had been fired onto wall tiles at each corner. It was Andalucia and all I wanted was to go home to *Hacienda del Sagrado Corazon*.

The docks wouldn't have won any prizes compared to Cadiz. The few headed for the Mother Country milled about nervously waiting for the crew to row, and that was it. The pageantry accompanying a ship sailing the Atlantic was missing, which was unfortunate because it would've been nice to have had musicians obliterate the silence during the time de la Cruz was supposed to be begging me to stay.

It was difficult not to look at the ex-priest pirate. One peek at those puckish blue-gray eyes and I doubted I would've gone anywhere. But, the stubborn son-of-a-fisher who had made love so sweetly the night before didn't say or do anything. He let me get into that boat with the others.

I could still feel him inside me when he dropped the bag with a thud and let go of my hand. My perspiring palm went cool. I had become so accustomed to de la Cruz being there, the moment he set me free, I almost lost my balance.

Tethers were tossed on shore and the few passengers headed for Spain were pushed away to the rhythmic grunts of a seaman signaling the rowers to splash their paddles into the briny.

Oars plunked. Clenching my fists to keep from looking back to shore, I sat quietly staring out the ship that waited for its sails to be unfurled.

I was fine for a while. Then, it was as if I had just tossed a coin into a well and as it left my hand, the sound of it hitting the bottom became an unwelcome echo. I leapt from my seat, twisted around like Lot's wife destined to be salt, and screamed, "Salvador!" with such force, the woman next to me put her hands over her ears and shook her head.

"Woman, sit and be still!" one of the mates shouted.

Seeing de la Cruz galloping off in the opposite direction opened a hole in my chest.

Too far away to hear my cry above pounding hooves, the horse's tail went high, and the pirate disappeared around the corner of a narrow street.

I flumped back down on the bench. The splashes of insistent oars striking the water weren't enough to drown out the sobs that wetted my hands hiding my face.

FRIDAY, 13 APRIL 1781

B etween re-loads and flying Apache arrows, I prayed for boredom, a request granted after five weeks at sea.

The ship lived a life of its own, foul and fresh like the bittersweet of our lives, translated through the stench of human and animal excrement, sweet smell of damp wood, salty air, spices, and suppers past. Hemp twisted into ties bound sails of flax that gently thumped when they caught the wind just right.

The tedium was welcomed at times. But when I lay awake in my bunk at night to the scratching of tiny vermin toenails, or watched the wake from the railing, each minute the finely hewn wood of the *Santa Niña de Atocha* creaked upon the water, I was that much farther away from Salvador de la Cruz. No day passed without thinking of him. I tried to alter the last scene of our final act together, watching him ride off, the vision turning over in my mind so many times always had the same ending -- tears had to be in his eyes as he disappeared around that corner. How could it have been otherwise?

I consoled myself by rationalizing that I would be far better off without him, and tried to leave it at that.

We made the crossing in record time, thanks to favorable currents and the skill of Captain Francisco de Somovilla at the wheel. Unfortunately, the extra days gained were quickly lost when, lured by the intoxicating thought of seeing the lime-washed walls of Hacienda del Sagrado Corazon, only an hour or two from Sevilla's docks, I made the decision to sail from Cadiz to Sevilla instead of taking the highway. So, while the boat waited for conditions that had to be just right in order to get up the Guadalquivir, I was forced to wait in the filthy port city where a woman alone was, of course, perceived as a whore.

Sitting by myself at a seaside taverna, I put a stranger's face to the end of my dagger more than once, making up some story about waiting for my husband.

It wasn't until the little ship set sail up the river that I actually felt as if I were going home.

Lifting the gold chain around my neck, I tugged the arrow in and out of its slot in the heart charm, stopping only to swipe a tear. I was scared. What if things weren't as I had remembered? What if they were? Sevilla was a place that didn't exist without Armando. It wasn't a city, it was a world. Everything reminded me of him. I couldn't stop the feeling.

We were getting close -- the water was murky from silt. Then, *Torre del Oro,* the huge tower guarding the entrance to Sevilla, appeared like a nub on the far edge of the Guadalquivir. I could hardly believe it. I was home.

"I remember the other one," the wrinkled old man next to me said, leaning his elbows on the rail.

"The other one?" I asked, thinking he might've been daft.

"The other tower," he replied, with his wiry beard moving around with each word as if the hairs had been stiffened with egg whites.

"There were two?"

"Yup, looked just like that one," he said, pointing to the Tower.

"What happened to it?"

"It come down. That quake turned it to gravel. You're too young to remember that earthquake, aren't ya? You wasn't born yet, was ya?"

"I had no idea there had been another tower, that's the only one I've ever seen."

"Guess those Moors could only build one good one! They had a huge chain strung across the harbor between both those towers, worried 'bout the Christians invading, I suppose. Didn't do 'em much good though, one of the towers done come down and so did the Christians, from the north!"

The old man's shoulders popped up and down laughing at his own wit. Scuffing the deck with ragged shoes, he walked away mumbling to himself.

Sevilla was in full bloom. The air thick with sweet blossoms bouncing into each other, hanging over the river banks in the sun-warmed breeze. I'd forgotten how beautiful it was.

The vessel had been secured, the flurry of disembarking past, and I was still staring as if I'd never seen civilization. I was alone. The streets were empty. No carriages waited. Where was everyone?

Cobblestone bumps pressed through the worn soles of my boots as I walked toward the center of the city. I felt like a stranger from another world.

A young gypsy boy in garments more tattered than mine sat in the street playing with sticks.

"Where are all the people?" I asked.

"They're watching the Procession," the boy replied, without looking up.

"The Procession?"

"*Semana Santa,*" he said, crunching another stick on the stone.

"Good Friday," I whispered, dropping the sack with the few things I had.

Running through the streets, I saw gypsies in a church doorway vying for a handout. A courtyard beyond an iron gate was empty, and tangerines lay decaying on the ground beneath their branches.

I stopped to catch my breath. The smell of candle wax and slow rhythmic drums of a funeral march echoed against buildings somewhere on another street. The penitent beats became louder as I turned the corner. People appeared on rooftops, under awnings, on balconies, and more lined the streets. Suddenly, the drums stopped.

Marcher sinners dressed in blue robes with faces masked by tall pointed hoods with eyeholes cut into the fabric accidentally anointed the path of the Lord's followers with their candles dripping hardened dots on the cobblestone.

Men hidden beneath the skirts of the effigy barge panted in exhaustion, while old women dropped to their knees, crossing themselves at sight of the post Crucifixion. A single white cloth draped over a huge cross covered with blood, under which the bloodied Santo of Christ lay lifeless in the arms of His Weeping Mother.

Gyrating candelabra mounted on each of the barge's four corners struck their dangling crystals against each other with the delicate tinkling of tiny fingernails swats on a fine wine goblet. The hidden bearers, having caught their breath, lifted the weight and moved on.

I searched faces for someone I knew – anyone.

My feet stung through the holey soles of my boots as I ran past the green and gold sign of the old taverna where Armando used to drink with friends, the same place he had been stabbed by an ex-lover. I had to stop. Catching my breath, I bent over and put my hands on my knees.

Up ahead down a narrow passageway barely wide enough to accommodate a carriage, a man on horseback had just turned the corner.

"Wait! Please wait!" I yelled.

The rider pulled up. It was, Sebastian, the messenger.

"La Condesa?" he asked, as if not sure it was me.

"Yes. Yes, it's La Condesa. Can you take me home, please?" I replied, gasping for air.

I was filthy, my hair tangled, wearing pants, torn boots, and a man's shirt. Lord only knew how bad I must've smelled. Sebastian said not one word about it. He pulled me up onto his horse without question and called me Senora Condesa. Suddenly, the frontier never happened.

Outside La Puerta de Carmona we picked up a canter. The music of hooves beating on the hardened dirt played all the way to the final turn.

Andalucia was in celebration. Insects couldn't wait until dark to hum in the tall grasses blossoming into yellow, pink, purple, and white.

Starting down the road leading to the house tears joyously dripped down my face.

I recalled coming home late one night. I had fallen asleep in Armando's arms on the rear seat of our coach after seeing Voltaire's *Eriphile* and lifting a glass at the Red Door afterward. With my head on his lap, the change in direction when the driver steered the team onto our road woke me. The ruffles on the cuff of Armando's sleeve tickled my face as he held me, leaned over, and put his mouth on mine. Pulling up in front of the house, he was still kissing me.

Wounded, filthy, sore, sitting behind the messenger, coming home wasn't quite as alluring. Albeit far more welcomed.

Holding in the wave, I said to Sebastian, "I'd like to walk the rest of the way."

Hoof beats faded behind me as I stood beneath the arch of the limed herald. The shiny brass and copper Sacred Heart medallion hanging overhead was moss green. Weeds sprouted everywhere. The iron gates, rusted in place, were frozen open.

Had the trees lining the drive not been where they were, I wouldn't have recognized them. I used to think it was silly to make vegetation look like huge balls. Workers meticulously groomed those citrus trees every day until they resembled perfect spheres on sticks. Armando joked about it, saying that the unnatural grooming was the only way the tree would know it was in noble soil. Not one leaf was out of place when he was alive. It was as if the branches knew he was gone.

Those same trees had been home to tiny frogs darting back and forth across the drive the previous summer, belching little gulps in a musical score to endless nights of love-making.

My God, how am I going to do this?

Barking turned into a cordial dabbing of wet noses and licks once my scent was confirmed. Then there he was, running from the house.

"Adelio" I shouted.

The gray wiry would-be cur couldn't contain himself. He knew better, but without a second of hesitation, the hound lifted his paws onto my shoulders and about knocked me over with wet kisses.

Wiping the dog spit from my lips with the back of my hand, I gave the number one canine a huge hug.

The crunching of the crushed stone under my boots ceased for a moment or two each time I was forced to administer pats on a furry head or rump when a cold nose slid under my palm. Surrounded by wagging tails from aristocrat canines, stable curs, and Armando's beloved Adelio, I went the way to the house wiping back the tears.

Walking with me were not only the Deerhounds that were Armando's prized hunting dogs, but also the barn dogs of indistinguishable parentage abandoned as a litter destined to die on a back street.

One night after a performance of *Il re pastore*, Armando had seen the motherless pups in the gutter, stopped his coach driver, and promptly brought all of them home.

My eyes were so wet I barely noticed the front door crack open. Hands clapped loudly once and Maria yelled, "My God…you're alive! You've come home. Praise the Lord!"

She turned and yelled inside, "La Condesa is home – Léna is here!"

The yellow asphodel neatly tucked in the dark hair that had grayed on the sides while I was gone fell to the ground. Maria ran to me, threw her arms wide, and the stoic demeanor she managed to hold onto, even when Armando died, evaporated. We cried in each other's arms.

Holding my face in her hands, she gazed adoringly into my eyes as if I were her own, and through her tears said, "I knew you would come home. Arturo never let me speak of it. But, I just knew you were coming back."

A gray-haired man, loose locks falling to his shoulders, came running from the courtyard. At first, I didn't know who it was.

Covering my mouth trying to keep the wail in, I threw my arms wide and shouted, "Papa!"

The hug lasted until words could be spoken. My father, who had gone nearly completely gray since I last saw him, whispered between sobs, "I couldn't stay on the farm without your mother."

Neither of us could talk about her. Holding me in his arms, he rubbed my back and said, "You're home now, it's all right. Where are your things?"

"I lost Armando's baby!" I sobbed, expecting Papa to cry with me.

His smile held back the tears and he said, "All will be well, you'll see. Maria is making duck with far more saffron than anyone needs."

"Oh my God, I can't even imagine. You have no idea what I've been eating these past months. There were more times than I care to say that I had no idea what I was eating," I replied, losing my tears.

"The floor still hasn't come clean," Maria said, as we went past the blood stain where Armando nearly killed Henri.

Thinking everything was fine didn't last long. Adelio, as if it were his routine obligation, trotted by the library and casually growled at a man I didn't recognize.

Nervously rubbing her hands together, the head-housekeeper explained that the dog regularly made noises at the intruder who had apparently been in the house for quite some time. And with somewhat less than her usual enthusiastic manner, she somberly introduced the Marquis de Lyon, a Corsair employed by the Duke.

The self-appointed title sounded fancy, but he was merely an opportunist bastard who had been a tailor before taking up mercenary duties.

During my absence, the Duke tried to exercise his right over Armando's property, citing a clause within some Sevilla document permitting assumption of the Hacienda, if Armando died or his family failed to inhabit the house. A small article I was certain Armando knew nothing about.

The overdressed, satin-clothed, hired pirate was smiling inside his bearded chin and turned-up moustache as I ran upstairs.

Armed with a thing of beauty far greater than what I learned with, I returned with the gun I never thought I would ever pick up, let alone point at anyone. The weapon, a work of art with gold inlaid scrolls imbedded in the handle, looked as if it should've been in a frame on the wall.

The Corsair's smirk faded as he watched me fill the pan with gunpowder, slide the lock into place, and stick the end of the barrel inches from his nose.

"Get out of my house!" I said, knowing exactly how intimidating it was to be looking down the hole of a firearm.

I didn't expect the war to be over, but was grateful the Marquis saw it upon himself to depart without having his head blown off.

Maria and my father's eyes were wide as Pieces of Eight.

Lowering the gun, I grinned and said, "A couple of tawdry bits from the New World rubbed off."

"You will have to tell me of your trip," Papa replied, as he went to change clothes for supper, minus the enthusiasm to make me think he truly wanted to know.

The wheel-crunch of an unannounced carriage along with a single lengthy horse-snort came through the door left ajar by the Marqui's hasty retreat.

Setting the gun down to peer through the crack, I saw a woman placing her driving whip in its holder. Several locks fell from the combs on her head as she wrestled with the carriage brake and hopped to the ground. Luisa.

She picked up the ruffles of her under skirt and ran toward the house, the little bag tied to her wrist bouncing back and forth all the way. Stopping to catch her breath on the step, she popped her head around the door and peeked inside. "Someone saw you in Sevilla,"

The expression on her face turned to one of despair. Her husband was nowhere in sight, and my silence must've harbingered her worst fear.

Luisa threw her arms around me. Together, we slid to the floor and cried for two chimes of the quarter hour.

Not knowing of Maximo's fate, Maria assumed our tears were from happiness. With wand burning in hand to light the torches, she unwittingly said something about how lucky Luisa was to have Max home. After which the blacksmith's widow ran out wailing.

Lifting her skirt just enough to free her scurrying feet, Luisa clumsily twisted her ankle on the stone, climbed up to the driver's seat of the single-horse carriage, yanked the whip from its holder, and cracked the animal on the butt as if it were his fault her husband was dead. Startled from rest, the horse took a tiny rear, laid his ears back, and galloped into the descending night with wheels rattling like they were about to fall off their axles.

Even if we were going to be only ones at the table, Papa and I decided to dress for dinner.

A smile during the loving touch of the satin I hadn't worn in such a long time became a laugh aloud after putting it on, for the gown I recall not being able to breathe in was comfortable.

Light leaked from the portico as I walked past the splashing fountain sparkling in the torches on my way to supper. Surely that idiot Corsair didn't have the audacity to return, so I went out there to snuff the candle being wasted. Turning the corner, I stopped in my tracks.

A man was seated at the little table where breakfast was usually served. My first notion was that he was yet another one of the Duke's freelance soldiers. But to look at him, you'd have thought he missed too many meals to instill fear in anyone.

Confidently surging to his feet, the scrawny character caught me in the eye with a flash like a sun twinkle on an ocean swell, and in a voice half-a-tone higher than masculine said, "I am Janko, the world's greatest swordfighter!"

SATURDAY 14 APRIL 1781

Arturo patiently waited for the wax to harden on the letter seal. Staring at the library rug, he was the vision of humility. Maybe he felt guilty for having squelched his wife's hope of ever seeing me again. Perhaps it was because he knew I was master of the hacienda. Whatever made him so amenable worked just fine -- much needed to be accomplished. I wasn't about to allow anyone in my household to sit and sip chocolate until the Velazquez legacy was secure.

Looking up from Armando's desk, I said, "See to it that the trees are trimmed along the driveway today, Arturo. The front entry hinges are rusted open, fix that first. The medallion needs a good cleaning, too. Never mind the High Holy Days, you must take this letter to our counsel now. Bring him back here to see me in person, right away. Most importantly, be certain he has no obligations to the duke. If our legal advisor has any ties whatsoever to that malefactor, you are not to let him see this letter under any circumstance. Make up a story and leave at once."

The gold Velazquez sealing emblem clunked to the desk. I smiled and said, "The duke is already serving his punishment for being a subversive idiot. He's married to the duchess, penitence no one should have to endure. And where is Janko? Find the World's Greatest Swordfighter and tell him to come see me. He's been here how long? Three months and hasn't done anything yet?"

"Yes, Señora Condesa. Very good, Señora Condesa, right away. I am going now, Señora Condesa,"

Moments later, standing at the threshold, the skinny swordsman pulled the hat from his head, bowed, and said, "Janko is here."

Thwarting a grin as if it was an emerging cough, I covered my mouth and asked "Where are you from, Janko?"

"Romania."

"I thought Arturo said you were from Transylvania."

"Yes, Romania."

"Well then, how did you come to be here?"

Janko walked over, brazenly put one leg over the edge of the desk, and replied, "Count Armando de Velazquez hired me to serve as fencing master. He had offered me the position many times before, but I was unable to accept. Your husband must've been determined to make his point because he finally sent me one year wages in advance. I travelled months just to get here. When I arrived, I was told El Conde was no longer alive. But alas, I'd already been paid. So you have me here where I will be for the rest of the year."

"Enjoying Maria's cuisine?"

"Oh yes, she is a wonderful cook. She made *Pollo Paprikas* for the world's greatest swordfighter."

"You are not the world's greatest swordfighter."

"But I am, Señora Condesa."

"Call me Léna," I said, getting up from my chair and carefully lifting Armando's cherished weapon from the shelf behind the desk.

I put the gleaming blade into Janko's hands and said, "*Now* you are the world's greatest swordfighter. You will be permitted to use this weapon only as long as you work for me. I'm allowing that because this steel isn't ready to retire to the wall just yet."

Janko held Armando's sword as if it were a baby at its baptismal. Carefully running his fingers over the edge, he quickly wiped the smudges with his sleeve and said, "This is the most magnificent thing I've ever seen.

"My husband is dead. That is probably the only reason you'll be able to hang onto your title. You've already been paid for your services, so you will stay on as my teacher. You're going to instruct me in the art of fencing, and maybe deal with the duke's corsair if need be. When I am able to do it justice, I will take back that weapon for myself. We begin this afternoon at 3, and will continue our lessons everyday promptly at that time from now on. You will stay on as my personal coach until I have progressed to the point where it becomes necessary for me to hire someone else because I've mastered everything you know."

Luisa walked in. She was drunk. The whites of her eyes veined in red, she shook a finger at me and staggered toward the desk.

"Max would be alive, if you hadn't come here. Not only would my husband be fine…Armando would be alive if you had stayed the hell away! Why don't you go back, where you came from!"

Alleviating Janko's stare, I told him to leave us in private.

"What are you talking about, Luisa? Max was killed by pirates."

"You killed him!" she sobbed. "You were the one who killed Max!"

"Luisa, I truly understand your pain, perhaps better than anyone. But it's too early in the day to drown in a bottle. Why don't you go home and we'll talk later when you feel better?"

"Maximo was in love with you. It drove him insane," she cried, slouching onto the floor, covering her eyes.

"Luisa, Max loved *you,* not me," I replied, hoping it was convincing enough.

She looked up and said, "You didn't know him. You didn't live with him. Max was livid that Armando hadn't killed him during their duel. Maximo was drunk out of his mind that night. I couldn't believe the way he was talking when we got home. He told me he was in a living death without you. He said he'd relinquish his soul to hell for eternity just to be granted one night with you. Max was consumed by the woman from France! Since he could never be with you, because you were in love with Armando, his life meant nothing. Léna, he was willing to do anything to change that, including murder. He screamed about enduring any price just to be with you. I told him he was sick, but it just made him angrier. I know he did it, Léna."

"Did what, Luisa?"

"Killed Armando."

"That's ridiculous! Max was with Armando when it happened -- and two others!"

Luisa's head wobbled. Her eyes half closed and she said, "Just ask Hansen, his blacksmith pal from the guild, who came into some unexplained coin. And who just happens to be an expert with the crossbow."

MONDAY

I needed to ride. Hours went by, not knowing where I was going or where I was.

My boots struck earth on a narrow monastery road.

Beyond a pair of old rusted gates, I walked with horse in hand. Flies knowing no honor buzzed around lifeless little ones of all ages and sizes one after the other on both sides of the drive. Bodies of dead children with cherubic faces that told of dying in peace had been deposited by impoverished families, knowing the monks would provide burial free of charge.

Lifting the enormous iron clangor, I let it drop onto the massive door. The echo inside faded. The towering portal creaked open.

Using just his expression, a tonsured monk questioned my intent without saying a word.

"Is there a garden here with a fountain?" I asked.

He motioned for me to come in and follow him through a maze of huge rooms, none of which contained a stick of furniture.

The faint chants of men in harmony came from another building as brown-robed monks scratched their brooms on the stone.

Disregarding the actual cleaning of the floor, instead they dedicated their total being to the task of sweeping endlessly in one spot.

The padre opened his arm toward a path of primitive stone steps set into the earth before a garden on the edge of the forest where I was allowed to wander alone.

Crude stone benches rested at odd locations along the gravel that wound its way past santos, plaques of prayers, and religious offerings that had been left to be reclaimed by nature. Rosemary and wormwood leaked from meticulously kept beds of herbs and flowers smelling of spice and medicines.

I must've walked past the fountain several times before filling my cupped palm under the flowing clear water. My reflection rippled as I lifted a sip. Could it have been the same fountain Armando drank from during our six-day separation?

In a bed of rue, Jesus with outstretched arms watched over a huge rock, much larger than anyone would care to dig up and cart away.

I knelt down to touch six crudely carved notches in the giant stone, so innocent in appearance, they looked like engravings made by a child, perhaps someone using an unwieldy blade or possibly hands weak from starvation.

Were the cuts a calendar devised to log days spent without food?

I stared at the gouges in the stone for the longest time before I realized the six random notches were, in fact, three crucifixes.

Rain began falling gently in little weak thumps on the grass. The world was weeping with me.

It might have been said that Armando whisked into my life, sliced my chest open, stole my heart, and left me bleeding. But he did not take without replenishing. What he gave was a heart beating so strong, it could go on in spite of being pierced by an arrow, similar to the heart that pounded long enough for him to breathe life into me with the last of his own.

Rain mixed with the water falling from my eyes as I sat in a heap holding onto the rock.

Someone knelt behind me. One of the monks offered the comfort of a hand. Surprisingly, it didn't end there. The kindness went so far as a break in the vow of silence. Gently touching my shoulder, he whispered, "Rest your soul my child, your heart is in the Hands of God."

Hidden by the generous hood of a flowing brown robe, the monk helped me to my feet. I wanted to thank the man who violated his vow to offer consolation to a crying woman. But before I could say anything, he surprised me even more by pulling me into an embrace.

I strained to see this man of God daring to have his arms around a strange woman in a downpour.

Heavy from the soaking, the hood of the monk's wool robe fell to his shoulders, revealing a face in need of a razor.

"*De la Cruz*! I thought you said you were never coming back to Spain! And by what magic did you get here so quickly?"

With the smile he could no longer hide, he casually replied, "It was no magic. Just a rather nimble little ship formerly called the *Dolorosa*. And, as you know, occasionally I encounter difficulty keeping my word."

"Did you not deny a life devoted to God? What are you doing here in a monastery of all places?"

His light eyes sparked, and he quipped, "Sometimes it becomes necessary to say fuck it, and just take the next thing that comes along no matter what it is -- along with the fact that old habits have a way of not dying easily."

I reached up for a feel of the familiar scratchy face I missed to death and said, "Am I really touching you? This cannot possibly be. Here in the absolute last place in the world I'd ever have expected to see Salvador de la Cruz. Are you real?"

He squeezed me tighter. And, with his lips practically on mine, whispered, "Let me show you how real I am."

www.ingramcontent.com/pod-product-compliance
Lightning Source LLC
Chambersburg PA
CBHW070800180626
46818CB00001B/32